Murder

with

Wine

Murder
with
Wine

Anita Dickason

Mystic Circle Books

Publisher: Mystic Circle Books
Cover Design: Mystic Circle Books & Designs, LLC

ISBN:
978-1-958464-09-0 (paperback)
978-1-958464-10-6 (hardback)
978-1-958464-11-3 (eBook)

Library of Congress Control Number: 2025909833

Acknowledgments

To my daughter, *Chris,* your help with the plot and cover design made the difference.

To my daughter, *Julie,* thank you for your unwavering support.

To my sister, *Cheryl Pochert,* and my friends, *Kimberly Werntz, Kristine Hall, Pat Pratt,* and *Crista Walker,* thank you for your invaluable suggestions and critiques.

My heartfelt appreciation and love to all of you.

Deceit Runs Deep

Danger Runs Deeper

CHAPTER 1

An unexpected jolt of intrigue shattered the monotony of sorting the day's mail. *How odd*, she thought. Tori Winters' hand hovered over a plain envelope. No stamp or addresses, only her name scrawled across the front in jagged, uneven strokes. A detail that spoke of haste. Or secrecy. Was the erratic writing yet another attempt to mask the sender's identity, Tori wondered.

Whoever had placed it in the mailbox hadn't simply dropped it inside. Instead, the envelope was buried deep within the pile of magazines, letters, and advertisements. Almost as if the person hoped it would remain hidden, unnoticed by all except the one individual meant to find it—the owner of the mailbox.

Before she could quell the spark of curiosity, the rich scent of coffee curled through the air, momentarily distracting her. Mia O'Brien strolled in with a steaming mug in each hand. "Thought you might be ready for a coffee break."

Tori smiled and set the envelope aside. "Oh, what an enticing aroma. What's today's pick?" They'd been testing different brands and flavors for their new venture, The Red Door Inn.

"Cinnamon pralines," Mia replied, passing a cup across the desk and easing into a chair.

Tori took a deep swig, savored the spicy, nutty flavor, and sighed with pleasure. "This one's a keeper."

Over the rim of the cup, Mia eyed the stack of mail. "Anything interesting?" she asked before taking a sip.

"Mostly trash," Tori replied, gesturing toward a disheveled heap of papers. "Though this one is a mystery." She set her cup aside and reached for the plain envelope. "Someone stuck this in the mailbox. No stamp or addresses."

Mia leaned forward for a closer look.

Tori slit it open, removing the contents. With a puzzled expression, she held up a small piece of cardboard. "Whatever I was expecting, it certainly wasn't a ticket for the *Walking Ghost Tour*."

Mia eyed it with interest. "Someone wanted to make sure you got it today. It's for tonight's tour. The date's written on the back."

Tori flipped the ticket over. "Why would someone anonymously give me a ticket to the ghost tour?"

Mia sipped her coffee before saying dryly, "If I had to guess, it's probably from Vada Struthers. She owns the tour and loves a good marketing gimmick. A subtle way to nudge you into adding the tour to our recommended activities list." She hesitated before adding, "Still, this seems a bit extreme even for Vada."

"You're probably right," Tori replied. Since word had spread about her plans to convert the historic mansion she'd inherited into a bed & breakfast inn, Tori had been inundated with flyers, phone calls, and salespeople.

"Are you going?"

With a shrug, Tori said, "Why not? Who can resist a good mystery? And a ghost tour is a lot more fascinating than spending the evening dusting wine bottles. Besides, I've wanted to do this since I got to Granbury. Want to come? I can probably snag another ticket."

A grimace crossed Mia's face as she leaned back in her chair. "I can't. Mom's got a family dinner scheduled for tonight, mandatory attendance, no excuses."

Tori chuckled softly. "Sounds intense."

"You have no idea. And if I don't show up, I'll never hear the end of it." Mia's eyes sparkled with mischief. "Why don't you call David? I bet he'd jump at the chance to go with you."

A warm glow trickled through Tori as she mulled the suggestion. "Hmm, maybe so. Something to think about."

Mia smirked over the rim of her mug. "And how's it going with David?"

Tori rolled her eyes. "We're just good friends."

"In a pig's eye," Mia muttered, stifling a laugh. She set her mug down and shifted gears smoothly. "Anyway, I do have one piece of business. We need another storage unit. The one we have is stuffed to the gills, and another truckload of paper supplies is on the way. We're out of space. I'm leaving to rent a second unit."

Tori frowned slightly. "Is one more unit enough?"

"Could be iffy."

"Might as well rent two then," Tori said decisively. "We haven't even started stocking canned goods and other food supplies for the inn yet. Plus ..." She paused as an idea took shape. "Maybe we should think bigger. What if I bought a warehouse instead of renting more storage units? That could solve a lot of problems."

Mia raised an eyebrow. "What a great suggestion. It would give us more space, that's for sure. With storage units, we'll waste time and energy moving boxes to get what we need. A warehouse would be more efficient."

"And less frustrating," Tori added. "Do you know any good realtors?"

Mia tapped a finger on the edge of her mug as she thought. "Harley Landis at Landis Realty. She's sharp and honest. Won't try to upsell you because you're Tori Winters, the millionaire heiress."

Tori snorted. "I'm hardly a sucker, and anyone who's tried to take advantage has learned the hard way."

Mia grinned. "True enough. Want me to call her?"

"No, I will," Tori said, her voice thoughtful. "The more I think about it, the more I like the idea of a warehouse. But it might take time to find the right one. You'd better go ahead and get two more units."

The transformation of the Leichter mansion into a boutique B&B had proved more challenging than Tori anticipated. The main house needed extensive renovations, and the dilapidated guest house had been torn down. The replacement would house a museum, gift shop, and offices for the inn.

While construction was underway, Tori and her team, Mia, Heidi Grant, Cammie Dodd, and Tina Lopez, had been busy turning plans into reality. Though their grand opening was still a ways off, they intended to hit the ground running once the construction was complete.

"Oh, I got a call from Cammie," Mia said, pulling Tori from her thoughts.

Instantly interested, Tori asked, "And?"

"She aced her baking class."

Tori laughed. "Of course she did."

Already an exceptional cook, Cammie had taken advantage of the downtime to enroll in a culinary school in Fort Worth. She wanted the diploma and chef's hat to enhance the inn's credibility. Tina was up north at another college, sharpening her photography and graphics design skills. At the same time, Heidi signed up for a hotel management course. For now, it was just Tori and Mia holding down the fort.

"You mentioned the wine bottles. Have you heard when your expert will arrive?" Mia asked.

"Later this week, which is why I planned to spend the evening down there." A sizable basement was in the house her great-grandfather, Frankie Leichter, a notorious Dallas crime lord, had built in the 1930s. Her grandmother, Elly Leichter, had transformed it into a climate-controlled wine cellar for her extensive and valuable collection. Though Tori had never taken a complete inventory, estimates placed the number of bottles in the thousands. Since her previous experience with wine only extended to the occasional under-ten-bucks variety, she'd hired an expert to catalog and appraise the collection.

Mia stood and picked up the cups. "There are sandwiches in the refrigerator. I'll see you in the morning."

After looking up the realtor's number, Tori picked up her phone.

A woman answered, "Landis Realty."

"May I speak to Harley Landis?"

"This is Harley. How may I help you?"

"Ms. Landis, this is Tori Winters. I own the Leichter mansion, which I'm turning into a B&B. I'm looking for a warehouse for the inn's inventory. Mia O'Brien, my general manager, suggested I contact you."

Harley didn't bother to hide her enthusiasm. "I'd be happy to help you! Do you have an idea of the size you're looking for?"

"I want plenty of room for shelves to store boxes of supplies for the inn. Easy access is also important. I figure this will be one of those—I'll know it when I see it."

Harley chuckled. "Got it. I'll pull some listings for you and email them. When would you like to look at them?"

"As soon as possible. I already have trucks arriving. One storage unit is full, and we're starting on a second."

"Are you free tomorrow?" Harley asked.

"Absolutely."

After agreeing on a time and providing her email address, Tori disconnected, filled with a quiet sense of satisfaction. Another problem was neatly on its way to being solved.

She picked up the ticket. Should she go? *Why not,* she thought. It had been weeks since she'd taken a break. Her finger tapped the speed dial. When a deep male voice answered, she pressed the speakerphone button.

"Tori, how's the construction coming?" David asked.

"Since Colt is your best bud, you probably know more than I do. It's coming is about all I can say. When it will end is a mystery."

David laughed. "At the last poker game, Colt was pretty upbeat about the progress."

"He's not living with the construction like I am. But I'm not complaining." She would readily admit one of her better decisions had been to hire Colt McLean to oversee the renovations to the house and the new construction.

"What's up?"

"I was wondering if you'd like to join me on the ghost tour tonight."

"You finally got suckered into that," he said.

"I got a free ticket in the mail. How can I resist?"

With a rueful tone, he said, "I wish I could, but I'm in Austin. I won't be back for another couple of days. Why don't you wait, and we can go another night?"

"No, I think I'll go tonight. My options are an intriguing ghost tour or dusting wine bottles."

David laughed. "I'd probably choose the ghost tour, too. I've got to go, but I'll call you tomorrow."

As she disconnected, she felt the familiar tingle of

anticipation. David Tucker, though not a relative, had been raised by Tori's grandmother. He'd become a special person, though she still wasn't ready to admit to how special. For now, he was a good friend. The friendship was all she needed, or so she kept telling herself.

****

Later that evening, Tori zipped into a parking space in front of the courthouse. With an unexpected eagerness, she hopped out of the car and briskly strode toward the ghost tour office. Since a damp, chilling fog had risen, Tori was glad she opted for a jacket.

Shrouded by the dark mist, the hazy shimmer of streetlights cast an eerie glow over a group standing on the sidewalk. As Tori joined them, a young girl, her steps muffled by the fog, darted toward her. After collecting Tori's ticket, she announced the tour guide, Vada Struthers, was ready to begin.

Dressed in a black 1800s-style dress and a black hooded cloak, a woman stood in front of the group. Her unnerving presence added a spectral aura to the gathering.

Vada's voice, low and serpentine, coiled through the fog like a living thing. "The night holds many mysteries. What lurks beyond our senses is hidden in dark places. What you may see or feel are only the shades of those who didn't pass on. But! Beware!"

Tori couldn't stop the shudder rippling through her. The woman was undeniably talented, though the dramatic fog clinging to the streets heightened her eerie demeanor.

It felt as if the night itself conspired with her, weaving an unsettling tapestry of shadows and whispers.

As she threaded her way through the dense mist, a spark of apprehension flickered to life. The sensation of unseen eyes watching her prickled at the back of her neck.

Her gaze flitted over the group and the swirling haze surrounding them as she searched for an explanation. No one appeared to be looking her way, yet the unease lingered. She exhaled slowly, forcing herself to attribute the tension to Vada's eerie words and the creeping fog.

Near the end of the tour, the group gathered in front of the Hood County Jail Museum, a looming structure that seemed to absorb the faint light around it. The building, constructed in the late 1800s, had been converted into a museum. Yet its weathered facade bore the scars of its grim past.

Vada's voice drifted through the shadows, recounting chilling tales of prisoners who had supposedly never left the jail.

Entranced by the vivid stories of restless spirits, Tori barely noticed the people around her until a sudden, unexpected jolt sent her stumbling. Startled, she spun.

A young woman glared at her, eyes sharp and accusing. "Why did you hit me? What's wrong with you?" As her piercing voice rang out, heads snapped toward her, their glances tinged with unease.

Tori froze, her breath catching in her throat. A wave of disbelief washed over her. "What?" she stammered, her voice barely audible amidst the crowd's murmurs.

The woman's eyes narrowed, her anger flaring as she shoved Tori again. While Tori struggled to keep her balance, the woman inched closer, her harsh voice growing louder. "No one hits me and gets away with it," she spat. Her hands curled into tight fists.

In a low, commanding tone, a voice said, "Stop!" A man stepped forward. His gaze darted nervously at the spectators before settling on the angry woman. "I saw what you did. You shoved her. She didn't touch you."

The woman faltered mid-step, confusion glinting in her eyes. When he moved closer, her aggressive demeanor wavered. Her lips parted as if to argue, but instead, she let out a sharp, dismissive snort. With a quick toss of her head, the woman turned on her heel and stormed off. Her hurried steps betrayed a sense that she was escaping.

Vada clapped her hands sharply, commanding the group's attention as she resumed her tale. The moment passed, and the onlookers turned back to the guide.

Tori exhaled softly, quiet relief filling her voice as she whispered, "I'm not sure what this was all about. Thank you, though, for noticing what happened and coming to my rescue."

The man leaned in slightly, his tone tinted with desperation. "I didn't just *happen* to see it, Ms. Winters."

Her brow furrowed, her earlier unease creeping back. "How do you know my name?"

"I've been following you," he admitted.

His unsettling admission sent a wave of anxiety through her. Tori stumbled back a step, her voice rising.

"Following me? What for?"

"I had to find a way to warn you," he whispered, his words clipped and urgent. "Your life is in danger, trust no one!"

"Danger! What do you mean," she blurted, throwing up her hands as if to shield herself. The icy dread pooling in her stomach had nothing to do with the mist clinging to the air.

The man's expression froze. His eyes darted over her shoulder, his body stiffening.

Tori twisted instinctively to follow his gaze. Nearby, a woman stood with her hand raised, a cell phone pointed directly at them.

Whipping back around, Tori found herself alone. Scarcely visible, the man slipped away in the mist. His warning, though, echoed ominously in her mind. "Your life is in danger, trust no one." What did he mean? Unconsciously, she rubbed the goosebumps rising along her arms while her eyes scanned the thinning crowd.

The woman with the cell phone was nowhere to be seen. Most of the others had already dispersed, their muffled voices fading into the quiet night.

Left alone on the sidewalk, Tori was struck by a profound foreboding. Determined to push the unsettling feeling aside, she made her way toward Vada.

Once a couple finished gushing about how they'd enjoyed the tour and wandered off, Tori stepped forward with a polite smile and extended her hand. "Hello. I'm Tori Winters. I've heard a lot about your tour, and it certainly lived up to the hype. I appreciate the ticket you sent."

The woman's fingers brushed Tori's lightly but withdrew almost instantly. "I know who you are," Vada said, her tone neutral. "But I didn't send you a ticket."

This wasn't an auspicious start, but Tori forged ahead. "I'm sure you know I'm turning the Leichter mansion into a bed & breakfast inn. If you're agreeable, I'd like to discuss adding your tour to the inn's event calendar."

Vada shrugged. "I don't see why not."

"Then, either Mia O'Brien or I will give you a call."

"I heard Mia was the general manager," Vada said, her lips curling faintly. "Definitely a step up from working in a grocery store and cleaning houses."

Tori bristled at what sounded like snark. Her voice sharpened as she responded, "Mia was a store manager and owns a successful house cleaning business."

She could feel her temper smoldering, but another couple approached Vada before she could say more. They were a convenient excuse to end the uncomfortable conversation.

"I'll let you get back to your tour," Tori said and turned on her heel.

On her way to her car, she made a mental note to ask Mia about Vada's attitude. But her thoughts quickly shifted to the peculiar encounter with the man and his bizarre warning. "Your life is in danger, trust no one," he'd said. The memory of his words sent another chill skittering down her spine.

CHAPTER 2

Through the breakfast nook windows, Tori watched the soft morning light chase away the night's shadows across her sprawling property. Yet, the brightness outside did little to dispel the shadows clinging to her thoughts. With a weary sigh, she leaned forward, resting her elbows on the table as she pressed her fingers to her temples, kneading gently to ease the stubborn tension.

Haunted by the cryptic warning, she'd spent the night tossing and turning. Who was the man? What did he know? Why was she in danger? Relentless, the questions swirled in her mind. When she flinched at the slam of the front door, Tori knew her nerves were frayed.

A familiar and lively voice called out. "Tori, it's me." A few moments later, Mia strolled in. "What a lovely morning," she said in a cheerful voice, setting sacks onto the center island. "What happened last night? With all the fog rolling in, did you give up on the tour?"

"No, I went," Tori said, rising to refill her cup.

Her attention focused on the groceries, Mia asked,

"Did David go with you?"

"Couldn't. He was in Austin."

She reached inside the sack. "So … what's the verdict? Did you enjoy the tour?"

Tori hesitated, then set the glass pot on the burner. "Enjoy isn't how I would describe the experience."

Mia's hands stilled, and she shot a questioning look at Tori. "Uh-oh. I know that tone. What happened?"

"Something totally unbelievable," Tori said with a troubled tone. "A woman bumped into me. Then she shouted that I hit her and shoved me again."

"What?" Mia's jaw dropped. A head of lettuce slipped from her grasp and rolled across the countertop.

"If a man hadn't stopped her, I think she planned to slug me." Tori settled back onto her chair.

With both hands braced on the counter, Mia knit her brow in disbelief. "That's crazy! Why would someone do that? Who was she?"

"I have no idea why, and I'd never seen her before. Mid to late twenties, tall with dark hair is about all I remember," she added, sipping her coffee.

"Thank goodness someone stepped up to help."

"Yeah, well …" Tori's voice trailed off as the disturbing details replayed in her mind.

"Well, what?" Mia prompted.

"This is where it really gets weird." In a neutral tone to hide her uneasiness, she detailed the encounter with the unknown man.

By the time Tori finished, Mia's lips had pressed into a thin line. "You're right. Not only weird but downright scary," she said, her voice tight with worry. "Do you think what the man said was tied to what happened with the woman? Could she have been the threat?"

"I don't know," Tori murmured as a shiver ran through her. "And I still don't know who sent the ticket. It wasn't Vada. By the way, what's the deal with her? She had an attitude. Did you two get crossways somewhere in the past?"

A grimace crossed Mia's face. "Let's say she's not on my list of favorite people. She's one of Carly's sycophants." Her hand reached for the errant head of lettuce.

Tori groaned. "Nuff said." Carly and her parents, Judd and Myra Swanson, had been a thorn in her side since she hit town. They'd been part of a ruthless scheme to force her to sell the property for some big real estate deal Judd had going. Just as ruthless and manipulative, Carly was proof the apple never falls far from the tree.

"What are you going to do?" Mia asked, opening the refrigerator door to drop the lettuce in a bin.

"I ... uh, don't know." The faint crack in her voice betrayed her unease.

Mia shoved the door shut. "At least tell Parker what happened."

While she pondered the suggestion, Tori took another gulp of the hot brew. Parker was head of security for the inn. After she inherited her grandmother's estate, circumstances arose that cast doubt on the motivation of the attorneys, Jonah Greer and his son Lincoln, and their management of her grandmother's estate.

Tori retained Daniel Foote, the attorney her grandmother hired before she was murdered. When her life was threatened, Dan enlisted the help of Parker Hayes, a private investigator and owner of Hayes Investigations. It wasn't long before Parker had become part of her team in charge of security. To put it mildly, they all adored him.

She nodded. "I'll tell him the next time I see him."

"Don't wait. Call him today," Mia insisted, her tone firm. "If there's anything to this threat, he needs to know now, not later."

"You're right," she said with a reluctant sigh.

In a casual tone, Mia shifted to another topic. "I found something interesting at the donut shop this morning."

"Oh? Do tell," Tori said, setting her mug down. She was more than ready for a distraction, and Mia had probably sensed it.

"How about a line of local jams for the inn?"

Intrigued, Tori straightened. "What a great idea, not only for the inn but for the gift shop. How do you propose to make that happen? We're not diving into jam-making, are we? Cammie's creative, but even she has limits."

"Never fear, I have a solution." Mia grinned.

Tori chuckled. "Of course you do. Let's hear it."

"A woman was pitching her jars of homemade jams to the owner, trying hard to make a sale. He wasn't interested, but I was. I thought we'd want to sample her product, so I bought a few jars: strawberry, blackberry, peach, and blueberry."

While she talked, Mia popped two croissants into the microwave. After heating them, she cut them into sections. She grabbed the jars from the counter and set everything on the table.

With raised eyebrows, Tori examined the cleverly designed label—*Shamrock Jams*. Behind a four-leaf clover, a mischievous-looking leprechaun peeped around a leaf. "What a clever label. I love it."

"So did I," Mia said. "Of course, with my Irish heritage, how could I resist?"

With plates in front of them and the jars open, Tori and Mia dug in. Tori scooped a generous dollop of strawberry jam onto a piece of croissant and took a bite. The flavor burst across her tongue, sweet and tangy with a hint of freshness. She groaned with delight. "O M G! This is incredible. It tastes like a strawberry fresh off the vine." Without pausing, she added a smear of blueberry to the next bite.

Mia started with blackberry. "Oh, this is a keeper. Cammie will go nuts over these. They'd be perfect for the breakfast buffet and our 'Tea and Crumpets' menu. We definitely need to stock these for the inn."

After swallowing the last bite, the mood shifted. Her tone turned practical, and Tori said, "We've got an appointment today. I talked to Harley, and she sent me a list of properties for us to look at. I'll need to let Colt know we're leaving."

The back door creaked open. "Ah, speaking of the devil," Tori said.

Colt strolled into the kitchen with an amused expression. "And what did I do this time?"

Tori chuckled. Colt, like Parker, had a way of gravitating to the kitchen. "How about a croissant with some new jams we may order for the inn? We could use your expert opinion."

"Toss in a cup of coffee, and you've got a customer." He pulled out a chair. Grey eyes twinkled with humor in a tanned, rough-hewn face. The dark scruff of beard covering a determined jaw added to his rugged good looks.

He was the epitome of a Texas cowboy, broad-shouldered and long-legged, with a proclivity for jeans, western-style shirts, cowboy boots, and a belt buckle the size of a plate. Though today, he wore jeans, a T-shirt, and work boots. A tool belt circled his waist.

Colt was one of David's closest friends. They'd both graduated from Texas A&M University with a degree in engineering. While David established an engineering consulting firm, Colt launched a construction business.

David had recommended Colt to oversee the renovations to the house and property. From the moment Colt stepped inside the house, Tori was certain he was the right fit. His good looks didn't win her over. What did was his love of old homes.

Mia heated a croissant in the microwave before setting the plate in front of him. Colt studied the jars lined up on the table, his gaze lingering on the colorful labels.

"Always had a soft spot for peach," he observed, reaching for a jar and slathering a large spoonful on the warm bread. He took a bite, his expression brightening. "This is good," he said around a mouthful.

After swallowing a swig of coffee, he looked at them both curiously. "What are you two up to that involves me?"

He reached for another jar, topping his croissant with the blueberry jam. He popped the piece into his mouth before grabbing the strawberry jar.

Tori grinned. "We wanted to let you know we're leaving. We have an appointment with a realtor to look at warehouses. We need one to store our inventory instead of renting storage units. If we do find one, and you have the time, I'd like you to inspect the building."

He swallowed the last bite with the blackberry jam. "These are all good, but peach takes the crown," he said, finishing his coffee. "I can easily add a warehouse to my list." He dusted his hands over the plate before pushing back his chair.

He rose and picked up the empty plate and silverware, setting them next to the sink. "Call me if you need me to look at one. I'll lock the back door on my way out. And thanks for the snack. I'm always up to a taste test," he said with a teasing look.

Mia said, "I'll get the kitchen cleaned up if you want to call Parker."

"It won't take long. Let me know when you're ready."

In her office, Tori plopped onto her chair, tapping the

speed dial. When Parker answered, he said, "What's up?"

"I had an odd incident happen last night." She described the ghost tour incident, recounting every uneasy detail. Parker listened in his usual manner, not interrupting until she finished.

"And you have no idea who this guy is?" Parker finally asked, his voice calm but with a subtle edge of concern. "Or why he was following you?"

"Not a clue. Never seen him before."

"Describe him."

She closed her eyes, trying to summon the image with clarity. "Mid-thirties with a narrow face, short dark hair, maybe five ten or so."

"What about the two women? Do you know them or have any idea what triggered this?"

"I've never seen them before and can't think of any reason."

"I'll contact the tour company," he said after a moment. "Maybe they'll have a record of who buys tickets. But until we get this figured out, stay alert." The line disconnected.

From the doorway, Mia asked, "Ready?"

"Yep." Tori pocketed her cell phone, then slung her tote bag over her shoulder.

On their way out, Mia asked, "What did Parker say?"

"Stay alert, though he's going to contact Vada."

With a dry note in her voice, Mia said, "Even as persuasive as Parker is, I doubt he'll get much cooperation from her."

Since the garage was blocked with construction equipment, Mia drove. The realtor's office was not far away, and she soon zipped into a parking spot in front of the building.

A bell over the door jangled when they stepped inside. Behind a sleek desk, an older woman in a tailored black pantsuit with a checkered blouse rose to greet them. "I'm Harley Landis," she said, extending her hand first to Tori. "Ms. Winters, nice to meet you." Then to Mia, "Good to see you again."

"Thank you for your quick response. And please, call me Tori."

Harley nodded. "Would you like to ride with me or follow in your car?"

Tori said, "Probably best if we follow you."

"The first location is two blocks away. Let's start there," she said, picking up several file folders.

While Mia followed Harley's car, Tori skimmed the listing sheet she'd printed. "This is the smallest one," Tori observed.

The building, situated on a corner lot, had a small parking area. By the time Mia parked, Harley had already opened the front door. She stepped aside to let Tori and Mia enter.

Tori walked the space's length while Mia gazed around.

"I think this one is too small," Mia declared, shaking her head. "By the time we set up shelves, there won't be much room left to maneuver."

Tori nodded. "And the location is too close to downtown. We'd have to deal with heavy traffic. Harley, we can scratch this one off the list."

The next three locations didn't fare any better. Once they reached the last property on the list, Tori hoped it wouldn't suffer the same fate.

But when they stepped inside, her mood shifted. "I like it," Tori said, her voice thoughtful. "This is large enough that we won't feel cramped. The location works, and accessing the loading dock isn't an issue."

Harley added, "Plus, this is the only property with a sprinkler system and security cameras."

Tori's eyes brightened. "A definite bonus." She thought for several seconds, then said, "Make the owner an offer twenty percent below the asking price."

Harley hesitated before saying, "I'm not sure he'll go for such a low figure."

With a decided air of confidence, Tori replied, "Tell him my offer is a cash deal contingent on passing inspection. And remind him the building's been on the market for eighteen months. He won't get a better offer."

She quickly scribbled a check for the earnest money, handing it and one of her new sleek business cards to the realtor.

Harley glanced at the card and the check, then back at Tori, her expression tinged with newfound respect. "I'm sure I'll have an answer today, one way or the other."

Mia chuckled as they climbed into the car. "I think the Red Door Inn just scored itself a warehouse."

Their euphoria lasted until they turned onto the street leading to Tori's house. Silence filled the car at the sight of a police car parked behind Parker's truck in the driveway.

Tori's muscles tightened as she stared at the vehicle, her pulse quickening. Her thoughts raced. What would prompt a visit from the police? A problem with the construction? Or something worse?

CHAPTER 3

Mia pulled into the driveway, braking to a stop. "They must be at the back of the house. I'll go inside and unlock the back door."

Tori threw open the car door and sprang out, anxiety propelling her toward the backyard. Her breath hitched at the sight of Andy Rodriguez with a large envelope under his arm, locked in conversation with Parker and Colt. Andy wasn't just any officer. He was the sergeant over the homicide division, and his presence could only mean trouble.

Colt was the first to spot her. "Here's Tori."

With more bravado than she was feeling, she said, "Andy, is there a problem?"

His gaze was unreadable. "I need to talk to you."

Mia appeared at the back door, her expression mirroring Tori's apprehension.

"Let's go inside," Tori said, her voice clipped.

While Colt strode toward the new building, Andy and Parker followed Tori inside.

As Tori passed Mia, she said, "Andy wants to talk to me. I want you in on this."

She stepped into her office, motioning to a chair. "Please have a seat."

Parker lingered in the doorway, leaning casually against the jamb, though his watchful eyes betrayed a hint of tension. With a nervous expression, Mia stood next to him.

Andy wasted no time. "I have a John Doe victim I'm hoping you can identify. A man, mid-thirties, five-eleven, one-eighty, and short brown hair."

From the corner of her eye, she noticed Parker stiffening. She stole a quick glance at him before asking. "What makes you think I can identify him?"

Andy inched closer, anticipation flashing in his eyes. Tori had the uneasy feeling he'd caught her glance at Parker. "A piece of paper in his pocket had your name and address," he told her.

"What?" Tori cried as Andy pulled a photograph from the envelope and slid it across the desk.

Andy's voice was insistent. "Who is he?"

Her fingers trembled as she slowly picked up the photo. She wasn't sure what to expect, but the reality hit like a punch to the gut. Despite the stark, clinical harshness of the autopsy photo, recognition struck, sharp and undeniable.

Tori struggled to make sense of what she was seeing. The man who had warned her was dead. His cryptic words took on a new sense of trepidation.

With a slight quiver, she said, "I encountered this man during the ghost tour last night."

Andy's voice sharpened. "What's his name?"

Dazed, her thoughts erratic, Tori muttered, "I don't know."

Parker stepped closer, leaning over the desk to peer at the photo. Mia was at his side instantly, her face paling as she studied the image.

"Either of you know him?" Andy asked, impatience creeping into his tone. When they shook their heads, he turned back to Tori. "Tell me what happened."

Tori described the encounter in halting detail while Andy scribbled in a small notepad he pulled from his pocket.

"And you say this took place in front of the old jail," he said, with an underlying tone of gravity.

"Yes. It was the last stop on the tour."

"Did you see him earlier?"

"No. The fog made it difficult to see the other people. How …" Tori gulped. "How did he die?"

"Shot," Andy declared.

The word spread an icy numbness through her limbs.

"His body was found in an alley this morning. His wallet was missing." Andy paused, his dark eyes studying her carefully. "The alley is three blocks from the jail."

Stunned, Tori stared at him, her pulse hammering loudly in her ears.

Andy circled back to his original question. "You're sure you don't know him?"

"Absolutely," she replied, her voice firmer than her nerves.

"Then why did he have your name and address, and why would he have been following you?"

"Andy, I don't know," Tori replied, her tone sharper than she intended. "When he told me he was following me, I asked why. I've already told you his answer. He said he had to warn me. 'Your life is in danger, trust no one.' It was the only time I saw him."

"What do you think he meant with his warning? Why would you be in danger?"

"I wish I knew, but I don't."

"Who was with you?"

"I went by myself. Someone put an envelope in my mailbox yesterday with a ticket to the tour for last night. I decided to go since we've," she nodded toward Mia, "been wanting to add the tour to our activities for the inn."

"Who gave you the ticket?"

"I don't know. I assumed it was Vada Struthers. She owns the tour company. But she denied sending it."

Andy's gaze hardened. "Let me get this straight," he said, his tone edged with disbelief. "You received a free ticket, have no clue who sent it, but decided to go by yourself anyway. During the tour, you had a confrontation with a woman who claimed you hit her. A man, now our John Doe, steps to your defense and says you didn't touch the woman. But he also tells you that he's been following you and warns your life is in danger."

His finger drummed against the desk, punctuating his words. "Next, he bolts when he sees someone recording the two of you with a cell phone. He has your name and address, but you don't know why. You don't know why he was following you other than he came to warn you for some unknown reason. You don't know who sent you the ticket, don't know the woman who accosted you, who the man was, or the woman with the cell phone. Does that sum it up?"

Hearing Andy lay it all out made what happened sound worse than she had realized, and the incredulity in his voice only made it harder to defend herself. All she could do was nod.

"What time did you leave?"

"I'm not sure. I waited to speak to Vada. Maybe around nine-thirty."

"The medical examiner estimates the time of death was between ten and midnight last night. Did you see the man again?"

With a hard edge to her voice, she replied, "No!" Her nerves were unraveling, becoming more difficult to hide.

Relentlessly, Andy pressed. "Do you own a gun?"

"No! I don't!" She forced herself to meet his gaze, though her mind raced as she recognized the implication behind his question.

Parker gave Andy a somber look, his jaw tightening. "Tori called me today and told me what happened. I'm concerned about the man's statement she's in danger."

"Not much I can do about it," Andy replied.

Parker's voice turned sharp. "Then I'd appreciate it if you would keep me posted on anything you discover. What about his prints?"

"Not on file." Andy flipped his notepad shut with a crisp motion, pocketing it. He slid the picture inside the envelope and rose. "For now, I don't have any other questions." He turned and walked out.

Already anxious about how Andy had interrogated her, his lack of response to Parker's request for information increased her uneasiness.

Mia trailed after Andy with worry etched on her face. Parker, with a similar expression, watched from the doorway of the office. Once he was certain Andy had left, Parker turned to Tori, his brow furrowed. "The direction of Andy's questions is unsettling, almost as if you're a suspect."

Tori's voice rose, disbelief trembling through her words. "How can he possibly think I shot the man!"

"Right now, you're the only person Andy can link to an unidentified murder victim. That's why he's got you on his radar."

Tori asked, "Then what do we do?"

Mia stopped in the hallway. "Anything I can do to help?"

His expression remained troubled as Parker said, "Not much any of us can do until the police identify the man. I'm sure Andy plans to talk to Vada Struthers, but I doubt he'll share the details with me. I'll follow behind him since I'd already planned on contacting her. I want to learn the names of the two women and find out who left the ticket in your mailbox."

He paused, shifting the computer bag slung over his

shoulder. "I wonder why the victim was spooked by someone taking his picture. That bothers me, bothers me a lot," he mused. With a shake of his head, he walked out.

After Parker left, Mia headed to the kitchen. Still jittery from the conversation with Andy, Tori strode toward the music room, her favorite place in the house. At its center stood her most valuable possession, a baby grand piano. She settled onto the bench, her fingers lightly brushing the keys.

Music had always been her anchor. A piano, a gift on her tenth birthday, sparked a passion for music. Tori spent hours practicing, eventually playing for weddings, school functions, and church services.

After her mother died, selling their furniture, including her beloved upright piano, had been a necessary but devastating decision. Watching it hauled away had felt like losing another connection to her mother.

But when Tori first stepped into the mansion and saw the baby grand, it was as if she had found her way back home. Now, the piano wasn't only a link to her mother but one to the grandmother she'd never known.

Elly had been a gifted pianist. Tori liked to imagine her grandmother sitting here, coaxing melodies from the keys. Perhaps her legacy lingered in the air, infusing the room with a sense of inspiration.

Her fingers transitioned seamlessly from classical pieces to show tunes, the music rising and falling in time with her emotions. She felt at peace until the doorbell's sudden ring shattered the moment.

As Mia appeared in the doorway leading to the dining room, Tori said, "I'll get it."

Four women stood clustered on the porch as she swung open the door. While a welcoming smile lit Tori's face at seeing Liz Talbot, the mayor's wife, the sight of two others sent a chill down her spine. Myra Swanson and her daughter Carly stood behind Liz, their postures rigid and their expressions aloof. The fourth woman was a stranger.

Tori mentally groaned. Dealing with the Swansons was not what she needed after an interrogation by a homicide detective. Pushing her unease aside, Tori stepped back. "Liz, nice to see you."

The first time Tori met Liz Talbot, there was an instant connection. Liz, a passionate antique aficionado, had fallen in love with the house and championed Tori's dream of turning it into a boutique B&B. Liz's warm enthusiasm was among the few bright spots in what often felt like an uphill battle.

The women brushed past her, stopping inside the entryway. Liz was quick to motion to the woman at her side. "Tori, I'd like you to meet Nora Evans. She's the director of the Granbury Opera House. Of course, you already know Myra and Carly."

Tori extended her hand to Nora. "Nice to meet you, Nora," she said. Then her gaze shifted to Myra and Carly, who stared at her contemptuously. "Myra, Carly," she added with a nod betraying none of her irritation.

Liz's tone held an apologetic edge as she spoke. "I

hope we haven't caught you at a bad time, but we wanted to discuss your plans for the inn."

"Not at all," Tori replied. "Today is one of the quieter days. All the construction is happening outside. Would you prefer to sit in the library or the living room?"

Nora had lifted her head to gaze at the chandelier with a wide-eyed look of delight. "Oh my. This is stunning, very similar to the ones at the opera house. I'd heard about your renovations, but this is breathtaking." She turned her attention to Tori. "Do you mind if I look around?"

"Of course not. You're more than welcome to explore," Tori said warmly.

Behind Nora, Myra and Carly shared a glance, their expressions tight with disdain. Myra sniffed, her nose tilting slightly upward. "We've seen it. We'll wait in the living room."

They started in the library, where Liz and Nora's voices rose with enthusiasm as they immediately launched into a lively discussion about the antiques. Their discussion continued as they moved to the living room.

Nora lingered, studying the portrait above the mantle. "Is this one of your ancestors?" she asked, glancing at Tori.

"Yes, my great-grandparents," Tori said. "Frankie built the house." She gestured toward the music room. "Shall we?" Myra and Carly rose, trooping along behind them.

Mia joined them, stepping gracefully in from the dining room. "Ladies." Mia greeted them with a smile radiating her warmth. "Nice to see you."

"Ah, Mia," Myra said, her tone laced with feigned sweetness. "Always devoted to Tori."

Mia returned Myra's smile with one of her own, equal parts charm and steel. "And rightly so."

Nora's attention, however, was drawn to the piano, her expression lighting up. "While all this is very impressive, I'd *really* like to know more about the piano. This is gorgeous," she said, her fingers lightly brushing the wood. "What a treasure."

"It's an 1881 Steinway," Tori explained. "Frankie bought it for my grandmother, Elly, when she was a teenager. She was an accomplished pianist."

Nora tilted her head, curiosity sparkling in her eyes. "When we walked up, we heard music. Were you playing?"

"Yes."

"If it wouldn't be too much trouble, I'd love to hear you play."

Before Tori could respond, Myra interjected, her tone adamant. "Nora, we shouldn't put Tori in an embarrassing position. Plinking out a melody is one thing, but Tori isn't a trained pianist."

Carly chimed in, echoing her mother. "I agree. It would only embarrass her."

A spark of anger flashed in Mia's eyes. "I beg to differ. Tori is exceptionally talented."

Myra's lips pursed. "Since you work for her, I doubt you would say anything different."

Her patience wearing thin, Nora said, "Tori, I'd still like to hear you play."

Tori's jaw tightened, though she managed a faint smile as she slid onto the bench. Myra and Carly's barbs were like waving a red flag before a bull. "What would you like to hear?"

Settled in a chair, Nora said, "Whatever you enjoy playing."

Liz sat alongside her, leaving Myra and Carly standing. After a moment, they sat.

"One of my favorites is *Rhapsody in Blue*," Mia suggested with a sly smile.

"Oh no," Myra protested, her voice sharp. "That's far too complicated."

Mia's eyes gleamed with mischief. "Not for Tori." She seated herself next to Liz.

For a moment, Tori's fingers rested lightly on the keyboard before one hand tickled the keys with the opening bars of the George Gershwin classic. Focused on the music, Tori forgot anyone was in the room. When she struck the final chords, she left her hands in position for a few seconds before lifting them from the keyboard.

A heartbeat of silence followed, then applause erupted. Nora clapped enthusiastically, her smile radiant. Liz and Mia joined in, their faces glowing with admiration.

Myra's lips puckered as though she'd bitten into a lemon, her expression sour with displeasure. Beside her, Carly glowered with annoyance.

Even though Tori ignored the two women, she

couldn't stop the faint smile tugging at the corners of her mouth.

"One more, Tori," Mia said, her voice light. "How about *Unchained Melody*? And this time, sing."

Nora gasped, her excitement evident. "Oh, you sing?"

The sight of Myra and Carly's disapproval only fueled Tori's resolve. She turned back to the piano, her fingers finding the opening notes. Her strong alto voice filled the room, carrying the melody with a haunting clarity. The song had been her mother's favorite, a link to her father, an Army Captain killed in Afghanistan. The memory lent her performance a quiet poignancy.

As the final note faded, Nora clapped even louder than before. "Absolutely … stunning!"

"Thank you. I enjoy playing, even more so on this incredible piano." Tori rose. "Let's go into the living room to be more comfortable."

Carly moved in closer as they strode toward the living room. In a low voice, tinged with mock concern and meant only for Tori, she murmured, "I thought you should know that after your debacle at the ghost tour, the gossip mill is running wild. Whispers about you are spreading like wildfire." A soft, gleeful chuckle erupted.

Tori's eyes darted toward Carly. How could she already know about the murder? Though her muscles tightened, she kept her voice even. "What *are* you talking about?"

Carly's eyes widened in feigned innocence. "Why, all that nasty business about you assaulting some woman."

Tori's jaw tightened. "If that's what you heard, then you should have also heard the woman lied."

"Well …" Carly dragged out the word, her smirk deepening. "You know the old saying, where there's smoke, there's fire." She gave a satisfied shrug and sauntered ahead.

In the living room, Nora, Liz, and Myra were engaged in a low, hushed conversation. When she caught the sharp shake of Myra's head, her curiosity piqued. Myra clearly wasn't pleased with whatever they were discussing. Abruptly, she turned away, visibly vexed, and sat stiffly on the couch beside her daughter. Leaning in, she whispered something in Carly's ear. While Carly listened, anger flashed in her eyes.

Once everyone was settled, Liz said, "Myra and I are on the Board of Directors for the opera house. During our last meeting, I broached the possibility of a liaison between the opera house and your inn, which is why we're here. But for now, we'd like to defer that to a later meeting. Instead, we believe you could help solve a more immediate problem."

Tori glanced at Myra as she sat stone-faced on the couch. She figured Myra had done her best to quash whatever Liz was referring to. Shifting her attention back to Liz, she asked warily, "What problem?"

Nora spoke up. "The country western band for our next event had to cancel after an automobile crash injured several members. This event is especially important because it's dedicated to raising money for a youth foundation." She paused, her eyes twinkling with excitement. "We need a replacement and believe we've found one. You!"

Tori blinked. "What! You can't be serious."

"I had the same reaction," Myra interjected sharply, using Tori's response to bolster her protest. "The opera house has a worldwide reputation, and having an unknown, untested performer could damage that beyond repair."

Her adamant gaze flicked between Liz and Nora. "I still say canceling and refunding tickets is the right decision."

Liz's tone conveyed a hint of steel as she said, "Myra, we've already talked about how this will affect the youth foundation. Canceling would deal a significant blow to their budget."

While Tori hated to agree with Myra, the woman had a point. "What Myra said is true," she admitted slowly. "I've never performed anywhere except for high school graduations, weddings, and church services."

Nora leaned forward, her tone laced with conviction. "What I heard tells me otherwise. Believe me, Tori, I know talent when I hear it. You're more than qualified. Please! Say yes."

Befuddled, Tori looked at Mia, seated next to her.

"I think you should," Mia said, her tone firm and supportive.

Myra crossed her arms, her expression hardening with annoyance. "I think this is a massive mistake," she said icily. "Playing in this house is one thing, but stepping onto the stage of the Granbury Opera House is entirely different. I shudder to think of the consequences."

Myra's words stung because, deep down, she wasn't sure they were wrong.

Then Carly opened her mouth, the venom unmistakable. "Mother's right, Tori. You're simply … not qualified for such a distinction."

The red flag fluttered. Tori's spine stiffened. "I'll do it."

Liz beamed. "Wonderful! I can't wait."

Nora answered confidently, "We have plenty of time to prepare, as the date is still about three weeks away. I'll need you at the opera house tomorrow to meet with the music director and discuss your musical selections. I'll start updating the advertising first thing in the morning."

They settled on a time, and the women rose to leave. Tori followed them to the door.

At the threshold, Liz clasped Tori's hands warmly. "I know you'll be a star, Tori. Thank you for saying yes."

As the door clicked shut behind them, Tori let out a long exhale, leaning her back against the cool surface. She glanced toward Mia, standing in the living room doorway. Her voice dropped to a murmur, "Mia, what the devil have I done?"

Chapter 4

The next afternoon, after parking her car in the lot across from the opera house, Tori remained in her seat, her body stiff with tension. Fingers drummed a jittery rhythm on the steering wheel as her gaze fixed on the imposing front doors. What possessed her to agree to such an insane idea? Myra and Carly, that's who.

She'd let herself be goaded into a catastrophic lapse in judgment. One she had stewed over ever since the women had left the house. The only solution was to claim a last-minute crisis and slink away.

With a heavy sigh, Tori finally opened the door. Her excuse disintegrated the moment her eyes landed on the sign displayed by the front door. Her name and the date of her performance were boldly printed for all to see. "Cripes," she muttered. "I'm stuck."

The heavy door creaked as she pushed it open, revealing the opulent interior. Chandeliers sparkled overhead. Twin staircases with plush carpeting curled gracefully to the upper floor, adding to the air of grandeur.

Behind a polished mahogany counter, a young woman

greeted her with a bright smile. "May I help you?"

Tori hesitated, her voice faltering. "I'm Tori Winters—"

Before she could say another word, the woman's face lit up in recognition. "Oh, yes, Ms. Winters. Nora is expecting you. Please, go up the stairs and into the main hall."

Her feet lagging, she climbed the staircase. With each step, her dread mounted. When she finally emerged into the grand hall, her heart plummeted.

Rows upon rows of seats stretched before her, their emptiness only amplifying the vastness of the space. She clutched the handrail for support as her pulse raced.

This wasn't stage fright, it was impending doom. *I can't do this. I just can't.* Despite the consequences, her only escape was the last-minute crisis.

A voice broke into her terrified musings. "Tori, come on down," Nora said from where she stood on the stage.

While every instinct said to run, Tori slowly trudged down the steps and onto the stage.

"I'm glad you're early," Nora said warmly. "Tori, this is Dwayne Radcliffe, our music director. I'm going to leave you in his capable hands. Everyone is thrilled about your performance. I've been singing your praises to the rafters."

After greeting the music director, Tori clenched her hands tightly and said, "Nora, I must talk—"

But Nora cut her off with an apologetic smile. "I can't right now. I'm already late for a staff meeting. Before you leave, we'll sort out anything you're unsure about." She bustled off the stage, disappearing before Tori could utter another word.

With a helpless feeling, she stared at the music director.

A look of sympathy gleamed in his eyes. "Nora said this is your first time to perform before an audience."

"Yes. I don't count playing the organ at a church service anywhere close."

Dwayne chuckled. "I think you'll discover this won't be as bad as you imagine." He moved to one side, gesturing. "I brought our piano out so you could get a feel for it."

When Tori turned, her breath caught. How she'd missed it, she couldn't imagine, other than she'd been so caught up in her fears. Under the stage lights, the magnificent instrument's polished surface gleamed, its curves radiating elegance. "Oh, my," she said softly.

"It's a Steinway concert piano," Dwayne explained. "We're quite proud of it. Nora mentioned you have a Steinway baby grand at home, so this should feel familiar."

An irresistible pull drew her closer as though the music within the piano beckoned. Tori circled the piano, her fingers gliding over the smooth wood. For a fleeting moment, her anxiety ebbed, replaced by a surge of longing to play.

His face wreathed with a knowing smile, Dwayne encouraged her. "Do you need music?"

"For my favorites, no," Tori said, dropping her tote

bag on the floor. Settling onto the bench, she adjusted her position and rested her feet on the pedals. Her fingers brushed lightly across the keys, playing a few scales to test their responsiveness. The piano was perfectly tuned, each note resonating with a clarity and vibrancy that sent shivers up her spine.

Dwayne said, "Play whatever you like."

Tori barely heard him. She was already immersed in the lilting opening chords of *Clair de Lune* by Debussy. The notes poured out effortlessly, like water from a stream, carrying her away from the weight of her nerves. From there, her hands seemed to move of their own accord, gliding into a medley of show tunes before transitioning seamlessly into Chopin's *Nocturne in E-flat Major, Op. 9, No. 2*. The familiar melodies swept over her. Each piece further eased her tension.

Not wanting to stop, her fingers danced across the keys, diving into Liszt's *Liebestraum No. 3*, then bouncing to the lively pace of Chopin's *Minute Waltz*. Finally, Tori let the grand crescendo of Gershwin's *Rhapsody in Blue* fill the air. The last chord echoed through the auditorium, lingering like a reverent whisper.

The sound of applause startled her. She shifted on the bench. To her astonishment, a small crowd was seated near the stage. Nora was among them, her face alight with pleasure.

Dwayne approached Tori, clapping as he moved. "My dear, your performance was utterly amazing. A sheer joy to listen to."

Heat crept up Tori's neck, and she couldn't find the words to respond. Her hands twisted nervously in her lap.

Nora almost danced onto the stage, her excitement bubbling over. "Didn't I tell you, Dwayne? She's incredible!" She turned back to Tori, triumphant. "See? I knew you'd blow us all away."

Dwayne nodded, clearly impressed. "Tori, I'd like to use the pieces you played for the concert, though we'll need to add a few more."

"Before you decide," Nora said, cutting in with a mischievous grin, "I'd like Tori to perform something else—one more piece. Tori, would you play *Unchained Melody* for us? And sing?"

Tori blinked, her heart skipping a beat. "Sing?" she echoed faintly.

"I wanted this to be a surprise," Nora said teasingly as she looked at Dwayne. She turned back to Tori, her expression softening. "Do you mind?"

Finding her voice, Tori nodded slowly. "I ... I guess not."

Sliding back, she adjusted her feet on the pedals and took a steadying breath. Her fingers hesitated for a fraction of a second, then found the opening chords. As the music flowed, she began to sing, her voice lifting and filling the cavernous hall. She poured every ounce of herself into the performance, the lyrics carrying her beyond her nerves.

When the final note faded, another round of applause erupted, louder this time. Breathing heavily, Tori looked up and caught Dwayne's awestruck expression.

"Oh, yes!" he declared. "We need at least two or three songs like this one in the program."

Nora shouted, "Ed, how did her voice sound up there? Do we need a microphone?"

From the farthest row, a young man stood and gave a thumbs-up. "Nope! Her voice is clear as a bell."

"I'd say we're good to go then," Nora said. She turned to Tori. "Still have a case of the nerves?"

Tori smiled, a flicker of humor lighting her eyes. "Not nearly as much as when I walked in here." Holding her thumb and forefinger close together, she added, "I was *this* close to walking out."

Nora chuckled. "I know. You looked like a deer caught in a headlight, absolutely terrified. Okay, I have to get to my meeting," she motioned toward the cluster of people in the audience, "along with the rest of my staff."

Dwayne pulled a couple of chairs from a corner and set them up. He picked up a clipboard lying on a podium. "Let's decide on the additional pieces you want to play. The concert is two hours plus an intermission midway."

His lips twisted with a teasing smile. "I have a hunch you have more."

Tori gulped. "Two hours!"

Dwayne's tone was reassuring. "You do realize you've already played for over an hour today. And without sheet music. That's quite a feat."

"I've found memorizing a piece of music was easier than fumbling with sheet music," Tori admitted.

"We'll start with what you played today and then fill in with a few more."

When they finished, Dwayne tapped the clipboard with satisfaction. "I'll make a copy of this before you leave. Any questions?"

Tori hesitated, then asked, "Is it possible to practice on this piano?"

"Most definitely. I'll also print out a schedule for the times the piano will be available."

When Tori walked out, she had considerably more confidence than when she entered the building.

Her state of euphoria lasted until her eyes landed on her car. "Cripes, just what I didn't need," she muttered. Fishing her phone from her bag, she tapped the speed dial.

"Hey, how'd it go?" Mia asked.

"Better than I expected," Tori said. "But I've got a flat tire. Do you know a wrecker service?"

"I sure do." Mia's tone carried a hint of amusement.

"I figured as much," Tori replied, a slight grin tugging at her lips. "There's not much around here you don't know."

"Where are you?"

"In the parking lot across from the opera house."

"Got it. I'll call you back."

When her phone buzzed, she assumed it was Mia. Instead, Harley's name flashed across the screen.

"Hi, Tori. Good news. The owner accepted your offer on the warehouse."

"That's great. Then, the next step is the inspection. Expect a call from Colt McLean. He's the contractor for the renovations on the house. He'll do the inspection. What about the contract?"

"I'll have it to you shortly," Harley assured her.

Satisfaction rolled over her as Tori ended the call. Moments later, her phone rang again. This time, it was Mia.

"The wrecker is on the way."

"Thanks. Just got a call from Harley. The owner accepted my offer on the warehouse."

"Super," Mia exclaimed.

Tori asked, "Is Colt still there?"

"Yes."

"Tell him we got the warehouse and ask him to call Harley and schedule the inspection."

"Will do."

As Tori pocketed the phone, the wrecker pulled into the lot. Tori waved to get the driver's attention. He stopped behind her car and hopped out.

"The right front tire is flat," she explained.

"Do you have a spare?"

"Yes."

Once the new tire was in place, the man rolled the old tire, examining it. "I don't see a problem other than the valve stem cap is loose." He fiddled with the valve stem. "I'll take the tire with me and let you know what I find. There might be some damage I'm not seeing."

After he drove off, Tori lingered beside her car, her gaze drifting across the parking lot. She toyed with sending the contract to her Fort Worth attorney, Daniel Foote. But after a moment's reflection, she decided to use the long-time family law firm. Letting Jonah Greer or his son Lincoln examine the contract would be faster. She strolled toward their office, a charming building located on the corner of the square.

Inside, Linda Keaton, seated behind the receptionist's desk, beamed as soon as she saw her. "Hi, Tori. What a pleasure to see you. What can we do for you today?"

"I need to run something by either Jonah or Linc."

"Linc is in court, but Jonah is in his office. I'll let him know you're here."

A few minutes later, a distinguished-looking man in his late fifties walked up. "Tori, good to see you." Jonah gave her a quick hug. "Come on back." While they strolled to his office, he asked, "How's the renovation going?"

"Still a work in progress," Tori said with a shrug. "But we're getting there."

"Now, what's this about you performing a concert?"

Tori stopped in her tracks. "Good grief, Jonah. How do you know about it?"

A humorous gleam sparked in his eyes. "Nora sent out a newsletter announcing your performance. She was overflowing in her praise," Jonah said with a chuckle. "Nora is very selective about who performs. The fact she's excited says a lot."

Tori's cheeks warmed. "I guess praise is always a matter of opinion."

"Not when it's coming from Nora," Jonah said,

waving off her modesty. "She has an exceptional eye for talent."

Once they were seated in his office, Jonah leaned forward. "What brings you by today?"

"I'm buying a warehouse," Tori said. "I'd like you to look over the sales contract."

"What prompted the purchase?"

Tori explained the issues she'd faced with storage units. "I need more space so we're not constantly moving boxes."

Jonah nodded approvingly. "That makes sense. Which building are you buying, and what was the purchase price?"

After she told him, Jonah leaned back with a hearty laugh. "How did you get old man Rickman to agree to the deal?"

"Cash, and the building's been on the market for over eighteen months."

"You got a steal. Good for you. Are you getting it inspected?"

"Yes. The sale depends on the building passing inspection. I'll send the contract as soon as I receive it from Harley Landis. I'm hoping we can wrap things up quickly. I'd like to avoid renting another storage unit."

"Don't worry. Once the paperwork is finalized, it won't take long to close. If needed, I can help nudge things along."

Rising, Tori thanked him and strolled out of his office. As she crossed the parking lot, a prickle ran up her neck, an unnerving sensation of being watched. The cryptic warning, "your life is in danger," surfaced in her thoughts, fueling a fresh wave of fear. *Ridiculous,* she told herself. How could she be in any danger?

It was broad daylight, and she was in the middle of a busy parking lot in downtown Granbury. Yet her gaze darted across the lot and sidewalks, scanning cars and faces for anything amiss. Everything appeared normal, but the unease clung to her, heavy and insistent.

Desperate to escape the unsettling moment, she quickly slid into her car and pulled out of the lot.

CHAPTER 5

When she arrived home, she was pleasantly surprised to see David's truck parked in the driveway. A warm burst of laughter greeted her when she opened the front door.

Tori dropped her tote bag in the office before strolling into the kitchen, where Mia was holding court. David, Parker, and Colt had gathered around the table. Parker, a hard-core coffee addict, had his usual cup of coffee, while David and Colt had glasses of Mia's sweet, iced tea.

Tori eyed empty jam jars and plates littered with crumbs of croissants and muffins. On a large platter in the middle of the table, a few muffins remained.

Mia laughed, her eyes sparkling. "Colt was bragging about getting to test the jams, and David wasn't about to let that slide. I think Parker egged him on when he sniffed the muffins I was baking, a new recipe, cherry nut. It turned into a full-blown taste test."

Tori turned to Parker. He met her gaze with wide-eyed innocence. Meanwhile, David flashed her a teasing, roguish grin, and Colt's raised eyebrows and lopsided smile practically screamed, 'Who, me?'"

After plopping into a chair, she asked, "Okay. What's the verdict?"

"Judging by how fast they dove in, I'd say the jams are a hit," Mia said, setting a cup of coffee, a plate, and a fork in front of Tori.

She helped herself to a muffin, taking a bite. The burst of sweet cherry paired with the nutty crunch lit up her senses. "Oh, this is good," Tori said, glancing at the jars. "Since those jars are empty, I should be grateful that at least a couple of muffins are left."

Unabashed, David grinned. "Should've got home sooner. How'd everything go at the opera house? Mia told us you got roped into performing. I can't believe you let Myra or Carly get to you."

Tori rolled her eyes. "Yeah. I came to the same conclusion." She popped another bite in her mouth.

"Okay, don't keep us on the edge of our seats here. What happened?" Mia said.

"I met the music director, and we set up the program for the concert. I'll be spending a lot of time there, practicing on their piano, a Steinway like mine, only bigger." She waved the fork at David. "And, for your information, I would have been home sooner if it weren't for my tire."

Ever the detective, Parker asked, "What happened to your tire?"

"It was flat. The wrecker driver who changed it wasn't sure why, but took the tire with him to fix." When David reached for the last muffin, she swatted his hand away.

"Oh, no, you don't." She scooped it onto her plate.

Colt rose. "I need to get out back. The men are ready to leave. Thank you, Mia."

After he left, Tori's tone turned serious. "Parker, have you heard anything more about the man who was shot?"

"Still a John Doe. Andy is planning to run a picture in the newspaper tomorrow. Hopefully, someone will recognize him."

David frowned. "What man?"

"A man Tori encountered at a ghost tour was shot in an alley after the tour ended," Parker replied.

David leaned forward, concern flickering across his face. "Someone needs to fill me in. I've been out of town and only got back a couple of hours ago."

After listening to Tori's explanation, David's concern turned to anger. "Parker, how could Andy think Tori is involved? What about the two women?"

Parker's expression darkened. "So far, we don't know who they are," he said grimly. "Andy's problem is that he's chasing shadows with no real leads, apart from the connection to Tori. He's grasping because he's desperate for answers."

His face tightened with concentration before he added, "None of this sits right. A warning too specific to ignore, the way the man bolted, the murder, and no identification."

He leaned forward as if to emphasize his words. "Plus, the timing's troubling. The warning followed so quickly by the murder is too much of a coincidence. I don't trust coincidences, and this one hits me in the gut. The man knew something, and someone silenced him."

Tori glanced at Mia, who had paused while loading the dishwasher. Their eyes met, and Mia raised an eyebrow, fear flicking in her gaze. Tori shrugged, though she couldn't stop the chill racing down her spine.

With a harsh voice, David asked, "What can we do?"

"At the moment, not much, though I'm trying to run down the identity of the two women." Parker stood. "I should get going. I need to check in with one of my investigators."

After Parker left, David exhaled, frustration lacing his tone. "As much as I hate to agree, Parker's right. There isn't much we can do until we know more." He rose. "I need to get going, too. I have several hours of work waiting at my office."

Tori followed him to the front door, where he lingered, wrapping an arm around her shoulders and pulling her close. "I'm sorry I was out of town," he said. "None of this would've happened if I'd been able to go with you."

She sighed, leaning briefly into the comfort of his embrace before stepping back. "Hopefully, Andy will get it all sorted out soon." Despite her positive spin, Tori was still troubled as she wandered back to the kitchen.

Mia, busy loading cups and glasses into the dishwasher, glanced up. "Are you okay?"

"Yes," she said with more confidence than she felt. "I'm sure this will all get cleared up. Like Parker said, the police need to identify the man."

"Then tell me about the opera house."

Tori let out a groan, sinking into a chair. "Mia, the concert is two hours long. My gosh, how am I supposed to pull this off?"

"Easy," Mia said confidently. "You do it all the time. I've heard you. You go from one song to the next. This won't be any different."

"Except," Tori countered, gesturing with her hands. "I'll have an auditorium full of people! I can't believe I let Myra and Carly goad me into this. Oh, and there's another problem. What am I going to wear?"

"Now … that is a *definite* problem," Mia said, dropping into a chair. She drummed her fingers on the table, deep in thought. Then, her face brightened. "What about one of your grandmother's gowns?"

Mia tilted her head, studying her. "You really do look like her, same long, russet hair, oval face, and deep-set grey eyes. Even your eyebrows, sharp and well-defined, match hers. I'd bet one of her gowns would fit you. You're built just like her."

"Maybe I do look like her," Tori admitted, her tone wavering. "But I don't know about wearing one of her gowns." She thought about the task that had fallen to her after moving into the house. Sorting through her grandmother's clothes had been bittersweet, and she hadn't been able to part with the dozen or so gowns. Instead, she had them cleaned, carefully packed in boxes, and stored them in the master bedroom.

Mia sprang to her feet, grabbing Tori's arm with the energy of someone on a mission. "Come on. Let's go look."

Laughing, Tori let herself be tugged out of the chair. Still chuckling, she followed Mia up the stairs to the master bedroom, where they opened each box, folding back the tissue paper. Oohing and aahing, they carefully spread the gowns across the bed.

Tori studied the exquisite dresses, her expression hesitant. "I'm still not sure about this. I've never worn anything like this before."

Mia placed her hands on her hips, fixing Tori with a determined look. "My friend, if there was *ever* a time to wear one, it's now." She held up a deep mahogany gown with a high collar and long sleeves tapering to the wrists.

"This one is truly timeless. The craftsmanship is exquisite, and the material enhances the red highlights in your hair. Will the sleeves be a problem?"

Tori took the gown, holding it against herself as she moved to the mirror. The fabric was soft and luxurious in her hands, and the reddish-brown tones glowed in the light. "No, they'll be fine," she said, her voice softening. "This is beautiful."

Mia beamed. "Then try it on. Let's see if it fits."

After stripping to her underwear, Tori stepped into the gown with Mia's help. A quick zip up the back, and Tori turned to face the mirror. Her breath caught. The gown fit snugly at the waist before flaring into a full, elegant skirt that brushed her ankles.

Mia circled her, appraising her with a critical eye. "Is

the length all right? Will you need to wear heels?"

"I'd prefer not to," Tori said, frowning slightly. "Heels could be a problem with the pedals."

"Hmm." Mia tapped her chin. "Walk across the room and then back. I'd hate for you to trip going across the stage."

"Thank you for putting that image in my head," Tori said dryly.

Mia laughed but watched her closely while Tori moved across the room. "It looks good. How does the skirt feel?"

"Seems fine," Tori said, glancing down as she walked. The hem brushed lightly against her shoes but didn't tangle.

"What about the others?" Mia gestured to the bed. "Do you like any of them better?"

Tori studied the remaining gowns, running her fingers across the luxuriant fabrics. After a moment, she shook her head. "No, I think this one is my favorite."

"Great! Let's see if you have a problem with the piano."

Gathering the skirt in her hands, Tori followed Mia downstairs to the music room. Mia pulled the bench out, giving Tori space to sit. Carefully, Tori adjusted the folds of the skirt before placing her feet on the pedals.

"Well?" Mia prompted.

After playing a few chords, Tori declared, "The skirt doesn't interfere with my feet, and the sleeves don't bind."

"Good. I'll get it cleaned again," Mia said as they

headed upstairs. She glanced at Tori. "You'll need to get your grandmother's jewelry out of the safety deposit box."

Tori moaned, "Not jewelry, too."

"This dress cries out for a diamond necklace I remember seeing in your grandmother's jewelry collection," Mia replied, her tone adamant. "We need to put your hair up, and then you can wear the matching earrings."

Tori shot Mia a sharp glare. "You're *really* enjoying this, aren't you?"

Mia grinned as she unzipped the gown. "Dang right, I am. An event like this is what poor mortals like me dream about."

Tori stepped out of the dress. "Then you need to figure out what you'll wear because I want you front and center."

"Oh, I don't need anything fancy." Mia waved her hand dismissively.

Tori gave her a sardonic look as she tugged on her shirt. "Oh, yes, you do."

"Well, dang," Mia grumbled. "I didn't expect I'd have to get all gussied up."

Tori smirked. "Tit for tat. Pick a dress. You're only a little taller than I am."

Mia froze, her face turning a shade paler. "I ... uh ... I can't wear one of your grandmother's gowns."

"And why not?" Tori demanded with her arms crossed.

"It … it wouldn't be right," Mia stammered, her voice barely above a whisper.

Tori emphatically pointed toward the bed. "Pick," she said with finality. Then, with a mischievous glint, she added, "And when I get the jewelry, we will decide which piece you're going to wear." She stepped to the side of the bed and gestured. "Come on."

Mia hesitated before murmuring, "I don't know. I've never worn anything like this either."

"Remember what you just said to me. We're both in the same boat. What about this one?" She lifted an emerald green gown with antique cream lace, delicately tracing the neckline and cascading down the front.

Tori helped Mia ease into the gown, carefully smoothing out the folds of the skirt. She stepped back, studying her friend with an appraising eye. Mirroring Mia's earlier movements, Tori circled her, taking in the dress. The style complemented Mia's curvaceous figure flawlessly. Her long blond hair, with its fringe of bangs, and dark blue eyes set in a round face made a striking contrast to the deep green of the gown. "Perfect. This one looks like it was made for you." Tori turned her toward the mirror.

"Wow!" Mia said, with a look of astonishment.

"I tell you what, in these gowns, we'll knock them dead, even if my music doesn't."

They replaced all the gowns in the boxes before carrying two to Mia's car. She left early to drop them off at the cleaners.

With the house quiet once again, Tori retrieved the list of musical selections from her tote bag. Settling herself at the piano, she began with the first piece, her fingers brushing the keys in a familiar rhythm. Between now and the night of the performance, her focus would be practice, practice, and more practice.

That is until the doorbell rang.

A tall man in his late forties stood before her when she opened the door. His salt-and-pepper hair was neatly combed. Above a strong, chiseled jawline, hooded eyes, dark and unyielding, studied her with almost clinical precision. His broad shoulders filled out a meticulously tailored dark grey suit, complemented by a crisp white shirt and a red-striped tie. "Ms. Winters?" he greeted, his voice smooth but cool.

"Yes."

"I'm Arthur Dubois."

For a moment, startled by his appearance, she hesitated. This wasn't the scholarly, bookish expert she'd envisioned from his correspondence. However, she quickly collected herself, stepping back to open the door wider. "What a pleasure to meet you, Mr. Dubois. Please, come in."

When he stepped into the entryway, a look of surprise crossed his face. "From the outside, the house is nice, but this," he waved a hand, "exceeds my expectations."

"Thank you. As you can tell from the construction, the renovations are still a work in progress. My office is this way."

She started toward the hallway, though her pace slowed as she noticed him pausing to peer into the library, then the living room. His gaze swept through the open doors of the music room and dining room.

Inside the office, his eyes scanned the room intently, lingering for a moment on her desk and the security camera monitor.

"Please have a seat. How was your flight?" Tori asked, sliding into her chair.

Dubois eased into one of the small, easy chairs, setting his briefcase neatly beside him. With a practiced motion, he snapped his cuffs and crossed one leg over the other. "Long and boring," he said.

"Have you checked into the *Inn on Lake Granbury?*" Tori had booked a suite at the hotel.

"Not yet. I came straight here from the airport. Since this is an inn, staying here would be more convenient than at another hotel."

Slightly surprised, Tori said, "I'm afraid that's impossible. The renovations upstairs are still underway. It will be several months before I open the inn for business."

She was sure she had explained this in one of her letters, but it might not have been clear.

A shadow of annoyance crossed his face, so brief Tori questioned whether she had imagined it.

"I'm sorry if my correspondence conveyed the impression the inn was open for business."

"How unfortunate. Then, before I leave, I need to look at the collection. Knowing what I'm dealing with is critical to organizing the project properly."

"I'm sorry. That won't be possible today." Tori's tone was polite but firm. The mechanism to open the door to the staircase leading to the basement was hidden in the kitchen pantry. The location was a secret known only to a few people.

This time, she was sure a flash of displeasure crossed Dubois' face. It was brief but unmistakable.

His fingers tapped the desk. "Then, I'll be here at nine in the morning." He rose, picked up the briefcase, and walked out.

His quick movement caught her by surprise, and she jumped up to follow. When he reached the front door, she asked, "Do you need directions to the hotel?"

He glanced at her with an aloof look. "I'm certain if I'm capable of traveling from France to Granbury, I can find the hotel. Good night."

Tori slowly closed the door. He wasn't the most cordial of individuals. But then, she'd hired him to appraise the wine collection. She didn't have to like him.

Chapter 6

Up early, Tori started the coffee pot before striding into the pantry. Colt had modernized the space, significantly increasing the storage capacity. However, what hadn't changed were the shelves mounted against one wall where the lever to open the cellar door was located. While Dubois was here, she planned to leave the door open. She shifted a few boxes, ensuring the lever stayed concealed.

After flipping on the lights, she descended the stairs, the wooden treads creaking faintly under her feet. Every trip to the wine cellar sparked the same awe she had experienced the first time she walked down the stairs. The overhead lighting bathed the room in a warm glow, illuminating wood-paneled walls and rows of freestanding shelves meticulously stocked with wine bottles.

Her grandmother's renovations included a system to control the temperature and humidity within the room, making it feel less like walking into a cellar and more like stepping into an upscale wine shop.

She'd come to grips with the shock that she was heir

to millions of dollars and the owner of a sprawling, historic mansion on ten acres in the middle of Granbury. After all, it was still just a house and money, though on a grander scale. The wine cellar, though, was an enigma. The collection left her feeling completely out of her depth with its high-dollar bottles.

When she hired Dubois, she'd hoped to learn more about preserving the wine. Now, she had to wonder if that plan was a lost cause. He didn't seem the type to be forthcoming with any helpful details.

From the top of the stairs, Mia's voice broke Tori's train of thought. "There you are. I wondered why the door was open." She bounded down the steps.

"Musing about the issues with the wine cellar," Tori replied with a decided tone of discontent. "My expert arrived late yesterday."

"That doesn't sound encouraging," Mia said. "I figured you'd be overjoyed when he showed up."

Frowning, she admitted, "So far, I'm not impressed."

Her eyes alight with curiosity, Mia asked, "Why?"

"He's very abrupt, bordering on rude. He expected to stay here, and I had to remind him we weren't open for business. He seemed put out by the fact."

With a puzzled tone, Mia said, "I thought you told him the inn wasn't open in your letter."

"I did, but I guess he didn't remember. Then he wanted to see the collection. I told him that wasn't possible, much to his dislike. I'd just as soon he didn't know how to open the cellar door. We need to make sure the door is open before he arrives and keep it open." Tori glanced at her watch. "I'd better get back upstairs."

No sooner had the words left her mouth than the doorbell rang. "Cripes, I bet that's him." Not wasting any time, she scurried up the staircase. As she raced to the foyer, she hoped her initial impression of Dubois had been unfair. After all, he'd flown from France and come straight to the house upon landing. She forced a cheerful smile, pulled open the door, and brightly chirped, "Good morning, Mr. Dubois."

He stepped across the threshold with a curt nod, his gaze cool and assessing. "I trust, *this time*, my arrival isn't inconvenient," Dubois replied, his tone clipped.

Her optimism plummeted. So much for attempting to view his demeanor in a better light.

"Not at all," she replied, her smile firmly in place. Tori motioned for him to proceed. "We have to go through the kitchen."

Mia looked up from unloading groceries as they entered.

"Mr. Dubois, this is Mia O'Brien, the general manager for the inn."

His nod was the only acknowledgment.

Though Mia's eyebrow raised, she politely said, "Would you like something to drink, coffee, sweet tea, or a soda?"

"I'll pass, thank you." His eyes shifted expectantly to Tori, who resisted the urge to sigh.

"Right this way, Mr. Dubois."

She led him into the pantry, where the open door to the cellar revealed a dimly lit staircase.

"Your correspondence led me to believe the collection was housed in a special room, not a basement," he remarked, his tone teetering on disapproval.

"It is, Mr. Dubois," she said politely, though her jaw tightened.

At the bottom of the stairs, she turned to observe his reaction. He paused, eyes sweeping the room with a stunned expression. For a moment, Tori felt a flicker of satisfaction at his apparent surprise.

She gestured toward a table and chair. "If you need a larger table, let me know. Also, feel free to help yourself to anything in the kitchen. We'll have lunch around noon. Do you have any questions?"

Dubois set his briefcase down beside the table. "I won't require lunch." With a pointed look at the stairs, he asked, "Is there a way to open the door from down here?"

"Yes, there is," she said, pointing to a lever on the staircase wall. "The lever will open and close the door."

He gave a curt nod and turned to the shelves, studying the bottles intently.

"Uh … I'll let you get started then," Tori said, feeling as if she had been dismissed.

When she entered the kitchen, Mia rolled her eyes and handed her a cup of coffee.

Tori stifled a laugh. "Let's take this into my office."

Once Mia followed, carrying a large glass of sweet tea, Tori closed the door.

"I see what you meant about his attitude." Mia settled into a chair, taking a long sip. "I heard his crack about the basement. He's not very friendly."

Tori shrugged, cradling her coffee. "He's not here to make friends."

Before Mia could respond, the doorbell echoed. Setting her glass down, she rose. "I'll get it."

A few minutes later, Parker strolled in with his typical calm, unassuming manner, a characteristic that made it all too easy to dismiss him at first glance. With his short frame, slightly overweight build, and bulldog-like features, he had the kind of appearance that made people underestimate him. Yet, Tori knew better. For a private investigator, his quiet demeanor was an asset, not to mention the tenacity lurking beneath the surface.

After he slipped the ever-present computer bag from his shoulder, Parker settled into a chair.

Mia soon followed, closing the door before handing him a coffee mug.

A brow slightly lifted as he glanced at Mia. "What's with the door?"

"The wine expert is in the cellar," Mia replied, dropping onto the chair beside him.

Parker swallowed a gulp of coffee, sighing with pleasure. "When did he get here?"

"Yesterday," Tori told him.

Suspicion shifted across Parker's face as he looked from Tori to Mia. "Okay. What's going on?"

With a slightly exasperated tone, Tori answered,

"Let's say we aren't impressed, though that doesn't matter. I'm paying for his expertise, not his personality."

"That still doesn't answer why the door to your office is closed."

"I'm leaving the wine cellar door open. I don't want him to see where the lever is located. Considering the issues with Andy, I don't want Dubois to hear our conversations."

"Ah," Parker said. "Makes sense. How'd you come across him?"

"Elly," she said simply. "I've been reading her journals. She described her trips to France and visits to a winery, Château du Montclair. While sorting through her records, I found invoices from the winery, and my curiosity got the better of me. I called and spoke to the owner, and to my surprise, he remembered Elly. "

She reached for her cup. "During our conversation, I mentioned I was looking for someone to appraise and inventory the wine collection. He recommended Arthur Dubois. Said he's one of the best in the field."

Parker said somberly, "I want to meet him, but first, the police released a picture of their John Doe this morning. Andy is hopeful someone will recognize him."

"Have you learned any more details?" Tori asked, her shoulders tightening with a familiar unease.

Parker shook his head. "No. I spoke with Vada Struthers. She claims she doesn't know the man's identity or the identity of the two women." A grim look crossed his face. "I think she's lying. Unfortunately, Andy is stonewalling me about his conversation with her. I don't know if he learned more than I did." He finished the last of his coffee. "Let's go see your expert."

Mia rose. "I'll be in the dining room. Still wrestling with the spreadsheet for the inn's inventory."

As Tori descended the stairs, she glanced around but didn't immediately spot Dubois. His briefcase sat unopened next to the table. "Mr. Dubois?"

He stepped out from between the shelves. "Yes, Ms. Winters," he said, his tone laced with annoyance.

Despite a flicker of irritation, her tone was polite. "I have someone I'd like to introduce."

Dubois' eyes shifted toward Parker with a piercing stare.

"This is Parker Hayes, head of security for the inn. If Mia or I are unavailable, Mr. Hayes can assist with any problems."

Parker extended his hand with a calm smile.

After a moment's hesitation, Dubois shook hands. "Head of security. Odd for an inn."

"There are valuable antiques in the house," Parker replied evenly. "One of which is this wine collection."

With a slight huff, Dubois replied, "That's still to be determined. I've only started my evaluation. Since the appraisal and cataloging of a collection is a lengthy process, I would appreciate as little interruption as possible."

Tori forced a polite smile. "We'll do our best to accommodate you, Mr. Dubois."

Back upstairs, as they walked toward the front door, Parker said, "You're right. He's not the most pleasant of individuals."

After closing the door behind him, Tori slowly strolled into the music room. Try as she might, she couldn't keep her mind from wandering to the murder victim and Andy's investigation.

The unsettling mystery shoved aside any concerns about Dubois' rude demeanor. She wondered if someone had responded to the picture in the paper and identified the man.

Troubled, she settled onto the bench, hoping the music would quiet her thoughts. Though she had each piece committed to memory, she had rummaged through the boxes she'd brought from Missouri until she unearthed her sheet music.

As she played, her eyes scanned the complex passages, reinforcing the accuracy of her memory. Lost in the process, time slipped away unnoticed.

It wasn't until Mia appeared in the corner of her vision that Tori's hands stilled on the keys.

"Aren't you getting tired?" Mia asked, leaning casually against the doorframe. "You've been playing for over three hours."

Flexing her fingers, Tori winced. "They are tingling. I didn't realize so much time had passed."

"I made sandwiches. Let's eat. Then you can get back to practicing."

She stood, rolling her shoulders to loosen the tension.

"I need to check on Dubois first. Have you heard anything from him?"

"Nope. He's still down there," Mia said, heading toward the kitchen.

Tori trotted down the stairs. She found Dubois seated at the desk, his briefcase open and a small laptop in front of him. At her approach, his head swiveled toward her. His hand quickly moved to close the laptop, placing it in the briefcase before shutting the lid.

"I'm leaving," he said curtly. "I need to enter what I've recorded into my computer. I will do better in my hotel room than here. Fewer distractions."

Considering he'd been in the cellar alone, Tori realized he must be referring to her music.

With a faint undertone of annoyance, he asked, "Is the music a daily event?"

Even though irritation bubbled at the confirmation of her suspicions, she calmly met his gaze. "I'm preparing for a concert."

Without another word, Dubois stood, briefcase in hand, and strode toward the stairs.

Her lips thinned to a tight line as she followed.

When they stepped into the kitchen, Mia held two plates, each with a turkey and cheese sandwich and a side of chips. "Are you joining us for lunch, Mr. Dubois?" she asked brightly.

He cast a disdainful glance at the plates. "I am not."

As Tori accompanied him to the door, she hoped for a more productive exchange. "What is your initial impression of the collection?"

"There may be a few valuable bottles, but any opinion at this time is idle speculation," he said, his tone dismissive. "I'll be back in the morning."

After closing the door behind him, she muttered, "What a rude man."

Halfway toward the kitchen, the sharp ring of the doorbell stopped her in her tracks. Frowning, she spun on her heel, wondering if Dubois had returned. When she opened the door, her breath caught in surprise. Sergeant Andy Rodriguez stood on the doorstep, his expression grave.

Without waiting for an invitation, he stepped inside. His voice was as grim as his demeanor. "Ms. Winters, I'm here to escort you to the police department for another interview."

Chapter 7

While his comment sent a surge of anxiety rushing through her, the formal use of her name startled her even more. "Good lord, why?" she exclaimed.

He cleared his throat before saying, "There are a few details we need to clarify."

With a steady look, Tori replied, "Do I have a choice?"

His body stiffened. "I'm here as a courtesy. If necessary, I will get a warrant."

Mia stepped into the hallway, wiping her hands on a towel. "I thought I heard your voice, Andy. Why are you here?" she asked as she approached them.

"I need to speak with Ms. Winters at the police department," he explained.

Mia quickened her steps, her voice harsh with urgency. "Ms. Winters? What's going on? I don't understand. Is Tori under arrest?"

"No, ma'am," he said, his tone neutral. "But she is a person of interest in the case."

He turned back to Tori. "Ms. Winters, let's go."

"At least let me get my tote bag," Tori snapped, her voice sharp. "It's in the office."

"I'll get it," Mia said quickly. "Anything else?"

"My phone is on the desk."

Once she'd slung the bag over her shoulder, she followed Andy out the door. As she eyed the police car with dismay, her steps lagged. Trying to inject some levity into the situation, she quipped, "Do I have to sit in the back like a prisoner?"

"No, ma'am," Andy replied, opening the passenger door. "That won't be necessary."

Tori glanced back to see Mia standing on the porch, her face contorted with anxiety while she talked on her phone.

When Andy pulled onto the street, a man darted from behind a tree, camera in hand. He stepped into the street, raising the lens as the squad car passed.

Startled, Tori froze. Too late, she realized he had snapped her face. "Who was that?" she asked, her voice tight.

Andy's expression darkened. "I don't know."

"You're not going to stop and find out?"

"Not with you in the car. There's nothing I can do right now," he said, his tone resigned.

She groaned, sinking into her seat. Just when she thought things couldn't get worse, they did. She wondered grimly which newspaper the photo would end up in.

Andy parked in a reserved spot outside the police station, then escorted Tori inside to a small conference room. "Please, have a seat," he said curtly. "I'll be right back." He closed the door behind him.

Tori settled into a chair, placing her tote bag beside her. Her gaze swept the room. The cold, sterile walls seemed to close in. A tingling unease crept over her when she spotted the cameras mounted in the corners of the ceiling. *Were they watching her now? Listening?*

Her phone buzzed. She quickly pulled it from her pocket. Parker's name flashed across the screen.

His voice carried a hint of urgency. "Mia called. Where are you?"

"I'm at the police station in a conference room."

"I'm on my way, and so is Lincoln Greer."

"Why is Linc coming? I'm not under arrest," Tori protested, though a hint of doubt flickered in her mind.

"I don't like how Andy handled this," Parker said bluntly. "He could have called and asked you to come to the station. I called Dan. He contacted Jonah since he or Linc can get there faster than Dan."

Disturbed by Parker's words, Tori frowned as she ended the call. Was this situation spiraling into something more serious than she had anticipated?

The door opened suddenly, and Andy returned with a voice recorder. Her stomach clenched at seeing it.

Not one to shy away from a confrontation, she squared her shoulders. "Is there a problem here I don't know about? Do I need a lawyer?"

Andy's impassive expression never wavered. "If you believe it's necessary, by all means." His even tone only deepened her apprehension.

Before she could respond, the door opened again. A uniformed officer stepped inside, his gaze flicking between Andy and Tori. "Lincoln Greer and Parker Hayes are here," he announced.

Linc pushed past the officer, striding into the room with Parker on his heels.

"What's going on, Andy? Why is Tori here?" Linc demanded, his voice sharp.

Ignoring Linc, Andy focused on Parker. "You can't be in here," he said.

Parker's jaw tightened, his lips pressing into a firm, unforgiving line. His eyes darkened, locking onto Andy's face with a cold, steady glare. Without a word, he turned on his heel and left.

Linc slid into a chair next to Tori.

"Linc, are you representing Ms. Winters?" Andy asked.

"Yes, I am. I'm still waiting for an explanation. Why is she here?"

Andy fiddled with the recorder. "After the picture of the victim was published, witnesses came forward with new information regarding Ms. Winters' encounter at the ghost tour, raising new questions."

"Who are these witnesses?" Linc snapped.

Andy shot Linc a disapproving glance. "You know I can't tell you."

"Have you arrested Tori?"

"No, I have not, though I will record this session."

Linc's jaw clenched, but he nodded grimly before

turning to Tori. "If I don't like a question, I'll object."

Andy switched on the recorder, his voice steady while he stated the date, the purpose of the interview, and the names of those present. Opening a file folder in front of him, he continued, "I have your written statement. I'd like to go over the details again."

With precision, he walked Tori through what had happened during the ghost tour. She answered each question calmly, though a suffocating tension gripped her.

"Do you still claim you do not own a gun?"

"I've never owned one," she said, her voice steady.

"I understand you moved here from Missouri. Did you own a gun there?"

"No, I didn't," she said, her voice sharpening with anger.

Andy's gaze was unyielding. "And you still contend you do not know the man?"

"Yes. The only time I saw him was at the ghost tour."

"What would you say if I told you two witnesses claim you and the victim had argued?"

Stunned, she leaned over the table. "That's a lie. There was no argument."

"What would you say if I told you one of them recorded the encounter on a cell phone?"

Her eyes blazed with anger. "I'm still telling you there was no argument. I've already told you what happened with the two women. If they're your witnesses, they're lying."

"Are you absolutely certain you didn't argue with the man?" Andy pressed.

Linc spoke up. "The question has been asked and answered. If you have evidence to prove otherwise, then produce it."

Andy's finger tapped a button on the recorder. "That's all I have for now."

Tori shoved back her chair and grabbed her bag.

Linc said, "Wait for me. I want to talk to Andy."

She marched around the table with her back straight and head held high. Angrily, she threw open the door.

Seated in the hallway, Parker and David rose as soon as they saw her.

David strode toward her, concern etched on his face. At her surprised look, he said, "Mia called me. Let's go."

She shook her head. "I can't leave yet. Linc wants to talk to me."

"Not here," Parker interjected firmly. "David, pull your truck up to the front door. I'm not taking a chance on a reporter lurking about."

Without hesitation, David turned and bolted out the door.

"What about Linc?" Tori asked, casting a nervous look over her shoulder.

His tone grim, Parker said, "He'll figure it out."

Near the front door, Parker shielded Tori from the view of anyone in the parking lot. When David's truck rolled to a stop, Parker hustled her outside and into the vehicle. Tori barely had time to close the door before David gunned the truck and tore out of the parking lot.

During the drive to the house, Tori filled David in on

what happened at the police station. "Andy said two witnesses saw me arguing with the man who was killed. And he's got a video. I bet they're the same two women I encountered at the ghost tour."

His brow furrowed with concern as he asked, "Did you find out their names?"

"Linc asked, but Andy refused to tell him."

After David parked in the driveway, Parker pulled alongside him. As they started toward the front porch, Linc drove in, his vehicle screeching to a halt.

He hopped out. His face tight with irritation, Linc said, "Tori, I *told* you to wait for me."

Anger flashed in David's eyes as he responded with a grim tone. "Getting her out of there was more important than talking to you."

The two men locked gazes, an unspoken challenge crackling in the air.

With a dismissive flick of his hand, Linc turned to Tori and said in a clipped tone, "We need to talk. I'll take you to my office."

Tori, tossing her head, said, "No. I'm not going anywhere. We'll talk inside." Without waiting for a response, she briskly walked up the porch steps where Parker and Mia stood.

Mia's anxious gaze swept over Tori, her lips pressed into a thin line. Without a word, she turned and walked inside.

Linc caught up with Tori in the entryway. "If you won't come to my office, then we'll use yours. But I must speak to you alone. Mia, Parker, or David can't be included," he insisted.

Tori replied, "No. This isn't a closed discussion."

"Tori," he demanded, "as your attorney, whatever we discuss must be private."

Still angry, she whirled. "Linc, someone lied about me. There is a killer out there, and it isn't me. I'm not leaving this up to the police, and I'm not leaving it up to you. Either get on board or get out of my way."

Chapter 8

Depressed, Tori stabbed the button on the coffee machine. She was still the prime suspect in a murder, not an encouraging way to start the day. After the relentless interrogation at the police department, the meeting in her office hadn't gone well. Without the identity of the murder victim or the witnesses, any investigation was stalled before it began.

Linc wasn't much help. He refused to enter into the discussion. Instead, he sat, stone-faced with crossed arms. Even Parker had little to contribute.

With another finger jab, she stopped the machine long enough to partially fill a cup before heading to her office. A knock on the back door had her changing directions. When she unlocked it, Colt stood on the stoop.

"I took a look at the warehouse yesterday," he said as he strolled inside, bringing the crisp morning air.

"Oh, my gosh, I forgot about the inspection. What did you think?" She motioned toward the coffee pot.

Colt grabbed a cup and filled it with coffee. He lowered himself into a chair. "The place is sound. I had a plumber and electrician examine the building. No problems there. The sprinkler system's in good shape, the foundation's solid, and I couldn't find any structural issues with the roof." He took a deep swig.

"That's good news. I can go ahead with the closing then. Once the sale is finalized, I'll need freestanding shelves installed. Do you have time to tackle another project?"

"Won't be a problem," Colt replied, taking another swallow of his coffee. "I can also send a couple of my men to move your inventory from the storage unit. Before we do anything, the place needs a good cleaning. Do you want me to handle it?"

"Please." Tori nodded with relief.

Colt finished off the coffee. "Let me know when you're ready." He rose, setting his cup in the sink, and walked out.

Tori refilled her cup and headed to her office. She had to let Jonah know about the inspection. But after the previous day's events, she wasn't up to talking to him.

When Linc left, he was infuriated that Tori had overridden his advice and gone ahead with a group discussion. He'd likely shared his ire with his Dad.

Instead of a phone call, she sent a quick email regarding the inspection, stating she was ready to proceed with the closing. Then, she sent a second one to the realtor.

The sound of the front door closing echoed. "It's me," Mia called out.

Her attention fixed on the computer, Tori said loudly,

"Good news! We've got a warehouse. Colt gave it a thumbs up."

Mia's response was clipped as she stepped into the office. "I can't say the same."

Tori's head snapped around at the blunt tone. The newspaper clutched in Mia's hands triggered an unwelcome flashback—the man snapping a picture. "Oh, no!" she groaned.

Mia waved the folded newspaper before slapping it onto Tori's desk. "Oh, yes! You made the front page. Picture and everything." She tossed her bag on the floor and sank into a chair.

Tori unfolded the paper as indignation surged through her. "Of course. Who else but the *Metro* with their scandalous innuendos?"

She read. *Murder in Granbury's Shadows. A disturbing encounter occurred between the infamous Granbury heiress, Tori Winters, and an unidentified man on a near-deserted street in the dead of night. Minutes later, the man was shot to death in an alley, a mere three blocks from where Winters and the man had argued. Has Winters become the prime suspect in the murder? Why else would the police transport the heiress to the police station for another round of questioning? What nefarious dealings is she involved in this time? It appears the heiress might have found herself in deeper trouble than even her wealth can get her out of."*

Enraged, she squealed, "Prime suspect! Nefarious! I bet that reporter, Phyllis, what's her name, is behind this. Isn't it interesting that she doesn't mention the ghost tour?" She tossed the paper on the desk. Not long after she arrived in Granbury, she became the target of the woman's spurious articles.

"Hess," Mia said. The disgust in her tone was unmistakable, as though merely uttering the name left a bitter taste behind.

Tori waved her hand dismissively. "Whatever."

Mia's brow furrowed with puzzlement. "How did someone get a picture of you in the police car?"

"When Andy pulled out of the driveway, some guy ran into the street, snapping pictures as we passed. That's how they got the dang thing." Fuming, she studied the picture of her sitting wide-eyed, mouth agape, in the front seat of a police car.

Mia leaned over the desk, tapping the newspaper with a fingernail. "Which raises the real question. How did someone know? No way the photographer was there by chance. This was planned. Who leaked the details, and who knew Andy was hauling you to the station?"

"It had to be one of the witnesses," Tori muttered.

The front doorbell rang. Tori groaned. "I bet it's Dubois. The last thing I need right now is a stranger in the house. I wonder if I should reschedule the appraisal."

The doorbell echoed again. "While you ponder the problem, I'll let him in. Did you open the door to the wine cellar?" Mia said.

Tori groaned. "No, I didn't. I forgot."

"Then keep him occupied for a few minutes," she said, rushing out.

Moments later, Dubois appeared in the hallway, his posture stiff and deliberate.

Tori cleared her throat. "Mr. Dubois, I'd like to speak with you briefly."

He stepped into the doorway, his sharp gaze landing on her.

To give Mia time to open the cellar door, Tori gestured to the nearest chair. "Please, have a seat."

"I'd rather stand," he replied curtly. "What is it you wanted?"

Tori swallowed her irritation, keeping her tone courteous. "I was impressed with your articles, especially the ones on proper wine storage methods. If there are any improvements I could make, I'd value your insight."

"I don't provide individual recommendations," he said, glancing at his watch. "If there's nothing else, I'll get started." Without waiting for a reply, he spun on his heel and strode toward the kitchen.

Tori had to concede his articles, peppered with witticisms, were far more appealing than the man himself.

A few moments later, Mia returned, closing the door behind her. "He's an odd duck, isn't he?"

"You're being generous," Tori grumbled. "Still, he's considered one of the top wine connoisseurs in the business. I felt fortunate I was able to hire him."

"Are you canceling the project?"

"No. Though having him in the house right now isn't the best timing."

A second sound of the doorbell had Mia dashing out

the door. This time, Parker strolled into her office.

At the sight of the newspaper in his hand, Tori frowned. "I guess you read the article."

"I did, which is why we need to talk." Parker sat and laid the paper on the desk. "I don't like the reporter's reference to an argument." He removed his laptop from the bag.

"It certainly didn't happen," Tori said firmly.

Parker nodded as he booted the computer. "I want to know every detail, starting with when you first arrived at the ghost tour."

Before she could begin, Mia strolled in and handed Parker a cup of coffee. "Unless you need me here, I'll be in the kitchen riding herd on our visitor."

Tori said, "I'd like for you to stay. Dubois is the least of my worries right now, but please close the door."

Before she started, Tori took a fortifying sip. As Parker listened, he typed steadily, occasionally pausing to ask a question.

When Tori reached the part about the confrontation with the woman, Parker's questions grew sharper, urging Tori to remember as many details as possible.

Once she finished, Parker kept typing, his fingers steady on the keys. Finally, with a sigh, he leaned back, swallowing the last of his coffee. "Here's what I think. You were set up. The ticket was bait to get you to the ghost tour so this confrontation could happen—and be recorded."

Tori's stomach dropped. "But why? What motive could they possibly have?"

"A couple come to mind. One, to embarrass you, painting you as the aggressor. The other? Far worse—an assault charge. The woman did shout you hit her."

Tori's shoulders tightened with tension. "You're right. It's already started. When the Swansons were here the other day, Carly made a point to let me know a new rumor was floating, and it was all about me. How I assaulted a woman at the ghost tour."

With a thoughtful expression, Parker leaned back. "Now, that's interesting. I wonder how she knew. Wasn't she here the day after the ghost tour?"

"Sure was. It doesn't take Carly long to spread bad news." She cocked an eyebrow. "But how could I possibly be charged with assault?"

Parker leaned forward, his voice low. "She was provoking you. If you'd raised your hands to defend yourself, and someone happened to film it, they'd have the perfect footage." He tapped the paper. "Same newspaper, different article."

Tori's face turned grim as the implications sank in. "You mean they wanted me to react, to make me look guilty." Her voice throbbed with anger and disbelief. "I can't believe this. Someone set a trap, and I walked right into it."

"What strikes me as odd is the victim's intervention. It doesn't seem like part of their plan, and that's where it gets dicey. Did one of the women kill him to frame you, or did they seize the opportunity when he was killed? Either way, they've put you on the hook for the murder, especially since the victim had a paper with your name and address."

Fear flashed in her eyes as Tori stared at him. "Parker, am I about to be arrested for murder?"

With a steady tone, he said, "A possibility since you *are* a person of interest. Do I think it will happen? No. Andy doesn't have evidence, a weapon, or even a motive to justify an arrest warrant. He hasn't even identified the victim, which is slowing him down. Right now, all he's got is two witnesses saying you argued and a video that supposedly backs them up."

Tori straightened, a glimmer of hope igniting. "The video should prove I'm telling the truth."

"There's the problem. It might not," Parker warned. "That's why I needed you to go over everything in detail. You mentioned you were shocked when the man said he'd been following you. I'm concerned your reaction could be twisted to support the accusation you argued with him."

Tori groaned, pressing her palms to her temples. "Oh, my gosh, can this get any worse?"

"Linc is pushing Andy to let him see the video and release the witnesses' names." Parker's brow furrowed. "But I doubt he'll get anything unless you're arrested, which means we have to figure it out ourselves."

He turned to Mia. "Do you know Vada Struthers? Can you get her to talk?"

"I do, but I doubt I'll have any luck. Vada's not who I would refer to as a friend." A thoughtful expression crossed her face. "There may be another way. We do have some friends in common. Vada was never one to keep a secret."

Excitement flickered in Tori's voice. "She might be gossiping about what happened?"

"Exactly." Mia nodded. "There's more than one way to skin a cat."

"Once we identify the women, we can piece together a motive." Parker shut his laptop and slipped it into his bag. "I'm also concerned about the *Metro's* role in this. Someone's feeding them information. That's a lead I can run down."

After Parker left, Mia turned to Tori, a determined look in her eye. "I'm going shopping. Some of those friends work in stores I frequent. Don't you need to be at the opera house today?"

"This afternoon."

"I'll be back before you leave."

After Mia left, Tori wandered to the music room, determined to make use of the time with a few hours of practice.

As her fingers rippled over the keys for the opening notes of the first selection on the program, the doorbell chimed. For a moment, she considered ignoring it, but the sound of the piano would have given her away. Yet, when she saw who stood on the porch, she wished she had left the door unanswered.

With one of her smug smiles, Myra said, "We hate to interrupt, but we need to talk to you." Without waiting for an invitation, she pushed past Tori. Carly followed, shooting Tori a scathing glance.

Tori motioned toward the living room. "Have a seat."

"We won't be here long," Myra said. Though she plunked down on the couch as if settling in for an extended visit.

Tori sank into an armchair, her legs crossed as she gazed at the two women. As always, they were impeccably dressed, with flawless makeup, perfectly styled hair, and four-inch heels that added to their polished appearance. Though taller, Carly was a younger version of Myra, with her short blond hair curving neatly around her chin.

From their self-satisfied expressions and cold look in their light blue eyes, they were up to no good. Tori folded her hands in her lap and waited with a calmness that was as fake as their smiles.

Myra cleared her throat delicately. "My dear, this is such a difficult task for us. But we felt we had no choice." She leaned forward. A hint of malice sparked in her eyes. "This must be dealt with quickly."

Tori waited with an unwavering gaze.

As the silence stretched, Myra fluttered her hand as if uneasy before rushing to say, "Of course, we don't believe the gossip." Her voice dripped with false assurance.

Despite Tori's inscrutable expression, her mind raced. The gossip could only mean one thing, the *Metro* article.

"Nevertheless, the severity of the accusations could be disastrous for the opera house," Myra declared. Her faint smile sharpened as her eyes gleamed with triumphant vindictiveness that she couldn't entirely conceal.

Tori arched an eyebrow, her voice cool. "Is there a point to all this?"

Carly's expression lit up with a gleeful smirk. "What Mother is trying to say, ever so diplomatically, is that since you're a suspect in a murder, your concert is canceled."

Anger flared within Tori, but she kept it tightly restrained, unwilling to give them the satisfaction of seeing her react. "And who made this decision?" she asked steadily.

"Regrettably, the board devoted considerable attention to your legal troubles, and rightfully so. The publicity you've already received is cause for concern," Myra said, her tone tinged with an unmistakable air of self-importance. "Since we know you, everyone felt it best to let us inform you."

Tori rose. "You've informed me. I'll show you to the door." She didn't miss the flicker of dismay on their faces at her lack of reaction. She stepped into the foyer and held the door open.

As Myra passed, she sighed. "So distressing, but, my dear, this is for the best. After all, it's not as if you're a professional pianist. You're just an amateur."

Carly shot one final barb over her shoulder. "You're simply not the kind of person who belongs here. And Elly's money will never change that."

Tori gently closed the door, though every fiber of her itched to slam it shut. Carly and her mother had thrown down the gauntlet with a vengeance, their hateful words cutting through her like a blade.

Anger propelled her toward her office, where she slumped into her chair, impatiently waiting for Mia to return. While Myra and Carly might believe they had the last word, Tori wasn't about to go down without a fight.

A sound in the hallway drew her attention. Dubois passed by her doorway, briefly nodding as he kept going. For once, his leaving early didn't irk her, though a disturbing thought flicked in her mind. Had he heard their declaration that she was a murder suspect? If he did, there wasn't much she could do about it.

Eager to leave, she grabbed a pen to leave a note for Mia. But the rumble of a car stopped her. Tossing the pen aside, she snatched up her tote bag and keys.

Tori intercepted Mia at the front door. "I've got to leave. Myra and Carly showed up to tell me the concert was canceled because I'm a suspect in a murder."

"What? Wait. Slow down. Where are you going?" Mia asked, her eyes widening as Tori flew down the porch steps.

"The opera house. Dubois has left. I'll call you," Tori said, racing toward the garage.

Traffic was light, and she soon parked on the square across from the opera house. When she reached the front door, she straightened her shoulders, a spark of aggressiveness igniting within her. She was Elly's granddaughter, and she had no intention of being underestimated.

Chapter 9

Resolutely, she shoved the door open and marched into the foyer. From behind the front counter, the receptionist's face lit up with a bright smile. "Good to see you, Tori. You're early, but I don't think that's a problem."

The greeting rocked her back on her heels, confusion flooding her senses. *What's going on?* she thought.

"Uh … is … Nora here?" she stammered.

"The last time I saw her, she was headed to the hall."

Without hesitation, Tori raced up the stairs, taking them two at a time. Inside the hall, she spotted Nora on stage, deep in conversation with Dwayne near the concert grand piano. Her footsteps echoed as she ran down the steps.

Nora looked up at the sound. "Tori!" she exclaimed, relief in her voice. "I'm glad you're here. I was about to call you."

Breathless, Tori skidded to a stop.

"Why are you quitting?" Nora demanded. "Myra called and said you decided to cancel the concert because of that awful *Metro* article."

A light went off in Tori's head. "Myra told me the Board canceled the concert because of the article."

Nora's expression darkened. "No, we didn't. We discussed the article but dismissed it as nothing but tripe. Myra must have misunderstood."

Yeah, right, Tori thought bitterly. *That woman didn't misunderstand anything. She lied through her teeth.*

Dwayne stepped in, his tone reassuring. "I'm relieved this is cleared up. Are you ready to go over the program?"

"You bet."

Nora placed a hand on her shoulder. "I'll be in my office if you need anything."

"Dwayne, I hope we won't need the sheet music," Tori said. In her rush to leave the house, she'd left it behind.

"If you don't, neither do I."

"I don't," she said confidently, setting her tote bag on a nearby chair.

For the next few hours, Tori played and sang, stopping only when Dwayne decided to take a break or requested that she replay a particular selection. The music worked its magic, soothing the storm of emotions Myra and Carly's malicious stunt had stirred.

As they wrapped up, Dwayne turned to her with an encouraging smile. "There's no way we'd consider canceling your concert. In fact, I think it will be the event of the year for us."

Relieved and grateful, Tori smiled. "I hope so."

The encouragement had her sailing out the door until

she approached her car. "Oh, no, not again," she wailed.

Unbelievably, she stared at another flat tire. How was that possible? With a sigh of resignation, she tapped the number for the wrecker service. When a man answered, Tori said, "Hi, this is Tori Winters. I've got another flat tire."

"Where are you, Ms. Winters?"

"The same place as before, the parking lot across from the opera house."

"I'm on my way, and I'll bring the other tire."

"Thank you." After settling behind the wheel, she called Mia.

With an anxious tone, Mia said, "Tori, I've been on pins and needles since you left. What happened?"

"Typical Myra, that's what happened," Tori spat, her words laced with contempt. "She told me the Board canceled the concert because of the article, then had the gall to call Nora and tell her I quit for the same reason."

"How sneaky and manipulative can one person be?" Mia fired back. "She'll probably excuse her behavior by blaming you. You misunderstood."

"No doubt. Also, I've got another flat tire. Can you believe it?"

"Oh, no. Where are you?"

"Same parking lot as before. I'm waiting for the wrecker."

"Seems bad luck is following you around."

"No kidding." She disconnected the call, leaning against the headrest as she stewed over Myra and Carly's vicious attempt to derail the concert. The honk of a horn broke into her musings. Her gaze shot to the rearview mirror. The wrecker driver had arrived. She hopped out and saw the driver lifting a tire from the back of the truck. He rolled it toward her car.

"Hi, Ted. What was wrong with it?" she asked.

"Nothing's wrong with the tire. All I could find was the loose cap on the valve stem."

She watched as he jacked up the car with practiced ease. Once he'd replaced the flat tire, he turned it, examining the sides and tread. "Umm … not seeing a problem with this one either," he said. "I'll let you know."

On the drive home, Tori couldn't shake her uneasy feeling. Mia's comment about bad luck didn't sit well. She'd had her fair share ever since she found the ticket in her mailbox. And what were the odds of two flat tires?

By the time she pulled into the driveway, everyone had left. With a weary sigh, she dropped her tote bag on a chair in her office before settling behind the desk. After booting the computer, she checked her emails. One was from Harley, with the date of the closing.

Tori stared at the message for a long moment as a realization dawned on her, rejuvenating her spirits. This was the first piece of property she'd ever bought. Everything she owned, this house included, had been inherited. A slow grin spread across her face. "By golly," she muttered, "this calls for a celebration."

With a glass of wine in hand, she meandered through the quiet house. It no longer felt foreign, as if she were simply occupying someone else's space. While she wandered, she paused in front of the portrait of her great-grandparents. She tipped her glass toward Frankie, the gangster who had left an unbelievable legacy.

The sound of the doorbell broke her reverie. When she opened the door, a warmth spread through her. David stood there, his familiar grin lighting up his face.

He glanced at her glass and quipped, "Any chance there's more where that came from?"

She laughed and stepped aside. "Sure is. Come on back to the kitchen. As a matter of fact, I've got a whole cellar full of the stuff."

David's voice took on a casual lilt as they strolled down the hallway. "Have you eaten?"

"Not yet."

"Could I interest you in a pizza?"

"Oh, it sounds perfect."

As she filled a wine glass, he was already on the phone ordering two fully loaded meat specials. They settled at the table in the breakfast nook, where the warm glow of the setting sun spilled across the room. Tori sipped her wine, watching the twilight's rosy hues slowly fade into deeper shades of color.

Across from her, David lounged in his chair, his long legs stretched under the table. For reasons she couldn't quite name, the world around her suddenly felt calmer, more grounded.

"How was your day?" she asked.

"Good. I have a short respite from the Austin project."

"Ah, more poker time, then." She grinned, teasing him about his weekly poker games. David and his friends took card-playing seriously, rotating houses for their gatherings. Even Colt had quickly become part of the group after moving to Granbury.

"Maybe," he said with a chuckle, "but hopefully more time for other things, too."

A faint flutter stirred within her when his gaze caught hers. It wasn't unpleasant, just mildly unsettling. But before she could linger on it, he said in a casual tone, "How's the practicing going?"

Relieved at the change in topic, she exclaimed, "You're not going to believe Myra's latest stunt."

David's expression tightened subtly. "I probably would. What did she do this time?" he said dryly.

Tori launched into the story. When she reached the part about the newspaper article, the reason for the two women's visit, David's casual demeanor disappeared. He straightened, his brow furrowing. "What article?"

"I'll grab it." She left and returned with the folded paper, handing it to him.

As his eyes scanned the page, his scowl deepened. "What rubbish. Who's behind this?"

"The culprit may be one of the two witnesses the police came up with. Andy is still not talking, though Parker is investigating, and so is Mia."

"What's Mia doing?"

Tori briefly explained.

When she finished, David said with a slight grin, "I'd

put my money on Mia." He gave the paper a shake. "Tell me the rest."

After recounting the events, she added, "Nora excused Myra's behavior as a misunderstanding."

David snorted. "Myra does nothing that's a misunderstanding. And that includes Carly."

Tori suppressed a smile, unwilling to examine why David's criticism of the women left her feeling oddly validated.

The sudden ring of her phone broke the moment. She pulled it from her pocket. It was the wrecker company. "Hello," she said after tapping the screen.

"Ms. Winters, this is Ted. I examined your tire, and there's no damage. The only issue was a loose valve stem cap, similar to the one on the other tire. If you can swing by the shop, I'll replace your spare and check the other two to be sure they aren't damaged."

"Thank you, Ted. I'll stop by tomorrow."

She disconnected and set the phone aside. At David's questioning look, she said, "That was Ted with A-Z Wrecker Service. I had another flat tire."

"With all the construction, it'd be easy to pick up a nail," David said.

"The tires weren't damaged." Her voice tightened with uneasiness. "All he found was loose caps on the valve stem."

When the doorbell echoed, David rose. "I bet that's the pizza. I'll get it."

As Tori pulled plates from the cupboard, she thought

about the tires. Could someone have tampered with them? The idea seemed absurd, even paranoid. After all, the parking lot in front of the opera house was always bustling, filled with people coming and going during the day. Surely, someone would have noticed anything out of the ordinary.

Yet, the unease persisted. A quiet, insistent whisper that Tori couldn't shake echoed the same unsettling prickle she'd felt in the parking lot days ago.

The mouthwatering aroma of onions, garlic, and pepperoni drifting through the air was a welcome distraction. David set the pizza boxes on the center island and flipped one open with an exaggerated flourish.

"Oh, that looks perfect," Tori said, eyeing the steaming pie.

"I'm starved." David grabbed a plate, piling on pieces. "Missed lunch again."

Once seated at the table, they ate in companionable silence, the quiet only broken by the occasional sound of crust crunching or the clink of a glass.

With a reluctant glance at the remaining half of the pizza, Tori declared, "I can't eat another bite."

David grinned and, without missing a beat, slid the slices onto his plate. His eyes gleamed with mischief. "I was hoping you'd say so. I'd already decided if you didn't stop, I'd have to order three pizzas next time since you're such a glutton."

She straightened, her face indignant. "I'm *not* a glutton. I have a healthy appetite."

"Sweetheart, for a five-foot-three, hundred-and-ten-pound dripping wet woman, you have an enormous capacity for pizza. In my books, that's a glutton."

She didn't know whether to be insulted at being called a glutton or euphoric over being called a sweetheart. Before she could decide, he shifted gears.

"Do you think someone tampered with your tires?" he asked, his voice serious now.

The chill she'd felt earlier crept back. "The thought crossed my mind," she admitted. "But how? The car's always in the garage when I'm home, and the parking lot in front of the opera house is always busy."

David finished the last bite of his pizza and sat back. "It does seem unlikely," he said, though his expression seemed doubtful. "What's on your agenda for tomorrow?"

"First, a stop at the wrecker shop. Ted said he'd replace the tire and check the other two. Then I have a practice scheduled at the opera house. I might also need to swing by Landis Realty to sign some papers."

A grin spread across her face as excitement bubbled up. "Oh, my, gosh! I didn't tell you my big news! You're looking at the proud owner of a warehouse."

David raised his eyebrows, clearly impressed. "A warehouse? That's a big move. What made you decide to buy one?"

"Well," she began, "we already have two storage units, and we'll need a third soon with how inventory's growing. Consolidating everything into one place made sense. It'll save us a ton of hassle in the long run."

"I'd like to see it when you get the keys," David said with a thoughtful smile. "We'll have to celebrate—properly."

The glint was back in his eyes, and this time, stirring something deep within her, something she didn't entirely know how to define. She smiled back, her heart skipping slightly. "I like the idea."

"Good," he said, standing and gathering their plates. "But for now, I'll help you clean up this mess. Then I need to head to my office. I have a report to finalize for a meeting tomorrow."

At the front door, he looked down at her, his fingers gently tilting her chin. His lips brushed hers in a light, lingering kiss, leaving her breathless.

"I'll probably see you tomorrow," he murmured, his voice low and warm.

With a deep sigh of contentment, Tori watched him stride to his truck and drive out before heading inside to check the lock on the back door.

As she passed the doorway to the pantry, she hesitated. The familiar disquiet she always associated with Dubois fluttered in her chest. On a whim, she opened the cellar door and trotted down the stairs. The stillness was unnerving. The table was bare, leaving no indication of what the man had done.

Her eyes drifted to the shelves of wine. Something about them felt ... off. Was it her imagination, or did most of the bottles look undisturbed? Tori sighed, brushing aside her misgivings. Talking to herself, she said, "I'm overthinking this. It's probably because I don't particularly like the guy."

Shaking her head, she climbed the stairs, closing the cellar door behind her. Determined to focus on her concert, she headed to the music room.

Soon, the rich piano notes swelled, filling the house with sound. The hours melted away as she played and replayed sections, each repetition bringing more confidence, smoothing over every minor hesitation or stumble.

With a sense of satisfaction, Tori finally stood. She ambled from room to room, turning off the lights, before checking the security system in her office. Secure in the belief that the house was protected, Tori headed to her bedroom.

****

A figure lingered motionless in the shadows of the trees bordering the property. Shrouded by the dense canopy, his breath formed faint clouds in the cool night air. When the final light inside the house flickered out, he retreated deeper into the darkness as silently as he had appeared. The time would be etched onto a growing list of details about the woman within.

Chapter 10

fter settling into her desk chair the next morning, Tori's first task was to check her emails. Among the usual clutter, one from the realtor caught her eye. Eagerly, she opened it. Several attachments were included, along with instructions for the closing. Relief washed over her when she discovered she didn't have to attend. Once finalized, Harley would arrange a time to drop off the keys.

By the time Mia arrived, Tori had returned the signed documents and issued the payment for the balance of the purchase price. Eager to share the news, she picked up her cup and shoved her chair back.

In the kitchen, Mia was unpacking a sack of groceries. She said, "I was just coming to see if you wanted a refill."

"I do. I just sent off the papers to close on the purchase of the warehouse."

Busy stacking boxes of cookies on the counter for the construction crew, Mia said, "That's great news. This went a lot faster than I anticipated."

As Tori picked up the coffee pot, Mia loudly cleared her throat.

Tori paused to glance up, catching the mischievous glint in Mia's eyes.

"I couldn't help but notice the two pizza boxes in the trash," she said. A sly smile crossed her face.

Though Tori's lips twitched, she ignored the remark and filled her cup.

Undeterred, Mia pressed on. "Guess you had some company last night. Dare I ask if your visitor was David?"

Tori smirked, sipping her coffee. "Nothing gets by you, does it?"

"I'll take that as a yes," Mia responded with satisfaction. "Any details you'd like to share, or do I have to rely on my imagination?" She waggled her eyebrows suggestively.

"Not much to share," Tori said calmly, not giving Mia any opening for another impish remark. She settled into a chair. "He ordered pizza, and we talked. There are no salacious details to brighten your day."

Mia chuckled. "Well, one can always hope." Stepping toward the coffee pot, her tone took on a reflective edge. "You know, one of these days, that will change." She filled a cup. "We both know David is more than a friend."

"Maybe," Tori admitted. "But I'm not ready. And, really, when would I even have time for a relationship? There's the renovation, launching a new business, and now I'm a suspect in a murder." She took a sip of coffee before adding with a note of indignation, "Not to mention the concert I got goaded into. I have more than enough on my plate."

Leaning against the counter, Mia regarded Tori thoughtfully. "We always make time for what's important. The real issue isn't how busy you are. It's that you're not ready. And that's okay." Another smile tugged at her lips. "The good news is, David isn't going anywhere. I see how he looks at you, and trust me, it's not as a friend."

Tori wondered if Mia was right.

Mia took a sip of her coffee. "So, what's on the agenda today?"

"I've got to stop by the wrecker company and get my tire. Ted, the wrecker driver, called last night."

"What was wrong this time?"

"Just another loose cap. He's going to check the other two."

With a look of puzzlement, Mia asked, "So, how did your tires go flat?"

"I don't know. I've wondered if it was deliberate, but the parking lot is a busy place."

Mia frowned. "Why on earth would someone mess with your tires?"

Before Tori could answer, the doorbell resounded. She set her cup down and straightened. "I bet that's Dubois. I'll let him in." The concerns from her visit to the cellar lingered, and she was determined to get some answers.

As she swung the door open, Tori said, "Good morning."

"Hello," he replied curtly, stepping inside without meeting her eyes.

"Mr. Dubois, I'd like to speak to you before you start." She led him to her office and gestured toward the chair opposite her desk. "Please, have a seat."

He lowered himself stiffly into the chair, setting his briefcase on the floor beside him. His demeanor was as chilly as ever. "Is this going to be a regular morning event? If so, I will adjust my schedule to accommodate your meetings."

Her tone was equally as cool. "Mr. Dubois, this is a very important project. It shouldn't be surprising to a man with your qualifications that I would expect a status report. And if there are any changes to your timeframes for finishing the project, I need to know."

His jaw tightened. "Any report or changes would be untimely, as the inventory is barely underway."

"You've been here for two days," Tori said firmly. "Surely you can provide some details."

Dubois' lips pressed into a thin line. "Quite frankly, I don't discuss a project until I'm finished. My reputation is based on accuracy, not premature conjectures." He rose, snapped up his briefcase, and strode out.

Tori exhaled sharply, tension radiating through her shoulders. She hadn't expected warmth, but his attitude was beginning to test her patience.

A few minutes later, Mia walked in, closing the door behind her. She took one look at Tori's face and winced. "Evidently, your meeting didn't go as planned."

"I haven't figured out if he's a prima donna or just plain rude."

Mia settled into the chair Dubois had vacated. "Probably a combination of both."

Her voice tinged with frustration, Tori said, "This certainly wasn't what I imagined when I hired him. While I don't like it, I'm probably stuck with him. After all, he's one of the top experts in his field."

"Can you get out of the contract?" Mia asked.

"Yes, though there is a penalty clause. The problem is that I'd have to start all over to find someone else. I wanted this done before we opened the inn." She shrugged in resignation. "I guess I can put up with him."

Her cell phone buzzed. Glancing at the screen, Tori frowned. "Uh-oh. I hope this isn't bad news," she muttered before tapping the screen. "Hello, Linc."

"Tori, if you have a few minutes, I'd like to stop by."

"How soon? I do have another practice at the opera house later today."

"I'm on my way."

A worried look settled on her face as she disconnected the call. "Linc's on his way over here. He sounded serious."

"Then you should let Parker know," Mia said.

"You're right." Tori picked up her phone and tapped the speed dial. When Parker answered, she said, "Linc is coming over for a meeting. Any chance you can sit in?"

"I'm already headed your way. I'll be there in a few minutes. Did he tell you why?"

"No, he didn't."

Parker disconnected, and Tori laid the phone aside. A

slow dread crept in, tightening around her chest. "Parker will be here in a few minutes. And I want you here too."

Mia nodded. "I'll be in the kitchen."

By the time the doorbell reverberated through the house, Tori's nerves were stretched tight. She jumped up and rushed out of the office. "I'll get the door!" she called out, her voice ringing down the hallway.

Linc and Parker stood on the porch. Tori stepped aside to let them in, her stomach churning with anxiety.

On the way to her office, Linc tugged her arm, stopping her. "Tori, I absolutely insist that we have a private conversation. What I need to discuss comes under attorney-client privilege. Our discussion must be kept confidential."

She gave him a hard stare. "Linc, I've told you before that's not happening. I want Mia and Parker to hear what you have to say." She marched off, leaving him in the hallway.

With a muttered oath, he rushed to catch up with her.

Once they were seated in her office, Mia shut the door behind her, taking a seat on the small sofa.

Linc, his jaw tight with annoyance, said, "Andy is making noises about a search warrant."

Tori's eyes widened, and her voice rose. "What! A search warrant? How can he possibly justify that?"

"Right now, he can't. He doesn't have enough evidence to get a judge to sign off on one. Still, I wanted to give you a heads-up." Linc paused, studying her face. "I'd like you to consider letting them search the house."

Horrified, Tori stared at him. "No! I can't. Do you know how much damage they'd do to my home, or how much time it'd take? Just the attic would take days. It would be a disaster."

She shuddered. "Then there's the *Metro*. Can you imagine the field day that reporter Hess would have? I can see her headline now." Spreading her hands wide, she announced dramatically, "Police search the mansion of murder suspect—Granbury heiress Tori Winters."

Linc held up a hand to stop her. "I understand your concerns."

"Do you really? Did you see the article in the *Metro*?" Tori asked, her frustration bubbling to the surface.

Linc nodded grimly. "Yes. When was the picture taken?"

"Right after we pulled out of the driveway," Tori said.

Linc's lips thinned. "Rather convenient that a photographer happened to be outside your house when Andy showed up to take you to the police station."

Parker frowned. "I did some checking with a contact at the *Metro*. The leak didn't come from the police. All my source could tell me is that it's a woman. Apparently, the reporter is the only one who knows her identity."

"It must be one of the witnesses," Linc said. "Who else would be privy to the details in the article and what the police planned to do? Just another reason why a voluntary search would help your case, Tori."

Tori's voice turned sharp. "As far as I'm concerned, there *isn't* a case."

Parker leaned forward. "Did this come from Andy? Did he suggest you get Tori to agree to a search?"

"No," Linc said. "This was my idea, not his."

"I agree with Tori." Parker's voice was adamant. "There's no justification for a search. Despite knowing there is no evidence, a search would do her more harm than good. It would just be fodder for more bad publicity."

Disturbed by the anger in Linc's eyes, Tori quickly said, "Linc, have you found out the identity of the witnesses?"

"No," he admitted. "Andy refuses to identify them."

Intensity sharpened Parker's voice. "There's another possibility you should put to Andy. I believe Tori was set up. Has been from the moment she got the ticket to the ghost tour. After hearing the details of her encounter, the incident was premeditated."

He paused, his eyes narrowing as he stared at Linc. "I'm certain the victim's intervention wasn't part of the plan. Did one of the women kill him to frame Tori? Or are they taking advantage of the situation to make her the prime suspect? We need the names of their witnesses."

Linc's brow furrowed. His tone was dismissive as he said, "I doubt your theory will get Andy to reveal the names." He stood. "Unless you have any more questions, I have to leave."

Mia rose. Opening the door, she nearly collided with Dubois, who stood in the hallway.

"Mr. Dubois," Mia said, arching a brow. "Can I help you with something?"

His gaze slid past her, landing on the group inside. "I need a notepad. Ms. Winters, do you have one?"

"Why, yes, I do." Tori jumped up and opened a cabinet drawer, retrieving a notepad. She handed it to him with a small smile.

Without a word, Dubois took it, his eyes briefly flicking to Parker and Linc before he turned and walked away. Mia followed him into the kitchen.

Linc asked, "Who was that?"

"The wine expert I hired to inventory and appraise the wine collection."

A look of approval crossed his face. "That's something that should have been done long ago. Dad advised your grandmother on more than one occasion to have the collection appraised. But as usual, Elly ignored him."

Tori's jaw tightened at the implied criticism. "But then, Elly didn't have a reason. She knew their value. I don't."

Tori led Linc to the front door, where he paused in the doorway. His eyes lingered on her, their intensity making her shift uncomfortably.

With a troubled tone to his voice, he said, "I'm concerned about the direction this murder investigation has taken. Tori, I don't want to see you harmed by the misguided efforts of others. Unfortunately, that's already happening."

His words struck a nerve, sparking a flicker of dismay. Was he talking about Parker?

Linc reached for her hand, holding it tightly. His voice softened. "I'm here to help you. I know what's in your best interest. You can trust me to guide you and make sure you're safe. But as your attorney and friend, I can't do that unless you listen to me and do what I say."

He let go of her hand. "I'll always be here for you." His fingers brushed her cheek. "I'll call you later." Turning, he walked out.

Disturbed by his words, her mind churned as she closed the door. For some time now, she'd suspected Linc wanted more than a professional relationship with her. Was he using the murder investigation as an excuse to get closer to her? His comment about others' misguided efforts felt possessive and deeply unsettling. Did he believe his voice should be the only one that mattered?

Tori couldn't shake the feeling that while dodging one threat, another was lurking around the corner.

CHAPTER 11

Tori strolled into the office, closing the door behind her. Parker was occupied with his computer. His fingers lightly tapped the keyboard.

Seated on the sofa, Mia shot her a quick glance. "Everything okay?"

"Yep," Tori replied with a brisk tone in her voice.

Mia's eyes narrowed in suspicion.

Her thoughts still circling around Linc's visit, Tori asked, "Parker, can Linc keep Andy from searching the house?"

In a matter-of-fact tone, he said, as he typed, "Andy has to have more than what he's got right now to justify a search warrant."

She groaned, leaning back in her chair. "Just the suggestion is enough to have nightmares about cops tromping all through my house, leaving a wake of havoc behind them. And the adverse publicity isn't helping. I've already had an issue with the opera house."

Parker's fingers stilled. His expression shifted into one of concern. "How so?"

"The Swansons struck again," she said, her words

tinged with frustration. She launched into an explanation, waving her hands as she recounted Myra and Carly's unwelcome visit and her conversation with Nora.

Parker leaned back in his chair, steepling his fingers as he considered her words. "They certainly seem determined to stop you from performing. I wonder." He paused, staring into the distance for a few seconds before asking, "What time will you be at the opera house today?"

She told him, then asked, "Why?"

"David and I cooked up a plan. We're going to watch the parking lot."

Her brow shot up. "What for?"

"David called last night, concerned about what's happened with your tires. I had to agree. It sounds fishy. Maybe one tire, but two? He said you had another practice today. We'll be keeping an eye on your car while you're inside."

Parker tapped a key, then closed the laptop's lid with a definitive click. "How long will you be there?" he asked, slipping the device into his computer bag.

"At least two to three hours," she replied. "Dwayne, the music director, likes to do a complete run-through of the program."

His eyes sparked with interest. "How are you doing?"

"Dwayne says good. Though I still get twitchy thinking about being on the stage with all those people staring at me," she admitted.

"I've heard you play. You're going to be okay." He slung the bag over his shoulder. "I'll see you later today."

He walked out, closing the office door behind him.

Tori barely waited for the door to shut before speaking. "Don't you think it was odd that Dubois was standing outside the door? I got the sense he was listening."

Mia tilted her head thoughtfully. "He sure seemed interested in who was in the room."

"I wonder why?" Tori mused.

"Could be he's just nosy."

"Hmm … maybe." Tori frowned. "His asking for a notepad seemed nothing but a way to explain why he was in the hallway."

"Admit it." Mia chuckled. "You don't like the guy, which makes everything look suspicious. I've got a question for you. What was with that odd look when you walked in?"

"Linc was hitting on me," Tori admitted, with a decided look of exasperation.

Mia roared with laughter. "Linc's problem is he doesn't get it that David's got the inside track."

"Maybe all he wants is a chance to one-up David," Tori observed.

"Could be," Mia said, sobering. "Their rivalry goes back to high school."

Tori hesitated before adding, "He also made a strange comment. He didn't want to see me harmed by others' misguided efforts."

Mia shot upright. "What a spiteful remark," she snapped. "And just who was he referring to?"

"I think he was talking about Parker," Tori said slowly. "Did you catch the look on Linc's face when Parker disagreed with him about searching the house?"

"Oh, I caught it," Mia said, narrowing her eyes. "Linc's always been the type to think he knows best, no matter the situation. He doesn't like someone disagreeing with him."

Tori shook her head, trying to push away the unease still gnawing at her. "Since I've got to stop by the tire shop, I'd better get a hustle on. I don't want to be late for my practice."

****

After leaving the tire repair shop, Tori texted David and Parker to let them know the tires were okay. Once she had parked, she took a few seconds to scan the parking lot. If they were there, she didn't see them.

Rushing inside, she gave the receptionist a warm hello before she hurried up the stairs and into the auditorium. Dwayne stood beside the piano, gesturing while he talked with Myra and Nora.

Tori groaned under her breath. "Great, just great." Myra was the last person she wanted to see or speak to. Irritated, she wondered what Myra was telling them this time.

Obviously, she was the subject of the conversation when Dwayne's voice rang out. "Here she is now."

"Have your ears been burning?" Nora asked enthusiastically. "Dwayne's been giving us an update on your performance. He's singing your praises."

The smile plastered across Myra's face never reached her eyes. "Oh, he's been quite eloquent. It appears your concert is a foregone conclusion. Regrettably, I can't stay." Though her tone remained polite, a glint of cunning flickered in her eyes as she turned away.

The look sent a chill racing over Tori. What scheme was she cooking up this time?

Oblivious to the undercurrents in Myra's demeanor, Nora had continued, her enthusiasm undiminished. "Everyone is excited about your performance. There are only a few tickets left. I've held back ten for you to give to your friends."

"How very thoughtful. Thank you."

Dwayne turned to her with a broad smile. "Are you ready to get started?"

Even though she nodded, the uneasiness from the look she'd seen in Myra's eyes still lingered.

"Let's do a full run-through like this was the live performance," Dwayne said.

"I'm going to stay for a few minutes," Nora told them. "Then I have a meeting with my staff. Is there anything else I can do to help you?"

"I can't think of anything," Tori said with a faint smile. "Unless you can figure out how to get rid of the nerves."

Nora and Dwayne laughed. "I haven't met a performer yet who didn't admit to a bout of nerves," Nora said. "It goes with the territory."

Tori dropped her tote bag on a nearby table and then

positioned herself at the piano, her feet instinctively finding the pedals. At Dwayne's nod, she began the opening notes of *Rhapsody in Blue*. The melody rippled under her fingers, soft at first but growing with intensity. With each note, the knot of anxiety loosened. The music consumed her, quieting her restless mind.

****

David pulled onto a side street where he could see Tori's car. Parker was nearby, though David wasn't sure where. He settled back in his seat, preparing for a long wait. This was a long shot. Neither he nor Parker fully believed someone was tampering with her tires. Though two flats in quick succession were too suspicious to ignore. Still, the ring of his cell phone caught him by surprise.

"Got a kid on a bicycle," Parker said. "He's made two spins around the parking lot, each time slowing as he passed Tori's car."

David hopped out, holding the phone to his ear. "I'm headed to the parking lot." At a fast pace, he crossed the street, keeping an eye out for someone on a bicycle. "Got him. He's stopped behind Tori's car."

"I see him," Parker replied. "He's pulling his bike alongside her back wheel."

David pocketed the phone, sprinting across the lot. He spotted Parker moving in from the opposite direction. Between the two of them, they had the kid boxed in.

As David approached, the boy, thirteen or fourteen years old, knelt between the car's back tire and his bicycle. He crouched low, pretending to fiddle with the bike chain.

Anyone walking by wouldn't give him a second glance. Suddenly, the boy twisted, his hand darting toward the valve stem.

"Stop!" David shouted.

The kid leaped to his feet, clutching the bike's handlebars. Shoving the bike forward, he aimed for the sidewalk, but Parker stepped directly into his path and seized the handlebars.

"What were you going to do to the tire?" Parker demanded.

Blustering, the boy said, "I wasn't doin' nothin'. Just checking the chain on my bike."

"That's not what I saw," David said, his tone sharp. "You were reaching for the valve stem."

He bent and picked up an object next to the tire. "The lady who owns this car has had two flat tires. I bet you're the reason why."

He held up a nail. "Were you planning on letting the air out of another tire?"

A sullen expression settled on the boy's face. "I found it in the parking lot. Didn't want someone to run over it. Hey, I didn't do anything."

"I'll call the police," Parker said, pulling out his phone. "We'll let them sort this out."

The boy's eyes widened in fear, his voice breaking. "Oh, man, don't do that. My mom will kill me for sure."

Parker's expression hardened. "Either you tell us, or you tell the police. Your choice. Why were you messing with the tire on this car?"

The boy hesitated, his shoulders slumping in defeat. "I got paid to let the air out of the tires," he muttered.

"Who paid you?"

"Some woman. Never saw her before. Gave me a hundred bucks if I'd let the air out of a tire every time I saw the car here."

"How did she find you?" Parker asked, his gaze relentless.

"I'm always hanging around down here. Guess she saw me. Stopped me one day, asked if I wanted to make a quick hundred."

"What did she look like?"

The boy shifted nervously, glancing between the two men. "Just someone wearing a ballcap and sunglasses."

After more questions yielded few details, Parker got the boy's name and address before handing him a business card. "If you see the woman again and get a name, there's another hundred bucks for you. But if another tire gets damaged, you're on the hook. You'd better make sure that doesn't happen," Parker said, his tone leaving no room for argument.

The boy hopped on his bike and shot off like he'd been fired from a cannon.

"When Tori finishes, let's meet back at the house," David said. He glanced around the parking lot. "I'll send her a text message."

****

Tori had chosen *Unchained Melody* for the performance finale. As the final note rang out, her alto

~ 126 ~

voice soared in perfect harmony with the piano, filling the hall and lingering in the air before fading into silence. Her fingers stilled on the keyboard as she pulled herself back from the depths of the memories the music evoked. The song would be a tribute not only to her mother but to her grandmother.

The sound of quiet clapping broke into her musings.

"Oh, my dear," Dwayne began, his voice brimming with admiration. "Every time I hear you play, it's an absolute honor and privilege. Your talent is truly extraordinary. I should warn you to be prepared with at least three more pieces."

"What? Why?" she asked as her eyebrows shot up.

"Encores."

Tori moaned.

A gleeful chuckle erupted from Dwayne. "I fully expect the audience won't want you to stop. These can be shorter pieces. Bring the list with you tomorrow, and we'll add them to the practice session."

Tori picked up her tote bag and, with a quick goodbye, left. On the sidewalk, she sucked in a deep breath of fresh air and pondered the upcoming performance. Each time she practiced on stage, her comfort level rose.

At the sight of her car, Tori remembered David and Parker's undercover plot. Pulling the phone from a vest pocket, she checked for messages. David had sent a text about meeting her back at the house. Wondering what had happened, Tori called him, but the call rolled to voicemail.

Before getting in, she walked around the car, checking the tires. As she backed out, she didn't notice the shadowy figure hunched behind the wheel of a nearby van, watching her intently. Nor did she see the van pull out moments later to follow her.

By the time she arrived, Colt and his men had left, though David and Parker's vehicles were in the driveway.

Inside, Mia walked out of the library holding an empty box when Tori stepped into the house. "We received the books you ordered. I've already put them on the shelves. David and Parker are in the kitchen battling over a container of cookies."

Amused by Mia's description, she chuckled. "Is Dubois still here?"

"No," Mia replied. "He left not long after you did. He sure doesn't seem to spend much time in the wine cellar. How did the rehearsal go?"

"Oh, you're not going to believe this," Tori grumbled. "I've got to have at least three more pieces."

Though Mia laughed, her voice was curious as she said, "Good lord, why? Is there a problem with the ones you selected?"

"Encores," Tori exclaimed as if announcing the end of the world.

Another roar of laughter erupted from Mia.

"It's not funny!" Tori sniffed indignantly. "Dwayne said I should be prepared to play three more times."

Mia's eyes twinkled with amusement. "Give the man credit for knowing his job. If he expects three encores, I'd say you should be ready with even more."

Not getting any sympathy for her plight, Tori huffed down the hall with Mia still laughing beside her.

After dropping her tote bag on the desk in her office, Tori walked into the kitchen, where Mia was now expounding on the encores.

David and Parker were seated across from each other. In the middle of the table was a container of chocolate chip cookies.

Tori suppressed a smile as she wondered how they had positioned the container so evenly between them. Almost as if neither was willing to give an inch to the other. Tori shot a look filled with laughter at Mia, who only rolled her eyes.

David said, "I have to agree with the music director. Lady, you are going to knock them dead." He reached for a cookie, though from the crumbs on the plate in front of him, he'd already eaten several.

Parker nodded enthusiastically as he quickly grabbed another one.

Shaking her head at the antics of two grown men, she said, "The good news is I have ten tickets. Don't buy any." She settled into a chair next to David.

"Too late. Already did," David told her. He bit into the cookie. "Give mine to someone else," he mumbled.

"So did I," Parker said. "And Dan and his wife already have theirs."

"Hmm, after giving one to Mia, Heidi, Cammie, and Tina, I still have six left."

"How about Colt?" Mia suggested.

"Oh, my gosh, yes. Colt might want to bring a date. I'll check with him tomorrow." She reached for a cookie, although she didn't want one. Tori just wanted to see their reaction. They didn't disappoint. Both frowned as they eyed her hand dipping into the container.

Repressing a smile, she said, "Okay, what's up with the meeting?" Then, she took a bite of the cookie.

Parker glanced at David, who said, "Go ahead," grabbing another cookie.

"We caught the culprit letting the air out of your tires. A fourteen-year-old kid on a bicycle."

A look of astonishment flashed across Tori's face. "For heaven's sake, why? A prank?"

"No. Someone paid him," Parker said grimly.

Tori straightened in her chair. "Who?"

Parker's brow furrowed. "A woman. That's about all we know. She paid him a hundred dollars to sabotage your tires. He didn't know her, and all he could tell us was that she wore a ballcap and sunglasses." He popped a piece of cookie in his mouth.

"Did you turn him over to the police?"

Parker swallowed. "No." The grimness eased into a faint, wry smile. "I turned him into an informant. I'll pay him another hundred dollars if he can find out the woman's name. Though he's still not off the hook. He also needs to make sure no one else tries the same stunt."

Tori frowned. "Do you think it's one of the two women from the ghost tour?"

"That's a reasonable assumption," Parker replied. "But here's the thing, the tires are just petty harassment. Same with the trumped-up assault at the ghost tour. More harassment, a way to embarrass you. That doesn't align with a motive for murder."

Mia muttered, "Still, if someone's out to cause you problems, how far are they willing to go?"

"Maybe as far as murder," Tori asserted with a grave expression. "After all, I'm the prime suspect now. How long before the cops show up with a search warrant, or worse, an arrest warrant?"

Parker said, "Andy still has to have evidence. Without it, his hands are tied." He glanced at his watch, then rose. "I'd better get going." After saying his goodbyes, he walked out of the kitchen.

David rose to follow. "I need to leave too. Since I'm headed to Austin tomorrow, I have to finish a report."

As they strolled to the front door, Tori asked, "How long will you be gone?"

"Three or four days."

At the door, he gave her a quick hug, then said, "If you need me, call. I mean it, Tori. I don't like what's swirling around you, and I sure don't like having to leave town."

"I will, but hopefully, it won't be necessary."

Mia soon followed the others, telling Tori she'd see her in the morning.

In a pensive mood, Tori pulled a chicken casserole from the fridge and heated the container in the microwave. After setting the hot dish on the table alongside a glass of wine, she stared out at the backyard, watching as the last of the sunlight faded over the horizon.

Why would someone want to damage her tires? The vandalism seemed so petty. But then, why would someone try to pin a murder on her? Murder certainly couldn't be defined as petty.

Consumed by the puzzle, she was surprised when she stared at the empty dish. Once the kitchen was squared away, she ambled to her office.

Just as she settled into her chair, a loud knock echoed through the house. Tori sprang up, expecting to hear the doorbell ring. When it didn't, she quickly checked the front porch camera on her desk monitor. Seeing no one, she hurried to the door and cautiously pulled it open. The front porch was deserted.

Stepping out, Tori scanned the front yard and driveway. The faint glow of streetlights barely cut through the encroaching shadows. Nothing seemed out of place, yet unease prickled at the back of her neck.

Turning back toward the door, her gaze dropped. A folded piece of paper lay on the porch.

The chill in the air turned sharp as Tori cast another nervous glance around the yard, the stillness suddenly oppressive. Was someone hidden in the deep shadows, watching? Tori snatched up the paper and hurried inside, bolting the door behind her. She unfolded it. A shiver raced down her spine.

Scrawled in jagged letters: *The truth lies within the tour.*

CHAPTER 12

The dawn's bright light beckoned. With her coffee cup clutched in one hand, Tori wandered outside, hoping the crisp morning air would sweep away the remnants of another restless night.

She pushed open the door to the new building, inhaling the distinct aroma of fresh-cut wood and sawdust. More extensive than she had first envisioned, it would house the reception and check-in area for guests at the inn, along with a quaint gift shop, museum, office, and a cozy breakroom equipped with a small kitchen.

Tori paused while her eyes scanned the partially completed interior. Her shoulders relaxed, the tension fading as she envisioned the gift shop shelves filled with knick-knacks, clothing, and more. Bottles of local wines would be displayed in a corner wine rack. But the centerpiece of the building was the museum, aptly named Elly's Treasures, for the antiques her grandmother had lovingly collected over the years. Many were too valuable to leave in the house, where they could be damaged.

The hum of activity stirred her from her thoughts. The construction crew had arrived, their sounds breaking the morning's stillness. She turned back toward the house. After refilling her cup, she walked briskly to her office. The phone rang as she walked in. She hurriedly set the cup down to pick it up. "Tori Winters."

"Hi, Tori. It's Harley. Congratulations. You are now the owner of a warehouse. The paperwork was filed yesterday."

She settled in her chair and excitedly said, "Thank you for letting me know. How soon can I get the keys?"

"I can bring them by whenever it's convenient."

Tori considered, then said, "Better yet, I'm going to town this afternoon. I'll stop and pick them up."

"I'll be here." Harley disconnected.

The note she had dropped on her desk caught her attention as she set her phone aside. Tori slid the paper toward her. With her elbows braced on the desk and her chin propped on her hands, she carefully scrutinized it. The writing was jagged. Was it the same hand that had scrawled her name on the envelope? Unfortunately, she couldn't compare since she'd tossed the envelope away.

Mia appeared in the doorway with a cup in her hand. "Morning," she said brightly, her heels clicking softly as she crossed the room. She plopped into the chair across from Tori, her expression shifting quickly to one of curiosity. "What's got you occupied this morning?"

"Someone left this on the front porch last night." She slid the note across the desk to Mia.

Mia picked up the paper. While she studied the hastily scrawled message, her lips pressed into a thoughtful line. "How odd. Do you know who left it?"

"No. I checked the cameras, but all I saw was a shadowy figure. A hooded sweatshirt hid the face. I couldn't tell if it was a man or a woman."

Mia's gaze sharpened as she leaned back in her chair, the note held between two fingers. "Someone knows something," she murmured, her tone grim. "And they're trying to tell you. But why so secretive and underhanded? If they wanted to help, why not be direct? Why slink through the shadows, hiding their identity?"

Tori said, with an edge of frustration, "Makes me wonder if it's friend or foe. Is this another trap?"

With a resolute expression, Mia said, "I need to round-robin my sources again and even speak with Vada, though I don't think I'll get far with her."

In a voice unyielding and determined, Tori said, "Then I'll try. I have to go to the opera house this afternoon. Once I finish, I'll stop by her office. I want to hear what she has to say." Her voice lightened. "I do have some good news."

Mia smiled. "It's about time. We need some."

Tori drum-rolled her fingers on the desk, a wry smile tugging at her lips.

"Dang it, Tori, stop with the drum-rolling and tell me. Don't keep me on pins and needles."

Tori laughed, her fingers still thrumming the desk. "Wait for it … wait for it."

Mia's eyes narrowed. "Tori," she said with a note of warning.

"Okay, I'll stop. I now own a warehouse. Got a call

from Harley. I'll stop by her office on my way downtown and pick up the keys."

"Woohoo! Another problem solved," Mia exclaimed. "I talked to Colt about giving the place a good cleaning. He said he mentioned it to you. We'll need to turn the utilities on. I can do that while you're gone. Anything else on our agenda?"

Before Tori could respond, the doorbell chimed. Mia hopped up with a bounce. "Probably Dubois. Is the door open to the wine cellar?"

"Yes."

The man's voice soon echoed in the hallway. As he passed by the doorway, he nodded to her and kept walking. Mia followed him into the kitchen, then returned a few minutes later, shutting the door behind her.

"Do you have any idea how the inventory is going?"

A frown settled on Tori's face. "Not really. I've asked, but he won't say. Doesn't want to discuss the project until he's finished."

A tap sounded on the door.

"Come in," Tori said.

Parker stepped inside, a cup of coffee in one hand and the computer bag slung over his shoulder. "Came in through the back door. Bad timing?"

"Oh, no. Just a conversation that's better with the door shut," Tori said, gesturing for him to sit.

"Good, because I wanted to talk to both of you." He set his cup on the desk, slid the bag from his shoulder, and sank into the chair.

"I stopped by the police department this morning." He took a long sip of coffee. "An oddity in the investigation popped up—no vehicle."

Mia and Tori exchanged puzzled glances while they waited for Parker to explain.

"How did the victim get downtown?" Parker added. "The police have been looking for a vehicle. A car hasn't been abandoned. No car keys were found on the body. The man wasn't registered at any of the hotels. The police have already contacted taxi services and Uber drivers, but so far, nothing."

He leaned back, steepling his fingers. "That raises an interesting question. If he had a vehicle, what happened to it? The speculation is that someone drove him downtown, or the killer disposed of the vehicle. Tori, when he spoke to you, did you get the sense he wasn't from around here?"

Tori's face crinkled as she thought. "Now that you mention it, I think he did have a slight accent. His tone wasn't Texan—more formal, almost careful in how he pronounced words."

"Since no one other than two witnesses from the ghost tour claim to have seen him, it's likely he's not a resident. But he said he'd been following you. Which makes the missing vehicle even more of a mystery." With a pensive air, he mused, "I still keep coming back to why he didn't want his picture taken."

"There must be a way to identify the man," Tori said. "I can't believe the police can't do that."

"It's not for lack of effort," Parker assured her. "No ID, no fingerprints on file, only three people saw him, you and the two witnesses, no known method of transportation. It's almost as if he were someone hiding in the shadows, but for what reason? And why did he have a piece of paper with your name and address on it? " He took a sip of coffee. "I wonder," he quietly said.

"Wonder what?" Tori prompted.

A faint smile twisted his lips. "Just the odd notions of a retired cop."

"Then, I've got another riddle for you. Someone left a note on the front porch last night."

Mia picked up the paper from the desk and handed it to him.

Parker whistled. "This is interesting. Did you see who left it?"

"Nope," she said, tapping the keyboard for the camera system. "I saved the video from the cameras."

Parker hopped up and stepped around the desk to look at the monitor. Mia followed, looking over his shoulder.

"Run it again, this time slow the video down," he said.

Tori changed the speed setting.

Parker's sharp eyes scanned the screen intently. "That might be a woman."

"How can you tell?" Tori asked.

"Rewind," he instructed. Watching closely, he said, "Pause." Parker pointed at the screen, where the figure was silhouetted against a porch column. "Look at the height relative to the column—shorter build, narrower frame. This isn't definitive but does suggest the culprit isn't a man."

A grim expression crossed his face as he settled back into his chair. "Someone keeps stirring the pot, but why? Mia, where do you stand with your contacts?"

"Haven't heard back from any of them. I plan to talk to them again today."

Tori's voice hardened. "And I plan on having a heart-to-heart talk with Vada Struthers this afternoon after I finish at the opera house."

Parker swallowed the last of the coffee and stood. He motioned with the cup. "I'll put this in the kitchen."

Then he slung his computer bag over his shoulder and said, "Unless Andy comes up with something more substantial than he has now, this isn't going anywhere."

Tori sighed, her shoulders sagging slightly. "It's still a dark cloud hanging over me. The rumor is out there that I'm a suspect in a murder. If Andy doesn't find the real killer, I can't get rid of it."

In the doorway, Parker paused, his gaze firm. "Both of you—be careful. Very careful."

Mia rose, taking her cup with her, as she glanced at Tori with a worried look. "I'll be in the dining room, getting the utilities turned on at the warehouse."

Lost in her thoughts, Tori simply nodded. Parker's warning echoed in her mind as her unease deepened. Why did she feel like she was running out of time?

Footsteps interrupted her musings. Dubois passed by

the doorway without a word. She rose and caught up to him in the foyer. "Will you be back?"

"Not today."

His rudeness was a constant irritation, and she forced herself not to retort. Instead, she opened the door and watched him brush past the man standing on the front stoop.

Turning to the stranger, she asked, "May I help you?"

After a glance at Dubois' retreating figure, the stranger shot her an engaging smile. "I hope so. I'd like to speak to Tori Winters."

"I'm Tori Winters."

"Marvelous. I'm a reporter—"

Tori interrupted, "Not interested." She started to close the door.

"Wait, please," he said, raising a hand. "You should have received a letter from my editor."

Chapter 13

Tori hesitated, her hand tightening on the edge of the door. She took a closer look at the man standing before her. Of average height, with a lean yet athletic frame, he exuded confidence and charm. He looked to be in his mid-thirties. His deep-set hazel eyes sparkled with humor and warmth.

"I didn't receive any letter," she said curtly.

With an abashed look, the man said, "Then, I must apologize for dropping in unannounced. I'm Bartholomew Hempstead. I work for *International Vintner's Review* magazine. I'd like to interview you for an article featuring your wine collection."

"I'm still not interested," she said, her voice firm.

He didn't falter. Instead, he held up his hands as if to plead his case. "Please, could you give me a few minutes of your time? I understand you're in the process of turning your home into an inn. Our magazine has a global reach. An article like this could be excellent advertising for your new venture."

Advertising struck a chord in Tori's mind. She'd need all the help she could get to make the inn a success.

Frowning, Tori glanced at her watch. "Fine," she said, not entirely disguising her reluctance. "But I only have a few minutes to discuss your request."

An eager light ignited his eyes. "I'll take whatever time you'll give me," he said quickly, as though afraid she might change her mind.

Tori stepped back, motioning for him to come inside.

His gaze swept the foyer. "Wow! This is amazing. I've covered a lot of homes with private collections, but this is stunning. Even if you aren't interested in the article, the chance to see the inside of this house made the trip worthwhile."

His enthusiasm was disarming, chipping away at her earlier wariness. She felt her shoulders relax. "Come on back to my office," she said.

Mia stepped into the hallway. "I thought I heard a strange voice."

"Mr. Hempstead, this is Mia O'Brien, General Manager for the inn. Mia, this is Bartholomew Hempstead, a reporter for a wine magazine. He wants to interview me for an article about our wine collection."

Mia's eyes widened with a pleasant look of surprise. "How interesting, Mr. Hempstead. Such an article might be good advertising for the inn."

Hempstead latched onto her words with a gleeful grin. "That's what I told Ms. Winters. And please, it's Bart. Over the years, I've found Bartholomew is a mouthful for most folks."

Inside her office, Tori said, "Please have a seat."

Mia settled onto the small sofa.

Bart pulled a business card from his pocket and slid it across the desk. The card was thick, with embossed gold lettering. "Our magazine has a worldwide distribution, reaching over thirty-two countries. The main office is in Paris, though I'm based in the States."

Tori studied the card for a moment, admiring its sleek, professional appearance. When she finally looked up, her tone was measured. "How did you hear about my wine collection?"

"Actually, it was my editor. He heard about the collection and your plans to turn the Leichter mansion into an inn, though I'm not sure where," he explained, sitting a little straighter. "My editor believes the mansion's historical background would give the story extra pizzazz, which is why I'm here."

"What exactly do you want to know?"

Bart leaned forward, clasping his hands casually on the desk. "I'd like to examine your wine collection to see if it fits our readership. If it does, the article will delve into the collection, the history of this incredible house, and your future plans. Depending on your availability, I'd only need a day or two at most."

Tori tapped her fingers lightly on the desk, her expression unreadable. "Hmm ... I'll need to think about this."

Though his face fell slightly, Bart recovered quickly. "That's fair. When can I return?"

"Let's plan on tomorrow morning."

After they arranged a time, Bart rose with a faint smile. "I look forward to seeing you tomorrow."

After escorting him out, Mia walked back into the office and sank into the chair across from Tori. "So? What do you think?"

Tori tapped lightly on the keyboard, her gaze flickering to the screen. "The magazine is impressive. Several articles have his byline. This could be a great promotional opportunity for the inn."

"Then it will be interesting to hear what he has to say tomorrow." Mia rose. "I'd better get a move on. I have one more call to the water department before I can leave. I'm hoping one of my contacts can shed some light on what Vada's been up to. If I learn anything, I'll text you."

Tori glanced at her watch. "Yipes, same here."

"Get going, and I'll lock up," Mia said.

The bustling downtown traffic had picked up, but Tori quickly maneuvered through the streets. Soon, she pulled into the small parking lot outside Harley's office.

Inside, Harley greeted her with a congratulatory smile and picked up a set of keys, dangling them in the air. "All yours. I had a few extras made."

"Who'd have thought purchasing a warehouse could feel so … momentous?" Tori said, a grin tugging at the corners of her mouth.

"You'd be surprised," Harley replied, handing her the keys. "This is a solid investment. You'll see."

She also handed Tori an envelope. "Here's a copy of the closing documents. Jonah will send you the official set.

I thought you'd want them now."

"Harley, thank you," Tori said, her voice warm with gratitude as she dropped the keys into her tote bag.

Stepping outside, Tori glanced at her watch. There was enough time for a quick stop at the warehouse. The anticipation she'd tried to keep in check rose during the drive, lifting her spirits.

After parking, Tori strode toward the front door. Her fingers fumbled with the key before the lock finally turned, and the door swung open. A faint draft of stale air greeted her. As she walked, her footsteps echoed in the cavernous space. "This is mine," she murmured, her voice small against the vastness. "Dang, who'd have thought I'd own a warehouse?"

She slowly turned as she imagined rows of shelves brimming with supplies for the inn. Time tugged at her, and with a reluctant glance around, she locked the door behind her. As she pulled out, her thoughts on her new acquisition, she didn't notice the van following her.

When Tori pulled into the parking lot, a faint flutter stirred in her chest when she saw two police cars parked in front of the opera house. Grabbing her bag, Tori crossed the street, her curiosity laced with a growing sense of unease.

Inside, the receptionist, Emmy, sat behind the counter, dabbing at her tear-streaked cheeks with a tissue. Her shoulders shook as she tried to compose herself.

"Oh, my gosh, what's wrong?" Tori exclaimed, rushing toward her.

Her voice wavered as she said, "Someone vandalized the auditorium. The police are here now."

Tori's mouth fell open. "What? How bad is the damage?"

Emmy shook her head as she twisted a tissue in her hands. "I don't know, but Nora's really upset. She's on stage if you want to go in."

When Tori entered the hall, a sense of dread hit her. Small groups of people clustered on the stage, their murmurs rising and falling. Three police officers stood near the piano, their faces grave as they spoke with Nora and Dwayne.

As she stepped on stage, Nora caught sight of Tori and cried out, "Oh, Tori! Something terrible has happened." Her voice quivered. "Someone damaged the piano."

A chill raced down her spine. "Damaged?" Her gaze veered to the beautiful instrument. "How bad?" Tori asked, trying to maintain her composure.

Her eyes glistening with tears, Nora replied, "I don't know yet. Dwayne discovered the damage when he had the piano moved onstage for your practice. Several of the strings are cut."

While they talked, they edged closer to the cluster of individuals gathered around the piano. Tori leaned forward to peer inside the instrument. The damage was worse than she had imagined as she stared at the jagged ends of the wire strings. Anger and shock mixed with the sick feeling in her stomach.

She straightened, turning when Dwayne said, "This is Tori Winters. She's the pianist for the upcoming concert."

The officers briefly turned toward her, nodding in acknowledgment. As her gaze flicked to the one holding a notepad, she caught the name D. Edwards on his nameplate before he turned back to face Dwayne.

"Where do you keep the piano when it's not on stage?" Edwards asked, his pen poised.

"In a corner backstage," Dwayne replied, his voice unsteady.

"When was the last time you knew the piano wasn't damaged?" Edwards pressed.

"This morning, when I arrived. I raised the lid since I planned to move it onto the stage."

Edwards scribbled something in his notepad. "Who has access to the back of the stage?"

"Anyone who works here," Dwayne admitted.

Nora let out a faint moan, her hand rising to cover her mouth. "I can't imagine any of our employees would do something like this," she said, her voice trembling.

Officer Edwards softened his tone, glancing briefly at her. "I'm not accusing anyone, ma'am. I just need a clear picture of who's been coming and going."

Nora nodded, though her face was still tight with worry. "Today, we had several people backstage who don't work for the opera house. They were bringing in equipment for the next event on our calendar."

"Who were they?" Edwards asked.

"Members of a local theater group," Nora replied.

"How did they get in?"

Dwayne shifted uneasily before answering. "Through the back doors. I left them propped open. I suppose anyone could have walked in."

Edwards frowned slightly. "Is the group still here?"

"No," Dwayne said. "They left about an hour ago."

Edwards glanced at his notebook. "Do you have their names? We'll need to talk to them, along with all the employees who were here earlier today."

Nora dabbed her eyes with a tissue. "I don't have all their names, but I can give you the contact person for the group."

"Did either of you see anyone hanging around the piano?"

Nora shook her head. "I didn't, but I haven't been backstage much today."

"I was," Dwayne said, frowning. "But I didn't notice anyone."

Edwards stepped closer to the piano, motioning toward the damaged strings with his notepad. "How could someone cut the wires?"

"A set of wire cutters is all they'd need," Dwayne replied, his voice taut with anger. He shook his head, his lips pressing into a hard line.

"Any idea why someone would damage the piano?"

"No," Nora said. "This is so senseless. The only consequence is Tori's concert if the piano can't be repaired. We'd have to cancel. Even if it's repaired, we still might have to cancel since she's lost valuable practice time."

Edwards turned to Tori, studying her closely. "Who would want to jeopardize your concert?"

Was this more than wanton destruction? Tori's stomach tightened at the thought as two names jumped into her mind—Myra and Carly. But this seemed radical even for them. Besides, Myra was on the board. Surely, she wouldn't go so far as to condone a criminal act just to stop her from performing.

Tori swallowed hard, forcing her expression to remain neutral. She couldn't implicate them without evidence. "No. I can't."

Edwards slid the notepad into his shirt pocket. "Ms. Evans, once you have a damage estimate, please call the police department. I'll add the details to my report."

He looked at the other two officers. "Let's start interviewing the employees."

Once the officers strode off, Tori turned to Dwayne, her voice tight with apprehension. "Can the piano be repaired?"

Dwayne frowned. "I don't know. There might be more damage than I can see. And even if the piano can be repaired, the real question is how fast. Would it be in time for your concert?"

"What about my baby grand piano? Can we use it?"

"No, the sound wouldn't carry in a hall this size."

Her tone was bleak as Tori quietly asked, "Is there any point in continuing? Maybe you should cancel the concert."

With an adamant shake of his head, Dwayne said

firmly, "No. We're not giving up. Keep practicing. Let's not stop until we know for certain. I need to make a few calls." He strode off.

Nora said, "I'll call you as soon as I know more."

Still reeling from the shock of the wanton destruction, Tori slowly made her way toward the car. The image of the piano's jagged, ruined strings dominated her thoughts. Such a beautiful instrument might now be beyond repair. The thought left a hollow ache inside her.

After tossing her bag inside, she slid behind the wheel. Leaning back, she closed her eyes and took a deep breath. Who was responsible? And why? One possible answer was unavoidable and frightening. She was the reason.

Confronting Vada about the ghost tour took on an even greater purpose. There were too many loose ends and too many unanswered questions. She started the engine and drove out.

CHAPTER 14

When Tori turned onto the street where the ghost tour office was located, she eased off the accelerator, searching for a parking space. She spotted one at the other end of the block.

When she passed the office, the door swung open, and a figure stepped out. Her breath caught. Carly! Why was she visiting Vada?

By the time she'd eased into the parking space and hopped out of her car, Carly had already driven off.

As she walked toward the office, she couldn't shake the uneasy feeling Carly's presence at Vada's office was more than a coincidence.

A bell over the door tinkled as she stepped inside. The dimly lit interior seemed the perfect setting for the ghost tours. Aged furniture, the scent of old books, and a trace of dust created an eerie ambiance, blurring the line between reality and the spectral. The atmosphere, thick with mystery, raised the hackles on her neck.

Two desks occupied the room. Vada sat behind one, and a young woman typed on a keyboard at the other.

Vada's warm smile turned guarded, and her body

stiffened when she recognized Tori. "Ms. Winters. How may I help you?"

Tori said, "Hello, Vada," before directing her attention to the other woman. At hearing Vada's comment, her fingers had paused on the keyboard.

"Hello. We haven't met. I'm Tori Winters."

The young woman cast a quick, uncertain glance at Vada before accepting Tori's outstretched hand. "Gale Mills," she said with a faint smile. "Nice to meet you."

Tori returned the smile warmly before shifting her focus back to Vada. She slid into the chair in front of Vada's desk, setting her tote bag on the floor. "Please, it's Tori." She glanced around. "What a great way to advertise your tours. This office is perfect."

Vada, her gaze wary, only nodded.

Tori said, "I wanted to follow up on our conversation the other night about incorporating the ghost tours into my inn's event calendar."

"I thought Mia was going to call," Vada replied.

Tori folded her hands in her lap and politely said, "Since I have a few questions about the tour, I decided it was best if we spoke in person."

"What do you want to know?" Though her voice was even, a flicker of fear flashed in her eyes.

Tori, her body relaxed, casually asked, "How often do you conduct tours?"

Vada opened a drawer and pulled out a glossy brochure, sliding it across the desk. "This has all the tour information, times, and other details."

Tori picked up the brochure, giving it a quick glance. "How many people can you accommodate on a tour?"

"Twenty-five is the max."

"How far in advance do you sell tickets for a particular tour?"

Vada hesitated, her expression tightening. "That depends. Why are you asking?"

Tori kept her voice steady. "Since the ticket I received had a date on the back, I wondered if tickets had to be purchased in advance."

The woman shifted uneasily in her chair. "No. Tickets are available up to the start of a tour."

"Do you keep track of advance ticket sales?" Tori asked, leaning forward slightly.

"Yes," she replied.

"If a ticket was bought in advance, then you would know who bought it."

"No," Vada replied sharply. "All I track is the number of tickets sold for a particular tour, not the person who bought them." She leaned back in her chair, her tone becoming curt. "If this is about the ticket you received, I can't help you."

Ignoring the hostility in Vada's voice, Tori kept her tone even and patient. "The ticket I received did raise an issue about the necessity of purchasing tickets in advance. Guests at the inn would more likely purchase tickets on the day of the tour."

"There won't be a problem. If we exceed the number of tickets for a tour, then we run a second tour." She nodded toward the other woman. "Gale handles the overflow."

Tori glanced at Gale, who offered a small smile before resuming her typing. "Would you mind if I incorporated some of the elements from your brochure into our advertising?"

Vada's posture visibly relaxed, her shoulders dropping slightly. "Not at all. Use whatever you like. I can provide brochures."

"I'll take them," Tori said with a nod. "I've added a gift shop and museum. I'll put your brochures in the gift shop and include one in the gift baskets each guest will receive."

Vada's eyes widened slightly in surprise, but she recovered quickly. "A gift basket. A nice touch."

Tori smiled. "I think so, too. By the way, do you know Tina Lopez?"

"Oh, yeah," Vada said with a hint of condescension. "Went to school with her, like I did with Cammie Dodd, Heidi Grant, and Mia."

Tori offered an apologetic smile. "I keep forgetting what's new to me isn't to others. Tina is the advertising manager for the inn. I'll hand this off to her to coordinate."

She reached down, sliding the brochure into her tote bag. "I have one last request. Please check your records and tell me when the ticket I received was purchased."

Vada's expression darkened, her lips pressing into a thin line. "I've already been questioned by the police. I don't know anything about the women or the man. What difference does it make when the ticket was sold anyway?"

Tori leaned forward slightly, her gaze drilling into Vada's face with unrelenting focus. "Someone bought a ticket and sent it to me. Obviously, the ticket was purchased in advance, as the date was on the back. That ticket was the only reason I was on the tour, making the date and who purchased it critical pieces of evidence."

Her voice hardened, her tone clipped. "The contrived confrontation happened during your tour. Your tour is involved, and now, this isn't about a couple of women and their malicious stunt—it's murder. If you prefer, I'll call Sergeant Rodriguez, who is in charge of the murder investigation, and have him request the information."

Vada stiffened. "No, don't bother," she snapped as she angrily tapped the keyboard. Stone-faced, she said, "The ticket was bought three days before the tour."

Tori's brow lifted slightly. "How do you know it was my ticket?"

"Because only one advance ticket was sold for that tour," Vada replied curtly.

Tori's voice was incredulous. "You sold one ticket in advance and don't know who bought it?"

A brief spark of fear flashed in Vada's eyes. "No. I don't."

While she felt sure the woman was lying, she also realized she wasn't going to get any more information from her. Tori rested her hands in her lap and casually said, "I noticed Carly Swanson leaving as I arrived. Is she coordinating a special event? I know both she and her mother are deeply involved in community events. If she's planning something special, it might be a great addition to the inn's event calendar."

For a moment, a flicker of something unreadable passed over Vada's face. "Nothing specific, just visiting."

From the corner of her eye, Tori noticed Gale stiffen, her fingers pausing briefly over the keyboard. The subtle movement piqued Tori's curiosity, setting her mind racing. *Did she just react to Carly's name?*

"If you do hear of any special events, please let me or Mia know," Tori said, her tone light as she rose from her chair. Slinging her tote bag over her shoulder, she nodded politely at Gale. Though she kept her expression neutral, Tori couldn't shake the thought of the woman's peculiar reaction. Gale's avoidance of eye contact added to Tori's suspicions.

Tori was still mulling over her conversation with Vada when she reached her car. Before she could open the door, she saw Vada leaving the office, heading briskly in the opposite direction. Tori hesitated only for a moment before seizing the opportunity.

Gale looked up in surprise as Tori rushed in. "Did you forget something? Vada will be back in a few minutes."

"No, I wanted to talk to you."

"Me?" Gale blinked, her tone immediately defensive. "Why would you want to talk to me?"

Not wanting to waste time with niceties, Tori pressed, her eyes fixed on the woman's face. "I noticed your reaction when I asked about Carly Swanson. What do you know about her?"

With a nervous glance at the windows, Gale replied, "Nothing other than she and Vada are friends." Uneasy, she shifted uncomfortably in her seat.

"Why was she here?" Tori asked.

"I don't know."

Tori didn't believe her. Gale was seated two feet from Vada's desk. There was no way she didn't know why Carly had shown up.

Hoping to convince her to talk, Tori softened her tone. "I'm not trying to pry, but this could be important. A man's been murdered, and everyone connected with the ghost tour, including you, is involved."

Gale hesitated, her eyes darting around the room. "Carly and Vada have spent a lot of time together lately. That's all I know."

"Do you know who bought the ticket?"

A decided look of distress settled on Gale's face, though she quickly denied knowing.

"What about the names of the two women involved in the incident during the ghost tour?"

Her hands nervously twisted. "I don't know. I can't tell you anything," she exclaimed, refusing to look at Tori.

Even though Parker, not the police, came up with the theory, Tori didn't hesitate to say, "There's already a suspicion the two women might be connected to the murder. If you know anything, you need to speak up."

A mulish look crossed Gale's face. "I don't know

anything," she snapped. "I have to get back to work."

Though Tori knew Gale was holding back, she couldn't force her to talk. As she turned, the sharp jingle of the door's bell signaled someone's arrival.

Vada walked in, carrying a paper sack from a nearby deli. Her eyes narrowed, looking hard at Gale before turning to Tori. "What are you doing here again?"

Tori's mind raced, and she forced a casual smile. "I forgot the brochure. Thanks again."

On the way to the car, doubt and anxiety had Tori's nerves tingling. Did Vada believe her excuse? Did Vada see her slip the brochure into her tote bag? The worry she'd been caught gnawed at her, twisting her stomach in knots. Clearly, going undercover wasn't her forte.

When she slid into the driver's seat, her phone buzzed insistently in her bag. The quick glance at the screen triggered another jolt to her nerves. *Seriously? What else could go wrong?*

Taking a steadying breath, she answered, "Hi, Linc. I hope this isn't bad news."

"I do need to talk to you," he said in his familiar, even tone. "When can I stop by the house?"

Tori sighed, brushing a stray hair from her face. "I'm downtown. I'll swing by your office."

After ending the call and pocketing her phone, Tori started the engine. Her stress level was already maxed out, and after the way their last meeting ended, she wasn't sure if she was up for another go-round. Still, she didn't have much choice. He was her attorney.

CHAPTER 15

After parking near Linc's office, Tori steadied herself with a deep breath before striding inside. Linda greeted her with a warm smile.

"He's waiting for you. Go on in."

Linc rose when she walked into his office. "Tori, would you like coffee or something else?" he asked, his tone polite but carrying a hint of concern.

"After the day I've had, a cup of coffee sounds great," she replied, dropping into a chair with a weary sigh.

He sat and tapped the phone on his desk. When Linda answered, Linc asked for two cups of coffee before turning his attention back to Tori. "I heard about the vandalism at the opera house."

"Bad news sure seems to travel fast in this town."

"Sometimes," he agreed. "But in this case, Dad got a call."

While Tori wondered who had called, she didn't ask.

A soft knock preceded Linda's entrance, carrying two steaming cups of coffee on a small tray. She handed one to Tori and the other to Linc.

Tori wrapped her hands tightly around the cup as if the warmth might steady her frayed nerves. She took a deep swig, relishing the intense, rich flavor. "Have the police figured out who damaged the piano?"

"The latest Dad heard was they're still chasing down the individuals who brought the props for the upcoming play. I'm guessing your concert is up in the air."

Tori nodded, her shoulders slumping. "Yes." She exhaled sharply. "Linc, this is so senseless. Why would anyone want to damage the piano?"

Linc leaned back slightly. "Hopefully, the police will find out. But look at it this way. I know the concert, on top of the murder investigation, has put a lot of stress on you. This might turn out to be a blessing in disguise. After all, it's not as if you are a professional. You're an amateur. Honestly, I had to wonder at Nora even suggesting that you perform."

Tori stared at him blankly as his words sank in, her mind reeling with dismay. Linc not only parroted what Myra and Carly said but also agreed with them.

She knew the Greers had a long history with the Swanson family. Did Myra or Carly air their complaints to him? The idea didn't sit well, especially since Linc was her attorney.

She took another fortifying swallow of coffee as a slow burn began to build. "Why did you need to see me?" she asked with a hard edge.

He hesitated momentarily, then said, "I talked to Andy earlier today. Since he still refuses to release the names of the witnesses, I plan to talk to Vada."

She stared at him with a steady gaze. "Don't bother.

I've already talked to her. I just left her office."

Linc's jaw tightened as he leaned forward, his tone laced with annoyance. "What did she say?"

"She still claims she doesn't know the women's names. Personally, I think she's lying," Tori replied. "I did learn that the ticket I received was purchased three days before the tour. Vada keeps a record of advance ticket sales. She told me only one advance ticket was sold for the tour I attended."

Her tone turned grim. "Whoever's behind this clearly planned ahead, even delivering the envelope with the ticket to my mailbox on the day of the tour."

A shadow of doubt settled on Linc's face. "Maybe. If the ticket was connected to the incident during the ghost tour, it could suggest premeditation. In my opinion, the theory isn't plausible. What would have happened if you disregarded the ticket and didn't go?" he said dismissively.

Linc's gaze turned grave as he studied her. "I also wanted to talk to you because Andy is still considering a search warrant."

Indignant, Tori straightened in her chair. "For cripes' sake, why? There's nothing to connect me to the murder other than I talked to the man during the ghost tour!"

"That's what I keep reminding Andy. And he keeps reminding me they found your name and address on a piece of paper in the man's pocket," Linc said with an adamant tone. "But I got the impression he's being pressured to obtain a search warrant."

"Who's pressuring him?" Tori demanded, the frustration evident in her voice.

"I don't know," Linc admitted. "I'm waiting on a callback from the district attorney to find out." His tone sharpened. "Tori, as your attorney, I still recommend letting Andy search the house. While Parker means well, I believe this is in your best interest. A voluntary search shows you are willing to be upfront with your cooperation."

That comment about Parker made her wonder if Linc's purpose was to divide and conquer. Did Linc really believe he could convince her if Parker wasn't present?

Her voice clipped, Tori said, "No! I'm not changing my mind. Quite frankly, I can't believe you still think the search is in my best interest. The adverse publicity is already tearing me apart, and I won't let anyone take another shot at me. This isn't open for debate." She paused before snapping, "Anything else?"

In a tone sharp with irritation, Linc said, "No."

"Then I need to go home." She drained the last sip of coffee, setting the cup on the desk.

Linc's demeanor abruptly shifted. With a slight smile, he added, "Let's put all the irritating issues aside. Why don't you stay in town, and I'll take you to dinner?"

After the remarks he'd thrown at her, Tori couldn't believe he suggested dinner. She gathered up her tote bag, her fingers tightening on the strap. "I'm spending the evening practicing," she replied.

He raised his eyebrows. "I thought the concert was canceled."

"Not yet." She didn't bother to explain. Rising, she slung the bag over her shoulder and turned toward the door.

Linc quickly shoved back his chair. "I'll see you out."

They made their way to the front, where Linc opened the door. Before she could step outside, he leaned in slightly, his voice low. "I'm very serious about a dinner date."

There would never be a dinner date, but now she had to question whether he should still be her attorney. Tori's face stretched into what she hoped was a noncommittal smile before she eased through the doorway.

The hair on her neck prickled as she strode toward her car. Tori glanced over her shoulder, half-expecting to see Linc watching her. But his door was shut. With a nervous twitch, she glanced around the still-busy parking lot. Nothing seemed amiss.

While Tori wanted to dismiss the feeling as leftover stress from a terrible day, it nagged at her, a reminder this wasn't the first time she'd felt someone watching her.

During the drive home, the anxiety clung to her, twisting her thoughts into a tangle of unanswered questions.

When Tori pulled into the driveway, all the cars were gone except for one. Parker stood leaning against his truck, his posture relaxed, but his expression preoccupied as he talked on a cell phone.

He had a key but refused to use it, claiming the house was still her private home until she officially moved into the new apartment Colt had built over the garage. He wouldn't enter unannounced.

When she braked to a stop, he slid the phone into a vest pocket, reaching inside the vehicle to grab his computer bag. After she exited, he said, "I heard you had quite a day," his voice carrying a mix of curiosity and concern.

"Way more than you know," she replied. "Come on, let's go inside."

Parker stepped beside her, and they walked toward the front door. Inside, she dropped her tote bag in the office before heading into the kitchen.

On the counter, a handwritten note from Mia caught her eye. After reading it, she said, "Mia made lasagna and garlic bread. All I have to do is heat them. Would you like to stay for supper?"

Parker, hovering by the kitchen doorway, pulled out a chair. "How fast can I say yes?" he said with a chuckle. "I haven't stopped since I left my house this morning, and breakfast is a dim vision in my rearview mirror. And I still have work waiting at my office."

Though she softly laughed, moving toward the coffee machine, she knew Parker was a workaholic. He seldom mentioned it, but his wife and daughter were killed in an automobile accident, a tragedy she suspected was the reason for his long hours. She jabbed the start button.

With a heavy sigh, Parker leaned back in the chair,

stretching his legs out in front of him. "I heard about the opera house," he said, his gaze meeting hers. "Tell me what happened."

While talking, Tori turned on the oven, slipping the container of lasagna and foil-wrapped garlic bread inside. The coffee machine beeped, signaling the brew was complete. She poured steaming coffee into two mugs, setting one in front of Parker.

"Is there still a possibility the concert is a go?"

"Yes," she said, leaning against the counter with the mug cradled in her hands. "Dwayne wants me to keep practicing. Until told otherwise, I will."

"What else happened?" he asked, with a slight tilt of his head as he watched her.

"I had a visit with Vada Struthers, which was exceedingly interesting," she said, her voice sparked with a hint of intrigue.

Parker raised a brow as he listened to the details. "I've tried to have another go at her, stopping by a couple of times, leaving messages to call. Even though I had already talked to her, her refusal to return my call was surprising. There's no reason to avoid me unless she's involved. However, the business with her employee, Gale Mills, opens up a new lead."

Tori nodded, taking a sip. "I think Gale knows something, even the names of the two women. I might've learned more if Vada hadn't shown up when she did."

His gaze sharpened with thought. "Do you think Mills could've left the note?"

"I don't know. It would make sense if she did. Based on her reaction, Gale's definitely nervous about getting involved. But why? Is she afraid of losing her job, or is there something more sinister? I don't see that I have much of a chance to find out."

Tori's eyes narrowed. "That's not all. I had another meeting with Linc. He called as I was leaving town, so I stopped by his office." With a note of bitter frustration, she added, "The search warrant is still rearing its ugly head."

Parker frowned slightly, setting his mug down. "Did he say why?"

"Someone is pressuring Andy to get a search warrant. Linc doesn't know who, but he's trying to contact the district attorney. He's still pushing me to let the police search the house."

Parker's eyebrows shot upward as a concerned expression crossed his face. "And?" he prompted.

"I pushed back and told him a voluntary search wasn't happening."

Even though he nodded in approval, his brow furrowed, and his voice was grim. "Someone keeps stirring the pot to keep you at the forefront as a suspect."

Before he could say more, the timer on the oven dinged. Tori set the cup aside and grabbed the oven mitts to retrieve the lasagna and bread. The savory aroma filled the room as she cut two portions and plated them, setting the dishes and silverware on the table.

Parker inhaled the rich steam from the lasagna, sighing with pleasure before grabbing his fork and digging in. For a few minutes, the conversation stilled as they ate. When Parker finished, he leaned back, nursing the last sip of coffee. "Utterly delicious."

"There's more if you want another helping. Mia made enough for several people," Tori replied with a small smile, gesturing to the kitchen counter.

"Even though another helping is tempting, I've had enough. I wonder if Cammie has any idea Mia is a close second to her when it comes to cooking."

Tori chuckled. "I'm sure she does. Mia's amazing. There isn't much she's not good at." She popped the last bite of bread into her mouth.

"I have to say, with the three of them gone, it's pretty quiet around here," Parker remarked.

Another laugh bubbled out of Tori. "Enjoy this while you can. Once they're back and we kick into high gear for the grand opening, I expect this place to get loud and hectic."

Rising, Parker grabbed their mugs and refilled them. A somber expression crossed his face as he settled in the chair. "Back to the issue with the warrant. Andy knows he can't justify searching the house. If he is being pressured, he's between a rock and a hard place. In the morning, I'll stop by his office. He might open up."

Tori frowned slightly, swirling her coffee absently. "I wish we could get the names of the witnesses. I can't help but feel their identity is the key to whatever's going on."

"Did Linc have anything else to say?"

Still raw from Linc's insinuations about the concert,

she didn't want to discuss them. Instead, she said, "No, he mainly wanted to talk about the search warrant."

She shifted gears, her tone lightening. "I picked up the keys to the warehouse today. Mia left a note that the utilities should be on in the morning. I hope Colt can start cleaning and installing the shelves tomorrow."

"Then I need to look at the security system and see if I need to make any modifications."

Tori said, "Before you leave, I'll give you a key."

"New locks on all the doors are the first item on my agenda," he replied. "When you talk to Colt, tell him I'll be at the warehouse in the morning."

He took a sip of coffee. "How's the inventory going?"

A flash of irritation crossed her face. "I don't have a clue. Dubois won't tell me anything until he's finished. I regret hiring him, but I'm stuck if I want the inventory done. On paper, the man's credentials are very impressive. In person, he's the south end of a northbound mule."

Parker choked mid-sip, setting his mug down as laughter erupted from him. "That bad?" he asked, his voice tinged with amusement.

"Oh, yeah," Tori replied, shaking her head. "At least he keeps to himself. When he's here, he stays in the wine cellar."

She leaned back, crossing her arms. "I had another visitor today. A reporter for the *International Vintner's Review* magazine. He wants to interview me for an article in the magazine. I told him I'd think about it. The magazine is very impressive, so I've decided to go ahead with the interview. The article will be good publicity for the inn."

"How long will he be around?" Parker leaned forward slightly, his curiosity piqued.

"I'm not sure."

"Let me know when you plan to do the interview," he said. "I'd like to meet him."

Her brow furrowed slightly as she studied him. "You don't think there'd be a problem with him?"

"No, not at all," Parker assured her. "But I like to know who's coming and going."

Tori chuckled as she remembered the police officer at the opera house had made the same comment. "I knew there was a good reason why I hired you as security director."

He smiled, rising from his chair. "Okay, I've got to go. I need to stop by my office. Thank you for dinner. I'll see you tomorrow."

Before he walked out, Tori retrieved the warehouse keys from her bag, handing him one.

While Tori cleaned up the kitchen, she pondered the bizarre events of the last few days. Too restless to sit, she headed downstairs to the wine cellar.

Tori intently scanned the neatly aligned bottles while she wandered along the rows, trying to discern if they had been disturbed. Surely, Dubois had to pull them out to document each brand and type. Yet, it still seemed the bottles were untouched.

She pulled out a bottle and then slid it back. The

bottle's appearance didn't change. Maybe she was just seeing a problem where none existed. Still troubled, she headed back upstairs.

She eased onto her chair, intending to check her emails. Instead, she reached for her notepad. Starting with the ticket to the ghost tour, she jotted down the details, including the tires and piano, then settled back to study the list.

On the surface, they seemed completely unrelated. What did someone hope to gain by such a heinous act as murder to something as trivial as letting the air out of her tires?

The answer, the key, lay in understanding—WHY! She wrote the word in big block letters, repeatedly circling it with her pen.

Chapter 16

Tori stood in the backyard, her arms crossed against the chill of the early morning breeze as she spoke to Colt. Behind him, the whine of a table saw echoed inside the new building.

After Tori handed him a key to the warehouse, he slid it into his pocket. "I'll start this morning." He motioned with his hand toward the ongoing construction. "I'm far enough along that I can easily pull a few of my men from here. Besides, I doubt getting the building cleaned and shelves installed will take more than a couple of days."

"Parker will be there this morning working on the security system. Plus, he plans to change the locks."

"Good idea," Colt said.

From the back stoop, Mia's voice rang out. "Tori."

She turned to see Mia waving a newspaper.

"Oh no!" Tori groaned, agitation seeping into her voice. She stomped toward the steps. "The *Metro*?"

Her lips tightly pressed, Mia curtly nodded. Once inside, she handed Tori the newspaper and turned silently toward the counter, where she filled two cups with coffee.

When Tori finally looked up, devastation gleamed in

her eyes. The newspaper rustled in her hands as her voice broke with disbelief. "Oh, Mia, this is awful. Hess insinuates the police believe I'm a murderer, but they're doing nothing to bring a killer to justice. She even questions their refusal to search the house. And why? Because I'm the heiress to the Leichter estate. She even drags in my great-grandfather, suggesting a criminal streak runs in my blood."

Mia's hands tightened around the cups, a tremor sending ripples across the steaming brew. "I'd love to know who's feeding that reporter this rubbish," she said, her voice seething with outrage. "She doesn't care about the truth. All Hess wants is a scandalous headline. The fact that the police don't have any evidence is unimportant."

Tori sank into a chair. The surge of fury pushed back the tears threatening to overwhelm her. "I doubt the words, truth or evidence are *even* in her vocabulary. Not when she can spin a story fueling suspicion. Libel and innuendos should be her byline."

Mia carefully set the cups on the table before settling into a chair across from Tori.

After tossing the paper aside, Tori reached for a cup. "You know what's truly unsettling? This story ties right into what I discovered from Linc yesterday." She took a deep swig of coffee, hoping to calm the roiling anger inside her.

"I stopped at his office on my way home. He said Andy was being pressured to search the house. Linc's waiting for the district attorney to call, hoping to find out who is pushing the police. Could the pressure be coming from the newspaper?"

Mia frowned. "I wouldn't think so. What's even more alarming, though, is how the murder investigation is being publicized. This is nothing but a calculated smear campaign, deliberately aimed at harming you."

Tori's fingers anxiously drummed the table. "Why is there pressure to search the house when we all know there's no evidence?"

"What immediately comes to mind is the next headline in the newspaper," Mia said, her tone tinged with annoyance.

A chilling thought struck Tori, sudden and sharp. Her back stiffened. "Oh, my gosh, Mia, there's another possibility. Do you think someone planted evidence in the house? Could that be why?"

Mia's eyes widened, her expression taut with alarm. "You might be on to something."

Tori leaned forward, her voice urgent. "Do you remember who has been here since the murder?"

With a thoughtful air, Mia said, "Myra and Carly visited twice. Once with Liz and Nora. Then there's Dubois and the reporter. But other than Dubois, no one was ever left alone."

Tori's brow furrowed as she pressed further. "Could Dubois have gone anywhere in the house without us knowing?"

Mia's fingers tapped the edge of her cup as she thought. "I can only think of one time. Remember when I opened your office door, and he was in the hallway?"

Tori nodded, shoving back her chair with determination. "Let's start searching. I'll take the wine cellar and work my way toward the front. You start in the library. If something has been planted, I'd bet they stashed it somewhere that can easily be found."

An hour later, they met in the dining room.

"I scoured the cellar, kitchen, pantry, and my office. I even checked under the seat cushions and rugs," Tori said, her voice edged with relief. "Nothing."

"I did the same. If someone intends to leave a little gift for you, they haven't done it yet." A grim expression crossed her face. "From this point forward, we've got to make sure no one we don't know or trust is left alone."

As they made their way to the kitchen, Mia said, "While we're on the subject of trust, what about Linc?"

Tori hesitated. The disquieting uncertainty from his earlier comments crept back into her thoughts. While she didn't want to cast undue suspicion on him, at the same time, she couldn't say she fully trusted him either. Finally, she admitted, "I don't know."

Mia nodded decisively. "Then we put him in the untrust category until we know for sure. We don't leave him alone."

While Mia filled a glass with her sugar-laden iced tea, Tori refilled her coffee cup before settling into a chair.

"With all the unpleasant drama surrounding the *Metro* article, I haven't had a chance to tell you about what happened at the opera house or my visit with Vada."

Mia set her glass on the table before opening a cabinet door. "I heard about the piano. Got a call from a friend last night who works at a restaurant downtown." As she talked, she pulled out a container filled with cookies. "The entire square was avidly enthralled by the police cars in front of the place. It didn't take long for the news about the vandalism to hit the gossip mill."

"Why would anyone damage a piano?" Tori still couldn't quash the anguish she felt.

"How about to sabotage your performance?" Mia countered, a sharp edge in her tone. "And we both know who doesn't want you on stage."

She settled into a chair across from Tori and, with a decisive, almost aggressive snap of her wrist, she popped the lid from the container.

Tori eagerly reached for a chocolate chip cookie. She nibbled a bite before saying, "The thought did occur to me, but going so far as to damage a valuable piano seems extreme even for Myra or Carly."

"Not to me," Mia said, shaking her head. "What are the cops doing?" She reached for a cookie.

"Interviewing everyone. The piano was stored behind the stage, and the back doors were propped open for a theater group bringing in equipment. From what I heard, anyone could have walked in and snipped a few wires."

"Is the concert a lost cause?"

"Not yet. I'm hoping Dwayne will call today," Tori said, frustration flickering in her tone. "He's trying to get the piano fixed. I offered to use mine, but he said it wasn't suitable for a large hall. Still, he wants me to keep practicing."

Mia gave her a keen-eyed look. "So, tell me what happened with Vada."

Tori waved a second cookie in the air. "Oh, my visit was quite intriguing. What do you know about Gale Mills? She works for Vada."

Mia took a sip of tea, her brow furrowed as she thought. "I've heard the name, but I've never met her. I think she moved here a couple of years ago. Why do you ask?"

After recounting the details of her visit and subsequent conversation with Mills, Tori added, "I think Vada and Gale know more than they will admit."

With a knowing look, Mia said, "That wouldn't surprise me at all."

Tori took a long sip of coffee. "What did you find out from your contacts?"

"A dead end, which I also found intriguing," Mia replied. "They haven't heard anything about the two women, but the rumor mill is alive with talk about you as a suspect in the murder. Someone's definitely fueling the fire. If they figure out who, I'll get a call."

Tori frowned. "Mia, this is all so puzzling, a tangled mass of contradictions. The only common link is me. Last night, I kept thinking, what does a murder have to do with dang tires?"

"When we figure out the why, we'll know the who," Mia said with quiet conviction.

"That's exactly what I thought," Tori said.

Mia's eyes narrowed as she mused, "I keep thinking about Carly walking out of Vada's office. Vada is a hanger-on. I can't see Carly dropping by for a casual visit unless she wanted something from Vada."

The doorbell rang. Tori rose. "I'll get it since that's either Dubois or the reporter." She added, almost absentmindedly, "I left the cellar door open."

When she opened the door, Dubois stood on the front porch. "Good morning, Mr. Dubois." Determined to maintain a cheerful tone despite his dour expression, Tori added, "A beautiful day, isn't it?"

He gave her a withering look. "I suppose so." Without waiting for an invitation, he walked past her. "I hope there won't be any interruptions today."

"There might be one. I may need to show the cellar to someone."

His tone sharpened with irritation. "You do realize these interruptions only delay my progress."

Tori held her ground, her voice steady. "Then, we'll both have to work around the problem, won't we?" She gave him a sweet smile.

He grunted in response, heading into the kitchen.

Dubois grunted again at Mia's sunny greeting before disappearing into the pantry.

Tori paused in the kitchen doorway, giving a half-hearted shrug. "I'll be in my office." She had barely taken a step when the doorbell echoed through the house. With a flicker of anticipation, she hurried toward the foyer.

Opening the door, she was greeted by a friendly smile.

"Good to see you again, Ms. Winters," Bart Hempstead said with an easygoing tone.

"Nice to see you, too, and please, it's Tori. Let's head back to my office," Tori replied, stepping aside to let him enter.

As they walked toward the hallway, he cast an appreciative glance at the library and a quick sweep of the living room. "I'm really hoping to get the grand tour today. Hard to believe this was built in the 1930s, considering how well the house has held up."

"My grandmother kept it meticulously updated, and I've added a few modern improvements." She gestured toward a chair as she moved around her desk.

He slipped the strap of his briefcase from his shoulder and settled into a chair.

From the doorway, Mia asked, "Would you like a cup of coffee?"

He shifted in the chair to look at her. "I'll pass, thank you."

Before she could leave, Tori said, "Mia, please stay. I may need your input."

Mia settled onto the small sofa with a watchful gaze.

Bart's eyes flickered for a fleeting moment, but the emotion, whether irritation or something else, vanished as quickly as it appeared. Then he smiled. "Now, please put me out of my misery, Tori. Are you going to let me do the interview?"

"Yes, but I insist on final approval on the questions."

"Of course," Bart replied smoothly. "That goes without saying. Our magazine takes pride in ensuring our interviews are accurate and satisfactory."

"Do I need to sign a contract?" she asked.

"I have one with me," he said, picking up his briefcase and placing it on his lap. With a quick spin of the lock, he cracked the lid, slipping his hand inside to retrieve a document. He snapped it shut, relocked it, and set the case on the floor.

"This is a standard agreement commonly used by most magazines," he said, sliding the document toward Tori.

For a few moments, she studied the simple contract. The content was concise and straightforward. She agreed to a complimentary interview for *International Vintner's Review* magazine, with the condition that she had final approval for the article.

Satisfied, she set the document aside. "You mentioned the interview hinges on the wine collection. Let's make sure you still want to move forward after you've seen it."

"From what I've seen of this house, I'm sure I will," Bart replied. "I'd like some time to study the collection to learn more about the different vintages for the article."

"That's impossible. The collection is being inventoried and appraised by a wine expert."

His face sagged with disappointment. "How long will he be here?"

"Several weeks. I can't allow his work to be interrupted."

"Of course, I can understand. Still, I'd like to examine what you have." He rose, picking up his briefcase.

"You can leave your case here," Tori suggested.

"Thank you, but I may want to take some notes."

When they entered the pantry, Bart's gaze immediately locked onto the open door to the cellar. "This is unusual," he murmured, narrowing his eyes as he moved closer.

Bart paused to study the door and fittings, running his fingers lightly along the edges. "I can't say I've encountered a setup like this before. How do you open it?"

"The door is controlled from another part of the house," Tori said, stepping through the doorway.

As they descended the stairs, he asked, "What happens if the door closes while you're down here?"

"There is a lever in the cellar that will open the door," she assured him.

When they reached the bottom, Bart abruptly stopped, his gaze sweeping across the room and rows of bottles. An avid gleam sparked in his eyes. "This is far more than I expected."

Dubois was seated at the table with his laptop open, staring at them with annoyance. Before he rose, he closed the computer.

Tori said, "Mr. Hempstead, this is Arthur Dubois. He is cataloging and appraising the collection."

Bart hesitated, reluctantly tearing his gaze from the bottles and directing an interested look at Dubois.

Disregarding Dubois' frown, Tori said, "Bartholomew

Hempstead is a reporter for *International Vintner's Review* magazine. He's writing an article about the collection."

With an engaging smile, Bart extended his hand, keeping it outstretched until Dubois, after a moment's pause, shook hands. "Nice to meet you," Bart declared enthusiastically.

Not bothering to wait for a reply, Bart turned back to the bottles. "This is astounding." He glanced toward Dubois. "What's the value?"

Dubois stiffened. "Any opinion would be premature and simply conjecture. I'm still assessing the collection."

Tori's lips thinned. Whenever she'd been down here, it seemed like Dubois was doing anything but assessing.

Bart set his briefcase near the staircase, then began slowly strolling along the first row, occasionally pausing to inspect a bottle before continuing his steady pace.

Tori moved to where she could watch him and hopefully answer any questions.

Dubois, meanwhile, glanced repeatedly at his watch. At last, he huffed and said in a tone heavy with aggravation, "Ms. Winters, I simply must get back to what I was doing."

Bart stepped out from between the rows with an apologetic smile. "I didn't mean to take up so much of your time, but this," his hand swept toward the shelves, "is mind-boggling. I'd say you've got some very valuable bottles, Tori."

He walked back to retrieve his briefcase before turning his attention to Dubois. "How long will it take to complete your assessment, Mr. Dubois?"

"I hardly believe it's relevant," Dubois said stiffly, his tone edging into rudeness.

"Oh, but it is," Bart countered smoothly, his expression curious. "I'm sure our readers would love to know more about cataloging and appraising a collection like this."

Dubois sat, his annoyance barely concealed. "Ms. Winters can provide you with the information."

"Ah, right. Okay," Bart said with a nervous chuckle, his hands briefly fumbling with his briefcase.

"Ready to see the rest of the house?" Tori asked.

"I sure am," Bart replied, his energy undiminished.

Bart kept up a steady stream of questions as they strolled through the rooms downstairs. His curiosity seemed boundless, his energy almost exhausting.

Stopping before the painting, he tilted his head. "This must be the infamous Frankie Leichter and his wife. From what I've read, he was a ruthless gangster."

Tori wondered about his comment, bordering on admiration, but then Frankie's infamous career might hold interest for a reporter. "Yes, these are my great-grandparents," Tori said, folding her arms. "He left quite a legacy with this house."

Bart turned away from the painting, glancing toward the staircase in the foyer. "What about the upstairs?"

"Sorry. The rooms are still under renovation."

A momentary look of disappointment crossed his face before his engaging smile reappeared. "I'm definitely in for the interview. And I'd love to spend more time here, soaking in the atmosphere."

"Let's head back to my office," Tori said. "I'll sign the agreement and make a copy, and then we can schedule a time for the interview."

"You can't do it today?" he asked with a hint of frustration.

"Sorry, not today," Tori replied, her tone firm but polite.

With a forlorn expression, he asked, "What about tomorrow?"

She chuckled lightly. "Yes, I can."

Tori signed the agreement, then made a copy and handed it to him. He quickly unlocked his briefcase, sliding the document inside.

Once they arranged for an afternoon session the next day, he said, "Thank you again for your time. This was very informative." He quickly added as she rose from her seat. "I can show myself out."

"I don't mind," Tori replied, following him to the front door.

On the porch, she inhaled deeply, enjoying the crisp air. Bart lingered in the driveway, his eyes scanning the garage and construction. For an instant, his expression shifted, becoming sharp and unreadable, before he caught sight of her watching. His features softened almost too quickly, settling into his bright, cheerful smile as he gave her a wave and strode toward his car parked at the curb.

Tori strolled back into the house, going to the dining

room, where Mia was perched in front of her computer.

Mia glanced up, rolling her eyes. "I wonder if he ever runs out of energy."

"You have to give him credit," Tori said, leaning against the doorframe. "He's certainly enthusiastic about his job. But I wonder if the article is worth all this effort?"

"Having second thoughts already?" Mia asked with an arched brow.

"No … maybe."

Mia's gaze turned searching. "Well, which one?"

"I don't know," Tori admitted with a sigh. "I guess it will be okay. I think I'm just jumpy, seeing spooks where there aren't any. I'm going to practice."

CHAPTER 17

Lost in the music, the time passed unnoticed, and only when her fingers ached for a break did she stop. Stretching her hands, she slid off the bench, startled to find Parker sitting in a chair not far from her.

"When did you get here?" she asked.

"Not long ago," Parker replied with an easy smile. "I didn't want to ring the doorbell. I went to the back door instead. Anytime I can hear you play is a treat."

A spicy aroma drifted toward her as he spoke, catching her off guard. "What is Mia baking?"

"She's experimenting with burnt sugar and orange muffins."

"Oh, my god," Tori said with mock despair, "it's a miracle I don't weigh more. Mia's as bad as Cammie."

From the kitchen, a cheerful voice rang out. "I heard that! Better be nice if you want one."

Laughter rippled between Parker and Tori as they ambled to the kitchen, where Mia was pulling a tray of golden, fragrant muffins from the oven.

Parker's eyes sparkled with anticipation. "I bet those would be right tasty with a cup of coffee."

Mia shot him a playful look, reaching for a plate and flipping two muffins onto it. "Don't think this is because of the shameless hound-dog look you've perfected, the droopy eyes, the pitiful smile, and the whole 'I'm completely innocent' act. You really have that down to a science."

He laughed, holding up his hands in mock surrender. "No, ma'am, I wouldn't dream of it."

Then Mia plated two more muffins for Tori. "Dubois left while you were practicing. I made him go out the back door so he wouldn't disturb you. He wasn't too pleased."

Tori raised an eyebrow but said nothing, distracted by the steaming muffin she was already tearing into. Parker poured coffee for all three of them, and soon, they were seated at the table.

Tori popped a piece of muffin into her mouth, savoring the explosion of flavors. "Oh, my gosh," she said. "These are amazing. We have to add them to the menu. Where did you find the recipe?"

Mia, chewing thoughtfully, swallowed before answering, "These are a variation of one I found online. I wasn't sure the changes I made would work."

"Whatever you did," Parker said, gesturing with his mug of coffee, "make sure you've got it written down. These are too good to lose. Wait until Colt hears what he missed."

Tori turned the conversation, glancing toward Parker. "What did you think about the warehouse?" she asked as she forked another bite of the steaming muffin.

"The building's solid," Parker said, leaning back in his chair. "The security system is adequate, but I'm adding two cameras at the back. The existing camera only covers a small section of the back doors. The cleaning crew was starting on the windows when I left."

He took a sip of coffee before continuing, "The shipment of shelves arrived. I expect Colt will have them installed today. The locks have been changed, and Colt has a new key. I've got extras for you in my bag."

Tori nodded. "Did you see the article in the *Metro*?"

"I didn't until Colt mentioned it," he said, his tone sharp with disdain. "I grabbed a copy on my way here. That reporter, Phyllis Hess, excels at scandalous headlines."

Tori glanced at Mia. "Should we let him finish eating before we tell him what we did?"

Parker's fork froze mid-air, and his eyes narrowed suspiciously. "Do I really want to know?" He shoved the last bite of muffin into his mouth as if bracing himself.

"We searched the house," Tori said.

A look of approval crossed Parker's face. "You think someone planted evidence. I'd say what you did was heads-up thinking."

Rising to pick up the plates, Mia said, "We thought so."

Tori leaned forward. "From what Linc told me about the pressure on Andy and then the newspaper's innuendos, it made us wonder if someone expected the police to uncover something."

"Where did you search?"

Tori described how they divided the rooms.

Mia added, "There's nothing here now, and we're making sure no one gets the chance to hide anything."

"Good." He rose. "I need to check in with one of my investigators." Parker slung his computer bag over his shoulder. "I'll leave the keys on your desk, Tori."

"Oh, I almost forgot," Tori said. "The interview is tomorrow afternoon."

After asking about the time, Parker said, "I'll be here." He walked out, and the closing of the front door echoed a few minutes later.

Tori turned to Mia, her eyes alight with purpose. "Since we don't have to babysit Dubois, let's check out the warehouse. I'd like to see what Colt's done."

"What a great idea," Mia said.

"I'll grab my tote bag and meet you out front," Tori said, her steps quick as she disappeared down the hall.

Minutes later, Mia pulled out of the driveway.

As they neared the intersection, Tori's phone rang. She pulled it from her pocket, glancing at the screen. "Hello, Dwayne. What's the news?"

Dwayne said, his voice upbeat, "It's good. An expert in repairing pianos will be here tomorrow. The repairs should only take a few days. Though here's the question. You won't get much practice time. Are you still comfortable with going ahead with the concert?"

Tori's grip on the phone tightened slightly. "Since I can still practice on my piano, I think I'll be okay."

A sigh of relief echoed over the line before Dwayne said, "Wonderful. I'll keep you posted on the progress."

"Thank you for calling," Tori said, disconnecting the call and slipping the phone back into her pocket.

Mia glanced over, her curiosity evident. "I'm guessing that was good news about the piano."

Tori smiled faintly as Mia navigated the left turn at the intersection. "Someone will be there tomorrow to start the repairs. The piano should be ready for the concert."

Mia nodded. "How do you feel about it?"

Tori hesitated, gazing out the window. "Just thinking about the concert sets off a flutter of nerves," she confessed, her voice tinged with emotion. "But then the anger takes over. Was someone so consumed by malice they'd destroy a valuable piano just to keep me from performing?" Her jaw tightened. "If sabotaging my concert is what this is all about, I'm not letting them win. Come hell or high water, I'll be on that stage."

"Yes!" Mia exclaimed, throwing her fist lightly into the air.

"Remember this when you're squeezing into the gown," Tori teased. "I don't want to hear any complaints."

Mia's laughter bubbled up, filling the car. "You know, the rest of our team will be there. I talked to all three of them. Heidi was adamant about doing your nails, hair, and makeup for the concert."

"I've got tickets if they want to bring a friend."

"I asked, but they said no."

As they turned the corner, Tori glanced out the

window, and her eyes widened. "Look! Is that Dubois?"

"Where?" Mia said, her head snapping toward the direction Tori was pointing.

"Up ahead, at the convenience store." Tori leaned forward, her eyes fixed on two men.

Dubois stood beside a car parked near the storefront, deep in conversation with a tall man wearing baggy pants and a ratty-looking hoodie.

"Oh, my gosh, it is Dubois," Mia said.

"Slow down." Tori leaned closer to the window, trying to get a better look as they passed. "It looks like they're arguing."

With a curious tone, Mia said, "What's a French wine expert doing here? This is mostly a warehouse district."

"Considering I'm paying him to be in my wine cellar, I want to find out," Tori said with a grim note. "Park, and let's see what he's up to." Tori motioned with her hand. "Pull into that parking lot. We can watch from there."

Mia zipped into the lot, turning to face the street. "Should we get out?"

"Um … no, he might see us if we do. Better yet, slide down a bit."

Mia's eyebrow arched as she adjusted her position in the driver's seat. "This is more animation than we've ever seen from Dubois. What's going on?"

As they watched, Dubois grew increasingly agitated, leaning forward with his hands gesturing as if to emphasize something. After a few heated moments, the man wearing the hoodie spun on his heels, heading toward a nearby van. Thin-lipped and with a heavy frown, Dubois watched for a few seconds before marching to his car. When he drove out of the lot, he headed in the same direction as the van's driver.

"Well, that was enlightening," Tori said, sitting up straight. "Dubois didn't like whatever they were discussing."

Her eyes followed the car until Dubois disappeared around a corner. "Did you recognize the other man?"

Mia started the car, her expression troubled as they pulled onto the street. "No," she admitted. "But he looked ... unsavory." There was a heavy pause before she added quietly, "Why do I have this creeping sense of trepidation?"

"Whatever the reason," Tori said, her voice tinged with unease, "it's contagious because I have the same feeling."

When they reached the warehouse, Mia pulled alongside Colt's truck. The front door was ajar, and inside, a bustle of activity greeted them. Men maneuvered hand trucks, hauling boxes from the loading dock, while others assembled the metal shelves.

In the center of the chaos stood Colt, clipboard in hand, his voice rising above the din as he directed the placement of the freestanding shelves. When he spotted Tori and Mia hovering at the entrance, he pocketed his pen and strolled toward them.

"What do you think?" He motioned with his clipboard. "All this will be finished today, and I can start moving your inventory tomorrow."

"Wow, what a change," Tori said as she scanned the room.

Colt grinned. "Any preferences on where you want the different products?"

Tori exchanged a wide-eyed glance with Mia. "Oh, my gosh, that's something we haven't discussed," she admitted.

Mia's eyes narrowed as she studied the shelves. "Start with the heavier items on the bottom shelves in each row and go up. I've got a list of the inventory at the house. Are you coming by in the morning, or do you want me to drop it off here?"

"I'll stop by the house," Colt replied.

Mia nodded, still studying the shelves. "They are taller than I envisioned. We'll need a good sturdy ladder."

"I'll pick one up tomorrow," Colt said, though his focus shifted when one of his workers shouted, and he quickly walked off.

"Not much we can do here except get in the way," Tori observed.

"True," Mia agreed, glancing toward Colt, who was engrossed in overseeing the placement of another load of boxes. "Anywhere else you want to stop before we go home?"

Tori slid into the car. "Nope, I'm good." She buckled her seat belt as Mia pulled out of the parking lot.

Near the intersection, Tori suddenly yelped, "There's the van!"

Focused on turning, Mia shot her a startled look. "What van?"

Her tone laced with astonishment, Tori said, "The one the guy was driving. The one who argued with Dubois. Back there!" She jabbed a finger at the rear window.

Mia's eyes darted to the side mirror as she navigated through the intersection. "I don't see a van. Where is it?"

Tori's voice rose. "It's backed up against an empty building. I think I saw someone inside." A chill rippled over her skin, unease creeping into her voice. "Mia, I think he's watching the warehouse. Pull over! We need to get that license plate number."

Chapter 18

Mia pulled to the curb and threw the gearshift into park. "We can circle back around. I'll go slow so you can get a picture of the plate."

"Not a good idea since he probably saw us drive by, and I don't think there's a front plate," Tori admitted with a frown.

"Then, how do you figure we're going to get the plate number?" Mia asked, her tone laced with skepticism.

Tori nibbled her bottom lip. "I'm working on it. We need a way to get closer—without being seen," she said, her mind racing.

Mia sighed. "Why do I have this feeling I'm not going to like whatever plot you're hatching?" she muttered, her voice tinged with resignation.

As her gaze swept the street, Tori spotted a narrow alley. "I've got it!" she said excitedly. She unbuckled her seatbelt to lean forward. "There," she pointed. "The alley runs behind the buildings. We can get to his vehicle from there."

Mia arched an eyebrow. "What? You're not *actually* suggesting that we walk up on this guy?"

Energized by her plan, Tori eagerly nodded. "We drive down the alley. You stop, and I'll hop out, run up on the side of the building, and take a peek."

"Hate to burst your bubble, but driving in there is a bad idea. It's an easy way to get a flat tire—then what? Plus, he might hear the engine and wonder why someone's creeping through the alley. So much for your stealth approach."

Frustrated, Tori slumped but refused to abandon the idea. "Okay, fair points," she admitted grudgingly. Her finger tapped her lips as she thought. "Then, how about this? Turn onto the next street and park. We can go between the buildings and cross over the alley."

Mia groaned, letting her head fall back against the headrest. "Let me get this straight. We'll walk between two buildings, cross an alley, and sneak up on the side of a building on the other side. Just to get a license plate. Have I got it right?"

Though undeterred, Tori grinned at Mia's dramatics. "That's better than driving straight up to the guy."

Muttering under her breath about reckless ideas, Mia shifted the car into drive and turned at the next street.

"Park there," Tori said, pointing to a spot across from two buildings separated by a narrow strip of ground with more weeds than grass.

After turning off the engine, Mia's fingers drummed an irregular beat on the steering wheel as she eyed the buildings. "And you think we can do this without being spotted?"

Tori reached for the door handle. "I don't know," she admitted, glancing briefly at Mia. "But what do we have to lose?"

"I don't want to think about the answer to that question," Mia muttered.

She opened the door and stepped out, looking at Tori over the top of the car. "What are we going to say if someone comes out of one of these buildings and wants to know *why* we're prowling around? What's the genius explanation, Sherlock?"

Tori's face lit up with mischief as she strolled around the front of the car. "How about I'm looking for another building to buy?"

"Oh, right! Fantastic plan. This one will *really* work. You're so dressed for real estate negotiations," she said dryly, her eyes sweeping over Tori's outfit—jeans, a T-shirt, vest, and tennis shoes. "If you haven't noticed, they're not for sale."

Grinning, Tori waved her hands dismissively. "Minor detail. Come on."

With a roll of her eyes, Mia locked the car, then followed as Tori dashed across the street, her sneakers scuffing against the uneven asphalt. The sunlight felt glaringly bright, making their hurried movements more exposed. They slipped between two buildings and stopped at the corner.

Tori peeked around the edge, scanning the alley with sharp eyes. The faint smell of garbage lingered, and a lone soda can rolled lazily in the wind. Satisfied the alley was safe to cross, she darted ahead, dodging the ruts and debris scattered along the way. Mia followed, her steps quieter, slower, her skeptical gaze flicking upward toward the windows of the buildings looming over them.

When they reached the back of the vacant building, they pressed close to the wall and eased along its side, the rough bricks scraping their arms. At the corner, Tori stopped again. Her heart thundered in her chest as she cautiously peeked around.

Tori froze. She was right. There was someone in the van. The man sat motionless, slumped low in the driver's seat. An elbow rested on the open window frame. From her angle, she could only make out the curve of his shoulder and the side of his face.

Still, the casual stillness of his posture somehow felt deliberate, even dangerous. And across the street was her warehouse. A wave of unease prickled over Tori's skin.

Swallowing hard, she stepped back, pressing her shoulder into the wall. Leaning forward, her lips close to Mia's ear, Tori whispered, barely audible, "There's a man behind the wheel. His window is open. We can't get any closer than this, and I can't see the license plate. If we wait, he may drive off."

She pulled out her phone, muted it, and motioned for Mia to do the same.

They took turns peeking around the corner, careful to make each movement slow and precise. The minutes dragged by, each one feeling like a small eternity.

The man in the van didn't budge except to lean

forward occasionally when someone exited the warehouse. Each time he moved, Tori stiffened, her muscles coiling with fresh tension.

She was about to tell Mia they should call it quits when the man leaned forward, shoving a cell phone to his ear. Tori's pulse quickened. She turned back to Mia and waggled her hand, mimicking the action of holding a phone to her ear.

While his voice wasn't loud, from their position, they could easily hear. "The crew is leaving." A brief pause followed before he added, "Both of them were here. Didn't stay long, looked around, then left." Another beat, then, "I'll find out later."

The engine's rumble broke the momentary lull, snapping Tori into motion. She quickly glanced around the corner of the building. But before she could grab her phone from her pocket, the driver had already sped out of the lot. From her brief glimpse of the plate, it was obscured by dirt. Was that deliberate? Tori wondered.

Disgusted, she turned back to Mia, her voice tight. "The plate's covered with dirt, and I wasn't fast enough to get a picture. Let's get back to the car."

As they carefully crossed the alley, Mia said, her voice filled with concern, "I think he was talking about us."

Tori nodded grimly, her lips pressing into a thin line. "I think you're right. He was definitely watching the warehouse. But why?" His cryptic words, "I'll find out later," sent a fresh chill down her spine.

Occupied with their thoughts, the drive back was

quiet, though Mia finally broke the silence. Her question echoed what had been rolling in Tori's thoughts. "What's the connection to Dubois?"

"I've been wondering the same," Tori admitted.

Her hands tightly gripped the wheel as Mia said, "This wasn't some random guy lurking around your warehouse. We need to figure out how they're connected."

Tori let out a sharp breath, frustration flickering across her face. "Yeah, well, the problem is, I don't exactly have a game plan."

Mia glanced at her sideways. "Maybe Parker will. He's good at this kind of thing."

When they pulled into Tori's driveway, the familiar surroundings did little to ease her sense of foreboding. Before she exited the car, Tori said, "I'll see you in the morning. Maybe we'll have an epiphany overnight."

Still troubled by her thoughts, she unlocked the front door and wandered inside. On the way to the kitchen, she dropped her tote bag in the office. After pulling the remains of the lasagna from the refrigerator, she slid the dish into the microwave. With a glass of wine in hand, Tori sank into a chair. While she gazed out the window, she brooded.

She was a suspect in a murder, a target of relentless harassment, and now, some guy, connected to her wine expert of all people, was watching her warehouse. Her grip on the wine glass tightened at the thought.

The beep of the microwave stirred her out of the doldrums. She retrieved the lasagna and returned to the table. While she ate, her mind kept circling back to Dubois. From the beginning, he'd been uncooperative, insisting he couldn't provide any updates until he finished his work. Now, Tori had to wonder if he had another agenda.

Unable to finish the meal for worrying, she pushed the plate aside and fished her phone out of her vest pocket. When Parker answered, she asked, "Did I catch you at a bad time?"

"Not at all. Handling some paperwork at the office. What's going on?"

"Mia and I had a strange encounter today." She hesitated momentarily, pulling her thoughts together before launching into the details. When she finished, she added, "I think the license plate was deliberately covered with mud."

Parker's voice took on a grave tone. "If it was deliberate, someone is trying to hide their identity, and that makes it dangerous. Tori, you shouldn't—"

"I know," she cut in quickly. "I felt trying to get the plate number was a risk worth taking. I still do."

Parker let out a noticeable sigh of exasperation. "Tell me every detail you remember about the van and the driver."

When she finished, there was only silence on the other end. Tori shifted uneasily, the stillness unnerving her. "What are you thinking?" she finally asked, her tone quieter than before.

"I'm thinking I'm worried," Parker said, his voice low. "A man claiming to have been following you, warning you that your life is in danger, winds up dead. Now, your French wine expert is talking to someone who is clandestinely skulking around your warehouse. This reeks of something much larger and far more dangerous. Which raises an alarming question. Is there a connection between Dubois and the murder victim?"

Tori sucked in a breath. "You think Dubois might have killed him?"

"At this point, it's sheer speculation. What I can't get around is that one man was lurking around you and is dead, and now there is a second one, and that man is linked to Dubois. I don't believe in coincidence, not when murder is involved. I'm going to make some inquiries."

His words sent a shiver down her back. "Should I fire Dubois?"

"Not yet. In the morning, the warehouse is my first stop. I need to activate the new cameras and set up a link to your security system where you can monitor the warehouse from your office."

Tori hesitated, her fingers tightening slightly around the phone. "You don't think there's any real danger to the warehouse, do you?"

"Unlikely," Parker admitted, though his tone wasn't entirely dismissive. "I can't imagine what anyone would gain. Still, there's no reason to take any chances. I'll see you tomorrow."

After the call ended, she set the phone aside. Parker's assessment and the unanswered questions swirled, refusing to settle into anything coherent. The uneasiness she'd felt listening to him twisted and churned, refusing to let go.

She reached for the list. Names and events she'd scrawled. Adding Dubois, the van, driver, and warehouse to the list, she leaned back in her chair, studying the words and connections that she'd tried to piece together. This was like staring at a puzzle with missing pieces. The more she tried to make sense of the conflicting maze of details, the less they seemed to fit together. And no matter how long she stared at the words, the gaps didn't just remain, they seemed to widen, increasing her foreboding.

Her eyes lingered on one word—WHY. Whatever the reason, the enigma seemed to be gathering strength, moving at a frightening speed, but to what end? All she could sense was the danger felt closer with each passing moment. And, she had no way to stop it—or did she?

Chapter 19

After another restless night, a grim determination settled deep within her. The epiphany had struck, but not about the warehouse. Impatient, not even coffee calmed her nerves as Tori waited. The moment the hour hand reached eight, she grabbed her phone and tapped the number.

When a warm, familiar voice answered, Tori said, "Hi, Linda, it's Tori. Is Linc in?"

"Yes, he just walked in. Hold on."

His voice radiated enthusiasm when he came on the line. "Tori. What a pleasant surprise. I like hearing your voice so early in the day."

Unwilling to waste time on niceties, she said, "You may not after you hear why I called. Did you talk to the district attorney?"

"I did. I planned to call you this morning," Linc replied.

She straightened, gripping the phone tightly.

"He's not issuing the warrant unless something changes. There's no evidence to support one," Linc said.

His statement did nothing to alleviate her anxiety.

Instead, it steeled her resolve. "That's not what I consider as reassuring. Since I'm still a suspect when I shouldn't be, I don't like the 'unless something changes' bit," Tori declared with conviction.

Her voice sharpened with anger. "If someone's leaning on Andy or the DA to search my house, there must be a reason. Does someone have a plan to make sure that evidence is found? I want it on record that it doesn't exist."

A pause stretched over the line. "Does this mean you are willing to let the police search?"

"No! Absolutely not. I want *you* to search my house," Tori said firmly.

"What? Whatever for?" His voice, usually so self-assured, wavered with confusion.

"Mia and I have already searched the house, but I want a second search. This time by you," she explained.

With a calm and unnaturally patient tone, he replied, "Tori, just let the police search."

"I've explained why that's a bad idea," Tori said. "I'm not going over the same ground again."

"Look, I know how concerned you are about the search and the adverse publicity. But … don't you think this borders on paranoia?"

While she bristled at the word, Linc's measured tone made her pause. Was she overreacting? A relentless whisper simmered in her mind, *trust no one.*

Her voice sharp, Tori pressed, "What do you have on your schedule this morning?"

"Tori," he said, the frustration evident in his tone. "I

really don't think my searching the house is necessary."

"Well, I do," she fired back. "Who would believe me, or even Mia, for that matter? They'd say she's biased. But your testimony carries weight. When you searched, you found nothing. That matters."

"Even so, a search is still a waste of time. It has no legal standing," Linc countered, his tone verging on impatience. "If Andy claims to have evidence to support a search warrant, nothing you or I do can stop him."

Tori's voice hardened. "Linc, I fully understand what I'm asking isn't legal proof. But this isn't about what's legal or not legal. It's about me being proactive, not reactive."

Frustrated, she sighed. What she couldn't tell him was her overwhelming, almost desperate urge to act, to grasp at any semblance of control over events spiraling beyond her reach.

Instead, in a tone laced with determination, Tori said, "I want to head off whatever scheme someone has cooked up. Look at the facts. I'm a suspect in a murder, there's pressure to get a warrant for my house, my tires have been sabotaged, a piano was viciously destroyed, and now some creep is watching my warehouse."

"What?" His shock was unmistakable. "I know about the piano, but what's this about tires and your warehouse?"

Quickly, she filled him in, each detail painting a clearer picture of the threats closing in around her. When she finished, she added, "I'm the common link here. And if I am a bit paranoid, I think I'm dang well entitled. When can you come to the house?"

"I'm on my way," Linc said before abruptly disconnecting.

Mia walked into the room, her curious gaze locking onto Tori. "What was that all about?"

"I'm plotting and scheming," Tori replied, leaning back and propping her feet on the corner of the desk, her expression grim.

Mia sank into a chair, her face tightening with concern. "I only caught the tail end. Why do you want Linc here?"

"We're searching the house again," Tori said. "This time, Linc will be our witness. If Andy actually has evidence, this won't stop him. But if someone comes forward claiming there is evidence in the house, and Andy finds it, at least we can argue that Linc's search proves it was planted."

"I think it's a good idea," Mia said with a look of approval.

"Linc doesn't think so. Says I'm 'paranoid.'" The words rippled with irritation as she raised her fingers to mimic air quotes.

"Well, that's a lawyer for you," Mia said with a shrug. "When will he be here?"

"He's already on the way."

"What prompted this?" Mia leaned forward slightly, her tone curious.

"I had an epiphany." Tori swung her feet off the desk

and sat upright, her determination glinting in her eyes. "I called Linc about searching the house. That's when he told me that he'd spoken to the district attorney, who has no plans for a search warrant—unless there's a change."

Mia nodded, her expression turning serious. "And a change means a search warrant."

"Exactly." Tori's voice sharpened. "Which only reinforced my reason for a second search. Are you planning on going anywhere?"

"No. I stopped by the store on my way here."

"I need you to stay in the kitchen. Make sure Dubois doesn't wander out."

"Then you'll need another witness. What about Parker?"

"I talked to him last night. Told him what happened at the warehouse. He's there activating the new cameras. I think that's more important than being a witness to the search. What about Colt?"

"He's out back."

The doorbell rang, sharp and jarring.

"Probably Dubois. I'll let him in." Mia said, rising.

Tori's gaze darkened as she said, "I've got a few questions for him."

Mia stopped mid-stride and shot her a wary look. "Tori," she warned.

"Don't worry. I'm not going to let Dubois know we saw him. Especially after Parker raised the notion that Dubois might be connected to the murder."

Stunned, Mia exclaimed, "What?"

The doorbell jangled again.

"I'll tell you later." Tori rose to wait in the doorway.

Mia opened the door, and Dubois strode in without waiting for an invitation. He nodded briefly but pushed past her with an air of irritation.

"Mr. Dubois," Tori said as he neared. "I'd like to speak with you before you get started."

She stepped back, returning to her chair, her gaze fixed on him. Though she kept a polite smile, she couldn't help but wonder if she was looking at a murderer.

When he hesitated, she said with a hard edge to her voice, "Please. Have a seat."

With an unfriendly look, he set the briefcase down with a noticeable thud. He lowered himself into the chair stiffly, his back ramrod straight. "What is this about?"

Tori tilted her head, giving him a bright look. "I've never asked. Is this your first time in Texas?"

His eyebrows shot up, the question clearly catching him off guard. "Yes. Why?"

While her expression never changed, she watched for any flicker of reaction. "I was curious if you knew people in the area."

His jaw tightened slightly. "Why are we talking about this?" he asked, his tone clipped.

"I can't help but notice the limited number of hours you've spent working on the inventory. Is it because you have other business or friends in Granbury?"

Dubois frowned, shifting in his seat. "No, I don't. The only reason I'm in Granbury is your wine collection. Is that all you wanted to discuss?"

What she really wanted to ask was why he was meeting some shady character in the warehouse district when he should have been appraising her collection. Especially when the shady character was watching her warehouse.

Instead, she met his gaze head-on and said, "Yes, there's more. I'm not satisfied with the progress of the inventory. In fact, I haven't seen any signs of progress at all. Quite frankly, after our correspondence, I expected a more hands-on involvement. That hasn't happened. I'm considering terminating the contract."

He stiffened, a flash of something unreadable flickering in his eyes. Anger, wariness, or perhaps both. "You can't cancel."

"Yes, I can. And if I do, then I expect an inventory of what you've accomplished to that point, along with the value of the wines, even if the list is incomplete. Of course, as per the contract, I will pay the full fee upon receipt of the documentation."

His expression tightened further. "Ms. Winters, I don't appreciate having my methods questioned. However, I am committed to this project and will continue until I'm told otherwise."

His lips pressed into a thin line as he stood abruptly. In one swift motion, he snatched up his briefcase and locked his gaze on her for a fleeting moment before turning and striding out.

Tori's eyes narrowed with suspicion. What was he

hiding? She rose and followed him into the kitchen.

After he stomped past Mia, she rolled her eyes at Tori. A few seconds later, footsteps thudded on the staircase.

"I need to talk to Colt," Tori said. Before she walked out, she leaned close to Mia. "Did you hear?"

With a look of worry on her face, Mia nodded.

When Tori stepped onto the back porch, Colt was striding into the backyard, his boots crunching softly against the gravel path.

"I was coming to talk to you and grab a cup of coffee," Colt said, a faint smile tugging at his lips.

"I also want to talk to you. Let's go to my office."

Colt's curiosity flickered in his eyes, but he didn't ask. Inside her office, Tori closed the door as Colt sank into a chair, cradling the coffee mug Mia had handed him in the kitchen.

After swallowing a swig, he said, "We finished the inside of the warehouse yesterday."

Tori nodded as she sat in her chair. "That's part of what I wanted to talk about. Colt, someone was watching the warehouse yesterday."

His eyes widened. "How do you know?"

Tori explained about seeing the argument between Dubois and another man, then added, "After we left the warehouse, we spotted a van, the same van the man arguing with Dubois was driving, backed into a lot across the street."

Colt frowned. "Are you certain he was watching the warehouse?"

With a smug smile, she said, "Mia and I snuck up on him. We even heard him talking on the phone, telling someone you and your crew were getting ready to leave. And this isn't all. He also said he saw Mia and me there, looking around."

Stunned, he set his mug down with a decisive thump. "Does Parker know what the two of you were doing?"

She nodded.

"I bet the notion didn't make him happy," he mused. His frown deepened. "And you're saying your wine expert knows this guy? And now this guy's got eyes on your warehouse."

"Yes," Tori replied, her voice firm.

"Describe the man and the van." He pulled a small notepad from his pocket. As Tori talked, he jotted down the details. When she finished, he flipped the notepad closed and tucked it back into his pocket.

"I'll watch for him," he assured her. "I'll be at the warehouse most of the day, moving your inventory."

"Can you hold off for an hour or so?" Tori asked, her tone shifting slightly into a quiet request.

"Sure," Colt replied, taking another swallow of coffee.

After explaining about the search, she added, "I'd like an independent witness, though you could end up in court."

Unfazed, Colt said, "That's not a problem. I'll stick like glue to Linc."

Before Tori could respond, the doorbell chimed. She rose, heading to the foyer. When she opened the door, Linc strode in, his expression thunderous.

"I still say this is unnecessary," he began, his words clipped. "The district attorney has assured me there won't be a search warrant."

Tori replied, her annoyance matching his. "His assurance may be good enough for you, but not for me. I want added insurance, and this is one way to get it."

Linc hesitated as if suddenly reminded of his manners. "I'm sorry. I didn't mean to burst in like this," he said, though his tone was still edged with frustration. "It's just ... this seems excessive."

"Well, let's agree to disagree on this one. Would you like a cup of coffee before we start?"

"No," Linc replied, shaking his head. "I don't have much time. Let's get started."

Tori turned to see Colt walking up.

Linc's eyebrows lifted in surprise as he shot Colt a questioning look.

"Didn't Tori tell you?" Colt said, his tone casual. "I'm going to be another witness to the search."

Linc glared at Tori, crossing his arms over his chest. "No, she didn't. How many people do you plan on getting involved in this insane idea of yours?"

With an unrepentant smirk, Tori said, "Just the three of us. It won't take long."

"Mia's not in on this caper?" Linc asked.

"No, she's doing something else. We'll start with the wine cellar. Linc, you can meet the wine expert."

The two men followed her, the wooden steps creaking

slightly as they descended the staircase.

Dubois stood in front of a rack, carefully sliding a bottle into place. He looked up at their entrance, his brow creasing in mild surprise.

After introducing Colt and Linc, she said, "They're going to examine the room."

Though his eyebrows twitched upward, he didn't comment as he moved to the chair behind the table. While his expression remained composed, Tori didn't miss how his gaze darted between the two men, his posture subtly rigid.

The search didn't take long since the wine cellar offered few places to conceal anything. Back upstairs, they moved methodically through the pantry and utility room before stepping into the kitchen.

Once they finished, Linc asked, "What about your bedroom?"

"I keep the door locked," Tori informed him.

They continued their slow pace from room to room, pulling open every drawer, scanning every bookshelf, and checking any other possible hiding place. The process was tedious but necessary, leaving no stone unturned.

When they finally paused in the foyer, Linc's eyes drifted toward the staircase. "What about upstairs?"

"Until the renovations are finished, no one is allowed up there," Tori said firmly.

"Garage and construction areas?" Linc asked.

Colt spoke up. "The garage is kept locked, but we can walk through the construction area."

"I'll take a quick look, then I need to leave."

"I'll meet you out back." Colt turned and walked away.

Linc glanced at Tori. "While I still believe this was unnecessary, I can attest that there's no evidence in this house related to the murder. I hope that satisfies you."

Her tone unwavering, she said, "It does."

After shutting the door behind him, Tori headed to the kitchen, her steps a touch lighter.

Mia, her hands full of wrapped sandwiches, used her hip to close the refrigerator door with a soft thud. Though she shot Tori a questioning look, she only said, "Dubois left, muttering about the interruptions to his work. I made him go out the back door so he wouldn't see what you were doing."

"Between Dubois and Linc, my brain feels fried." Tori reached for a coffee mug, filling it to the brim.

She took a deep swig, welcoming the warmth spreading through her. "Nothing like a shot of caffeine to recharge."

"Now, explain what Parker said about Dubois," Mia said, her tone adamant.

Tori went over the gist of Parker's comments about a link between the murder and Dubois. "He did say it's only speculation."

With a worried expression, Mia set plates on the table. "If Parker is questioning Dubois' connection to the murder victim, I'd consider his assessment more than speculation. Are you going to fire Dubois?"

"Parker said to wait, though when I mentioned canceling the contract, Dubois' reaction was sharper than I expected."

At the sound of the doorbell, Tori hopped up, heading to the door.

Mia grinned. "Probably Parker, and it is lunchtime."

Tori chuckled as she walked toward the door. But the moment she saw Parker, his face grim instead of his usual smile, her laughter faded.

Chapter 20

Parker strode inside with his computer bag hanging off his shoulder. With a somber tone, he said, "I picked up someone nosing around the warehouse on the camera system."

He headed down the hallway, his footsteps echoing softly against the floor. "I need to connect the warehouse camera system to the one here. I think I can get a better look at the video on the larger monitor."

Inside her office, he set his computer bag on the desk before dropping into her desk chair. He rapidly tapped on the keyboard for the camera system.

Mia walked in. Her eyes sparked with curiosity. "What's going on?"

Tori, who had been watching Parker, turned to answer. "Parker saw someone on the warehouse camera system. He's linking the two systems together."

A few minutes later, a new screen appeared on the monitor for the cameras. "If you toggle this icon," he pointed to the screen, "you can switch between the two systems."

After a few more keystrokes, the video began to

rewind, the footage flickering with each frame as Parker deftly navigated the controls. He clicked the play button, his gaze locked on the screen. Though the video was dark, faint shadows and muted outlines revealed the back doors of the warehouse.

"Wait," he muttered, his voice tight. He paused the video, his finger hovering over the keyboard. "There."

Tori leaned forward as Mia moved closer to peer over her shoulder. Parker advanced the footage in slow motion. On the screen, a hooded figure emerged from the shadows, slipping along the back of the warehouse. The faint beam of a small light flickered on, briefly illuminating the lock on the back door. The light vanished almost as quickly as it had appeared, leaving only the vague silhouette of the figure slipping out of view.

Tori gasped, "This might be the guy we saw arguing with Dubois, the one in the van. He was wearing a hoodie. What do you think, Mia?"

"Maybe," she replied.

Parker, watching the video again, said, "Odd. All he did was look at the lock, then left."

Tori and Mia exchanged uneasy glances as they stepped away from the desk.

With a worried tone, Tori said, "Parker, the man in the van said he'd find out later."

Mia exclaimed, "You're right. He did. Was this what he meant? Finding out something about the locks."

Parker shrugged. "Still doesn't make sense. Why would the warehouse be a target? Not much demand on the street for the stuff you've got stored there." He rose, pushing the chair back.

"Have you eaten?" Mia asked.

Parker blinked, glancing at his watch with mild surprise. "Nope, lost track of the time again."

Mia laughed, already turning toward the kitchen. "Come on. I made sandwiches."

After Mia set another plate on the table, they settled into chairs.

Frowning, Tori asked, "What do we do about this guy?"

"I'll talk to the police and ask for extra patrol. There's not much else we can do unless you want to put guards on site," he said between bites.

Tori chewed while she pondered the thought. "I could, but honestly, there's nothing of value in the warehouse to justify the expense."

"Agreed, but I wanted to put the option out there." He took a deep swig of coffee, glancing between Tori and Mia. "Since we're discussing this in the kitchen, I assume Dubois isn't around?"

Mia waved a chip in the air. "No, he's left. He doesn't like interruptions."

"Music again?" Parker asked, half-joking.

"No," Tori said with a chuckle. "This time, Linc was the interruption. I had him search the house. Since you were at the warehouse, I roped Colt in as a witness."

Parker paused mid-bite, raising an eyebrow. "What prompted this?" He popped the last bit of sandwich in his mouth and shot a rueful look at his empty plate.

Tori shoved her plate aside. "I wanted independent witnesses to prove there is no evidence in this house tying me to the murder. If it shows up, then it was planted."

"Smart move." Parker's voice carried a note of admiration. "How'd Linc react to your request?"

"Not well," Tori admitted. "He thought a search was a waste of time. He's convinced the district attorney won't get a warrant."

"Better safe than sorry," Parker said, finishing his coffee. "Heads-up planning."

Resting her elbows on the table, Tori asked, "What about Dubois?" She relayed the conversation she'd had with the man. "He lied. While he may have thought it wasn't any of my business, I don't think that was his motive. Plus, he didn't want the contract canceled, even when it meant he would receive full payment. In fact, he was adamant that he meant to stay until I told him to leave. Don't you find that odd?"

Parker leaned back, rubbing his chin. "I do. So, why would he want to stay in this house?"

With a troubled expression, Mia said, "If you think he's connected to the murder, I'm concerned about Tori's safety."

"As little time as he seems to spend here, I don't think he's a threat. Besides, whatever he's hiding, it's easier to keep an eye on him here."

The chime of the doorbell interrupted them.

"That's probably the reporter," Tori said, standing

and pushing her chair back. "And just a heads-up, I might put you on the spot to answer questions."

With a soulful expression, Parker said, "Then I need to be fortified, that is, if I can talk Mia out of another cup of coffee."

Mia's lips humorously twitched as she replied, "He's annoyingly good at the hound-dog look."

Striding into the hallway, a roar of laughter erupted from Tori. She shot a parting remark over her shoulder. "Well, it works."

At the door, Bart greeted her with an exuberant grin. "Hello! I've been looking forward to this."

With his case slung over one shoulder, he all but bounced through the doorway. He extended a hand, and Tori shook it. "Seldom have I been excited about an interview as I am this one," he said, his voice brimming with unfeigned excitement.

While Tori felt awkward when his handshake lingered a little too long, she couldn't help returning his smile. His genuine enthusiasm was oddly charming.

"Well, I hope I don't disappoint," she said, her tone light but steady, as she gently reclaimed her hand.

Bart's eyes sparkled as he took in his surroundings with an ardent glance. "Disappointment? Impossible! Shall we get started?"

"Absolutely. Let's begin in the living room," Tori said, motioning toward the archway. "Please have a seat, and you can tell me how you want to proceed."

Bart swung his case onto the sofa. Before he could sit,

Parker walked in. Bart's eyes flitted toward him with an intense, almost probing look.

"Bart, this is Parker Hayes. He's in charge of security for the inn. Parker, this is Bartholomew Hempstead, a reporter for *International Vintner's Review* magazine."

As Tori spoke, she caught a fleeting glimmer in Bart's eyes. Something elusive, perhaps, a flicker of calculation concealed behind his cheerful emotion. The moment quickly passed, leaving her to wonder whether it had been real or merely her imagination.

Bart extended his hand, his enthusiasm undiminished. "Pleased to meet you," he said warmly.

Parker, his expression neutral but polite, grasped his hand. "Are you based stateside or overseas, Mr. Hempstead?"

"Call me Bart," the reporter replied with a friendly grin. "Home is New York City, but I'm rarely there. I spend most of my time on the road, especially in Europe."

His eyebrows lifted slightly as he glanced around the room. "I wouldn't expect a bed-and-breakfast inn to have a security director. But then, this is my first experience with one. Is security for an inn common?"

While Bart talked, Tori couldn't help but notice how Parker's intense gaze scrutinized Bart's face or the faintest edge of warning in his tone. "Given the history of this house and the value of the antiques, naturally, security is a priority."

Bart nodded, his face lit up with what seemed to be genuine interest. "That certainly makes sense, especially with a valuable wine collection," he said as he dropped onto the couch.

Parker sat in a chair across from him. Tori settled in next to him.

Bart turned his attention back to Tori. "First, I'd like to record the interview. Even though this will be a printed piece, I find a recording helps ensure accuracy."

He paused, his eyes flicking around the room again. "We can start here, then finish in the wine cellar. I'm really excited about the opportunity to see your collection again. My first glimpse whetted my appetite to learn more."

"I should warn you. I'm not very knowledgeable about wines," Tori admitted, her tone light but tinged with hesitation.

"Your novice perspective will make the article even more compelling," Bart enthusiastically replied, leaning forward. "I'll add a slant about the challenges you've had to overcome."

He reached for the case, settling it onto his lap, and unlocked the lid. He slid a hand inside and pulled out a recorder, followed by a compact camera. "I'll also want to take a few pictures," he added casually as he shut and locked the lid.

Tori stiffened. "Bart, you never mentioned pictures. You can't take any."

He looked up with a surprised expression. "Oh, boy. This gets back to the letter you didn't get. My editor mentioned the pictures. It never occurred to me to bring the subject up again. Is there any way we can work something out? I only need a couple of shots to go with the story?"

The determination in Tori's voice didn't waver. "I can't. This is a security issue," she said with a rueful smile that was more polite than apologetic.

The doorbell rang. Tori rose. "Excuse me," she said and walked toward the front door.

When the door swung open, she fought the urge to groan. Carly stood on the doorstep with two women in tow. Her expression, one Tori knew all too well, exuded an air of self-importance.

Before Tori could draw a breath to stop her, Carly breezed past, trailing a gust of perfume in her wake.

"Hello, Tori. My friends are very eager to see the house. I assured them you wouldn't mind," Carly said, tossing the words over her shoulder as though she had the right to guarantee their entry.

The trio had barely stepped inside when Carly's gaze zeroed in on the men in the living room. She cooed in a tone laced with saccharine. "Oh, you have company. How lovely." She breezed into the room as though she belonged there, her friends trailing dutifully behind.

Parker and Bart both stood. Ignoring Parker, Carly honed in on Bart, her sharp gaze gleaming with interest. Like a hawk spotting prey, she strutted toward him, her smile radiating practiced charm. Extending her hand, she tilted her head coyly. "Hello. I'm Carly Swanson, and you are?"

Bart responded with equal charm, his smile polished

but intrigued. "Bartholomew Hempstead, but please, call me Bart," he said, clasping her hand with a casual confidence.

Carly, eyes sparkling with anticipation, leaned in ever so slightly, her grip lingering long enough to hint at more. "How delightful," she purred. "What brings you to our lovely inn?"

As Tori watched, annoyance simmered inside her. Carly was up to her usual tricks. But this time, Carly wasn't going to get away with her rude conduct.

With a polite tone that belied the determination etched on her face, Tori stepped forward and said, "Carly, you and your friends need to leave. This isn't a convenient time for a visit." She motioned toward the door.

Carly's lower lip puffed out in a practiced pout, her expression an artful mix of faux innocence and annoyance. "Now, Tori, we don't plan to stay long, but I'm certain you won't disappoint my friends. You and your friend can show them the house while I entertain your visitor."

She turned toward her companions as if to draw them into the conversation, but her eyes flicked to Tori with a fleeting, malicious glint.

With a dismissive wave of her hand toward Tori, she turned to face Bart, her expression smoothed into a predatory interest. "What business are you in, Bart?"

"I'm a reporter with the *International Vintner's Review* magazine," Bart replied.

"Why, how … very impressive." Her hand preened her hair while the other fingered the strap of the handbag over her shoulder. "And I bet you're interviewing this sweet person. How kind of you. I know Tori needs all the help she can get," Carly said, her voice oozing in a Texas drawl laden with sarcasm.

"Carly," Tori said again, her tone sharpening like a blade. "I must insist that you and your friends leave."

Parker, still standing near the couch, took a purposeful step forward. "Ms. Swanson, I'll escort you to the door," he said, his voice calm but leaving no room for argument.

Chapter 21

Faced with a man clearly intent on removing her, Carly's expression faltered for a fleeting moment before shifting into one of feigned politeness. "Well, of course, if you insist. Before I leave, I'd like to use the ladies' room."

Tori, seeing through the transparent ploy, folded her arms. "I'm sorry, but the guest bathroom is out of order due to the renovations."

"How ridiculous," Carly huffed. "I'm sure there must be at least one working bathroom in this place."

Before Tori could respond, Parker stepped beside her, his calm gaze shifting to Carly's companions. "Ladies," he said, his tone courteous but firm as he motioned to the door.

Carly's friends, lacking her boldness, exchanged hesitant glances before quietly turning toward the front door. Left with no backup, Carly had no choice but to follow. She pushed past them in the foyer, swinging the door open in a burst of indignant fury before storming outside. Her friends trailed behind, their faces flushed with embarrassment.

Tori, who had followed, shut the door firmly, letting the tension in her shoulders ease slightly. She resisted the urge to lean against it. From the hallway, Mia watched with a grim expression, arms crossed tightly as if sharing Tori's outrage.

Without a word, Tori straightened and returned to the living room. "Bart, my apologies for the interruption," she began, her voice steady despite the lingering irritation. "Continuing with the interview today isn't a good idea."

A flicker of annoyance crossed Bart's face, though he quickly hid it behind a polite smile. "Can we reschedule?"

"How about tomorrow at the same time?" Tori offered.

"That would be wonderful. Would you object if I took a few pictures of the outside of the house before I leave?" Bart asked, his charming smile returning in full force.

Tori glanced at Parker.

He said, "Pictures of the outside aren't a problem."

"Thank you," Bart said, his smile widening as he unlocked his case, sliding the recorder inside. He stood, slinging the camera around his neck and the case over his shoulder. "I'll see you tomorrow."

Tori walked him to the door. "Again, thank you for understanding," she said.

She closed the door, and this time, Tori did lean against the wood.

Mia marched into the foyer with fire in her eyes. "The nerve of that woman. I wanted to yank her by the hair and drag her out of here."

Tori managed a small laugh, though the aggravation hadn't faded. "She is obnoxious."

She straightened when Parker stepped into the foyer, his face troubled.

"Parker, thanks for your help," Tori said. "I wasn't sure I'd get her to budge until you entered the fray."

"I wonder why she was here," he said, his voice low, as if speaking more to himself than her.

"Snooping would be my guess," Tori said.

"Maybe," he said, a note of doubt creeping into his voice. His eyes narrowed slightly, and he nodded toward the hallway. "Let's go to your office. I want to keep an eye on Bart."

"I've got a batch of chocolate chip cookies fresh out of the oven," Mia said. "Anyone interested?"

"Oh, my gosh, how perfect," Tori said, her chuckle breaking through the lingering tension. "A chocolate fix is exactly what I need to soothe my rattled nerves."

"Count me in," Parker said, his tone lightened while a faint smile tugged at his lips. "I could use something to calm down. Chocolate would definitely soothe my nerves after all the excitement."

Mia snorted, turning toward the kitchen. "As if any of us has ever seen you with rattled nerves."

In an even, mild tone, Parker replied, "There's always a first time."

Their shared laughter rippled through the hallway, lessening the strain of Carly's rude behavior.

Inside the office, Parker moved to the window that

overlooked the driveway. "What is this all about?" he muttered.

Tori stepped beside him. Outside, Carly leaned against her car, ignoring her friends as they climbed into another vehicle. Engaged in a lively discussion with Bart, her gaze was locked on his face. She playfully reached for the camera strap, lightly tugging on it with a pleading look. Bart threw back his head, laughing. He stepped back, motioning toward the front of the house. Carly adjusted the strap of her large shoulder bag and followed him, her steps quick and eager.

Tori crossed her arms, her voice edged with sarcasm. "Looks like she's going to play photographer's assistant."

When Mia strolled in, carrying a large plate of cookies, an enticing aroma wafted in the air. Her eyes drifted toward the window as she set the plate on the desk. "What's she up to?"

Tori shrugged, her annoyance thinly veiled. "I don't know, but she's following Bart like a puppy."

Parker's jaw tightened, his usual calm replaced by a resolute tone. "Whatever she's planning, I don't like it. I'll be outside."

He strode out, his steady steps echoing faintly. A few moments later, the front door slammed shut with an unusual force.

"Okay, that's a first," Mia said, her eyebrows lifting in surprise. "He didn't even look at the cookies. He's worried about something."

"If Parker's worried, so am I." Tori rushed toward the

living room, where she could watch through the front window.

In the front yard, Parker stood near Carly and Bart, pointing with animated gestures toward the house. Carly's eyes narrowed with dislike as she glared at Parker.

Mia, stepping next to Tori, muttered dryly, "If looks could kill, Parker would be toast. She absolutely hates not being the focus of attention."

Still talking, Parker moved toward the driveway. Forced to keep up, Bart wasn't taking any pictures. Ignored by the two men, Carly trailed behind them. With each step, her sour expression deepened.

Once the trio disappeared from view, Tori and Mia scurried to the back of the house to peer through a kitchen window. In front of the new building, Parker was deep in conversation with Bart, while Carly hovered nearby. Each time she attempted to interrupt, Parker would pause, fix her with a polite yet unyielding look, and then continue his conversation with Bart.

"She looks like she's about to blow a fuse," Mia observed. Her eyebrow arched as amusement danced across her face.

Outside, Carly's patience had reached its breaking point. Arms tightly crossed, she stood off to the side, her features contorted with anger. With an exasperated huff, she finally spun on her heel and stomped toward her car, sliding behind the wheel.

Bart shot a look over his shoulder. After a brief, tense handshake with Parker, he jogged after her. Tori and Mia ran to the office, watching Parker slowly stroll along the driveway behind them. Bart stopped by Carly's car, leaning slightly as she lowered the window. Whatever she said was sharp enough to dispel his easygoing demeanor, leaving a look of contrition. Her tires squealed as she tore out of the driveway. Bart hopped into his car and followed.

A few minutes later, Parker entered the office. "She was up to something," he observed, his voice calm but tinged with certainty. His eyes swept over the plate of cookies, and he grabbed one with an almost childlike enthusiasm. A look of contentment crossed his face as he took a bite and chewed. "Colt's missing out again," he said with a chuckle.

Mia smirked. She didn't have the heart to ruin Parker's fun by telling him she'd set some cookies aside for Colt as she had with the muffins. Instead, she said, "There's a fresh pot of coffee."

"Ah." Parker's faint smile widened. "Doesn't get any better than cookies and coffee—unless it's those muffins."

As Mia rose, Parker motioned for her to sit back down. "Stay. I'll get the coffee. Two cups, three?"

When he returned, he juggled three cups, setting one in front of Tori and Mia before dropping into a chair. "Any ideas why she was here?" he asked, his tone serious while his hand reached for a cookie.

Mia hesitated. "I'm not …" Her tone laced with uncertainty, her voice trailed off.

Parker's gaze sharpened as he looked at her.

"Whatever you're thinking, tell us." He bit into the cookie.

"There was something odd. Tori, did you notice anything different about her?"

Tori thought, replaying the encounter in her mind. "No, I didn't."

"The handbag," Mia said, her tone adamant.

"What was wrong with the handbag?" Parker asked, casually reaching for another cookie.

Tori's eyes met Mia's with the same dawning thought. "The bag was too big."

Parker shrugged, shaking his head. "Okay. A lot of women carry big handbags."

"Not Carly or Myra," Tori said with certainty. "They're all about those itty-bitty bags that probably only hold a phone, credit card, and a mirror. I remember Myra lecturing me once about my tote bag. How big bags pull on the shoulder material. As I recall, her exact word was ghastly. For those two, it's all about fashion statements. I've never seen Carly with a large bag slung over her shoulder. Never."

Mia added, "Tori's right." Her eyes narrowed as she picked up a cookie. "Here's what I think. Carly tried to get the two of you out of the way with that phony 'show my friends the house' gambit. And once she realized you were set on kicking her out, she suddenly insisted on using the bathroom."

Tori froze, her eyes widening in sudden comprehension. "You don't think that she had something in the bag she wanted to leave behind?"

"Hate to be the suspicious sort," Mia said. "But when it comes to Carly, that's a rock-solid feeling. She doesn't do anything that doesn't benefit her. And what could benefit her more than finding a way to cause you more problems, maybe even get you arrested for murder?"

Mia's words hung in the air with a frightening intensity.

"Then, she latches onto Bart. Since she didn't get a chance inside the house, she'd leave it outside," Tori said.

"Makes sense to me." Mia looked at Parker.

Gimlet-eyed, Parker said, "I think you may have struck pay dirt."

"Oh, my gosh," Tori breathed. "Do you think there was a gun in the bag?" The thought electrified her, sending a shiver down her spine.

Though his eyes held a hint of amusement at Tori's dramatic statement, his tone remained somber. "Doubtful, unless she killed the man. Otherwise, how could she have the gun?" He popped the last piece of cookie into his mouth, chewing slowly.

A bit disgruntled, Tori asked, "What else could she have?"

"A good question," Parker replied. "It would have to be something to give the police a reason to search the house. If causing you more embarrassment is her goal, a search would do it, even if the evidence wasn't enough to get you arrested."

"But how would the police know?" Tori asked, her tone worried.

"From another witness? Maybe one of the friends she had with her today." Parker rose, slinging his bag over his shoulder. His gaze lingered on the plate with two cookies left.

With a smile, Mia said, "Take them. There's more where they came from."

Parker grinned briefly, snatched the cookies, and headed toward the door. "I'll be back tomorrow. I want to be here when Hempstead returns."

After the front door shut with a decisive click, Mia shook her head and said, "I think we can assume Carly is behind the ghost tour debacle. And probably the other incidents as well. But still, I can't figure out how she'd connect to the murder."

"We did consider an idea someone might have taken advantage of the murder to cause more trouble," Tori replied thoughtfully. "Who better than Carly Swanson? Unless, of course, her mother is pulling the strings. Do you think Carly damaged the piano?"

"Maybe. Maybe not. Carly's always had a knack for getting other people to do her dirty work," Mia said, her tone heavy with disdain. She picked up the empty plate.

Tori picked up the coffee cups, following her into the kitchen. "I keep wondering what was in her bag."

"Since she didn't succeed today, she'll make another try," Mia replied grimly.

"What do you want to bet the pressure on Andy is coming from the Swansons?"

"Sucker bet. Probably coming from her father since

he's on the city council," Mia said as she stashed the dirty dishes in the dishwasher and pushed the start button. "Time I headed home."

Once Mia left, Tori wandered into the music room, hoping that playing would quiet her mind. But even after hours of practice, the restlessness lingered.

Finally, she gave up, rising from the bench and heading to her office. Her thoughts kept circling back to Carly. On the surface, the woman's motives were obvious, built on self-serving malice. But was there something darker, more insidious—murder?

Why had Carly shown up today carrying an oversized handbag? Coincidence? Or another calculated move to implicate her in a murder?

Tori felt like a puppet, her strings pulled by unseen hands, leaving her helpless in a game she didn't understand. *What else can I do?*

Settling into her chair, Tori stared at the camera monitor. A thought crept into her mind, driven by her sense of helplessness. After switching the camera system to the warehouse, she studied the grainy video for several moments. While her eyes flitted from one angle to another, nothing changed.

But what if someone was watching the place, just as she was? Did she dare find out? She frowned as she pondered the idea. After all, how dangerous could it be to drive around the warehouse?

Driven by resolve, or maybe desperation, Tori made her way to her bedroom. She quickly changed into a dark t-shirt, slipped on her boots, and grabbed a jacket from the armoire. Before heading out, she snagged a dark blue ballcap from the dresser. While the cap wasn't black, it would still blend into shadows. She draped her tote bag over her shoulder, snatched her keys, and headed toward the back door.

The night air, crisp and cool, brushed her skin as she turned the lock. After she pulled out of the garage, Tori slowed at the end of the driveway. Her gaze swept the street. Seeing nothing but quiet stillness, she eased onto the road. A cursory glance in the rearview mirror showed the same—empty, silent, reassuring. The sense of solitude steadied her.

But in the shadows, hidden and still, someone waited. When Tori turned the corner, a black truck rolled forward, quiet and deliberate, blending with the darkness, a hunter closing in on its target.

The drive to the warehouse seemed longer than before, though Tori figured that was due to her twitchy nerves. The closer she got, the tighter she gripped the steering wheel. There was nothing to cause any uneasiness until the warehouse came into view. The building loomed stark and foreboding against the night sky, adding a surreal feeling to her isolation.

She slowed as she approached the front, her eyes combing the parking lot where she had first spotted the van. Empty. As she ventured a few blocks further, her gaze scanned parking lots cloaked in impenetrable shadows. Still nothing. Pulling to the curb, she lowered her window to listen. The deserted streets now appeared menacing, every shadow seeming to whisper danger, and she was alone.

Should she abandon this idiotic plan and head home? The thought lingered momentarily before a spark of defiance flared within her. She couldn't give up. Still, an uneasy doubt crept into her mind. What would she do if she actually saw the van? Something she should have thought of earlier, but it was too late for second-guessing now. Despite the risk, she had to know if someone was watching the building.

As Tori turned onto the street behind the warehouse, the rumble of an engine shattered the oppressive silence. Ahead, a van, barely more than a shadow, shot through the intersection. Her heart slammed against her ribs as she stomped the accelerator. The car surged forward, tires screeching against the pavement. But when she reached the intersection, the van was gone, swallowed by the inky darkness as if it had never been there.

When she turned toward home, an unsettling thought refused to leave her mind, prickling at the edge of her awareness. She kept glancing in the rearview mirror, unease tightening her grip on the wheel. She knew the driver hadn't seen her. What spooked him? Had someone tipped him off? And if so ... who? Only one name came to mind—Dubois.

CHAPTER 22

Tori sat on the back porch step, relishing the crisp morning air. The quiet serenity, though, did little to settle her thoughts. Last night's events weighed on her, tangled in uncertainty. Why was someone watching her warehouse, and for what reason?

Colt strode across the backyard. The cheerful smile on his face was a welcome diversion.

"Any more where that came from?" He motioned toward the cup in her hand.

"Of course. Come on in."

Inside the kitchen, he filled a cup. After a deep gulp, he said, "We have one more load to move to the warehouse. I'd like for you and Mia to stop by. I hope we've arranged the products the way you wanted."

"Mia could probably go. One of us needs to stay here. I don't like leaving Dubois alone in the house. Plus, I have the interview for the magazine article today."

He topped off his cup, then plopped into a chair. "I thought that was yesterday."

"It was postponed, thanks to Carly. As usual, she showed up uninvited and unwelcome."

"Ah," he replied with a knowing look. "What dastardly deeds were on her mind this time?"

Leaning against the counter, Tori grunted. "She had two friends in tow who wanted to see the house."

"Suspicious," he remarked, his tone skeptical.

"It was odd since she never introduced them. But then, the reporter from the magazine was in the living room, and she got distracted."

Mia walked in, her arms loaded with paper sacks. "Hi, Colt. Are you two talking about Carly?"

"I'm getting filled in on her unexpected arrival yesterday. Did you ever figure out what she wanted?"

Tori took a slow sip from her cup, meeting his gaze over the brim. "We think she had something in her handbag she planned to leave behind."

Colt leaned forward, his sharp mind already connecting the dots. "Something linking you to the murder. But what could she possibly have?"

"That's the part we can't figure out," Tori admitted, frustration flickering across her features.

While they talked, Mia set her purse and bags on the counter. She opened a cupboard and retrieved a container. "One possibility is she killed the guy and had the gun," she said, setting the container on the counter.

Tori thought Colt was going to choke on his coffee. He coughed violently, waving off any attempts to help.

"Carly?" he managed, his voice rough. "The ever-so-elegant Carly? Lugging a gun around in her purse? Seriously?"

Mia sighed with disappointment, though a faint smile tugged at her lips. "Parker's already shot down the notion. But wouldn't that be something if she did?" She popped the lid off the container with a definitive click, setting it in front of Colt with a pointed look.

Colt's eyes widened as he stared at the contents. "Homemade?" he asked, a hint of anticipation in his voice.

"Made them yesterday. I put a few back for you. Otherwise, Parker would have scarfed them all down."

Colt eagerly reached for a cookie and then took a bite. "Hard to stay a step ahead of Parker. Dang, these *are* good," he murmured, savoring the taste. "What are you going to do about Carly?"

Tori's smile faded slightly as she considered his question. "I can't accuse her of anything outright, but she's not welcome here again," she said with conviction.

Colt raised an eyebrow. "Ha! Good luck with that. You know she has a way of worming her way in."

Mia muttered, "If I'm the one answering the door, I may be tempted to slam the dang thing in her face."

A gleeful grin crossed Tori's face as the image popped into her mind. "Good thinking."

Digging into one of the paper sacks, Mia asked, "How are you doing with the warehouse?"

Colt swallowed the last piece of cookie. "One more load to move. But I need one of you to tell me if anything needs rearranging."

"I told him you should probably go instead of me," Tori said. "You'll have a better idea of what works. And we can't leave Dubois alone in the house."

"How soon are you leaving?" Mia asked.

"I'm waiting on a delivery of paint," Colt replied. "Then, I'm headed to the storage unit to load the truck."

Mia said, "I'll meet you at the warehouse later this morning."

With a somber tone, Tori said, "Before you leave, I've got a video for you to watch. The cameras at the warehouse are linked to the system here. After Parker installed the new cameras, he caught someone messing with the back door."

Colt straightened in the chair. "Was this the same guy you and Mia saw?"

Tori nodded hesitantly. "Might be. The man we saw wore a hoodie, and so was the guy on the video." She paused, clearing her throat. "Uh … that's not all. I think someone was watching the warehouse last night."

Colt's expression darkened as his eyes locked onto hers. "Did he try to get in? Did you call the police? They'll need to see the video." His tone was sharp, laced with worry.

Tori shifted uneasily, taking a deep breath. "It's not exactly on the video," she admitted, her voice trailing away.

With an expression of disbelief, Colt said, "What do you mean it's not on the video?"

Tori wrinkled her nose and pursed her lips.

Mia stopped, her hand on the refrigerator door as she looked at Tori suspiciously. "I know that look. Tori, don't tell me you drove over there last night to snoop around?"

"Okay, I won't tell you," Tori replied with an impish grin.

Mia let out a dramatic groan and threw her hands in the air.

Without hesitation, Tori said, "At the time, it seemed like a good idea." Her face brightened. "And I did see the van hightailing it out of there."

As the two watched her with varying expressions, Tori was glad to hear the doorbell echo.

Mia said, "I'll go."

Tori nodded. "Come on, Colt. I'll show you the video." As they strode to her office, she added, "Just so you know, Parker planned to call the police and ask for extra patrol in the area."

When Dubois strode past the office doorway, Tori said, "Good morning, Mr. Dubois. I'd like to speak to you."

He turned, stepping into the room with a sour look on his face.

Undeterred, she said, "I don't think you've met Colt McLean. He's in charge of the construction."

After the two men shook hands, Dubois rudely said, "I need to get to work." He walked out.

Though Colt watched him leave with a bemused expression, he didn't comment.

Seated at her desk, Tori accessed the video. For several minutes, Colt studied the moment when the man stepped into view, shone the light, and slid away.

Stepping back from the desk, he said, "Not much to go on. The surveillance doesn't make sense. What could interest someone unless they believe valuable items are stored inside?" With a shake of his head, he headed back outside.

Tori settled in her chair, intending to check emails before taking advantage of the lull to practice. Since the concert appeared to be a go, she couldn't afford to pass up an opportunity. A knot of anxiety still twisted in her stomach at the thought of being on stage. The anxiety kept her practicing.

Before she could rise, her cell phone rang. She glanced at the unfamiliar number on the screen, hesitating for a moment before pressing the phone to her ear. "Tori Winters."

A voice, soft against a noisy, crackling background, said, "Ms. Winters, this is Gale, Gale Mills. I met you at Vada's office."

Though Tori strained to hear, the caller's name ignited a spark of anticipation as recognition flickered in her mind. "Can you speak up? I'm having a hard time hearing you."

"I can't," Gale whispered. "Someone might hear me. I need to talk to you." The urgency in her barely audible tone sent a chill down Tori's spine.

Despite the disquieting feeling, Tori couldn't pass up the chance to find out what the woman knew. "You're welcome to come to my home," Tori offered.

"No! Someone might see me. It's too dangerous."

"Where then?" While Tori's tone was steady, her unease grew.

"Library parking lot, tonight at nine," she said, the words muffled against the background noise.

Surprise slipped into Tori's voice. "What? A parking lot at night!"

"Please. It's urgent," Gale whispered.

"Why?" Tori asked.

"I can't tell you over the phone. Come alone, and don't tell anyone." The call ended abruptly.

In disbelief, Tori stared at the phone in her hand, her thoughts spinning in a whirlwind of questions and a growing sense of foreboding. Rising quickly, she strode toward the doorway.

"Mia?" she called out.

"Dining room," Mia answered.

Tori walked in, pulled out a chair, and plopped down. "I just got the oddest phone call."

Seated in front of her laptop, Mia shot Tori a questioning look. "From who?"

"Gale Mills. She wants to meet me at the library parking lot tonight at nine."

Mia's eyes widened. "Whatever for?"

"She wouldn't give me an answer. When I asked if she could come to the house, she practically panicked. 'Too dangerous,' she said. And she insists I come alone and not tell anyone," Tori explained.

Mia leaned back, alarm flashing across her face. "This sounds way too shady. You could be walking into trouble."

"I agree, and I don't like it," Tori said with conviction. She paused as the cryptic phone call replayed in her mind. "By nine, the library is closed, and the place will probably be deserted. But still, if there's a chance we could find out something, it may be worth the risk."

When the doorbell sounded, Tori sprang to her feet, her expression hopeful. "I bet that's Parker."

As he walked into the foyer, she greeted him with a burst of relief. "Boy, am I glad to see you."

His gaze flicked between her and Mia, who stood in the hallway. "Why do I get the feeling this isn't going to be good?"

Tori grabbed his arm, tugging him toward her office. "Confab time."

Mia followed, muttering as she went, "I'll get the coffee. I have a feeling this will take a while. Parker, you might need a caffeine boost before you hear what our illustrious heiress was up to last night."

Parker eased into a chair, setting his computer bag on the floor. His sharp gaze flicked to Tori as she lowered herself into her desk chair. "What's going on?"

"I got a phone call from Gale Mills."

A flicker of curiosity crossed his face. "The woman who works at the ghost tour?"

"Yes. She wants to meet me tonight at nine in the library parking lot."

He leaned forward with a gleam of interest. "Did she say why?" Engrossed in what Tori was saying, he didn't notice as Mia placed a cup of coffee in front of him.

"No. I'm supposed to come alone and not tell anyone." She couldn't disguise her uneasiness. "I tried to get her to come to the house, and she panicked. Said it was too dangerous."

With a thoughtful expression, Parker eased back, his hand absentmindedly reaching for the cup. He took a sip, then glanced at Mia, seated in the chair next to his. "Is she one of Carly's crowd?"

"I can't say for sure. She's only been in town a couple of years. But Vada certainly is."

His brow furrowed. "There are other places where you could meet during the day that would be private. Yet," he paused, his tone growing graver, "she wants to meet you at night in what's likely a deserted parking lot."

Despite the deepening sense of foreboding, Tori said, "I don't like the sound of it, but if there's a chance to find out what Gale knows, I think I should go."

Parker took a slow sip of his coffee. "You're walking into a trap. One thing is certain, you're not going alone. Is David still out of town?"

"Yes, he is. Why?"

"I'm thinking I'll need another person."

Tori perked up. "What do you have in mind?"

"I won't know for sure until I look at the parking lot." He swallowed the last of his coffee. His eyes took on an intent look. "Now, what did you do last night?"

"Found out someone is very interested in the warehouse. The van was back."

With a grievous tone in his voice, he said, "Tori, there

isn't any way you could see a van on the cameras. You were down there prowling around." With a resigned sigh, he said, "Tell me what you saw."

Her voice was steady as she talked, though tension flickered in her eyes.

She hesitated before adding, "There's something else. The way the driver took off was odd, almost like he didn't want me to see him. But he couldn't have known I was there. I think someone warned him."

He turned to Mia. "I think I need another cup of coffee."

Mia chuckled, her expression wry. "From the look on your face, your thoughts are exactly what Colt and I had when she told us earlier." Rising, she grabbed his cup and Tori's.

Parker asked, "Are you sure you saw the same van?"

"I'm not certain, but it looked like the one."

Before she could finish, Mia rushed back in, closing the door behind her.

She said, her voice low, "Dubois was in the kitchen. He may have been listening. I caught a glimpse of him when he ducked into the pantry."

Her tone turned grim. "And I didn't hear his steps as he headed down the stairs."

His face troubled, Parker tapped his fingers on the desk. With a quick shake of his head, he quickly rose, grabbing his computer bag. "I'll be at my office. I need to follow up on my inquiries about Dubois. I'll be back in time for the interview." He rushed out.

Mia said, "There's a man with a mission. And for the record, you're looking at a woman with a mission. From now on, if you decide on another nightly excursion like you did last night, I'm going! And that includes whatever Parker decides to do about tonight." With a huff, she rose and marched out.

CHAPTER 23

Alone in the office, Tori tapped her pen on the desk. The rhythmic sound punctuated the tangled web of questions that circled in her mind. She picked up the list she had compiled. While she studied the chaotic notes, she added the latest twist, Gale's phone call, to the growing puzzle.

Her pen hovered over the page before she circled a name—Gale. What could be so dangerous, so urgent, that the meeting had to be held in a deserted parking lot, alone and at night?

If there was ever a textbook setup for disaster, this was it. The whole situation screamed "trap" in metaphorical red ink. Gnawing on her lip, Tori drew lines between names on her list, Gale to Vada, Vada to Carly.

She'd bet her entire inheritance that Carly was behind this latest stunt. What was the purpose? Was another photographer poised to capture something compromising? An idea she'd run by Parker.

A flicker of movement in the hallway broke through her train of thought. Dubois moved briskly past her doorway, his gaze fixed forward as if she didn't exist.

Mia followed, watching him until the front door slammed shut, then stepped into the office.

Tori said, "Well, he didn't stay long."

"No, he didn't," Mia said with a thoughtful look. "A new record. I can't help but wonder why. But since he's left, do you want to go with me to the warehouse?"

She needed to spend the morning practicing, but a stronger need to get out of the house overtook her.

"Absolutely." Tori sprang to her feet and grabbed her phone and tote bag.

On the way to her car, Mia said, "I've got one stop I'd like to make in town. I got a call from Harriet Langford last night. She owns Langford Winery. They have a store, *Vintage Vibes*, on the square."

"I know the place. I stopped in there one day." Tori slid into the front seat, buckling her seat belt.

Mia started the engine. "She asked about the gift shop. Heard we planned to showcase local wines. I told her I'd stop by her store and talk to her."

"Great. I was impressed with the store. I'd also like to stop at the opera house and check on the repairs."

When they reached the downtown, Mia eased into a parking space.

As they walked into the store, a few customers browsed the well-stocked shelves, occasionally pausing to examine a bottle. A warm, rich scent of oak and berries lingered in the air.

"This store is very well-organized," Tori observed. "Plus, I like how all the accessories are artfully tucked in alongside a grouping of bottles."

"Marketing is one of Harriet's strong points."

As they stood near the entrance, a woman in her mid-forties moved through the shop, greeting customers with an easy charm. Her auburn hair was swept into a casual twist, and though she was dressed in jeans and a soft sweater, she exuded an air of confidence.

Her warm smile widened as her gaze landed on them. "Hello, Mia. I didn't expect to see you this soon, but what a nice surprise." Her eyes flicked curiously to Tori.

"Harriet, this is Tori Winters."

"I figured as much." Harriet extended a hand. "Welcome to *Vintage Vibes*."

"Nice to meet you," Tori replied, shaking her hand. "I love your store, though this isn't my first visit."

Harriet's smile grew at the compliment. "Something I always love to hear. Please browse around. If you have any questions, don't hesitate to ask."

"Mia mentioned you were interested in our plans for the gift shop," Tori said.

Harriet gave a slight nod. "I am. Turning the mansion into an inn is nothing short of brilliant."

A warm glow spread through Tori. "Thank you. Though you may be in the minority. I've encountered some resistance to the concept."

"I'm not surprised." Harriet's tone became thoughtful. "A project like this doesn't just change a building. It shifts the dynamics of the whole community and places you in a position of influence. However, not everyone's ready to embrace the change."

She paused, her gaze steady as though weighing her next words carefully. "But honestly, one that's overdue. Someone with a fresh vision and a willingness to shake up the status quo is what this town needs. And whether they admit it or not, many people will benefit from what you're doing, which is why I'm interested in your gift shop."

A spark of enthusiasm crept into Harriet's tone. She gestured broadly as her gaze swept the store. "This isn't only about selling items. There's an opportunity to highlight the products from our local businesses and showcase what makes them unique. Your inn and gift shop will be a huge draw for tourists. I see it as a way to pull more customers to the square. Frankly, I think the entire concept could be transformative for the business district."

"That's exactly what we hope to achieve," Tori replied, her voice quiet but resolute. "And I have an incredibly talented team to make it happen."

Harriet laughed. "I know. Tina's already hit me up, which is why I called Mia. I'd love to collaborate with you for Langford wines. I think we could put together something really special."

Tori's face lit up with a wide smile. "I do, too. We have several ways to feature your wines, including the gift shop, food events, and gift baskets for our guests. As we get closer to the grand opening, we'd love to have you visit the mansion and work out the details."

"Let me know the date and time, and I'll be there with

bells on." She glanced over Tori's shoulder. "Ah, I see a customer with a questioning look. Feel free to browse. Before you go, please accept a complimentary bottle of wine—pick your favorite." She moved past them.

"Which one should we pick?" Tori asked as she wandered past the wine displays, eyeing bottles of Merlot, Chardonnay, Riesling, fruit wines, and more.

"I don't think we can go wrong with any of them. Langford wines have quite a reputation."

Behind them, a voice said, "Well, well, look who's here. Granbury's latest scandal."

The words sent an icy shiver down Tori's spine as she turned.

Carly leaned against a counter with her arms crossed while one of her usual hangers-on hovered nearby. Her eyes, fixed on Tori, gleamed with malice, sharp and unrelenting.

Mia stepped closer to Tori's shoulder.

"Ah, your watchdog." Carly cast a hateful glance at Mia.

Tori's voice dropped low. "Carly, I'm curious. Did you acquire your spiteful attitude growing up, or is this a genetic defect, one you were born with?"

Carly gasped. Red streaks blossomed across her cheeks.

Tori figured no one had ever had the nerve to tell Carly to her face how spiteful she was.

"How dare you!" she exclaimed.

"Oh, there's more if you want to hear it."

Carly straightened, her tone biting. "It won't be long until everyone knows you for what you are. You'll never be anything in this town."

"Your posturing is becoming rather irrational, considering I am Elly Leichter's granddaughter. An honor I can claim, but you could never come close to emulating."

Carly flipped her hair back with anger. "We'll see." She started to turn, then paused, her eyes narrowing. "By the way, you can forget your ridiculous concert. It's been canceled. Seems the insurance company doesn't want to pay for the repairs. How sad. Poor little Tori Winters won't have a piano."

Tori's lips pursed, then curled in a wicked smile. "You think so? I guess you forgot your poor little Tori Winters is quite the opposite. I'll gladly pay for the repairs. Thank you for the heads-up."

Carly's stunned expression quickly morphed into angry chagrin, and she spun on her heel to storm out of the store.

Mia chuckled. "Hoisted by her own petard."

"Yep. Let's say goodbye to Harriet and head to the opera house." They quickly selected a bottle of wine. Harriet met them at the cash register, her warm smile lighting up as she bagged the bottle.

"It was nice to meet you," Harriet said as she handed over the bag. "I'm looking forward to seeing all the good things you'll do for this town."

Mia and Tori both thanked her again, promising to stay in touch. As they headed out the door, Mia said, "I'll put this in the car and meet you inside the opera house."

They separated, and Tori, walking briskly, soon entered the building.

Emmy greeted her with a cheerful smile. "Hi, Tori! Are you here to see Nora?"

"I am," Tori replied. "Where can I find her?"

"She's in the auditorium."

"Thanks, Emmy." Tori bounded up the stairs, her tote bag bouncing against her side. As she entered the grand hall, she saw several people clustered near the grand piano. While she recognized Nora and Dwayne, the other three had their backs to her.

Dwayne was the first to spot her. "Here comes Tori now. We won't have to call her."

The rest of the group turned, and Tori's stomach tightened when she recognized Myra. "Great. Just great," she muttered under her breath. One confrontation with a member of the Swanson family was enough for a lifetime, and now she'd have two on the same day.

She strode onto the stage and greeted Dwayne and Nora with a warm smile. When she nodded curtly at Myra, the woman's self-satisfied smirk only deepened, like a cat toying with its prey.

Tori's jaw tightened, but a flicker of satisfaction lit within her. She knew she was about to knock the smug look off Myra's face.

"Tori," Nora began, her distress evident in the tremble of her voice, "we have bad news. The insurance company is refusing to pay for the repairs to the piano.

They claim the piano should have been better protected. I guess we'll have to cancel the concert after all."

Myra's smile grew while a spark of triumph flashed in her eyes. "Yes, what a pity."

Tori shifted the tote bag on her shoulder and smiled faintly. "I heard what happened."

Nora blinked in surprise. "How did you find out?"

With a measured glance at Myra, Tori replied calmly, "I ran into Carly on my way in. She was kind enough to fill me in." Then, turning back to Nora, she said evenly, "I'll be happy to pay for the repairs."

Nora gasped, one hand flying to her chest. "Oh, my gosh. Tori, we can't expect you to do that."

"I want to," Tori said firmly. "I hate that this beautiful instrument was viciously damaged."

Tori looked at the others standing on the stage, her gaze briefly lingering on Myra, whose face flushed as red as her daughter's had earlier. Myra tightly pressed her lips together as she struggled to maintain her composure.

"I'm also interested in the opera house," Tori continued, her tone steady and resolute. "This is a way to show my appreciation. What's the status of the repairs?"

Nora straightened slightly as relief washed over her face. "Oh, my goodness. With all the upset, my manners have gone begging. Tori, this is Norman Singleton and his son, Marcus. They're the experts we hired to repair the piano. Gentlemen, this is Tori Winters, the pianist for our concert."

She shook hands with the two men.

Norman said, "We need another two or three days. But we'll make sure the piano is ready to go with time to spare."

Tori pulled out a small leather case from her tote bag and handed a business card to Norman. "Please send me the bill."

Then Mia arrived, her eyes sweeping across the group. "Hope I'm not interrupting."

Nora said, "Hello, Mia. Not at all. Tori has very graciously offered to pay for the repairs." She introduced the two men before adding, "And they have assured us the piano will be ready in time for the concert."

"That's wonderful news," Mia replied. "Many people are eagerly looking forward to Tori's concert." She shifted her attention to Myra with a polite smile. "Don't you agree, Myra?"

Myra, ignoring Mia's comment, said, "Since that's settled, I must leave." For the briefest moment, her gaze locked onto Tori's. A flash of hatred flickered in her eyes before fading into something shrewd and calculating. She turned to go, her lips curved into a cryptic smile.

CHAPTER 24

Nora's voice pulled Tori's attention away from the woman marching off. "I'll call you to let you know when you can resume your practice sessions."

Tori nodded absently, her thoughts still shadowed by Myra's departure. After exchanging goodbyes, she and Mia made their way out.

Once they were in the car and headed toward the warehouse, Mia's voice turned somber. "You pulled the rug out from under Myra once again. If looks could kill, you'd be dead."

Tori's expression darkened, her voice low and grim. "I know." She paused, her gaze fixed on the passing scenery. "There was a look on her face when she left. She's planning something, but what?"

Silence settled in the car as the weight of Tori's words lingered. When they arrived at the warehouse and stepped inside, both women paused. The sight before them caught them by surprise.

The space had undergone a transformation. Neatly stacked products lined the rows of shelves, creating an orderly, efficient appearance that had seemed impossible only days before.

Her face alight with excitement, Mia said, "What a difference. This actually feels like we're getting close to the grand opening."

Colt strolled over. "Anything you want moved, let me know," he said. He motioned toward the large doors propped open at the rear of the warehouse. "A few more boxes, and we'll be finished."

"Colt, you've done an amazing job," Tori said, her voice warm with appreciation. "The way you arranged the shelves will make finding a product easy."

"If you need more racks, I can move these closer together and add another couple of rows," he replied.

As Tori viewed the empty spaces on the shelves, she said, "It's good to know we can expand if we have to, but it looks like we have plenty of space." Tori's expression turned serious. "Have you noticed anyone in a van hanging around?"

Colt's smile faded. "I haven't spotted anyone with an undue interest."

Before she could respond, her phone buzzed. As she pulled it from her pocket, Parker's name flashed on the screen. "This is Parker. I'll be outside," she told them.

When she answered, he said, "Are you at the house?" His curt tone immediately put her on alert.

"No. Mia and I are at the warehouse."

"What happened to Dubois?"

"He left not long after you did."

Parker muttered, almost to himself, "Odd behavior for a so-called wine expert." His voice rose. "When are you going to be home?"

"We're getting ready to leave," she replied.

"Any sign of surveillance?"

"Colt said he hasn't seen anything suspicious."

"I'll meet you at the house." He disconnected. The abrupt end to the call left her feeling unsettled.

She turned to go back inside, only to find Mia already walking out.

"Ready to go?" Mia asked, her tone light, though her sharp gaze lingered on Tori.

Once Mia pulled onto the street, Tori said, "Parker wants to meet us at the house."

"Did he say why?"

With a worried expression, Tori shook her head. "No, but you know how tight-lipped he can be sometimes."

Mia chuckled. "I guess that comes from being a homicide detective for so many years. He and Andy are cut from the same cloth."

Though Tori smiled, her mind lingered on Parker's tone. There was urgency there, something he wasn't saying. Her nerves sparked at the thought of what waited for them at the house.

When they pulled into the driveway, Parker was already there. Seated in a chair on the porch, one leg crossed over the other, he waited patiently, exuding an air of quiet authority.

As they strode toward the house, Mia said, "I've often

thought this isn't a man I would want for an enemy."

Tori nodded in agreement. "Once again, our minds have run along the same track."

Parker rose as they walked up the steps. His gaze, sharp and assessing, swept over them. "I'd say something unpleasant happened."

Tori glanced at Mia, suppressing a grin at his uncanny perception, and caught the same expression mirrored on Mia's face.

Tori unlocked the door, and they trooped inside. She asked, "Did you look at the parking lot?"

"I did, and that's part of what I want to talk about."

"Then let's take this to the kitchen and discuss it there," Mia said. "It's lunchtime."

Parker's face lit up with a broad smile.

Tori dropped her bag in the office, then followed Mia and Parker into the kitchen.

"Anything I can do to help?" Parker asked.

"Nope," Mia told him. "I picked up sandwiches from the grocery store deli this morning." She punched the button to start the coffee machine. The rich, enticing aroma of coffee soon wafted in the air.

"What did you find out?" Tori asked as she grabbed plates, cups, and a glass.

"Since the library closes at seven, the place should be deserted by nine."

While Mia placed the sandwiches and chips on the table, Tori filled two cups with coffee and then the glass with ice and sweet tea.

Once Mia and Tori were seated, Parker picked up where he left off. "The terrain around the library is difficult to secure. Too many places where someone could hide. I plan to use two of my men. They've got the experience. I'll be in a vehicle parked on the street. When you drive in, I'll have three sets of eyes monitoring what happens." He took a bite and chewed.

Mia leaned forward, her expression grim. "Four."

Parker looked at her in his calm, unassuming way before nodding. "You can go with me. I want everyone in place by eight. Whatever they're up to, I plan to be there ahead of them. Tori, is the interview still on for this afternoon?"

"Yes, as far as I know. Are you staying?"

He nodded, taking another bite.

Tori munched on a chip. "Anything on Dubois?"

He swallowed. "Other than a few articles, there's not much about him online. I'd already contacted an FBI agent I've worked with in the past, asking about Dubois. Still waiting for him to call me back. The delay is unusual and makes me wonder why."

Tori leaned in with curiosity, but a glance at the wall clock reminded her of the time. She'd have to defer her questions until later. "I'd better get ready for the interview," Tori murmured. She set her empty plate on the counter and headed to her bedroom. After freshening up, she practiced until the doorbell rang.

When she opened the door, Bart greeted her with an eager smile. "I'm early. I hope that's okay."

"Of course, come on in," she said.

As he stepped into the foyer, he asked, "Was that you playing?"

"Yes. The piano is one of my favorite pastimes." She gestured toward the living room.

Walking alongside her, he said, "You're very good."

"Thank you. Please have a seat."

He settled on the sofa with his case alongside him.

Tori perched on a chair across from him. Too nervous to relax, her fingers were clasped tightly in her lap. "How did the pictures you took of the outside turn out?"

"I only had a couple, but they're quite good. I usually have a photographer with me, but he couldn't make this trip for personal reasons."

As Bart spoke, he eased the voice recorder from his case before relocking it. "May I set this on the table?" He gestured toward the one in front of him.

"Certainly."

With a reassuring smile, he glanced at her. "This will be very easy. I'll ask a question. If you're uncomfortable, say so, and we'll move to the next one. As I mentioned yesterday, the recorder helps me maintain the accuracy of your answers."

Tori managed a small smile, grateful for his understanding tone. She shifted in her seat, feeling more at ease.

"As I mentioned yesterday, while the article's main focus is the wine collection, the history of this house is very intriguing. Are you ready?"

She took a deep breath and nodded.

He pushed the record button. "Interview of Tori Winters, heiress and owner of a historic Texas mansion and wine collection."

Then he looked at Tori. "From my research, I understand you didn't know about your grandmother or her estate. How did you feel when you first learned of your inheritance?"

"I think the best word to describe my emotions would be 'unbelievable.' It was such a shock—like stepping into a dream I didn't know I had."

"How big is the mansion?"

"Quite large. There are six bedrooms, two attic rooms, and four bathrooms split between the floors. There's also a library, living room, dining room, music room, study, kitchen, and even servants' quarters."

"You're right. That is large, and I would add, quite magnificent. There is also a building under construction. What is it for?"

"The new building will be a gift shop, museum, and office for the Red Door Inn. The museum will feature many of the house's antiques, which I think will help preserve the unique history for guests to experience."

"What prompted you to turn the mansion into an inn?"

Tori chuckled softly, glancing briefly around the room as if taking it all in. "Actually, the idea came from my close friend, Mia O'Brien. She's incredibly sharp and saw potential in the house that I hadn't considered. I realized she was right. The notion of an inn seemed to fit the mansion perfectly. Its history and charm were meant to be shared, not hidden away."

"When do you plan to open the inn?"

"Hopefully, in the next few months. Renovation is still underway on the second floor, along with other construction projects. We have quite an event planned for the grand opening."

Bart smiled, clearly intrigued. "If possible, I'd certainly like to make another visit. Could you tell me more about the house's history? Over the mantle is a painting of your great-grandparents."

She laughed. "My great-grandfather, Frankie Leichter, wasn't on the right side of the law. During the early 1900s, he was a crime lord, running alcohol during Prohibition and then later the Dallas gambling syndicate. He built the house as a testament to his success or his ego. Many of the antiques in the house date back to his era."

"A crime lord, huh? How intriguing," Bart said, raising an eyebrow. "Did the wine collection start with him?"

Tori shook her head. "No, it didn't. According to my grandmother's records and journals, the collection was entirely hers. She had a genuine passion for wine and loved collecting rare vintages. Some bottles date back to the mid-1900s."

"How fascinating that your grandmother wrote about the collection," Bart said, leaning forward. "What prompted her to start collecting wines?"

Tori replied. "Her trips to France and visits to the wineries. The house originally had a basic cellar, but she renovated the space into a proper wine cellar. She paid meticulous attention to every detail, including humidity, temperature, and light. Everything is carefully controlled to preserve the integrity of her collection."

"How many bottles are we talking about?"

"I'm not sure exactly, as I haven't tried counting them," Tori admitted. "But there are thousands. That's why I'm having the whole collection cataloged and appraised."

"Your grandmother sounds extraordinary," Bart said. "Did she pass on her passion for wine to you?"

"I have to be honest and say I don't know much about wine, but I'm learning." She paused, a hint of pride in her voice. "It's hard not to develop an appreciation for something my grandmother cared deeply about. The wine is not only a collection but also a legacy."

He nodded enthusiastically. "What a fascinating story, family legacy, incredible history, and now, a new chapter with the inn. Almost poetic. Do you have anything you'd like to add?"

She shook her head no.

He clicked off the recorder.

Tori leaned back with a sigh of relief.

"This went very well," Bart said as he carefully slid the recorder back into his case.

"When do you expect the article to be published?" Tori asked.

"I'm not sure. After you approve the interview, I'll send my article to the editor. Once we have a firm date, I'll contact you. Would you mind if I took another look at the wine cellar? Now that I know more of the history, I'd like to get a closer look."

"Not at all." She rose. "You can leave your case here."

"No, I'll take it with me," he replied, slinging the strap over his shoulder.

When they walked into the kitchen, Parker was seated at the table, his eyes darting briefly toward Bart before settling back on Tori.

"Bart is going to take another look at the wine cellar," Tori said.

Parker rose and silently followed them. His steps echoed faintly as they descended the wooden staircase into the brightly lit wine cellar.

Tori settled into the chair as she watched Bart wander toward the shelves.

His eyes avidly gleamed as he scanned the labels like a connoisseur admiring fine art. Occasionally, he would pull out a bottle, tilting it slightly to read the label before holding the bottle up to the light.

"I could spend hours down here," Bart said, his voice tinged with genuine admiration as his fingers trailed along the shelves. "This is an exceptional collection."

Parker had stood where he could easily watch Bart. Though his posture was deceptively casual, Tori couldn't miss seeing the quiet intensity in his eyes as he observed the man's every move.

Bart paused, pulling out a bottle of Bordeaux wine. Turning the bottle gently in his hands, he let out an appreciative whistle. "You don't come across treasures like this often."

"You might be wise to set the case down," Parker calmly said. "Before you knock a few bottles over."

With a look of chagrin, Bart replaced the bottle and stepped out from between the rows. "My apologies," he said, setting the case on the floor. "I'm so used to carrying this over my shoulder, I didn't think about it." He turned back to his perusal.

"Do you recognize any of these vintages?" Tori asked.

Bart turned, nodding thoughtfully. "Tori, your grandmother obviously had a remarkable eye for quality wines."

He stepped to the middle of a row and pulled out a bottle, holding it up. "This is one I spotted, a 1945 Chateau Lafite Rothschild. Not only is the wine incredibly rare, but the bottle is in pristine condition. A find like this could command an exceptional price at auction." Bart carefully slid the bottle back onto the shelf.

He seemed to collect himself and smiled faintly. "I've taken up enough of your time." Reluctantly, he reached for his case.

In the foyer, Tori said, "I'm looking forward to seeing the article. I'll make sure there are copies of your magazine for our guests to read."

"I'll be in touch," he replied with a polite nod.

From the window, Tori watched as he strolled to his

car. He opened the door, then paused to glance back at the house. His face seemed to shift in the fading light, shadows etching sharp, almost sinister lines across his features. His eyes appeared darker, his expression unreadable. His appearance carried a disquieting edge.

She frowned, shaking her head. It was nothing more than a trick of the light. "Great," she muttered under her breath. "Now I'm imagining things, turning a cheerful, chatty reporter into some kind of lurking threat. Ridiculous."

Yet even as she dismissed the thought, the nagging unease refused to be ignored.

CHAPTER 25

Stepping back inside, Tori found Parker in the foyer. "I need to finalize a few details about tonight. I'll be back later." His lips twitched in amusement as he glanced toward Mia, who was striding toward him, before dashing out the door.

When Tori glanced at her with a questioning look, Mia said with a dry tone, "I'm headed home to change clothes." Mia glanced down at her bright yellow t-shirt and purple jeans. "I was told I'm too noticeable." Muttering to herself about demanding males, she stomped outside.

With a soft chuckle at Mia's indignant protest, Tori locked the door and strolled to her office. Her steps quickened at the sound of her phone ringing.

A warmth blossomed within her when she heard David's voice.

"I had a break and wanted to see how you were doing," he said.

She settled deeper into her chair. A small smile tugged her lips. "Where are you?"

"Still in Austin. I'm hoping to wrap this up in another

couple of days. I'm ready to come home. What happened with the opera house?"

"Still a go," she said. "I stopped by there earlier and met the two men repairing the piano. They assured me it'll be ready in time." She decided not to mention the insurance issue.

With an easygoing tone, he said, "That's good to hear. I'm looking forward to the concert."

With a slight hesitation, Tori shifted the conversation. "Do you know a Gale Mills?"

"No. Who is she?"

"She works for Vada at the ghost tour. She called me today and wants to meet me. She was quite insistent."

"Do you think she knows something?"

"Yes, I do." Tori went on to explain about her visit to Vada's office.

"It's good, then, that she reached out to you."

"Umm … yes and no. The only problem is that Gale wants to meet me tonight at the library parking lot. She also told me to come alone and not to tell anyone."

David's voice rang with fear. "You're not going, are you?"

"Yes. But Parker will be there along with two of his men. It's likely another trap like what happened at the ghost tour."

David sighed, relief mingling with the worry in his voice. "A good assumption, especially after your picture sitting in the police car showed up on the front page of the *Metro*. I'd hate to see you caught up in another contrived confrontation. Are you certain you need to meet her?"

Her voice filled with conviction, she said, "I have to go. Gale might know something that will unlock this entire puzzle."

The doorbell rang. "David, someone is at the front door. I've got to go."

"Tori ...," David began but then fell silent.

"Yes?" she prompted, her heart racing at the urgency in his tone.

"Please be careful." His voice was low, almost pleading.

"I will," she promised, though his lingering hesitation stayed with her. As she ended the call, a quiet question whispered in her mind. What had he stopped himself from saying?

The doorbell rang again, sharp and insistent, jolting her from her scattered thoughts. She sighed, rushing out of her office. When she swung the door open, Linc greeted her with a grim expression.

"I didn't want to call," he said, stepping inside without waiting for an invitation. "There's been a new development. Let's go to your office."

Linc didn't wait for her response. His body radiated tension as he strode along the hallway. Tori trailed behind him, her stomach tightening. Something was wrong—very wrong.

Once they reached her office, he settled into the chair opposite her desk, his posture anything but relaxed. "Are you alone?"

Caught off guard by the question, Tori blinked. "Yes. Mia had an errand to run. She'll be back, though."

While her answer was the truth, Tori deliberately withheld the rest. She wasn't going to tell him about the phone call or the meeting. He'd made his opinion of the search of the house quite clear, and she didn't need another argument.

Even though he nodded, she sensed her answer didn't matter. Linc's refusal to meet her gaze said more than his words.

"I received a call from a contact in the district attorney's office," he said, his voice clipped. "The police either have new evidence or expect to obtain new evidence implicating you in the case."

Tori's heart seemed to seize mid-beat. "What evidence?" she demanded, her voice shaking with fear and disbelief. "There is none. There can't be."

Fixing her with an icy stare, he said, "I don't know the specifics, and neither did my source. All I was told is the district attorney is prepared to issue a warrant for your arrest, which means they'll search the house."

For a moment, the room tilted, and her surroundings blurred. She clutched the edge of the desk, her nails biting into the polished wood. She gulped in a deep breath.

"Tori, are you okay?"

"Okay?" she echoed, her voice dripping with sarcasm. "No! I'm not okay. How can I possibly be okay when you told me I might be arrested for something I didn't do?"

A defensive look flickered across his face, his jaw tightening. "I know this is a shock, but I wanted to be sure you weren't going to faint or something."

Her eyes flashed with anger. "For heaven's sake, Linc. Shock is an understatement."

His silence lingered a second too long before he spoke again, his words deliberate. "As your attorney, I have to ask. Have you told me everything you know about the man who was killed?"

Still reeling from the devastation of his revelations, her head jerked back as if he had slapped her. "Of course, I've told you everything."

"Tori, whatever you say to me is covered by attorney-client privilege. I'm the only one who will know. You must tell me if there is a connection between you and the victim."

Stupefied, she gaped at him. "Linc, read my lips. I … do … not … know … that … man. How many times do I have to tell you? My only contact with him was that brief moment during the ghost tour. I don't know how to make that point any clearer."

He persisted. "The man had your name and address in his pocket. I cannot properly defend you if you don't tell me the entire truth."

Tori barely managed to contain the sharp edge in her voice. "I don't know why he had my name and address." Then, a horrifying realization hit. "Oh, my god! You don't believe me."

For an instant, mistrust flickered in his gaze before he

averted his eyes, his features settling in a polished, unreadable expression. "Of course, I believe you," he said evenly.

But Tori wasn't convinced. Her gaze remained hard and unyielding, even as distress twisted in her gut. Why did she have this nasty feeling he was lying? "What do I do now?" she asked.

"We wait. My hands are tied until I know what the new evidence is." He stood abruptly, the chair scraping across the floor.

"I have to get back to the office." He turned and walked out, his footsteps echoing in the hallway.

She followed him to the front door, her mind numbed with disbelief.

At the threshold, he paused, his tone clipped and impersonal as he said, "I won't know you've been arrested until after it happens." Without another glance, he stepped outside.

Tori slowly closed the door, the click of the latch reverberating through the silence. For a moment, she stood frozen, staring at the wood grain. Her world had shattered. Her heart pounded as she struggled to breathe. Fear seeped into every corner of her being. *Arrested!* The word echoed in her mind, cold and relentless. And Linc believed it would happen.

Her legs barely supported her as she made her way back to her office. Collapsing into the chair, she buried her head in her hands. Events were spinning out of control, each twist tightening the grip of helplessness.

Linc's visit replayed in her mind, feeding the certainty that her attorney didn't believe her.

But how could they have new evidence? It wasn't possible. She struggled to recall what Linc had told her, evidence they had, or evidence they expected to have. The distinction gnawed at her. Then the reason struck, sharp and jarring—the meeting at the library. There had to be a connection.

The timing was too perfect for the district attorney to suddenly be ready to move forward with a warrant for her arrest. Parker always said he didn't trust coincidences, and Tori had to agree. This one blazed like a warning beacon. Anger surged, flushing away the fear and sense of helplessness.

Determined, she jumped up and strode to her bedroom. While Parker hadn't mentioned anything about her attire, she couldn't shake the feeling that blending into the shadows would put her in control. After rifling through her wardrobe, she settled on a black t-shirt, a vest, dark jeans, and her hiking boots. Whatever awaited, she was ready to meet it head-on.

Chapter 26

When the murmur of voices echoed at the front of the house, Tori drew in a deep breath, steadied herself for their reaction to Linc's visit, and strode into the hallway.

Mia, her outfit noticeably subdued, spotted Tori and headed toward her, followed by Parker and two strangers. A flicker of anxiety rippled across Mia's face. "Something's happened."

Parker moved alongside Mia, his sharp gaze focused on Tori's face. With a steady tone, he asked, "What is it, Tori?"

She hesitated, her eyes darting to the strangers. "I'll tell you later," she said finally, her voice even, although a faint thread of unease lingered.

Even though a troubled expression crossed his face, Parker only nodded. "I'd like to use the dining room table," he said, walking into the room.

Mia stepped inside and, without a comment, cleared the table, stacking papers and catalogs into neat piles.

The two men, both in their early fifties, pulled out chairs as Tori and Mia took seats across from them. Parker stepped to the end of the table, placing his computer bag and another bag down with a light thud. He unrolled the paper he was carrying and used catalogs from Mia's stash to hold the corners in place. After a quick glance around the table, he introduced the men.

"Blake Phillips and Mitch Bolton," he said, nodding toward them. Then he gestured toward her. "This is Tori Winters, owner of the house and the one we're guarding tonight. You've already met Mia."

He turned his attention back to the table, smoothing out the map. "This is a satellite image of the terrain around the library," he said.

Everyone leaned forward for a closer look.

"There are two parking lots. The main one is on the north side in front of the building. The second is behind the library." He pointed with his pen.

"From the street on the west side are three driveways. One leads to the front parking lot, and the second is behind the library. It continues behind the adjacent buildings to the third driveway near the end of the block."

He tapped again. "Next to the main parking lot is a large open field. On the east side is the Hike and Bike Trail."

He moved his pen to the street. "I'll park here, near the main entrance. I'll be able to see the main parking lot and the driveways. Tori, when you pull in, park in the middle of the lot." He tapped the map.

"Turn the car to face the driveway so you have a straight shot onto the street. Leave the engine running and the lights on. When you get out, leave the car door open. You don't want to be fumbling to get into the car if you need to make a fast exit."

She nodded, her expression resolute.

He turned toward Blake and Mitch with a sharp look. "Our biggest risk is someone slipping in on foot. That's where the two of you come in. Stop anyone from sneaking onto the parking lot."

His pen tapped the map decisively. "Blake, I want you behind the library, positioned at the southeast corner. You should be able to spot anyone coming from the east or the end of the block. Keep to the shadows and stay out of sight unless you need to act."

He shifted his focus to Mitch, pointing at the map again. "Mitch, you'll cover the north side of the library, watching for anyone approaching from the east or across the field. Position near these buildings," he said, tapping a spot on the map.

His gaze flicked between the two men. "From this point forward," Parker said, his voice lowering slightly, "we play it by ear since we don't know what we're walking into."

Tori shifted her gaze to Parker, her brow slightly furrowed. "How do we communicate?"

Parker said, "We'll be using an earbud with a wireless mic. I brought a set for you." From his computer bag, he pulled out a small plastic pouch, holding it up for her to see.

"The earpiece fits snugly into your ear and is nearly

invisible. Clip the mic on your clothing." After showing her how to activate them, he handed her the pouch.

Parker reached for the second bag and, from inside, pulled out a ballistic vest, laying it on the table.

At the sight, Tori froze. Suddenly, the reality of the danger sank in. Next to her, Mia gasped.

Tori's gaze locked onto Parker's unyielding eyes. "You really think I need this?"

"Murder is involved." His tone was adamant as he said, "I'm not trusting anyone. Put it over your shirt, then wear a lightweight jacket, zipped up. The mic can be clipped to the jacket collar or the inside of a front pocket."

His stare held hers, reinforcing the gravity of his next words. "If you hear me say move, you move. You drive out. No hesitation." His voice deepened, leaving no room for doubt. "This might turn out to be nothing. But I'm not taking any chances. Understand?"

Tori nodded, her mouth a firm line of determination, though she couldn't stop a surge of apprehension.

"I want you in the parking lot by eight-thirty. I don't want to risk Mills getting there first. The rest of us will be in position by eight. And, if someone tries to approach on foot, I expect it will happen before Mills arrives."

He paused, his expression tightening as though weighing his words. "Someone might be watching the house to see when you leave. One of my men will be watching to see if someone is tailing you, which is why I don't want us all leaving from here."

He rolled up the map, securing it with a rubber band

as he spoke. "Mia, go home at your regular time. I doubt anyone will follow you, but be alert. Meet me at the grocery store where you used to work at about seven-thirty. We'll leave your car there."

He glanced around. "Questions?" When no one responded, Parker shifted his attention toward his two men. "This is probably a good time for you to leave. I expect the construction crew is getting ready to quit for the day. You'll blend in. I'll meet you back at the office."

The men nodded in unison. Without a word, they stood, their chairs scraping lightly against the floor.

Mia walked out with them. After locking the door behind them, she turned, rushing back to the dining room. "Talk!" she said, her tone laced with worry.

Tori hesitated for a fraction of a second, taking a steadying breath. "Linc showed up. The district attorney is ready to issue an arrest warrant."

Shock rippled across Mia's face.

Even Parker's stoic demeanor cracked, his face momentarily slack with surprise. His eyes, however, sharpened quickly, and his tone was taut when he asked, "Did he say why?"

The tension in Tori's neck and shoulders spread down her spine as she nodded slightly.

"The police either have new evidence or expect to receive new evidence."

Parker's jaw tightened. The anger underlying his clipped words was unmistakable. "Did this come from the district attorney? Or from Andy?"

With a quick shake of her head, she said, "No. Linc said the information came from a contact in the district attorney's office."

Parker leaned a hip against the table's edge. His lips pressed in a tight line as he thought.

Tori watched him, her mind turning over what she had come to know about him since they first met. Parker's methods were never haphazard; every action, every word carried purpose. Over time, she had come to trust him. His ability to anticipate and account for even the slightest possibilities wasn't a skill—it was a mindset honed by years in law enforcement.

Her voice tight with unease, Tori asked, "Parker, is this connected to Gale's call?"

His gaze flicked back to her as he refocused. "I'd say so. If Andy or the DA had evidence, they wouldn't beat around the bush. Since it was Linc and not the police who showed up, that tells me the police don't have it. Which only strengthens the connection between the meeting at the library and this so-called new evidence."

He straightened, his tone laced with authority. "Change in strategy. Mia, I need you to stay here."

A mulish look crossed her face, but he raised his hand before she could argue. "Hear me out. I don't want to leave the house unguarded. Someone needs to be inside. As soon as I can make a call, one of my men, Orville Mason, will be on the way here. But I need his presence to look natural. That's why I need you to stay."

Tori's voice wavered, anxiety creeping in. "Do you

think someone would break in and plant evidence while I'm gone?"

"While I don't, I'm not taking a chance that this meeting is an excuse to get you out of the house." His jaw was set, his movements brisk as he gathered his bags and map. Without another word, he strode out, his fast steps echoing in the hallway before the front door slammed shut.

Stunned, Mia and Tori exchanged a glance.

"I don't think I've ever seen Parker move so fast," Mia observed. While her tone was light, her eyes were shadowed with worry. "Come on. We both need a glass of wine, but since that's not a good idea, we'll settle for coffee."

Tori picked up the pouch and vest. "I'll drop these in my bedroom."

When she walked into the kitchen, a carton of eggs sat on the counter, and Mia was placing a pan on the stove.

"I think an omelet with toast sounds perfect right now," Mia said, dropping a pat of butter into the pan and turning on the burner. The butter sizzled softly, its rich aroma soon curled into the air.

Tori absentmindedly reached for the loaf of bread, her thoughts still on the meeting at the library. For a moment, her hands stilled. "What possible evidence could someone come up with that would lead to my arrest for murder?" she exclaimed.

Mia shot her a sharp glance as she briskly whipped the eggs in a bowl. "There's still the gun," she said.

Her gaze fixed on the toaster as she slid the bread inside, Tori pondered the idea. Finally, she exhaled. "The gun? Nah, just wishful thinking. There has to be something else. But I can't imagine what."

Mia tilted her head slightly, carefully pouring the whisked eggs into the hot skillet. "What about one of those thingamajigs you see in the cop shows, a burner phone?" She sprinkled a handful of cheese over the bubbling eggs.

Tori snorted in disbelief. "That doesn't make sense. What could someone do with a burner phone?"

"I don't know." With a quick flick of her wrist, Mia deftly flipped the omelet, then set the pan back on the burner. "Maybe fake calls to another burner phone."

Tori shot her a disbelieving look.

Mia's hands flew into the air. "I'm just saying. Makes about as much sense as Carly having the gun."

Tori said in a decidedly grumpy tone. "I don't think either of us is cut out for detective work."

"Hey, speak for yourself. Who spotted the handbag?"

"Okay, I'll give you that point."

Tori pulled out the evenly browned bread, spreading butter on each slice before setting them on a plate. She filled two cups with coffee, the rich aroma mingling with the scent of melted butter.

Mia slid the omelet onto a plate, cut it cleanly down the middle, and slid half onto another plate. She grabbed a bowl of strawberries from the refrigerator, selecting a few to add a splash of color and taste to each plate. With a practiced ease, she set the plates on the table.

Tori sank into the chair, hands curling around her cup. Her voice dropped. "You want to know the worst part?" A pause. "What I couldn't tell Parker?"

Mia froze, her fork suspended in mid-air. "There's more?" she asked, her tone edged with worry.

Tori's gaze drifted to the window. The darkness pressing against the glass seemed to imprint itself inside her. "Linc kept asking if I had told him everything I knew about the murdered man. It was as if he didn't believe what I'd already told him," she replied. "He said he couldn't properly defend me if he didn't know the absolute truth."

Her throat tightened, and she swallowed hard. "From the way he questioned me, I don't think he believes I'm innocent. He seemed certain I'd be arrested."

The fork slipped from Mia's fingers, clinking against the plate. Her expression turned grim. "Why … *that* rat! I've known him for most of my life. Linc's always been ambitious, always looking out for himself first. But this may be a new low, even for him."

She picked up the fork, took a bite of omelet, and chewed thoughtfully. "Here's the issue. You're no longer Tori Winters, a hospice nurse. You're Tori Winters, an heiress. You've moved into a position of prestige in this town, causing a ripple. Some resent it."

She jabbed the air with her fork, a strawberry dangling precariously at the tip. "That's what Harriet told you. You've upset their perceived status quo. I hate to say it, but the Greers may be part of it." She popped the strawberry into her mouth.

"But, you know, I'm not looking for power and prestige, Mia. I'm not trying to change anything, and I certainly don't want to be one of the movers and shakers in this town," Tori exclaimed.

"I know that, but others don't. All they know is there's a new Elly in town, and she's a force to be reckoned with." Mia forked up another bite of omelet. "You come by it naturally. You are more like your grandmother than you can imagine. Remember, I knew her." She stabbed another strawberry. "So, why didn't you want Parker to know what Linc said?"

Tori shrugged, tearing off a piece of toast. "I guess because I was embarrassed," she admitted. "I value Parker's good opinion."

Mia snorted. "I think Parker's already got Linc's number. And I suspect he doesn't think highly of the man."

A spiteful grin crossed her face. "I've got a feeling the two of you are going to kick somebody's butt tonight. Dare I hope it's Carly?" she added with a teasing glint.

CHAPTER 27

Once the kitchen was cleaned up, Mia dragged out the makings for cookies. "I need something to keep me from going crazy while you're gone."

When the doorbell echoed, Tori rose, rushing toward the foyer to open the door.

An older man smiled politely before saying, "Ms. Winters, I'm Orville Mason. I work for Parker Hayes."

"Please come in, Mr. Mason. We're in the kitchen." Turning, she caught sight of Mia standing at the end of the hallway, watching silently.

As the man stepped inside, he glanced around with a decided air of interest. "This is a beautiful house," he said. "I have to admit, the interior is even more impressive than I expected."

Mia had already stepped back into the kitchen. When they entered, Tori made the introductions, then said, "Please, have a seat. Would you like a cup of coffee?"

"No, I'll pass, but thank you. And please, call me Orville."

Tori glanced at the clock on the wall. "I'd better get ready." In her bedroom, she dropped the vest over her head, settling it on her shoulders before fumbling with the Velcro straps on the sides.

Mia, standing in the doorway, asked, "Need some help?"

"Yes, please. I can't seem to get the straps in the right place," Tori said gratefully.

Mia quickly adjusted the straps, then stepped back. "How does it feel? Is it too tight?"

Tori gave herself a shake. "No, I don't think so. But how would I know? I never thought this would be a choice of attire," she quipped, though her wavering voice gave her away.

Her eyes glittering with worry, Mia spotted the jacket. Picking it up, she handed it to Tori. "Let's see how it looks."

Tori slid into it, zipping it up.

Mia studied the fit before nodding. "It's loose enough that you can't tell you're wearing the vest."

Tori sighed. "I suppose that's good." She opened the pouch. Following Parker's instructions, she soon had the earbud and mic in place and activated. She'd clipped the mic to the inside of the front pocket. After stuffing her phone and a small flashlight in her other pockets, she said, "I guess I'm ready to go."

Mia, worry etched on her face, took a quick step and gathered Tori into her arms. The hug was fierce and unyielding, as if she could shield Tori from any dangers that lay ahead. "Be careful," Mia murmured, her voice barely above a whisper, yet laden with unspoken fears.

Tori hesitated, the words catching in her throat. She leaned into the embrace, her arms tightening around Mia for a fleeting moment. "I will," she whispered back. She grabbed her tote bag and keys and rushed out.

Settled in the car, Tori pulled to the end of the driveway, pausing while her eyes scanned the street. Seeing nothing unusual, she eased onto the road. Once she was moving, she called Parker.

"I just left the house," she said when he answered.

"Good. Did Orville get there?"

"Yes. He's in the kitchen with Mia. She's making double chocolate fudge cookies."

An odd sound rippled over the phone. Did Parker groan? Then he said, "Lucky man." A faint smile touched her lips, easing some of the tension in her shoulders.

"Have you seen anyone?" she asked.

"Not yet," he replied.

Traffic was light, and Tori arrived in less time than expected. A pang of nervous energy surged through her. What should she do? She was way too early.

Her voice was tentative, wondering if Parker could hear her. "Ah … I'm early. Do you want me to circle the block?"

"No," Parker said, his steady voice reassuring in her ear. "If anyone's watching, they might think you're leaving. Go ahead and pull into the parking lot."

She slowed as she turned onto the street leading to the library, keeping to a cautious crawl. Her headlights swept across the shadowed buildings as her gaze darted between corners, seeking any flicker of movement, any figure lurking in the night's depths.

Up ahead, she spotted an unfamiliar vehicle parked on the street, though she guessed the truck was Parker's.

Her grip tightened on the steering wheel as she turned into the parking lot, her eyes combing the area. The beam of her headlights briefly illuminated the trees and buildings. Everything seemed still. Empty. Silent.

Parker's voice echoed in her ear. "Stay in the middle of the lot."

Following his instructions, she turned and parked to face the driveway. While the headlights' unwavering glow cut through the murky night, they did little to alleviate the darkness pressing against the windows. Only the steady rumble of the engine broke the oppressive silence as she waited. The minutes slowly ticked by.

"Anything?" she finally asked, needing to hear Parker's voice.

"Nothing yet," came the calm response.

A burst of static crackled through the earpiece, followed by Blake's voice. "Car turning onto the street."

Parker's reply was instant, clipped. "Got it."

Tori stiffened, her senses sharpening. She hoped Gale's request to meet would be nothing more than a brief conversation. While she desperately wanted to discover what Gale knew about the events at the ghost tour, she had no desire to prolong the meeting.

Her eyes caught the flash of headlights as the car approached.

Blake's voice reported, "Only one person visible."

The tension twisted in her chest. Did this mean someone could be hidden inside the car? The possibility hadn't been explicitly covered in Parker's instructions, though he'd mentioned playing it by ear.

The car slowed and turned into the parking lot. Tori watched the vehicle with as much trepidation as she would watch a coiled snake about to strike.

The driver stopped near the entrance. Tori's breath caught, and her voice rose, tinged with alarm. "Parker, the driveway! It's blocked! What do we do?"

Parker's tone had a grim edge. "Don't worry. It won't be a problem."

Tori waited, unwilling to get out, and the other driver was staying put. Her hands clung to the steering wheel as the moments stretched.

Then, the other car door slowly opened, and a figure emerged.

"Is it Mills?" Parker asked.

Tori squinted. Foreboding surged through her as recognition dawned. "Oh, my god, no! That's Carly Swanson."

Carly's head swiveled as her gaze swept the street and parking lot before she casually leaned against her car, arms crossed, her smirk unmistakably provocative.

"I'm getting out," Tori muttered, gripping the door handle. Leaving the door ajar, she moved purposefully to the front of her car, her eyes locked on Carly's smirking face. "What are you doing here?"

Carly chuckled, the sound tinged with condescension. "Oh, Tori, were you really expecting Gale?" Her voice dropped, her tone laced with fear as she mimicked, "Someone might hear me. I need to talk to you. Too dangerous. I'll have to meet you. Please, it's urgent."

A stunning revelation flooded her senses as Carly's sardonic laughter rippled in the night air. "That was you, not Gale," she shot back.

Carly's smirk widened. "Bingo! Give the woman the brass ring," she said with a sneer. "It's almost too easy to play you."

With more bravado than she felt, Tori said, "Whatever you're planning, you won't get away with it."

Her voice laced with sarcasm, Carly said, "Oh, I already have. You'll be finished in this town when *I'm* done with you."

Carly's blatant confidence sent a spark of anger through Tori, and she didn't hold back. "What a shocker, coming from someone who always lets others do the dirty work. Just goes to show how wrong you can be about people," Tori retorted with biting mockery. "Though I'll admit, I'm stunned you had the nerve to crawl into the light."

The woman's demeanor shifted in an instant. Carly straightened and unfolded her arms before taking a step forward. She said coldly, the amusement gone from her voice, "You just don't get it. The town's newest darling, Tori Winters, is about to be arrested for murder. Imagine the headlines, the stares, the handcuffs. You might even be rotting in a cell by the end of the week." Her laughter followed, sharp and cruel, as she stepped closer.

"Even if your money buys your way out," she hissed, "you won't be able to step outside your house without people whispering behind your back, wondering if you murdered a man. Maybe you'll finally get the message to sell the monstrosity you live in and get out of town."

Even though the venom in Carly's words twisted in Tori's gut like a knife, sharp and unrelenting, Tori pushed back the anger seething inside her. She hadn't been kidding when she said Carly let others do her dirty work.

Yet, Carly impersonated another woman to lure Tori to the library. Whatever else she had in mind, Carly wanted to flaunt her brilliance, to bask in her triumph. Her arrogance would be her downfall.

Tori had to keep pushing, goading her to talk. "Somehow, I can't buy into your grand scheme."

She crossed her arms, tilting her head as she studied Carly's face, letting the moment stretch. "No, Carly. You're not that smart," Tori taunted, shaking her head.

Carly's eyes glittered with malice as her voice cut through the air, clipped and cold. "You really are clueless. Who do you think orchestrated all this—the ticket, the scene at the ghost tour, the man who was killed? I even left you a note, keeping you exactly where I wanted you."

She took another step forward. "It didn't take long for you to show up at Vada's and then to have that little talk with Gale. Sure made a phone call from her believable. I set up the perfect trap, and you walked right in. And, now, all the evidence points to you."

A jolt of adrenaline coursed through Tori. Her instincts screamed a warning. Why did Carly keep inching closer? What was she planning?

While she casually eased away from the car to avoid being cornered, Tori baited her. "That's where your so-called perfect plan will fall apart. What happens when the police find the real killer? Or didn't you think ahead?"

Carly's lip curled into a sneer as she flicked her head dismissively. "Ah, yes. The murder. That was so very convenient, wasn't it? The man who tried to save you gets shot. But then, I don't have to worry. The police already have their killer—you. Why would they be looking for another? Especially since I've made sure you're their only suspect."

Tori didn't flinch. Instead, she pressed, provoking Carly. She shrugged her shoulders as if Carly's words were meaningless. "Nothing's going to happen despite all your plotting and scheming. I'm innocent, and nothing you say or do will change that simple fact."

In a clipped, vindictive tone, Carly gloated, "Who do you think is going to believe you? The police? You're the one they dragged in for questioning. They've got statements from two women and a video. After tonight, they'll have all the evidence they need. I've heard the district attorney is ready to issue a warrant for your arrest."

"So, this is the reason for your ridiculous little

charade, another trap." Tori chuckled with amusement. "This is nothing but another fabrication. You don't have any evidence because there is none."

The anger blazed in Carly's eyes. "Oh, I do, and soon everyone will know it. I wonder what your picture will look like on the front page of tomorrow's *Metro*. How about the Granbury heiress in handcuffs? Oh, that would be a good one."

Tori's voice rang out. "Hate to break the bad news, Carly, but this time, your malicious stunt won't work." Her voice deepened with a hard edge of undeniable confidence. "Here's what else you didn't consider. The truth will come out."

Tori's words were relentless as she fanned Carly's growing rage. "When your viciousness is exposed, you'll be the one on the outside—exiled. You won't be the high and mighty Carly Swanson with your devoted pack trailing behind. They'll all scatter, too scared to stick around and get dragged down with you."

Carly's face contorted with fury. "You little upstart. You can't touch me," she snarled. "Trust me, Tori, this is a night you will never forget."

Her eyes sparkled with a deadly intensity as her steps quickened.

Refusing to give way, Tori flung her hand up. "That's probably the only true statement to come out of your mouth. I'm sure I won't forget tonight, but you'll wish you could. Did you really believe I would let you or your friends get near me without protection?"

Carly faltered, confusion flickering in her eyes.

Blake's voice rang out from behind the library, "Stop!"

Carly's head whipped toward the sound.

Another voice shouted, "Take your hands off me!"

Carly's mask of malice shattered, replaced by something primal—fear. Without hesitation, she spun on her heels and bolted toward her car. Her footsteps slammed against the pavement in her frantic attempt to escape.

An engine roared as Parker's truck slid into view, its tires skidding to a stop, effectively blocking the driveway.

His voice rippled in her earpiece. "Tori, behind you."

Tori turned, squinting into the dim light. It took a moment for her eyes to adjust to the deep shadows stretching across the parking lot. Movement caught her attention. A man was sprinting away from the rear of her car, his silhouette barely visible in the dark. Mitch was hot on his heels as they headed toward the large grassy field bordering the parking lot.

Carly's furious voice pierced the night. "Get your truck out of the way! I'm leaving!"

Tori whirled to see Parker striding toward Carly's car.

Before Carly could make a move, Parker said, "You're not going anywhere until the police get here."

"The police? What are you talking about?" Carly's voice rose, laced with anger and a hint of desperation "I haven't done anything wrong! You have no right to keep me here. I'll sue you for every dime you have!"

She leaned forward, her voice teetering on hysteria. "I demand you move your truck so I can leave."

From around the side of the library, two figures emerged. Blake had a firm grip on the arm of a man who struggled against him. A camera hung from the stranger's shoulder, its strap twisted in Blake's grasp. With an iron-clad grip, Blake marched him into the center of the parking lot.

Stunned, Tori recognized him as the man who had taken her picture in the police car.

"Caught this one sneaking around the back," Blake announced. "He says he's with the *Metro*."

"Blake, watch them," Parker barked. "Mitch is after someone."

As Parker turned on his heel to rush after Mitch, the sharp sounds of a scuffle rang out. Mitch's voice boomed, rough and commanding, "Get on the ground!"

Parker took off at a dead run with Tori right behind him. Ahead, Mitch stood in the center of the field, his flashlight cutting erratic arcs in the dark. Skidding to a stop, Parker yanked out his flashlight, and its beam landed squarely on Mitch's face, illuminating a sizeable red abrasion on his cheek.

Still breathing heavily, Mitch said, "Sorry, boss. Thought I had him. He got in a lucky punch. But don't worry, I got in plenty more." His voice was laced with frustration as he aimed his flashlight at the ground. "He was carrying this."

CHAPTER 28

Parker looked down, then dropped to one knee. His sharp gaze intensified as he studied a gun lying on the ground. His voice lowered to a murmur, "What do we have here? If I'm not mistaken, this is the same caliber used in the John Doe shooting." He stood.

Tori stumbled to a halt beside him. The sight of the gun stole the air from her lungs. Gasping, she asked, "Was he going to shoot me?"

"Doubtful," Parker said with a thoughtful air as he continued to study the weapon at his feet.

Mitch spoke up. "He wasn't headed toward you, Ms. Winters. He was running toward your car."

Parker assessed the parking lot where the chaotic scene had unfolded. The headlights of the two cars cast long shadows while Blake stood guard over a deflated reporter. The Swanson woman stood rigid, her defiance unmistakable. His gaze shifted back to the gun.

With a harsh, sharp-edged voice, he added, "If this is the gun used to kill the John Doe victim, it would have been enough to arrest you for murder."

Tori's heart thudded as his words sank in.

"If I had to hazard a guess," Parker continued, "The plan was to toss it inside your car while you were distracted by Carly. I bet after she created a scene, the police would have shown up. Of course, they would have looked in your car, and lo and behold, there, neatly waiting for them in plain view—their new evidence, a gun. All while a reporter conveniently stood by to take pictures. The bigger question is, how does Carly connect to the gun?"

He whipped out his phone, scrolling through his contacts until he found the one he wanted.

"Andy, it's Parker Hayes. I'm at the Hood County Library and have a gun I think you might be interested in." He listened, then said, "I'm not leaving."

"He's on the way. Mitch, you stay here. Don't let this gun leave your sight until Andy Rodriguez arrives."

Mitch gave a curt nod, his expression resolute. "I won't."

Parker then turned to Tori and gestured back toward the parking lot. "Tori, let's head back."

Still shaken, Tori followed his lead, but her mind was racing. "Did you hear what Carly said?" she asked.

"Every word, and I've recorded it. Carly Swanson might have sealed her own fate. Especially if the gun turns out to be the murder weapon, and she was gloating about her new evidence for the cops."

With a steady pace, Parker closed the gap toward the reporter. His gaze was icy, his voice clipped. "What are you doing here?"

The man bristled, but his bravado wavered under Parker's scrutiny. "I don't have to answer your questions," he blurted, his voice rising defensively. "I didn't break any laws! I can go where I want. I'm doing my job."

"Then you can talk to the cops when they arrive."

The man's defiance crumbled, his face paling. "The police? I didn't do anything wrong. I'm following orders."

"What orders?" Parker's tone was relentless.

The man hesitated, darting a nervous glance toward Carly. "My editor got a tip. Something about Tori Winters."

"And who gave your editor the tip?" Parker pressed.

"I don't know," the man protested. "I go where he tells me."

"What were you supposed to do?"

"Take pictures, that's all." With a panicked expression, he said, "Something was going to happen involving Winters that would prove she murdered a man. Some new evidence. That's all I know."

Parker turned his piercing gaze to Carly, whose defiant expression flickered with unease.

Another car screeched to a stop on the street. When the man hopped out from behind the wheel, Tori groaned. "Great, just great. That's Carly's father, Judd Swanson."

Carly, catching sight of him, immediately shifted gears. Her bravado and defiance melted away, replaced by a calculated display of fragility. She stumbled toward her father, collapsing dramatically against his chest, her sobs loud and theatrical.

"Daddy," she wailed, her voice ringing with faux desperation. "They won't let me leave! I don't know why!"

Swanson's jaw tightened as he patted her shoulder, his anger bubbling beneath the surface. "Don't worry," he said, his voice a low growl. "I'll get to the bottom of this." He turned his icy glare on Parker and squared his shoulders. "Who are you?"

Parker didn't flinch. "Parker Hayes. Hayes Investigations."

Carly sniffled, still clutching her father. "He works for her," she said, her voice dripping with disdain.

Swanson's glare deepened. "Is that true?"

"I'm Tori Winters' security director," Parker replied.

Swanson's voice rose. "I demand to know why you've detained my daughter!"

"I'm waiting for the police to arrive. We'll let them sort it out," Parker said, his calm demeanor unshaken.

"The police?" Swanson barked. "My daughter says she was lured here by Tori Winters, and now you're holding her against her will!"

Parker's voice dropped an octave, the intensity of his words cutting through Swanson's outburst. "Mr. Swanson, you'll hear a different story when all the facts come out. I'm not going to debate this with you. As I said, we'll let the police handle it. Sergeant Andy Rodriguez, Homicide Division, is on his way."

"Homicide?" Swanson's voice faltered, disbelief replacing his earlier fury. "What does a murder investigation have to do with my daughter?"

Parker's eyes tightened, his sharp gaze unwavering. "The police will decide." His words, though calm, carried the weight of undeniable certainty.

"Daddy," Carly whined, her voice carrying the right note of desperation. "Why do we have to wait? I didn't do anything wrong. I want to leave."

"We are," Swanson replied harshly, his tone leaving no room for argument. His sharp eyes swept the parking lot. "Whose truck is that?"

Carly tilted her head toward Parker, her expression shifting to one of loathing. "It belongs to him," she said with venom, each word a dagger aimed at Parker.

Swanson turned his glare on Parker. "Move your vehicle, Hayes."

Parker didn't respond, unfazed by the demand.

Swanson's voice rose an octave, his irritation boiling over. "Fine. Come on, Carly. I'll take you home. Lock your car. We'll come back for it tomorrow."

"You can leave," Parker said smoothly, his eyes still locked on Swanson, "But be prepared. It won't take long for the police to show up at your house to question your daughter."

Swanson's tone turned icy as he marched toward Parker, his finger jabbing the air with each word. "I don't know what game you're playing, Hayes, but hear me loud and clear. If you or that woman you work for messes with me or my family, I'll bury both of you."

Before Parker could reply, the piercing sound of sirens cut through the tense air. A squad car pulled to a screeching halt at the edge of the parking lot, its blue and red lights painting the scene in harsh, flickering colors. Moments later, another car arrived.

As the sirens died away, a uniformed officer exited the first car and jogged toward the group. "What's going on here?" he asked.

Swanson, shooting another hard look at Parker, stepped back as he gestured. "You'll have to ask him. I'm Judd Swanson, city councilman, and I want to take my daughter home." He motioned toward Carly, leaning heavily against her car, her tears flowing freely now.

Another officer approached. His piercing gaze quickly assessed the group. "I'm Sergeant Andy Rodriguez. Mr. Swanson, you or your daughter can't leave until I've had a chance to figure out what happened here."

"This is outrageous!" Swanson exploded. "Unlawful detention! I'll have your badge for this!"

Andy's expression remained neutral, though a flicker of exasperation glinted in his eyes. "I'm certain you can try, Mr. Swanson," he said, his voice level, "but I have a job to do. And I'm going to do it. I'd appreciate your cooperation while I sort out the facts."

"Parker," Andy said, shifting his attention. "Show me what you found."

"Found? I want to see whatever this man claims to have found," Swanson interjected, his voice sharp.

Andy held up a hand. "Please stay here, Mr. Swanson. This is official police business."

Parker turned to Tori. "You'll need to stay here. You

might want to wait in your car." Then he turned to Andy, saying, "Over there."

****

As they walked off, Parker said with a note of sympathy, "That's one of the reasons I retired."

"I can't. I've still got at least ten to go. Start talking."

Parker detailed the phone call Tori had received, walking Andy through the chain of events leading them to the library parking lot. They reached the grassy field where Mitch stood waiting, the beam of his flashlight aimed toward the ground.

After Parker introduced Mitch, Andy crouched. He studied the gun for a few seconds before glancing up at Parker. "Let me guess. You think this is the gun used to kill the John Doe victim?"

Parker nodded, his voice steady but grave. "It's a strong possibility."

He stood, keyed the mic on his shoulder, telling someone to bring him an evidence bag and gloves. Then he turned his attention back to Parker. "Finish your story."

Parker continued, recounting the tense moments before the discovery of the gun.

Andy listened intently, his expression grim. Once Parker wrapped up, Andy turned his attention to Mitch. "All right, tell me exactly what you saw."

Mitch shifted his stance, gesturing toward the buildings opposite the library. "I was watching the parking lot from the corner over there. I saw a guy running across the field, staying low. Ms. Winters wouldn't have seen him since he came up behind her. I don't know about the other woman. She could have. He was making a beeline for Ms. Winters' car."

Andy held up a hand, stopping him. "How can you be sure he was targeting her car?"

Mitch didn't hesitate. "The angle he was moving, diagonal, went straight toward her car. Ms. Winters was in front, a good distance away. He wasn't after her. He was headed toward the vehicle."

The tension was unmistakable in his voice as Andy asked, "What happened then?"

"I ran toward him, but he spotted me. Took off running. Almost had him, too. When I tackled him, the gun fell to the ground."

"Can you describe him?"

"Not much detail," Mitch admitted. "Tall, about my height, five-ten. Slim build, moved like an athlete. He was wearing a hoodie sweatshirt, ball cap, and gloves. I never got a good look at him."

Parker grunted.

Andy shot him an expectant look. "Do you have anything to add?"

"Tori recently purchased a warehouse for her inventory for the inn. Twice, a man wearing a hoodie was spotted watching the place."

Andy said, "You think there's a connection?"

"I don't know," Parker said, "Though I don't like the similarity."

Andy glanced down at the weapon, his expression

hard. "But you're sure the man was carrying this?"

"Yes. I grabbed him around the waist and felt the gun in his waistband. When he twisted, the weapon slipped out, landing on the ground," Mitch told him.

Andy nodded sharply. "Since he was wearing gloves, I'd bet we won't find any fingerprints. I'll need a typed statement from you in the morning. Stop by my office."

An officer jogged over, handing Andy gloves and an evidence bag. After gloving up, Andy crouched. For a moment, he studied the gun with an impassive expression before sliding the weapon into the bag.

He sealed the pouch, initialed it with the date and time, and passed it to the waiting officer. His voice carried a quiet authority. "Get this to the lab—top priority. I want a report on my desk as soon as possible."

The officer nodded, moving swiftly toward the squad cars as Andy turned to Parker. "If this gun is tied to the John Doe murder, things are about to get complicated."

As the men strode toward the parking lot, Andy broke the silence. "What happened to the woman who called?"

Parker's tone turned thoughtful as he replied, "Tori expected to meet her, but from what I heard, Mills didn't call Tori. The caller was Carly Swanson."

"And you've got all their conversation recorded?" Andy asked, his tone tinged with curiosity.

"Yes. You'll hear a very different version than the story the woman and her father will try to spin."

At the edge of the parking lot, Andy came to a stop. His gaze lingered on Parker, a flicker of trust in his measured expression. "What's your take on this?"

Parker, unwilling to speculate, had stuck to the facts. But since Andy asked, he told him. "This was a setup to frame Tori. Drop the gun into her car and then create a scene to force a police response. The gun would've been found, and conveniently, a photographer was standing by to capture it all. Instant evidence. I've heard rumblings about new evidence being expected, and the DA was primed to issue an arrest warrant for Tori."

Andy's brow furrowed, his expression hardening as he absorbed the implications. "I'm not going to ask how you know," he said, his voice flat, "but we've tried to keep a lid on this case from the beginning."

Parker nodded. "What happened tonight puts significant holes in any arguments that Tori is a suspect in the murder. Carly was adamant she had evidence that would have Tori arrested for murder. Sure does make me wonder about Carly's connection to the gun."

Andy exhaled slowly, his lips curving into a grim smile. "Even though your theory might be right, I suspect it will be difficult to prove a case against the Swansons."

He squared his shoulders and glanced toward Carly and her father. "I'll talk to them, but I can't hold them. There's not much I can do until we know if this is the murder weapon. I'll need to speak with Tori before she leaves."

"Do you need my men to stay?"

Andy shook his head. "No, they can leave." He marched toward the Swansons.

Parker turned to Mitch, who stood waiting nearby. "You heard him. Go home. I'll let Blake know, too." As Mitch walked off, Parker added, his voice warm, "By the way, good work tonight."

Mitch glanced back, a faint grin breaking his serious expression. "Thanks, Parker."

****

Next, Parker shifted his attention toward Tori's car. Her driver's door was still ajar, though the engine had been turned off. Tori stepped out, wrapping her arms tightly around herself.

"What's happening?" she asked, her voice carrying a nervous edge while her eyes darted toward the figures locked in a heated conversation.

"Andy has sent the gun to the lab. Once he finishes talking to Carly and her father, he'll want to talk to you," Parker said, his tone low and reassuring.

"I called Mia to let her know I was okay." Tori exhaled softly, nodding toward where Andy calmly stood while Swanson angrily gestured at him. Carly still clung to her father as if he were her lifeline. "She's going to lie," Tori said, her tone tinged with quiet certainty.

"Andy knows, and when she does, that helps us. We've got the proof she's lying," Parker replied, stepping closer, his eyes locking on hers with steady resolve. "He's already put a rush on the lab work for the gun. Until we know the results, there's not much he can do. But if this is the murder weapon," he paused, letting the weight of his words sink in, "everything changes."

CHAPTER 29

Tori's eyes scanned Parker's face as if searching for reassurance. "What do you think?" she asked, her voice barely above a whisper.

Parker's steady gaze met hers. Without hesitation, he said, "It's the murder weapon." His hand gestured toward the Swansons. "If it's not, then none of this makes sense."

Her heart raced, fearful to ask the one question burning in her mind. "Will I still be a suspect?"

His answer was emphatic. "No!"

The breath she hadn't realized she'd been holding escaped in a shaky sigh, her shoulders loosening under the weight of relief. "Carly was behind all this," she said, her words tinged with disbelief. "I wonder if she did kill him."

"Still unknown. There is no evidence to tie Carly to the gun. Right now, all we can say is that she set you up to take the fall."

From across the parking lot, Andy hollered at Parker. "I need you to move your truck!"

Parker turned and trotted toward his vehicle. Tori watched him until the buzzing of her phone drew her attention. She glanced down to see David's name flash across the screen, a text asking if she was okay. She typed a quick reply, promising to call when she got home. A response immediately appeared—*doesn't matter how late, call.* The simple message brought an unexpected flicker of comfort before she turned her attention back to the Swansons.

Across the lot, the argument with Andy reached a crescendo. Carly's sharp and defiant voice sliced through the night air while her father's tone was harsh with anger.

While she watched, she slid off the jacket. Her fingers pulled the straps apart on the sides of the vest, and she slipped it over her head. With a sigh of relief, she dropped it on the back seat. As she slid the jacket back on, her gaze turned toward the group by Carly's car.

Carly's head turned. A shiver ran down Tori's spine when their eyes met. The woman's enmity felt like a living, tangible web, floating and tightening around her.

In that instant, Tori was certain. If Carly thought she could get away with it, she wouldn't hesitate to pull the trigger.

Once Parker's vehicle was out of the way, Carly and her father left, though Judd took a final swipe at Andy as he threatened to escalate matters to the police chief. Andy stood his ground, his expression stoic, but the tension in his stance betrayed his frustration.

Once they were out of sight, Andy turned on his heel and headed purposefully toward Parker, standing near Blake and the reporter. After a short, hushed exchange, Blake and the reporter departed.

Tori's stomach churned while she watched Andy stride toward her, his jaw set and eyes fixed on her with determination. She took a deep breath, trying to steady the pulsating nerves surging through her.

When he stopped, his voice was edged with intensity. "Tell me what you know, starting with the phone call you received."

Tori nodded and began explaining what had transpired on the call, which she believed was from Gale Mills. At first, her voice faltered but gained steadiness as she spoke.

Andy's brow furrowed slightly as he listened. When Tori finished, he asked, "How do you know Mills?"

"She works for the owner of the ghost tour business. I met Gale a few days ago at Vada Struthers' office. I was asking questions about the ticket I received. Throughout my conversation with Vada, Gale seemed nervous. After I left, I saw Vada also leave the office. I took advantage of her absence to go back and talk to Gale. While she claimed she didn't know anything, I had the sense that Gale did. After that conversation, though, we thought she might have left the note."

Andy's head snapped up from what he was jotting in his small notebook. "Note! What note?"

"Someone left a note on my front porch. It read, 'The truth lies within the tour.' So, today, when the caller identified herself as Gale Mills, I was hopeful that I'd find out who was behind what had happened. But Carly admitted tonight that she left the note."

Andy nodded, continuing to write. "Do you remember what day you got the note?"

"It was the day before I went to Vada's office."

"And when did you talk to Vada and Mills?"

"The same day the piano was damaged at the opera house," Tori replied.

Andy's gaze sharpened. "Was the call on your cell phone?"

"Yes."

"Is the number still there?"

Startled by the question, she quickly opened the call log. Relief washed over her when she found the number. "This is it," she said, holding the phone for Andy to see.

He jotted down the date, time, and number. His jaw tightened as he said with an adamant tone, "Don't erase the call log. Why didn't you go to where Mills works and talk to her there?"

Tori replied, "The caller insisted I had to meet her tonight. Even said it was too dangerous to come to my home when I offered. The call was disturbing, and I felt something was brewing. I just didn't know what."

His voice turned sharp. "Then why *did* you show up?"

Tori crossed her arms, not bothering to hide her exasperation. "For cripes' sake, you were ready to serve me up on a platter as your prime suspect. I learned that I was about to be arrested because of new evidence. I knew I was being set up ... again."

Bitterness added weight to her words. "I had no choice but to take a chance on meeting her. Of course, I know now that Carly was the caller, not Gale Mills. The woman sure put on a good act. But then, she excels at it."

Parker, standing nearby, stepped toward Tori, placing a steadying hand on her shoulder.

Andy's sharp gaze shifted from his notepad to Tori. "How do you know the caller was Carly?"

"She admitted she made the call, even quoting what she said to me on the phone. All part of her plan to entrap me."

Though his gaze softened for a fleeting moment, his questions still carried an unrelenting edge. "I get the impression there's more going on here than you being a murder suspect."

Parker spoke up. "Andy, Tori's been the target of a relentless string of harassment incidents. It started with the staged assault during the ghost tour but didn't end there. Twice, someone tampered with her tires downtown while her car was parked across from the opera house. You may not know, but Tori is the featured pianist in an upcoming concert."

A quick flash of surprise flickered across his otherwise stoic face. "No, I hadn't heard." Andy glanced at Tori. "Congratulations. That's quite an honor," he said before shifting his gaze back to Parker. "But what does her concert have to do with any of this?"

"Just another piece of the puzzle," Parker replied. "A few days ago, David Tucker and I kept an eye on Tori's car while she was at the opera house. We caught a kid on a bike about to let the air out of her tires. When I confronted him, he admitted a woman had paid him a hundred dollars to tamper with her tires whenever he saw the car in the parking lot."

"Did you file a police report?" Andy asked, arching an eyebrow.

Parker shook his head. "You and I both know your department wouldn't have been able to do much. The kid didn't know the woman, but I'm paying him a hundred bucks if he finds out. And then there's the vandalism to the piano at the opera house."

Andy nodded slowly. "I heard, though the offense isn't part of my department."

"Myra and her daughter have been very vocal with their objections to Tori's concert. They've even attempted to use the fact she's a murder suspect as leverage to get the concert canceled."

"And you think all of this ties together?"

"I do," Parker said with conviction. "This was a calculated act of malice against Tori from the moment she received the ticket to the ghost tour. Especially when you factor in the negative publicity Tori received and the presence of a *Metro* photographer tonight. Add Carly's threats, and you'll see the same pattern I do. The Swansons are the spiders at the center of this web."

Andy's lips quirked upward. "Interesting analogy."

Tori couldn't help but agree with Parker's portrayal of the Swansons, considering his words echoed her earlier thoughts. But the mention of the Swansons, not just Carly, struck a nerve for some reason. Enlightenment hit with sudden clarity. Carly had made an odd comment. One that resonated with an unsettling significance.

"Andy," she began, her voice steady but carrying an undercurrent of urgency, "Carly said something strange. About how I would 'finally get the message to sell the monstrosity I live in and get the hell out of town.' Ever since I arrived in Granbury and learned I'd inherited the Leichter estate, the Swansons have made a concerted effort to force me to sell the house and leave."

Parker sucked in a sharp breath, an uncharacteristic reaction. "She's right, Andy. We know her mother is involved in the smear campaign, but what about Judd?"

Andy's eyes narrowed as he flipped his notepad shut with a quick motion. "I get your point," he said, his tone carrying more weight than before. "Both of you need to be in my office early, around eight tomorrow. Tori, I'll get your statement then. I'd also recommend Lincoln Greer be there."

Tori nodded, but a flicker of apprehension remained. She watched Andy stride toward his car, wondering what the next day would bring.

The uncertainty still lingered in her thoughts as Tori pulled into the driveway. After parking in the garage, she grabbed her tote bag and vest. Her shoulders slumped with fatigue, each movement feeling heavier than usual. She walked out, jabbing the remote to close the door.

Parker stepped out of his vehicle, his steady gaze locking onto her while he waited. Tori's pace slowed as she moved toward him. Without a word, he rested a hand on her arm, removed the vest from her hand, and then gently guided her up the porch steps.

Light spilled onto the porch, wrapping Tori in its warmth as if the house itself welcomed her home. Mia stood in the open doorway, her eyes scanning Tori's face with a mix of worry and relief. Behind her, Orville waited. As she stepped into the foyer, she swallowed hard, choking back the tears threatening to rise.

Ever attuned to Tori's emotions, Mia slid an arm around her shoulders. "I've got the perfect remedy—hot coffee and double chocolate fudge cookies."

With a playful tone, Parker asked, "Orville didn't eat all of them, then?" He dropped the vest on a table by the front door.

Orville chuckled. "Believe me, I tried. Now that you're here, if it's okay, I'll take off."

"Absolutely. I'll see you tomorrow at the office."

Mia held up a hand, stopping him mid-step. "Wait, don't leave," she said, darting down the hallway. Orville exchanged a puzzled glance with Parker.

When she returned, she handed Orville a plastic container of cookies. "A few cookies to thank you for making an unbelievably difficult evening a little easier. And don't worry about returning the container. We have plenty."

A blush crept up Orville's cheeks as he accepted it. "Thank you, ma'am. This was a pleasure," he said before he turned and hurried out the door.

Tori dropped her tote bag in the office before joining

the others in the kitchen. She sank into a chair with a heavy sigh, pulling the zippered bag from her pocket and handing it to Parker. "Dang things worked really well."

Mia placed three steaming mugs on the table and motioned toward a plate piled high with cookies. "Help yourselves."

Tori stared at the plate in disbelief. "Did you spend all evening baking?"

Mia flushed, a sheepish grin spreading across her face. "Yeah, pretty much. Now," she said, sliding into a chair and leaning forward to pick up a cup, "One of you start talking. I want to know everything that happened."

Her mouth filled with a piece of cookie, Tori motioned for Parker to speak. He began detailing the events, his voice steady as the story unfolded. Half the plate of cookies had disappeared by the time he finished, and the coffee pot sat empty.

Mia, who had gone from worry to stunned amazement as she listened, leaned back in her chair. "I've got so many questions, but they can wait until tomorrow."

Parker rose. "It's time I left. I'll see you at the police department in the morning."

Tori stood as well, her expression earnest. "Parker, I don't know how to thank you for everything—"

He cut her off with a hurried wave of his hand. "No thanks are necessary. I'll see you tomorrow," he said, slipping out the door before she could respond.

As the front door closed softly, Mia remarked, "How lucky we are to have met him."

Tori sank back into her chair, exhaustion settling deep in her bones. "I know. If not for his foresight, tonight would have been a disaster. But I can't shake a feeling of trepidation. Parker's on Judd Swanson's hit list now."

Mia quipped, "Well, at least he's in good company. The two of us are there too." Gathering the plates and cups, she added, "What do you think Andy will do?"

Tori frowned thoughtfully, her hands resting on the table. "I don't know. That all depends on the gun. I guess I'll find out tomorrow if it's the murder weapon."

"Do you want me to go with you?" Mia asked, her tone tinged with concern.

Tori shook her head. "As much as I'd like you there, there's nothing you can do aside from waiting in the hallway. I need you here. Don't forget, we still have Dubois to deal with."

Mia started the dishwasher before turning back to Tori. "What are you going to do about Linc?"

"I've been sitting here wondering the same thing," Tori admitted. "I guess I'll call in the morning and leave a message. If he shows up, fine. If not, that's okay too. I've already decided I'm done with the Greer law firm. From now on, everything goes through Dan. I don't feel I can trust Linc after his earlier reaction."

Mia leaned against the counter, arms crossed. "If you want my opinion ...," she paused.

"Please. I do."

"You've made the right call. Are you going to tell them they're fired?"

"No point," Tori replied with a shrug. "I'll just stop using the law firm for legal advice."

With the kitchen cleaned up, Mia headed home. Tori grabbed her tote bag on the way to her bedroom, her feet dragging slightly with each step. The house was quiet, a welcome contrast to the tension-filled hours in the library parking lot.

She dropped her bag on the dresser with a heavy, shaky sigh. Stripping down quickly, she stepped into the shower, letting the steaming water cascade over her. While the tension in her shoulders eased, Tori's thoughts remained restless, churning from the confrontation with Carly.

Once she dried off, she slipped into a soft, oversized nightshirt and stacked her pillows. Settling in, she picked up her phone and dialed David's number. He answered on the first ring.

"I've been going crazy with worry. Are you all right?" His voice was laced with concern.

After reassuring him she was okay, his panic subsided. "What happened?"

Snuggling deeper into the pillows, her restlessness faded. Like Parker, David was one of those rare people who truly listened. He stayed silent while she talked about what occurred, though every so often, she heard the murmur of a faint curse, betraying his frustration.

When she finished, David let out a long breath. "I'm almost speechless. I've always known the Swansons were rigidly mired in their social standing, but it never occurred to me they'd go to such lengths."

"Most of this is still conjecture," she admitted.

"What's Parker's opinion?"

"They're responsible. But there's no hard evidence linking them to anything other than what Carly said tonight. While revealing, it's not proof. If the gun is the murder weapon, then I'd be cleared as a suspect. But there's no direct connection between the gun and the Swansons unless the police find the man who tried to plant the weapon in my car."

"Knowing Judd," David said, "he'll find a way to weasel out of this. You're tired. I can hear it in your voice. Hopefully, I'll finish up tomorrow and be able to leave. I'll call if it's not too late. If you're not busy, I'll stop by the house, and we can talk."

"What time it is doesn't matter. I'll be here."

"Uh ...," he paused, then added, "I'll see you tomorrow."

After the call ended, Tori frowned at the phone. The odd hesitancy in David's voice had returned, the same as before—like he wanted to say something but couldn't. What was he holding back? She yawned, deciding that his own worries were probably playing on his mind.

She set her phone on the bedside table, switched off the lamp, and pulled the covers over herself. As her eyes closed, her final thought was of David—and what he hadn't said.

Chapter 30

It wasn't the sound of construction that woke her. It was Mia pounding on her door. "Tori, wake up."

"I'm awake," she mumbled. "Come on in."

Mia pushed the door open, a mix of urgency and amusement on her face. "I hate to wake you, but you've got less than an hour to be at the police station."

"Cripes." Tori rolled over, squinting at the alarm clock. "I forgot to set the dang thing last night."

Mia laughed softly. "Not surprising. You were exhausted when you got home."

Spotting her phone on the table, Tori snatched it up. "Do me a favor, please. Stick this on the charger in my office. I'll be out in a few minutes."

Mia grabbed the phone and disappeared, closing the door behind her. Tori leaped out of bed, yanking jeans, t-shirt, and underwear from the dresser drawers. While she enjoyed the mansion's grandeur, she couldn't wait for the additional closet space her new apartment would offer.

Dressed in record time, she dabbed on makeup, swiped on some lipstick, and slipped into her vest and tennis shoes. In the kitchen, a cup of steaming coffee and a warmed bagel with strawberry cream cheese awaited her on the counter. Grateful for Mia's thoughtfulness, she glanced at the clock and realized she had time to eat before rushing out. She had barely finished when Mia walked in with Dubois trailing behind.

While many questions had been answered the evening before, one that hadn't was who killed the John Doe victim. Parker had mentioned that the man who dropped the gun was wearing a hoodie sweatshirt. A disturbing resemblance to the man Dubois had spoken to, the same man who'd been watching her warehouse. The possible connection to the gun, if it was the murder weapon, only added to her deepening suspicions about Dubois.

Oddly, he paused momentarily, his gaze sweeping over her sharply. Though all he said was, "I'm early."

When Mia slipped around him, heading toward the pantry, Tori knew it was to open the cellar door. To keep his attention, Tori rose, forcing him to step back and face her. "Please, have a seat and a cup of coffee," she offered.

"Thank you, but no."

By the time Dubois turned, Mia was opening the refrigerator door. "Mr. Dubois, would you like some orange juice?" she asked, her tone casual.

Telling her no, he brushed past her and disappeared into the pantry.

Tori glanced at Mia, rolling her eyes and shrugging. "I'd better get going," she said.

"Did you call Linc?"

Tori groaned. "Oh, no, I didn't. I still don't think it matters if he's there, but I'll call." She rushed to her office, relieved to see her phone fully charged. After tapping Linc's number, the call rolled to voicemail.

"Linc, this is Tori. I have to be at the police station at eight to meet Sergeant Rodriguez. He suggested you be there. If you can't, it's not a problem." Relieved that she didn't have to talk to him, she ended the call.

Then she saw the time. "Cripes," she muttered. She was going to be late. She grabbed her bag and raced out the door.

Thankfully, the traffic was light, and soon, she was pulling into the parking lot. As she hurried toward the front door, Parker was waiting to open it.

"I thought I was going to be late. Have you heard anything?" Tori asked, catching her breath.

"No."

A sudden thought flitted into her mind. "I forgot to ask Mia if she'd seen the *Metro*. I fully expected to be the headline on the front page."

"I saw a copy," Parker said. "The good news is you're not. Which makes me wonder why. There were plenty of juicy details the reporter could have used. Yet nothing was published."

Tori snorted in disdain. "Not surprising since the Swansons were front and center, not me."

Inside, an officer led them to Andy's office. When they entered, he rose from his desk and gestured toward the chairs. "Please, have a seat."

Her insides churned, a bundle of twitching nerves. Tori studied Andy's face as she sat, searching for any hint of what was to come. His expression revealed nothing.

He's as unreadable as Parker, she thought. *Must be a cop thing. They all seem to have the same traits.*

"Before we get started, this is the recording of what transpired between Tori and Carly last night." Parker slid a thumb drive across the desk.

"I'll listen to this later," Andy said, picking up the device. "Is Linc coming?"

"I'm not sure. I left him a message," Tori replied.

"Would you be agreeable to continuing in his absence?"

Tori straightened in her chair, her voice firm. "Andy, I've said all along I had nothing to do with the murder of that man. I saw him one time, and that was during the ghost tour. I have nothing to hide. And that won't change whether I have an attorney present or not."

Was that a smile? Tori could have sworn Andy's lips twitched upward but vanished almost instantly.

"Are you agreeable to having Parker present?"

Her eyes flashed with conviction as she met Andy's gaze head-on. "Absolutely. I trust Parker with my life."

Andy gave a short nod, seemingly satisfied. "Before we get to your statement, I have some news."

This had to be the gun. Her fingers dug into the chair's edge. Was it, or wasn't it? Tori swallowed hard, her pulse racing. She willed herself to stay calm, but the anticipation was crushing.

Everything—absolutely everything—hinged on a yes or no.

He paused, rifling through a stack of papers with slow, deliberate movements. The shuffling seemed unbearably loud in the small office. Tori's heart thudded, sharp and relentless. She couldn't breathe.

"Here it is, the ballistics report on the gun. No fingerprints. The gun had been wiped clean." He handed the report across the desk to Parker. "I thought you'd want to take a look."

Her nerves had frayed to the breaking point. Tori wanted to scream at Andy—just say yes or no. Pressing her lips together, her head snapped toward Parker, seated next to her.

His eyes slowly scanned the report. When Parker finished, he looked up at her. "It's the murder weapon."

Relief surged through Tori. She wanted to collapse into the chair and leap for joy all at once. Her gaze jerked back to Andy.

With a smile, he nodded. "I thought Parker might like to be the one to tell you."

She bent forward, pressing her hands to her face, breath shuddering as the weight of it all hit. Until this moment, she hadn't fully comprehended the fear she'd been living with.

While neither man spoke, Parker's hand rested gently on her shoulder. She drew a deep breath and raised her head, her voice unsteady. "I don't know what to say other than … what happens now?"

Andy leaned forward. "We record your statement." He picked up the phone and called for a recorder to be brought in.

A few minutes later, a woman entered the room. She sat at a desk in the corner, setting up her equipment. Once everything was ready, she gave Andy a nod.

He started with the date and the names of those present, then launched into the same questions he'd asked the night before. Surprisingly, the process went faster than Tori had anticipated. Once Andy was satisfied, the woman packed up her equipment and left without a word.

"Transcribing your statements won't take long," Andy said. "Once it's typed, you can review, sign, and be on your way."

Parker leaned back in his chair. "Where does the investigation stand?"

"I can confirm some details. Gale Mills denies calling you, and the number on your phone is from a burner phone," Andy replied in an even tone.

Tori muttered, "I bet the dang thing was in Carly's purse, though she did admit she called me."

Despite the sharp look Andy shot her, he only said, "The Swansons will be here today to give their statements." His phone rang. After a short discussion, he hung up the receiver, saying, "Excuse me for a moment." He stood and stepped out of the room.

"I wonder what happened to Linc," Parker mused.

Tori sighed. "I didn't call him until this morning. He might have a good reason, but honestly, it doesn't matter."

She hesitated, taking another deep breath. "Since this is over, I don't need an attorney. And if I do, I'll call Dan."

Parker's sharp mind caught the implication immediately. "Have you fired Linc?"

"No. I just won't use Jonah or Linc again for my legal services."

"Do you feel like sharing the reason?"

"I can't trust him," Tori admitted, her tone firm. "I don't think he ever believed I was innocent." She finally told him about Linc's questions.

Parker's expression was resolute, unforgiving. "I've had my doubts about the man. Knowing there was a strong connection between the Greers and your grandmother, I didn't want to say anything."

A sad look settled on Tori's face. "They've been the family's attorneys since my great-grandfather's time."

Parker's eyebrows lifted in surprise. "I didn't realize the relationship went that far back."

Her voice firmer, she said, "I don't want Linc to know the specifics of what happened last night."

"Ah, worried he might tell the Swansons?"

"I hope he wouldn't, but I can't afford to take the chance."

"Then what are you planning to tell him?"

"As little as possible. I'm sure Linc's ears will be full of the Swanson version soon enough," she said.

His tone somber, Parker said, "You need to tell Andy that Linc doesn't represent you anymore. Otherwise, he might assume he can talk to Linc."

Tori groaned. "Well, dang! I guess I have to fire him."

Before Parker could reply, the door swung open abruptly. This time, it wasn't Andy who stepped in. It was Linc. And he was furious.

"Tori, did you talk to Andy without me?" he demanded, slamming the door shut.

She stood, disliking the way he loomed over her. "Yes, I did."

Linc whipped around, venting his anger toward Parker. "You let her do this. If anyone should know better than to let a suspect talk to the police without an attorney, it's you. This is insufferable, even negligent. You should be fired."

Tori stiffened, her outrage rising to the surface. After everything she'd endured, Linc's attacking Parker was the final straw.

"Linc. Shut up!"

He spun back, his expression stunned. "What did you say?"

"You heard me. I told you to shut up. First, I'm no longer a suspect. And second—you're the one I'm firing."

The door opened, and Andy stepped in. "What's going on? Everyone in the hallway could hear you."

Tori's jaw tightened. "Sergeant Rodriguez, for the record, Lincoln Greer is no longer my attorney." Her gaze shifted to the papers he held. "Is that my statement?"

"Yes." Andy walked around the desk and set the papers in front of her. "Please review this carefully before you sign to ensure everything is correct."

Tori sat, ignoring Linc, who stood motionless, his mouth hanging open as if the floor had suddenly dropped beneath him.

"Wait a minute, Tori," Linc blurted, breaking free from his stupor. His voice wavered between desperation and disbelief. "You can't be serious. Before you do anything else, I need to speak to Andy. If this is just another of your attempts to sidestep the truth, that doesn't make it a legal reality."

Tori twisted in her chair to glance up at him. "That attitude is why I don't need or want your legal assistance."

"Tori. Wait just a minute. You can't do—"

Andy cut in, his expression unyielding. "Ms. Winters has released you from any obligations as her attorney. Respect her decision. Leave!"

Linc's hard gaze flashed toward Parker, then to Tori. His voice harsh with anger, he said, "Tori, you'll regret this. I hope you're ready to face the consequences." Spinning, he stormed out, the door slamming behind him.

Unshaken, Tori calmly read her statement. Satisfied, she signed the document and handed it back to Andy.

He smiled faintly, a gesture of quiet encouragement. "Thank you, Tori. I don't believe I will have any further questions for you."

Nothing he could have said would have been more reassuring as she gave him a bright smile.

As they exited the building, Parker said, "Don't be surprised if Linc comes back, trying to patch things up."

"I'm not expecting Linc," Tori said, a hint of bitterness

in her voice. "I'm expecting Jonah. Still, what I did felt right."

Before Parker could respond, his phone buzzed. He pulled it from his pocket, glanced at the screen, and answered, "Parker Hayes."

Tori watched as his expression shifted, his eyebrows lifting in surprise. He quickly pulled a small notebook from his pocket and jotted something down. "If this is accurate, you'll get your hundred dollars," he said.

When he hung up, a glimmer of excitement sparked in his eyes as he turned to Tori. "I just caught a fish."

Tori tilted her head, confusion flickering across her face. "Fish?" she echoed.

"This was the kid who let the air out of your tires," Parker explained with a tone of satisfaction. "He found the woman who hired him and got the license plate number for her car. I need to run this down at my office. I'll let you know what I find." Without another word, he hurried off toward his truck.

For a moment, she stood there. A cool breeze rustled her hair, and she inhaled deeply as she reveled in a newfound sense of freedom. With a lighter step, she made her way to her car.

When she pulled into the driveway, she screeched to a stop and hopped out. Her heart raced, thoughts tumbling over each other like dominoes as she bolted inside the house.

Chapter 31

Tori shouted, "Mia!" Her voice echoed through the house like a gunshot. "Where are you?"

Mia stepped out of the kitchen into the hallway. As she caught sight of her friend's breathless excitement, she blurted, "Oh, my gosh! That was the murder weapon, wasn't it?"

Tori skidded to a halt in front of her, grabbed Mia's hands, and twirled her in a jubilant circle. "Yes! Yes, it was! Oh, my god, Mia, you have no idea how good this feels. I'm finally not suspected of murdering someone!"

With their arms still entwined, they ambled into the kitchen, where Mia pointed to a chair. "Sit and tell me everything. Don't leave anything out."

Tori sank into the chair with a dramatic sigh, the giddy smile refusing to leave her face. "The huge weight is gone. I can breathe again."

Mia stepped to the counter and filled two cups with coffee, handing one to Tori.

"Oh, this smells good," she declared, curling her fingers around the handle. Tori took a deep swig, savoring the rich taste.

"Andy had the ballistics report. But instead of telling

me, he handed the report to Parker. I swear, I was a bundle of nerves waiting for one of them to say something. Andy finally confessed he wanted Parker to give me the good news."

With a probing expression, Mia leaned against the counter, holding her cup in her hands. "And what about the Swansons? Any updates there?" She took a sip.

"Not much," Tori admitted. "Gale Mills said she didn't call me, though we found that out last night. The number on my phone was from a burner phone."

Mia interrupted with a gleeful chuckle. "Ha, I knew it! I was right!" she declared. "There is a burner phone involved. I hate to be someone who says, I told you so, … but I told you so."

Mia laughed again. "And, just who kept bringing up the gun?" She set the cup on the counter, then huffed at her nails and polished them against her shirt, a smug smile tugging at her lips.

Tori joined in, and the laughter felt so good. "Yes, Watson, you were right," Tori teased. "The Swansons are supposed to be at the police station today for their statements. I'd sure like to be a fly on the wall during those meetings. Especially since Andy has Parker's recording from last night. Wonder how she'll lie her way out of that?"

Mia's lips curved into a wry smile. "Dang, that would be entertaining."

"Oh! I almost forgot," Tori said, her voice brightening as she straightened in her chair. "Parker got a call from the kid that he and David caught tampering with my tires. The boy found the woman, and he gave Parker a license plate number. Parker didn't waste any time leaving the station. I'm sure he'll be here later."

Mia walked over with the coffee pot, refilling Tori's cup. "You haven't mentioned Linc. Was he there?"

Tori's mood darkened slightly as she took a sip. "He showed up, and I fired him."

Mia's eyebrows shot up. "I thought you weren't going to fire him, just ignore him."

"Turned out it wasn't that easy. Before he arrived, I told Parker that Linc wasn't my attorney anymore and why. I also said I didn't want Linc to know any specific details about last night."

"Ah …," Mia mused. "You think he'll run and tattle to the Swansons."

"I hope not, but Parker brought up a good point. Andy had to be told. Otherwise, he'd believe he could discuss the details of my case with Linc. Then Linc walked in, and everything went downhill from there."

After she explained how Linc had gone after Parker, blaming him, Tori added, "I didn't have a choice. I fired him and told Andy he wasn't my attorney. Andy had to order him to leave."

"Even though I think you were right, this won't be the end of it."

"I know. Want to take a bet on how long it will take Jonah to show up?"

Mia laughed. "You know I don't take sucker bets.

Now that all this nasty business is behind you, what's on your agenda?" Mia asked.

"A concert," Tori replied with a grin. "I need to get in some solid hours of practice today."

"Don't forget we have the women's business league meeting tonight."

Tori groaned, smacking her forehead with the heel of her hand. "Cripes, I completely forgot. I can't be there. You'll have to carry the flag for the Red Door Inn."

Mia's eyes gleamed with avid curiosity. "And why not? When we got the invitation, you were excited about the opportunity."

"Um … something else came up."

With a sly smile, Mia asked, "Does something else have the initials DT?"

Tori's cheeks flushed. "Maybe?"

Mia burst into laughter, the kind that bubbled up from deep within. "Okay, okay. I'll take care of business while you play."

"It isn't that exactly, it's just …"

"Just what?" Mia teased, her laughter fading into a playful smirk.

Tori's hands flashed upward. "Oh, I don't know."

Mia raised her mug in a toast, her tone laced with humor. "Okay, I won't keep poking. For now."

Before Tori could say another word, footsteps pounded on the stairs. Both women turned as Dubois appeared in the doorway, his briefcase swinging from his hand.

"I'll see you tomorrow," he said curtly, his sharp tone as brisk as his stride as he crossed the kitchen and headed for the front door.

Silence hung in the air, punctuated only by the soft click of the door closing. Mia and Tori looked at each other with chagrin.

"How could I have forgotten he was here?" Tori groaned, slumping deeper in the chair.

Mia, her expression a mix of exasperation and amusement, said, "We both did."

Tori asked, "Do you think he heard everything?"

"If he did, I hope he found our comments entertaining."

Tori groaned again, pushing herself up from the chair. "I'll lock the front door. Then, I'm going to practice."

After positioning the bench, she settled into place. She closed her eyes briefly, her feet finding the pedals as her fingers hovered over the keys. Tori took a steadying breath and then began to play. The first notes poured from the piano, crisp and confident, rising and falling like a wave. Each piece blended seamlessly into the next. Everything faded, her focus narrowing to the keys beneath her fingers and the emotions swirling within the melodies.

The light tap on her shoulder jolted Tori back to reality. Startled, her hands stilled. She glanced up to find Mia standing beside the piano.

"You've got visitors."

Tori turned, spotting two men inside the doorway. Not only did Jonah show up, but so did Linc. Their faces were tight with determination, their posture stiff.

Resigned to the inevitable, Tori rose. "Let's go to my office," she said, walking past them into the hallway. Inside, she motioned to the chairs in front of her desk before taking her seat.

When Mia passed the doorway without stopping, Tori couldn't help but feel a flicker of amusement. Mia's refusal to offer refreshments was a small, silent act of condemnation that lightened her tension.

Jonah, seemingly uncomfortable, cleared his throat. "I had no idea you were so talented. What we heard was amazing. I understand now why Nora is excited to have you perform."

Tori nodded, though she glanced at Linc. The expression on his face was tightly controlled as he sat rigidly perched on the edge of the chair. Tori wondered if Linc remembered his earlier comments about her performance. Still, it didn't matter since she no longer cared about his opinion.

Undaunted by her silence, Jonah continued, "I understand there may have been a misunderstanding earlier today. I'm hoping we can resolve what happened."

Before Tori could respond, Linc leaned forward, his voice laced with regret. "Tori, I apologize for my outburst. Discussing this matter with the police without my presence was reckless and could have been dangerous. I've been so worried about these false charges against you that I overreacted."

His voice deepened. "Still, I shouldn't have let my

frustration over your well-being get the better of me. I'm truly sorry for any discomfort I caused."

"Thank you for the apology, but it doesn't change anything," Tori said, her tone steady but firm. "I will not be using your law firm in the future."

Jonah straightened. With a look of disbelief, he said, "I don't understand. What prompted this? Tori, as you know, the Greers have represented your family for many years. We have a long, deep-rooted history."

"Out of respect for the many years, as you phrased it, I will say this. Linc, I lost confidence in you. After your visit yesterday, I realized you didn't believe I was innocent. You didn't believe what I said to you was the truth. I saw the same disbelief in Andy's office. That's unacceptable."

Linc's voice rose, his tone tinged with desperation. "How can you even make such an accusation? Of course, I believed you."

Her gaze hardened as she looked at him. "We both know you didn't. You repeatedly questioned the truth of my statements. Today, I was exonerated of any wrongdoing. But I cannot have someone handling my legal affairs that I cannot trust."

She rose. "I don't believe we have anything further to discuss."

How could she explain when these two men were as deeply mired in the Granbury social environment as the Swansons? Despite her inheritance, Tori was still an outsider. She didn't have the deep roots that came from years of association and would never have them. Instead, Tori had to carve out a place uniquely hers and build her own relationships.

They stood, lips pressed into tight lines, brows drawn. Without another word, they walked out. Tori followed.

In the foyer, Jonah turned to her, his expression taut but polite. "Despite your decision, I hope that if there is ever any way we can be of service, you will let us know."

Tori didn't respond, only nodding curtly before opening the door. With a sense of relief and sadness, she closed the door behind them. She turned to head back to the music room, but the sharp ring of the doorbell stopped her in her tracks. Hoping this wasn't Jonah or Linc returning, she opened the door cautiously.

CHAPTER 32

Parker strode in, a knowing look on his face. "From their expressions, I'm guessing they didn't like what you told them."

"No, they didn't," Tori said, her lips curving in the faintest of grins.

"Well, I've got good news. I found the woman. Let's talk to Mia. I bet she knows her. Where's Dubois?"

"He's already left," Tori told him as they strolled toward the kitchen.

In the kitchen, Mia was laying out plates and silverware for lunch. She glanced up as they walked in. "Hi, Parker. I heard what you said. What's her name?"

"Evelyn Duncan," Parker replied, setting his computer bag on the floor by the chair he settled into.

"Well, dang," Mia said, setting down a stack of napkins. "Evie is one of Carly's BFFs. Her father is buddy-buddy with Judd Swanson in the real estate business."

Parker arched an eyebrow. "BFF?"

Mia chuckled. "Not up to date on the new lingo, are you? It means best friend forever."

With a glint of amusement, Parker said, "Uh … okay.

What can you tell me about her? I'd like to catch her by surprise."

Mia placed cups of coffee on the table, followed by a plate of sandwiches and a bowl of potato salad. "She works for her dad in his real estate office and lives not too far from the Swansons," she said, sliding into her chair.

"What would the two of you say to a little detective work this afternoon?" Parker asked, scooping a generous helping of potato salad onto his plate and then picking up a sandwich. His eyes sparkled with a mischievous twinkle as he glanced at them, a faint grin tugging at the corners of his mouth.

Mia's face lit up with enthusiasm. "Woohoo, I'm game!"

Sitting next to her, Tori exclaimed, "So am I. Sherlock and Watson, reporting for duty, sir," Tori declared with mock seriousness, adding a playful salute.

Mia raised her hand for a high-five. Tori met it with a satisfying slap. Their laughter erupted, unrestrained and contagious.

Parker gave them a bewildered look. "Sherlock and Watson? What am I missing here?"

Tori shot him a mischievous grin. "Inside joke."

Parker groaned audibly, rolling his eyes. "Maybe this isn't such a good plan."

"Nah, we've got you covered," Tori declared. She shifted, pulling her plate closer to her. "What's the plan?" She scooped potato salad onto her plate.

His lips twitched for an instant before his expression

turned serious. "Find Duncan and force her to come clean with Andy. The gun changed everything. What Carly did isn't harassment anymore. Now we're talking about murder."

Parker forked up potato salad. "Carly bragged about the evidence she had, and then the murder weapon shows up. That puts her smack-dab in the middle of a homicide, along with anyone else who's helped her."

Tori and Mia leaned in closer, their plates momentarily forgotten as they eagerly hung onto his every word.

With a wave of his fork as if to emphasize his words, he said, "We've got two incidents, the ghost tour and the tires. Do we have two or three women? My guess is two, and Evelyn Duncan was one of the two at the ghost tour. What does she look like, Mia?"

"You could be right. Evie fits the description of the woman who bumped into Tori, tall with long dark hair," Mia said with a thoughtful air.

Parker's lips curled into a faint smile. "When Evelyn Duncan realizes her BFF has embroiled her as a suspect in a murder investigation, she'll be sitting in front of Andy's desk singing like a canary."

Frowning, Tori picked up her sandwich. "What I don't understand is how Carly knew about the gun, and who was the guy who tried to drop it in my car? Was it the same man involved with Dubois?"

"I'm sure that's what Andy is very busy trying to figure out. I told him about the incidents with the warehouse." A look of satisfaction lit up Parker's eyes. "I'm betting we can help him, at least in dealing with Carly."

Tori swallowed the last bite of her sandwich. "What about Dubois?"

Parker leaned back with a thoughtful expression. After a moment, he said, "It's time to get him out of the house."

"Okay. I'll fire him tomorrow."

"I want to be here when you do," Parker told her.

Once they finished eating and tidied the kitchen, Parker grabbed his computer bag. "All right, ladies, let's get this show on the road."

After moving her car into the garage, she and Mia piled into Parker's vehicle. He started their hunt for Duncan's vehicle with a slow pass by the real estate office, a charming, renovated historic-style house with a wraparound porch and manicured landscaping.

When they spotted the car in the small lot, its sleek black finish glinting in the sunlight, Tori said, with an undertone of disappointment, "Cripes, this was almost too easy."

Parker's lips twitched in amusement before he said, "We may have gotten lucky. I'm hoping she's alone."

Inside, the faint sound of music filled the air. Behind a large, ornate desk sat a young woman, her fingers flying across the keyboard. She glanced up and smiled until her eyes focused on Tori and Mia. Her face paled.

"She's the one who bumped into me," Tori muttered.

Parker strode forward, his voice calm and professional. "Ms. Duncan, I'm Parker Hayes with Hayes Investigations. We'd like a minute of your time."

A mulish look crossed her face, though fear flickered in her eyes. "I don't want to talk to you. Please leave."

"It would be to your advantage to hear me out," Parker said, his tone measured. "We know you paid someone to tamper with Ms. Winters' tires."

Her voice rose. "I don't know what you're talking about! Leave, or I'm calling the police."

Mia strode forward, planting her hands firmly on the desk as she leaned in. Her gaze locked onto Evie's with a hard glare. "Get real, Evie. You're in deep doo-doo, and you know it. If you're smart, you'll talk to Parker. But if you really want to call the cops, go ahead. We'll be quite happy to talk to them instead."

Evie nibbled on her lip, her hands trembling as she looked away.

"Here's the pattern the police will see," Parker said, his tone calm but firm. "During the ghost tour, you accused Tori of assault. You had a woman ready to film the whole stunt. Who was she?"

With a wary glance at Mia, she said, "Marlene Wisner."

Her tone tinted with contempt, Mia said, "Another close, longtime friend of Carly's."

Parker nodded, picking up where he left off. "Then a man intervened, and the same man was later shot to death not far from where your contrived confrontation occurred.

When questioned by the police, the statements from the two of you implicated Tori in the murder."

His voice deepened, hammering each word. "Based on your testimony, Tori became the prime suspect, all while someone leaked the details to the press, causing more damage to Tori's reputation. Then you paid someone to tamper with her tires. And let's not forget the damage to a valuable piano to keep her from performing. You're tied to all of this, and you'll likely be considered a suspect in the murder."

As Parker spoke, fear and horror crept across Evie's face. Her hands clenched tightly together.

Her voice quivered. "No. That's not true. The ghost tour … that … that was just a prank Carly dreamed up. She said we'd get a laugh seeing Tori …" Her voice faltered, and her eyes darted nervously toward Tori. "With egg on her face."

Her voice dropped. "After we saw the man's picture in the paper, it was Carly's idea to take the video to the police. She told us to make it seem like Tori was arguing with him. Carly said Tori needed to learn that being related to Elly Leichter meant nothing. But Carly swore nothing terrible would happen."

She swallowed hard. "But then, the newspaper escalated the story about Tori as the prime suspect. Carly told Marlene and me not to worry. It would all blow over."

Despite the look of disgust on his face, Parker kept a calm, even tone in his voice. "Did you talk to anyone at the newspaper?"

"No! I didn't," she said.

"Did Carly?" Parker asked, his voice intense.

With another glance at Tori, she nodded. "I heard her on the phone one day. I think she was talking to someone with the newspaper. She said to be sure to get a picture of Tori in the police car."

"And how did Carly know?" Parker asked.

"I told her," Evie admitted. "When I was at the police department, I overheard the sergeant talking about it."

Anger and relief surged as Tori listened to Evie's revelations. They were finally getting truthful answers.

"Who came up with the plan to damage Tori's tires?"

Evie's hands twisted together in her lap, and she refused to meet Tori's eyes. "Carly. She was pissed about Tori's concert. The tires were one more way to cause Tori a problem. She gave me the money, and I paid the kid," she said, her voice cracking. "All he was supposed to do was let some air out. It didn't hurt anyone. And I had nothing to do with the piano."

"Was that Carly?"

"I don't know," Evie said, shaking her head frantically. "I swear I don't."

Parker's gaze darkened. "Did you know Carly planned to meet Tori at the library last night?"

Evie hesitated, her hands fidgeting. She looked up at Tori, guilt etched across her face. "Yes," she admitted, her voice barely above a whisper. "She said she finally had a way to get even."

"Did she tell you what she planned?" Tori asked, her

voice hard with anger as she leaned over the desk.

"No," Evie said. "She wouldn't say."

"Were you there last night?" Tori demanded.

"No," Evie said quickly, shaking her head. "I was at home."

Parker's expression hardened. "Evie, how far were you willing to go for your friend, Carly? You gave the police false information. You could be arrested. If you're found guilty, you'll go to jail. It would have been you on the witness stand, not Carly if Tori had been arrested. Lying on a witness stand is perjury. Were you willing to go to jail for your friend, Carly?"

What little color left in Evie's face vanished as she stared at Parker with a wide-eyed look of fear.

His voice tightened. "You're the one on the hook, not Carly. Where was she when you were doing her bidding? Do you really think she's going to support you?"

Mia let out a short, sarcastic laugh, her expression grim. "Carly will toss you to the wolves without a second thought, and you know it, Evie. Your only hope is to tell the police the truth."

The door opened. Evie gasped.

Chapter 33

Andy asked, "What are you doing here?" While his tone was mild, his eyes sparked with suspicion.

Parker turned. "After I left your office, I discovered who hired the boy to tamper with Tori's tires." He motioned toward the woman behind the desk. "Evelyn Duncan. She has information that you need to know."

He motioned for Tori and Mia to go ahead of him. Outside, they quickly strode toward Parker's truck.

Once they were settled inside the vehicle, Tori asked, "Do you think she'll admit everything to Andy?"

"I don't know, but he's a smart detective. I'm sure he already knows Duncan, and the other woman led him down the primrose path. And it won't make him happy."

After Parker dropped them off, Mia said, "I'm headed home since I'm attending that meeting tonight."

They stopped by her car.

Tori glanced at her watch. "I should be able to get another couple of hours of practice before ..." She stumbled to a halt.

With a mischievous look, Mia said, "Yes, before what?"

"Okay. I give up. Before David gets here. He's on his way back from Austin."

A hilarious burst of laughter erupted. "If you want a late-night snack, there's a container of cookies and muffins in the pantry. Tell David I said hi."

Still laughing, Mia climbed into her car.

Shaking her head, Tori strolled toward the house, wondering why it was hard to admit how she felt about David.

Uncertain when he might arrive, Tori decided to change clothes before starting on the piano. Standing in front of the armoire, she hesitated. Would wearing a dress make his stop on the way home seem like something more than it was?

Finally, she settled on soft jeans, a long-sleeved shirt, and sandals. A hint of makeup followed, just enough to feel polished without being obvious. Satisfied the balance was right, she turned and headed to the piano, her mind already on her music.

She laid the phone on a nearby table in case he called. She was on the second piece of music for the concert when it rang. Her heart leaped, and she eagerly reached to answer the call.

"As fast as you answered, I'm guessing David isn't there yet," Mia said.

"Not yet, but it's early. He wasn't sure what time he'd leave Austin. What's up?"

Her voice tinged with intrigue, Mia said, "You're not going to believe this. I had to call and tell you."

Tori's curiosity spiked. "Something juicy, I hope."

"Oh, yeah. Your not-so-favorite person."

Tori groaned, her frustration sharp. "Carly! It must be good for you to call."

"You'll never guess who she had dinner with. I'll give you a clue. Who did she meet the day she showed up with two friends in tow?"

"Bart?" Tori squealed. "Tell me you're kidding."

"I'm not. I got a call from a friend I had contacted about the ghost tour rumors. She saw Carly cozied up with a stranger at a restaurant near the lake. After hearing the guy's description, I knew it was Bart."

"Dang, that didn't take long. She had just met the guy."

"Carly's not known for waiting when she wants something. Got to go or I'll be late for the meeting. I'll see you in the morning." Mia disconnected.

Still pondering the thought of Carly and Bart, an unlikely combination, Tori reminded herself that he did work for an international magazine. Carly was the type to always keep her eye on the prize.

Back at the piano, her fingers easily picked up where she left off. Once she had completed a full run-through of the program for the concert, she let the final note linger in the air.

The house had grown noticeably darker, the evening's shadows swallowed by the night. She glanced at the clock. It was much later than she had realized. David was running late. Still, he'd call to let her know if he didn't plan on stopping.

Not wanting him to think she wasn't home, she wandered from room to room, flipping on lights. In the kitchen, she started the coffee machine, the low hum breaking the silence. When she opened the refrigerator for a snack, her stomach rumbled, a sharp reminder she'd forgotten to eat.

She hesitated, glancing toward the wall clock. Maybe she should wait. If David hadn't eaten yet, they could order a pizza. After a moment of indecision, she settled for a steaming cup of coffee and one of Mia's cookies. The rich taste of the chocolate helped curb the edge of her hunger.

In her office, she sank into her chair and booted her computer. While she waited, she could check her emails. The inbox was flooded with unread messages, but none seemed urgent.

As she scanned the list, the soft chime of an incoming text message interrupted her train of thought. She blinked, trying to remember where she had left her phone, then jumped up and headed to the music room.

The possibility that it was David lit a spark of anticipation. As she reached for the phone, she saw the message was from Mia.

Her thumb swiped across the screen, expecting something mundane, probably about how the meeting went. Instead, cold frissons shot down her spine as she read. *Meet me at the warehouse. It's urgent. Hurry.*

She froze, the words searing into her mind. This didn't make sense. Why would Mia send a message like this instead of calling?

With trembling fingers, Tori jabbed the speed dial. The call rolled to voicemail. The fact that Mia didn't answer after texting only sharpened the alarm twisting in her chest. Every instinct screamed. Something was terribly wrong. The thought blazed through her, galvanizing her into action.

Her heart thundered as she darted into her bedroom, kicking off her sandals. Her hands, clumsy with haste, frantically laced her boots. Tori threw on her jacket and shoved her phone in a pocket.

Another precious few seconds were lost as she hunted down her keys. They were on her desk. Tori grabbed them and her tote bag, bolting out of the room.

All the while, questions swirled, chaotic and unanswered. *What's happened? Why the warehouse? What is the emergency?* Panic clutched her lungs, its grip tightening with each passing second.

After locking the front door, she punched the remote door opener and raced toward the garage. Rolling under the door, slowly creaking upward, her lungs heaved with ragged and fast breaths as she jumped into the car. She jammed the key in the ignition. The engine roared to life. Once she cleared the garage, she hit the remote to close the door, not sparing a glance back.

When she turned onto the street, she punched the accelerator. The tires shrieked in protest, their sound cutting sharply through the night. She tried Mia's number again, but the call abruptly ended, leaving only an ominous silence. Was the phone off? Or something worse?

Her heart surged into her throat, terror twisting like a vice inside her. Should she call the police? But what could she tell them? She had nothing concrete, just a gnawing fear that something was wrong.

Instead, her foot pressed hard on the gas as she ignored the speed limit. Only instinct kept her from colliding with the maze of cars ahead as she zipped through intersections and squealed around corners.

She couldn't afford to hesitate. Every nerve in her body thrummed with the fear that time was running out.

When she turned onto the street leading to the warehouse, the sight ahead froze her breath mid-gasp. A crimson glow bathed the night, flickering erratically against the dark sky.

Flames leaped and danced along a rooftop, their movements almost alive, while thick, roiling smoke poured out like a living shadow, swallowing the air.

"No!" The cry was raw and harsh. Her warehouse was on fire.

Tori's hands tightened on the wheel while her eyes darted frantically. Relief surged when she spotted Mia's car near the front entrance, its familiar outline stark against the fiery glow.

She slammed on the brakes, the car fishtailing wildly before jolting to a stop. The moment she flung open the door, a wall of heat engulfed her. The crackling roar of the flames, a sinister, living growl, filled her ears. Thick, black smoke billowed, stinging her eyes and burning her throat with every ragged breath. The fiery light flickered erratically through the warehouse windows, casting eerie shadows.

She ran toward the car, hope surging with every step. But as she peered inside, the empty seats sent her heart plummeting.

"Mia!" she shouted into the chaos, her voice raw and desperate. "Where are you?"

Then she noticed the warehouse door was ajar, and terror clawed at her body, filling her with a fear she'd never experienced. Was Mia trapped inside the building? She raced to the door, shoved it open, and stepped into a living nightmare.

Mia lay motionless in the middle of the wide aisle between the towering rows of shelves, her body eerily lifeless against the concrete floor.

"Mia!" she screamed, though her voice barely rose above the roaring inferno clawing hungrily at the air. She stumbled forward, her knees slamming into the concrete as she collapsed beside her friend. The painful jolt of the impact went unnoticed, lost in the overwhelming tide of fear surging through her. *Was she dead?*

"No! No! You can't be!" she cried. Hot, acrid smoke burned Tori's throat as she bent over Mia's still form. Then she caught the faint, almost imperceptible rise and fall of Mia's chest, and relief crashed over her in a wave.

The moment was short-lived, giving way to a sharp, relentless urgency as the merciless blaze pressed in, its heat suffocating.

How do I get her out? Tori's eyes darted wildly around

the room, searching for an answer since carrying her wasn't an option. A deafening crash thundered above. Her head snapped upward, and her heart sank.

The towering shelves, stacked with combustible materials, were ablaze. Sparks rained down while thick, black smoke curled through the gaps. If the shelves toppled, escape was impossible. They'd be crushed. Her focus narrowed on one inescapable truth. Move or die!

Tori scrambled to her feet and crouched at Mia's head. Sliding her arms under Mia's armpits, Tori locked her hands over Mia's chest with a grim determination. The dead weight pulled at her arms, keeping her hunched forward. Bent at the waist, she stepped backward, her leg muscles straining and quivering. Inch by inch, she dragged Mia across the floor.

The concrete dragged at her soles, leeching every ounce of strength from each shaky step. Though her thighs burned with exertion, Tori pressed on, propelled by a single unwavering thought—*If I fail, we're dead.*

The air felt alive with fire, scorching her throat with every shallow, labored breath. Sweat streamed down her face, stinging her eyes. Her arms grew weaker, causing her sweat-drenched hands to slip against Mia's chest.

When her body slumped, Tori lunged, grabbing Mia's shirt. "No! No!" she muttered, her grip tightening with sheer panic.

Even as her body teetered on the brink of collapse, Tori didn't dare stop moving, didn't dare glance back to see how close the door was. If she did, Tori was certain her legs would buckle, and she'd never move again. Her feet became her focus, each backward step a battle against the dead weight of Mia's body and the fire that threatened to consume them both.

In her mind, she chanted over and over, one more step, one more step. The words became her lifeline as she fought to keep moving.

As the flames crept closer, their searing heat licking at her skin, the smoke thickened, curling like a suffocating shroud. It clawed at Tori's throat. Each breath burned, her lungs screaming for clean air. Her vision swam, and the edges of the room blurred as lightheadedness threatened to pull her under.

Amidst the overwhelming pain ravaging her body, Tori never heard the door crash open. Shoulders hunched, her body moved on autopilot, each step mechanical, driven by sheer will. It wasn't until the weight of Mia's body lifted away from her arms that Tori realized they weren't alone.

Men, blurred figures in the smoke, surrounded her. One of them cradled Mia in his arms as he rushed toward the door. For a moment, she was certain she was hallucinating.

Then, a wave of peace washed over her. Mia was safe. Nothing else mattered. Her body gave out. Darkness closed in as she crumpled to the floor.

CHAPTER 34

Someone patted her face. "Tori, wake up." The sensation was insistent, though she wished it would stop. She didn't want to wake. The heaviness pulling her down was oddly comforting. But the voice was relentless, the fingers against her cheek persistent.

"Come on, sweetheart. Wake up."

She groaned softly, forcing her eyes open, blinking against a bright light. Panic flickered, but a face leaned over her before the fear could take hold.

David looked at her with a worried expression. The sight of him sent a spike of fear through her. Memories flashed—Mia, the fire. Her heart lurched. She rasped, "Mia?"

His hand pressed warm and reassuring against hers. "She's alive," he said firmly, his voice softening. "She's on the way to the hospital. That's where you're headed."

Tori tried to focus, but the world around her felt foggy and disconnected. "What's on my face?" Her throat was dry and raw.

"An oxygen mask," David said.

Tori struggled, attempting to push herself up and see what was happening, but David's firm hand pushed her back.

"Don't," David said gently. "Everything is okay. There's nothing for you to worry about. Parker and Colt are here and are taking care of everything. I'm going to the hospital with you."

"I need to ask her a question first." Though the voice was familiar, it carried an unfamiliar note of authority.

David hesitated, a sharp edge creeping into his tone. "Make it fast." He moved aside.

A man moved into Tori's view. Her heart raced. The fear spiraled as the edges of reality seemed to waver. No, this wasn't real. He couldn't be here. She had seen things before, imagining him carrying Mia through the smoke and flames. This had to be another hallucination, a cruel trick her mind had conjured from the terrifying ordeal of the fire.

"This can't be real. You aren't here." Her voice quivered.

"I can assure you I am. Though I'm not Arthur Dubois. I'm FBI Special Agent Wilson Markle."

Her eyes widened. "FBI?" she repeated, disbelief and astonishment mingling in her voice. The sheer absurdity of the statement made her question whether she was hallucinating again.

Before she could make sense of it, he said with a firm tone, "I'll explain everything later. Right now, I need to know if you saw anyone when you got here."

Her mind struggled to recall. Details seemed unreal, hazy. "No," she murmured. "The building was on fire, and I found Mia inside."

From a distance, a voice said, "We're ready to roll."

David's response was immediate and firm. "That's enough."

The agent moved out of view, and she heard the doors close. The ambulance started to move, picking up speed. Tori closed her eyes, letting the motion lull her into semi-unconsciousness.

When the vehicle stopped, the jolt rippling through her snapped her awake. The rear doors swung open, and two men in white uniforms waited. The medic beside her said, "Okay, you can take her."

Her stretcher was slowly pulled from the ambulance, its wheels extending with a clatter. The cool night air brushed her face as they rushed her inside. David moved to her side as they rolled her along a hallway. He leaned over before she disappeared through large double doors into the emergency room. David's lips touched her forehead with a light kiss. "I'll be right here," he whispered.

Her eyes sparked with fear. "Mia?" Her throat felt like a swarm of bees had taken up residence.

"I'll find out," David said with conviction.

The stretcher rolled through the swinging doors where a nurse waited. Tori felt the prick in her arm, and everything dissolved into a swirl of muted sounds and fading light.

When consciousness returned, she was in a hospital bed. Machines on each side of her bed beeped. Though stiff, she struggled to sit up. The IV tugged at her arm as she shifted.

"No, not yet," a kindly voice said as a hand pushed her back.

She turned her head. A man in scrubs stood next to the bed. "I'm Doctor Suleman."

"Mia?" she gasped.

His eyes twinkled. "I was told that would be your first question. She's going to be fine."

Tori's eyes briefly closed as relief poured through her.

The doctor added, "She had a good-sized lump on her head, and we're keeping an eye on the injury. Like you, she breathed in a heavy amount of smoke."

"How long will we be in the hospital?" Tori rasped.

"Trying to get rid of me already?" He chuckled. "I expect both of you should be able to go home tomorrow. We're keeping you overnight to monitor the condition of your lungs. In a few minutes, you'll be moved into a room. Your throat will be sore for a few days. Take it easy on the talking. Any questions? Just nod."

She gave a negative shake of her head. "Good," he said approvingly and patted her hand.

Once she'd been disconnected from the machines and the IV removed, a nurse rolled her gurney into an elevator, taking her to the next floor and to a room with two empty beds. After she was helped into bed, the nurse raised it to a sitting position.

She handed Tori a cup with a straw. "Ice water. This will help ease the pain in your throat." She pointed to a container on the table next to the bed. "There's more there."

Tori took a sip. The relief was exquisite. She took another sip.

The woman tucked the covers, then handed her a small device. "Push the button if you need help."

She left the room, and a few seconds later, David and Parker strode in with similar expressions of concern. Their eyes quickly scanned her as if needing to be reassured she wasn't at death's door.

When they reached her bedside, David gripped her hand tightly. "The doctor said you're not to stress your voice. We'll talk. Mia is okay. The doctor wants to keep both of you overnight. Do you remember him telling you?" After she nodded yes, he continued, "They're going to bring her in here once she's released from ICU."

Tori's eyes widened, and a smile lit up her face.

David's eyes twinkled. "I knew that would make you feel better. I know you have questions. I'll try to anticipate them."

His expression shifted, his voice becoming somber. "You were gone when I got to the house. I called, but you didn't answer. Then I tried Mia. She didn't answer. Parker had heard a fire call over his police scanner and recognized the address, your warehouse. When he couldn't reach you or Mia, he called me."

He glanced at Parker before saying, "When we

arrived, two men had pulled you and Mia out of the building. One was, of all people, your wine expert, who turned out to be an FBI agent. Explanations on that will have to wait until you get home."

Parker had steadily watched her with a worried look. He said, "The fire was arson. The warehouse is a loss, though I'm sure you know it."

She gave an emphatic nod of her head in agreement. She reached for the container of ice water to fill her cup. David was quicker. After refilling the cup, he handed it back to her.

Parker, his voice intense, asked, "In as few words as possible, why were you there?"

After another sip, she sighed with relief. "Phone. Text from Mia," she rasped. She took another sip. Tori figured the words were indelibly engraved in her mind. She might never forget them. "Meet me at the warehouse. It's urgent. Hurry."

The intensity in his voice deepened. "I need your phone. Did you have it on you at the warehouse?"

Tori nodded. "Jacket."

"Then the hospital will have it."

"Mia? What happened?" she rasped.

With a grim look, Parker said, "She was abducted after leaving a meeting downtown. All Mia remembers is getting hit in the head on the way to her car. She was dumped inside the warehouse, and her car was left outside. Since you got a text from her, then whoever kidnapped her used her phone to send the message."

"Why?" She couldn't restrain the anger surging through her.

With a harsh tone, Parker said, "Thieves were after your wine collection. They used Mia to lure you to the warehouse to get you out of the house. The fire was meant to kill you both." He hesitated before saying, "They nearly succeeded. When the agents got there, the door was locked. They broke in."

As the implication of Parker's words slammed into her, the cup slipped from her grasp. For a moment, she was back in the warehouse, reliving the terror. They would never have been able to get out.

Parker quickly grabbed the cup while David gripped her hand. The warmth of his hand helped steady her.

Parker cleared his throat. "What you did, though, saved both of you. According to the agents, the reason you and Mia are alive is that you were so close to the door. They said you were dragging Mia. If you had been further inside the building, they would not have been able to get to you."

Reeling, Tori sank back.

Parker cleared his throat again before adding, "Your house was broken into. The police apprehended the gang as they were hauling boxes of wine into a moving van. Colt's at the house handling everything."

Before she could respond, the door opened.

A nurse stepped into the room. "Time's up. No more visitors until the morning."

"I'll be here to take you home," David said. He

brushed her cheek with his fingers, then leaned over to kiss her forehead. When he turned, Tori would have sworn she saw a glint of tears.

"I'll be here too. And reinforcements are on the way," Parker said. Like David, he quickly turned to rush out.

Tori leaned against the pillow. While questions buzzed in her head, her concern for Mia pushed them aside. Everyone said she was okay, but Tori had an overwhelming, almost urgent, need to see for herself. The panic she'd felt in the warehouse still lingered.

Noises outside her doorway had Tori sitting up in anticipation. The door opened, and a gurney was pushed in.

Pale but alert, Mia's eyes anxiously searched the room. "Tori," she rasped.

Tori's relief was instantaneous and all-consuming. She flipped back the covers only to be admonished by the nurse.

"Before you come charging over, let me get her onto the bed." Though her tone was stern, a twinkle gleamed in the woman's eyes.

Mia had been looking at Tori with an equal expression of concern. "All right?"

Tori nodded, her eyes never leaving Mia's face.

Once Mia was settled, Tori struggled out of bed. Her legs wobbly, she crossed the room.

The nurse grabbed Tori's arm. "Since you're determined, sit. I don't want to pick you up off the floor." She pulled a chair next to Mia's bed. Tori collapsed onto it, her hand reaching for Mia's.

Her arms crossed, the nurse said sternly, "Ladies, do not, and I repeat, do not stress your voices with a lot of chatter. You can talk later." She marched out with a faint smile on her face.

Once the door closed, both hands clutched Mia's as Tori's gaze searched the face she'd come to love.

Mia's other hand came over, grabbing onto Tori's. Her voice was raspy as she whispered, "They said you tried to pull me out of the building. You risked your life." Tears formed in her eyes.

"Hey, don't start, or you'll have me bawling," Tori croaked. "We're okay." Tori wasn't about to tell her how close the gap between life and death had been. Though she had a hunch, Mia knew.

The silence didn't need to be filled with talk. For now, it was enough that they were together, their hands clinging to each other. The questions and answers would wait for another day.

Mia's eyes slowly closed as she drifted to sleep. Tori never moved, never broke her grip on Mia's hand. Far into the night, she sat, watching over her friend.

CHAPTER 35

Reinforcements, in the form of Heidi, Cammie, and Tina, arrived early, bringing clean clothes for Tori. Mia was headed home under her mother's wing. Though, over her mother's protest, she promised Tori she'd be at the house later in the day.

Tori arrived home in grand style, escorted by David, Parker, and the three women. While Tina and Cammie still had a few last classes to finish and would be leaving, Heidi was back to stay. Since all she had left to do was submit her project, her professor released her from the remaining classes. Firmly entrenched at the house, she'd taken over for Mia, riding herd on Tori.

After walking into the house with David holding onto her, Tori's first task was a shower. Heidi stood by the bathroom door, ready to charge in if Tori needed help.

Under Heidi's watchful but worried gaze, Tori dressed. Though her voice didn't sound as gravelly as the night before, it still had a lingering harshness as she said, "Don't worry. I won't pass out."

"Humph, you let me be the judge," Heidi replied.

"Yes, ma'am," Tori said, then grinned. "Now, I need

to see how bad the damage is to my house."

The comment earned another admonishment. "Doctor's orders. You're not to talk a lot." As they walked out, Heidi's hand hovered protectively near Tori's arm.

As they passed the back door, Tori paused, watching two of Colt's crew repair the damage. The stark evidence, the splintered frame and shattered doorjamb, were haunting reminders of the deadly plot to kill her and Mia. The sight added another layer to the horrifying images from the night before.

Beside her, Heidi murmured, "Tori?"

With a mental shake, Tori moved forward. Seated at the kitchen table, Colt, David, and Parker had joined forces. As she strolled in, Tori was confronted with a wall of determined expressions that said she wasn't going to do anything.

Heidi poured a cup of coffee, handing it to Tori. As she sipped, the heat felt amazingly good on her throat.

Before she could ask a question, David said with a stern expression, "The doctor said for you to take it easy today. Don't talk unless you have to, and that's what you're going to do. Got it?"

She settled onto a chair, nodding.

Parker started. "The FBI agent, who has been masquerading as your wine expert, will be here later today to talk to you. Since we've only got bits and pieces, it's best to let him explain. The warehouse is a loss. We need to contact the insurance company."

"Call Jeff Archer, CPA. He has the info," she told him.

Parker nodded. "I'll take care of it. The repairs to the back door should be finished today. The thieves also took out the security system. I've got people coming to repair the damage."

"Who broke in?" she asked.

The three men quickly exchanged a look before Parker said, "That's part of what Agent Markle will explain."

Though Tori felt they were hiding something significant, she didn't have the energy to challenge them.

Parker said, "Your wine is undamaged. The gang was busy filling up boxes and hauling them to a large van when the police arrived. Even though the police wanted to keep the boxes that had been removed, I convinced them otherwise."

His voice adamant, Parker added, "Putting the bottles into their property room would damage their value. Instead, they took pictures after I assured them the bottles would be produced if required at a trial. They're back in the cellar. Thankfully, the crooks only had time to remove a hundred or so bottles. I know you have questions, but hold off until the agent gets here."

He rose. "I need to get to the police department and talk to Andy, but I'll be back."

Colt also stood. "I'm on my way to the warehouse to meet with the arson investigator. I'm waiting for him to give me the go-ahead to start the clean-up. Let me know if you need anything." He headed out the back door.

After the two men left, David said, "I can't stay either. I've got a meeting I can't cancel. But I'll be back once it's over. I want to hear what the agent has to say." His hand lightly brushed her hair before he strode out of the kitchen.

Heidi settled across from her with a worried look. "Are you sure you're okay?"

"I will be, but right now, this is overwhelming," she said.

"I spoke to Mia at the hospital and got the same reaction. By the way, she's itching to be here. Don't be surprised if you see her walk in. No matter the circumstances, she's not one to step back and take it easy. And I'm supposed to pass on a message."

Curious, Tori said, "Oh?"

"Yes, one word—practice."

Tori chuckled, ignoring the raw pain in her throat.

"Can I fix you something to eat?"

At the thought of trying to swallow food, Tori adamantly shook her head. "Not a good idea." Deciding to follow Mia's instructions, she headed to the music room.

Settled at the piano, her fingers danced over the keyboard, letting the music work its magic. Engrossed in the emotions of the notes, she didn't hear the doorbell. It wasn't until she felt a hand on her shoulder that she suddenly stopped.

Heidi said, "The FBI agent is here."

Tori stepped into the hallway to see a cluster of people—Parker, David, Andy, the agent who wasn't a wine expert, and a stranger. He seemed familiar, though she couldn't quite place him.

Behind her, Heidi said, "I'd suggest using the dining room. Otherwise, your office will be a bit crowded."

"Good idea. I want you to hear this, too," Tori said before striding toward the foyer.

The change in Dubois, no, the agent, she chided herself, was astonishing. The rude, cold demeanor had morphed into one with a calm, kindly look. He smiled as he walked toward her, extending his hand.

"We've not been formally introduced. I'm FBI Special Agent Wilson Markle." He held her hand for a moment. "I have a lot to talk about. I'd like you to meet Special Agent Neil Tate."

The other man stepped forward, and suddenly, the recognition clicked. Tori gasped. "You're the one who was driving the van, watching the warehouse."

With a sheepish look, he said, "Yes, ma'am, and you caught me."

Heidi, taking command, said, "Let's all go into the dining room, where there will be more room."

She led the way as everyone took seats. As Andy passed, Tori murmured a greeting. He smiled at her before saying, "I heard what you did at the warehouse, and so have most of the officers at the PD. We all wish you a very speedy recovery."

When the front door opened, Tori stepped out of the dining room. "Mia," she cried, rushing toward the foyer. They tightly hugged before Mia eased back, studying Tori's face.

Tori, stepping back, did the same thing, saying,

"You're not supposed to be here."

Mia grinned. "And you're not supposed to be talking."

Tori shot back. "Neither are you."

After laughing, Mia groaned. "God, that hurts." She sucked in a breath, then said, "I want to know what's going on."

"Our so-called wine expert, who's anything but just arrived." Tori tugged on Mia's arm. "We're in the dining room."

After Mia had been greeted by the others, though her eyebrows shot up at the sight of Andy, she settled into a chair. Heidi set a large tray with a coffee pot, a pitcher of ice water, cups, sugar, and creamers on the side table.

Once everyone was seated, Wilson stepped to the end of the table. "Hopefully, by the time I finish, I'll have answered most of your questions. While much of what I'm about to say is based on fact, there is some conjecture in connecting the dots."

He took a sip before continuing. "For several years, a ruthless gang of thieves has been operating in Europe, targeting high-dollar collections, art, jewelry, antiques, anything that would bring big bucks on the black market. About two months ago, the FBI received an alert from Interpol that the gang was headed to the United States, and their target was a wine collection. Interpol had an agent inside the gang, but the agent didn't know the location."

Tori and the others stirred at his words.

"We didn't discover the location until about two weeks ago. The agent managed to send a message to his supervisor that the target was here in Granbury. It didn't take long to discover your wine collection," he said with a pointed look at Tori.

Tori's face paled. "The man who was killed."

With a grim look, Wilson nodded. "Yes. Raul Spencer. While we don't know what happened, we suspect the gang leader discovered Raul was an undercover Interpol agent."

The harsh tone in her voice deepened to a growl. "They killed him." Sorrow bit deep as she thought about the man who tried to warn her.

"We didn't know he'd been killed until Sergeant Rodriguez ran his prints, which triggered an alert."

David leaned forward, his face twisted with anger. "Why didn't you contact the police department?"

His eyes sympathetic, Wilson said, "By the time we discovered the agent had been killed, Tori had already been implicated in the murder. We knew she was innocent since an agent was already watching her."

He nodded to Neil Tate. "If we had contacted Andy, a vicious gang would have disappeared. Many of the owners of the collections they robbed were murdered. This was as close as anyone had gotten to stopping them."

He paused as his gaze scanned the table. "The attempts to get Tori arrested were troublesome. Was someone in Granbury entangled with the gang? We had to wait, but we did it on our terms. Tori, when we learned you had hired a wine expert, Arthur Dubois, we had a way to get someone inside the house to learn more about the investigation. I took his place."

"How?" Tori asked.

"Let's just say we persuaded him," he said with a wry smile. "I have to admit, this was one of the more challenging undercover assignments I've experienced. Trying to pass as a wine expert was much harder than I had anticipated. I had to stall, keeping you at arm's length so you wouldn't be suspicious. You didn't make it easy. You were a little too efficient with keeping your office door closed."

Mia said with a droll tone, "Actually, we suspected you killed the agent."

Tori added, "And I planned to fire you."

"In the future, someone needs to remind me not to tangle with the two of you again," he said with an amused expression. Despite a few chuckles from around the table, the levity lingered for only a moment before his face turned serious.

Wilson shifted his gaze, giving Parker a respectful look. "When you called my office about Arthur Dubois, I knew you were suspicious."

Parker frowned. "I wondered why my contact was taking so long to call me back."

"We had to stall. We felt the gang was ready to make their move. My men found signs that someone was watching the house, though we were never able to catch them."

He took a sip of coffee. "When they did last night, we were waiting for them. We apprehended five men, including the head of the gang, as they hauled boxes of wine out of your cellar."

His expression darkened. "Despite our careful planning, we didn't anticipate they'd torch the warehouse or kidnap Mia and use her phone to lure Tori to the warehouse."

He paused to glance at Tori before continuing, "Tori, they had to make sure you were out of the way, occupied elsewhere. Stealing a collection the size of yours would take time to pack, and then the boxes had to be moved to their van. Their plan was even more insidious than what appeared at first glance."

Wilson shifted, taking a wider stance. "This morning, I talked to the arson inspector. Based on the type of contents in the warehouse and the accelerant, gasoline, the building went up fast, especially since the sprinkler system was disabled. Which told us someone didn't torch the place until you were a short distance away."

His expression turned grim. "If the fire was too far along, you wouldn't have been able to enter the building. Instead, they waited to start the fire. That's why they drove Mia's car to the warehouse."

His tone deepened. "It was bait. They wanted you inside the building. Then, to ensure their plan succeeded, whoever torched the building locked the front door."

Tori reached for Mia's hand. They exchanged glances as they clung tightly to each other.

Parker leaned forward, his tone laced with harshness. "Then they had someone following Tori. The person called whoever was waiting to set the fire. And they would have had Mia's keys to unlock the door, then relock it."

"That's the supposition, and it fits the timeline," Wilson said, glancing at Tori with respect. "The leader of the gang seriously underestimated you."

"How did you know they broke into the house?" Tori asked.

"I've had men watching both the house and you. Anytime you left, one of my agents followed you while the other stayed to watch the house."

Tori said, "I still don't understand, though. How did they know where the wine cellar was located?"

"You showed it to the ring leader."

Chapter 36

Tori's, "What! Who?" triggered a spate of coughing. Heidi sprang up and quickly filled a glass with ice water from the pitcher on the table, handing it to Tori.

"Bartholomew Hempstead," Wilson said grimly.

After a deep swig of water, Tori sputtered, "Are you saying he's not a reporter?"

"Oh, he's legit, a freelance reporter for several high-end magazines, like *International Vintner's Review*. A perfect cover for his real business, the mastermind of a vicious gang of thieves. His interviews gave Hempstead the perfect excuse to case the homes of his victims. Interpol is running down this lead."

With an aggrieved tone, Tori said, "And I did exactly that. Gave him a tour of the house and wine cellar. No wonder he looked at my collection like he'd found the Holy Grail. But he didn't know how to open the cellar door."

A wry look appeared on Wilson's face. "I hate to tell you, but I figured out how to open the door the first day I was here." He finished off the rest of his coffee.

Stunned, she sat back. So much for her and Mia's security efforts. She took another gulp of ice water.

"Two of his men are already talking, hoping for a lighter sentence. Especially since we found traces of gasoline in the trunk of one of their cars."

Parker leaned forward with an intense look. "What about the locals you mentioned?"

Wilson walked to the pot to refill his cup. "Andy has filled me in on his investigation. Even though the homicide occurred in Granbury, this is now a federal case. I listened to the recording from the incident at the library."

His brow furrowed. "That setup was certainly meant to trap you, Tori. While we're still investigating the actions of the three women, we don't have any evidence that links them to Hempstead. At this point, any charges for their role in the investigation are Andy's responsibility."

He took a sip, stepping back in front of the table. "The gun is the issue. We know the one found at the library was used to kill our agent. We surmise it was Hempstead at the library. Keeping the heat on Tori would be to his advantage. It would stop the police from looking in another direction for the killer. Planting the murder weapon in her car would have worked."

"I bet he had the gun with him when he was here," Tori said, her eyes flashing with anger. "He was always so careful about how he opened his briefcase. He planned to leave it here."

Parker said, "If that was his plan, you and Mia nixed it since you never left him alone."

Tori leaned back. Even though her voice rasped, the tone was laced with triumph. "I bet that ticked him off."

Wilson chuckled softly. "Probably did. His next move was at the library."

He took another sip before saying, "Unfortunately, we don't have a link between Hempstead and the gun, or Carly and the gun. Carly denies knowing anything about the weapon, the man at the library, or any evidence. Her attorney insisted she had only been bluffing about new evidence."

Wilson shifted slightly before continuing, "According to Duncan and Wisner, Carly was the mastermind behind the plot to damage Tori's reputation, but they also claim they didn't know about a gun."

A memory surfaced in Tori's mind. Mia's last phone call.

Before she could speak, Mia spoke up. "Carly Swanson had dinner with Hempstead the night before the meeting at the library."

Wilson stiffened. "How do you know?"

"A friend saw them at a restaurant."

"Give me the specifics." He jerked out a notepad and pen from his pocket, writing as Mia spoke.

Once she finished, he tore off the paper, sliding it across the table to Neil. "I want the witness who saw them brought in for a statement. Find out if the restaurant has cameras. If there is a video of Swanson and Hempstead, then pick her up for questioning."

Neil jumped up, rushing out the door.

The look that passed between Tori and Mia was nothing short of gleeful.

With a firm conviction in her voice, Mia said, "Knowing Carly, she filled Hempstead's ears with her vicious accusations about Tori. She likely bragged about the upcoming meeting and that Tori would be arrested for murder and who was killed. After all, Hempstead was this big-time international reporter. Carly would have relished the chance to sabotage the interview."

Wilson turned his gaze on Parker. "Who knew about the meeting at the library?"

A look of satisfaction crossed Parker's face as if he knew where Wilson was headed. "Myself, Tori, Mia, David, and three of my men." He glanced at Tori. "Did you tell Linc?"

"No, I didn't," she said.

The expression on Wilson's face matched the satisfied look Parker had. "This answers the question about how Hempstead knew about the library meeting. If we can tie Hempstead to the gun, then it could also connect to Carly."

Parker, who had stood to refill his cup, leaned against the side of the table. "I have a possible link for you. Have you seen Hempstead?"

"Yes, why?" Wilson asked.

"Does he have a bruise on his face?"

Wilson's eyes lit up with curiosity. "Yes, he does Know something about it?"

A slow smile crossed Parker's face. "One of my

investigators was involved in the fracas at the library. During the scuffle, Mitch hit the man. Mitch is a graduate of Texas A&M University. Aggies like to wear their class ring long after they have graduated. Mitch was wearing his. There might be a match between the injury to Hempstead's face and the ring. Plus, there could be DNA on the ring."

Wilson almost vibrated with excitement. "How soon can I get the ring? I'll have it sent to our lab for testing. If there's a match, we've got him."

"I'll make the call." Parker walked out.

"Why were you interested in the warehouse?" Tori said.

He smiled. "I wondered when you'd get around to asking. We were uncertain about your plans for the warehouse and whether any of the wine might be stored there. We kept an eye on the place until we learned the building was only for the inn's inventory."

He took a sip of coffee. "Parker said you caught me talking to Neil, then snuck up on his van and overheard him talking to me on the phone. Not sure he'll live that one down for a while. Your little trek to the warehouse caught us all off guard. I barely had time to warn him. But evidently, he wasn't fast enough since you still saw his van."

Parker stepped back into the room. "Mitch is on the way."

Wilson nodded. "Does anyone have any questions?"

Mia's eyes gleamed with mischief as she asked, "You

mentioned picking up Carly Swanson. How are you going to do that?"

Wilson gave her a long look before his easy smile crossed his face. "I think I'll impose on Sergeant Rodriguez to send a squad car to take her to the police station." He cast a glance at Andy.

Mia leaned back with a smug look.

Andy replied, "That can certainly be arranged. After all, this is a federal investigation, and the FBI wants to talk to her. I'll make sure she has a clear understanding of the situation."

Tori nearly choked on her laughter.

David said, "I'd like to suggest something else that would go a long way in clearing Tori's name."

"If there's something I can do, I will," Wilson said with an intense conviction.

"Issue a statement to the press about how Tori's cooperation in an FBI investigation was instrumental in bringing down an international ring of thieves that involved the murder of an undercover Interpol agent."

Wilson grinned. "That is very feasible. In fact, I'll make sure it's headline news in the *Metro*."

David gave Tori a slow grin.

Once Mitch arrived to hand off his ring, Wilson was ready to leave. Tori asked to speak to him alone. Andy had already left, and everyone else retreated to the kitchen.

Standing in the foyer, Wilson looked at her with a kindly expression. "Tori Winters, you are an amazing woman. When I came through the warehouse door, I don't believe I've ever seen such a look of determination as I saw on your face. You almost made it to the door. It's the only reason the two of you made it out of the building."

A cold glint settled in her eyes. "The thought of that locked door will haunt me for a long, long time, along with the memory of Raul Spencer."

Her throat tightened, but she forced back the tears. "Please send me any information you can share about his family. I'd like to reach out to them and let them know he tried to save my life."

His expression softened with sympathy. "As soon as I get back to my office, I will."

She hesitated, then said, "When Mia was carried out of the warehouse, I thought I was hallucinating. But it was you, wasn't it?"

"Yes. I got to you first, and Neil was right behind me. He carried you out."

"I didn't get a chance to thank him. Does Mia know?"

He nodded. "I talked to her at the hospital."

"How did you know we were there?"

"Neil followed you, though the way you were driving, he said he had a hard time keeping up. He suspected something was wrong when you tore out of your driveway. As soon as he realized you were headed to the warehouse, he called me."

Tori gulped back another threatening bout of tears. "You said there was only one reason we made it out of the building. By my count, I can add two more. There aren't enough words to thank either one of you."

He cleared his throat before saying, "None is needed." Wilson pulled out a small case from his pocket, removing a business card. On the back, he wrote a phone number.

"This is my personal cell phone. If you ever need help, please don't hesitate to call me. It was truly a pleasure to meet you and hear you play. Despite what I said, I enjoyed listening."

"How long are you going to be in town?"

"For at least a few more days. Why?"

"I'd love for you to be my guest for my concert at the opera house."

"I'd be honored."

"What about your men?"

"Other than Neil, the team is headed back to Quantico."

"Please extend the invitation to him."

"I will."

"Before you leave, I have one more question," Tori said. "How did they know about my wine collection?"

Wilson said, "Gossip."

At her puzzled look, he went on to explain. "You called the owner of the Château du Montclair. After your call, he checked the records of wine sales and discovered that among your grandmother's many purchases was a case of 1945 Montclair Nocturne, Pinot Noir wine. That wine has become one of the most valuable wines on the market. He spread the word among his associates that bottles of the wine might be in a collection in Texas."

"How valuable," Tori asked.

"Around half a million … for one bottle."

Tori almost choked. "And you think I have some?"

His eyes twinkled. "I believe you do."

"I can see Parker is going to be busy."

He chuckled as they shook hands. Tori stood on the porch watching him drive out, pondering his impact on her life and Mia's.

Suddenly, the future seemed much brighter. She still had a wine collection that had to be inventoried. She wondered if the real Dubois was still interested.

And, she had to break the news to Parker about the wines. She was sure her security would soon be ramped up.

Dwayne was on his way, needing to be reassured her hands weren't burned by the fire, and her voice wasn't permanently damaged.

And then, there was David. Something was up, and she was ready to know what.

Epilogue

Ten Days Later

Her insides were a bundle of twitching nerves as Tori waited in the wings. Since she woke that morning, she'd been a nervous wreck.

Mia, Heidi, Cammie, and Tina had arrived early with all their gadgets, lotions, shampoos, and makeup to get her ready.

Despite the ever-present tension of performing on stage, the day was joyous and filled with laughter. They pampered her and each other since they all planned to dress and leave from the house. While Elly's gowns wouldn't fit them, a shopping trip to north Dallas had solved that problem.

David had arranged for a limo to pick them up and transport them to the opera house. David and Parker would accompany them along with two of Parker's men.

He said the jewelry the five women would be wearing justified the additional security. In addition to Mia, Tori had insisted that the others each choose a piece of her grandmother's jewelry to wear.

Nora had called to check on her and to say the concert was sold out. They had to turn people away.

Tori suspected she was already plotting to convince her to do a second one.

Now, she waited, attired in her grandmother's gown. Heidi had piled her hair atop her head, with a few curls framing her face. Her grandmother's diamond necklace glittered around her throat, and the matching diamond earrings dangled from her ears. Tori felt far, far away from her career as a hospice nurse in Missouri. What an incredible journey, and now, she stood, about to perform on the stage of the Granbury Opera House.

Tori pulled the curtain to peek around the edge. The hall was rapidly filling up. Voices rose like waves. Front and center were Mia, Heidi, Cammie, and Tina, flanked by David and Parker. Dan Foote, her Fort Worth attorney, and his wife were seated next to Parker. Next to them were Wilson Markle and Neil Tate. Then she spotted Colt with an unknown woman on his arm. Interest piqued. Something to find out about later.

On the stage, the piano gleamed under the lights. Dwayne swore its sound was even better than before the vandalism. The police had never discovered the culprit, though Carly was the prime suspect. But the piano was the least of Carly's problems.

Hempstead had been charged with the agent's murder after a DNA match from Mitch's ring. The video of Carly and Hempstead at the restaurant put her in the middle of the murder investigation. Despite her repeated denials about the gun or what Hempstead planned to do at the library, Hempstead refused to back up her claims.

According to Parker, there was a very real possibility Carly would be arrested.

The tinkling of a bell, the warning for everyone to take their seats, pulled her from her musings. Nora and Dwayne walked up beside her.

"Ready?" Nora asked.

"As ready as I'll ever be," she said.

Nora walked on stage as the house lights dimmed. She stopped behind a podium at the corner of the stage. She paused, waiting for the murmurs to fade away.

When she spoke, her voice resonated. "Welcome to the Granbury Opera House. We are honored to have local resident Tori Winters performing for you tonight. You will find the selections Ms. Winters will be performing in your program. Please hold your applause until the end of the concert. Without further ado, I am proud to introduce Ms. Tori Winters."

Dwayne escorted her onto the stage, standing by the piano as she settled onto the bench. Everything had been set up earlier, including the position of the bench. He had threatened everyone with dire consequences if they touched it.

Tori didn't allow herself to be rushed as she ensured her feet were in the right spot on the pedals and she was comfortably in place. Once Tori was satisfied, she nodded. He turned and, with slow, methodical steps, walked into the wings.

For a moment, she held her hands in her lap, taking a few deep breaths to settle herself. Then she lifted her hands, and her fingers struck the opening notes for George Gershwin's *Rhapsody in Blue*. The music flowed, filling the concert hall. A surge of exhilaration swept through her. Lost in the joy of the music, the audience faded into the background.

Once she'd struck the last note, she paused, breathing deeply while resting her hands in her lap. Then, without hesitation, she launched into the next piece. Time lost all meaning, and the midpoint of the concert arrived before she even realized it.

Dwayne appeared at her side, assisting her as she rose. The rumble of voices filled the hall as they walked off.

In the wings, Nora greeted her with a cup of warm tea. "If I weren't concerned about messing you up, I'd hug you. You are fantastic, and the audience is loving it."

Tori took a few sips, though her throat felt fine.

With a note of concern, Dwayne asked, "How's your throat? Are you comfortable with singing?" They decided Tori would simply play if she felt her voice wasn't ready.

She reassured him. "Dwayne, my voice won't be a problem."

"Good," he said, lightly patting her shoulder.

A bell tinkled, and the house lights dimmed, signaling the start of the second half of the program.

Dwayne escorted her onto the stage, again waiting to ensure she didn't need help with the bench. Once she was ready, she nodded.

The first selection was *Let It Be* by the Beatles. As

Tori's voice joined with the music, a murmur stirred in the audience, which quickly died down. Her voice soared, filling the farthest corner of the hall. Her tone vibrated with passion and her love of music. After each piece, Tori paused, taking deep breaths before beginning another selection. For the final piece of music, Tori reached to move the microphone attached to the piano in front of her, pushing the small button to turn it on.

"This last song, I dedicate to my mother and my grandmother." She turned off the microphone, pushing it out of her way. For a brief moment, she closed her eyes while thoughts of her mother and grandmother filled her mind.

Then she started on *Unchained Melody*, singing as she had never done before. Her voice carried her heart and her soul. As the echo of the final words, "God speed your love to me," reverberated in the air, she dropped her hands back in her lap, choking back the tears.

For a few seconds, silence reigned, then the applause started, and it didn't stop. Dwayne stepped out, offering his arm for her to rise. He escorted her to the center of the stage. The house lights came up. The applause, accompanied by cries for more, rang out.

Dwayne leaned in and whispered, "I told you so."

Nora came on stage, carrying a large spray of yellow roses, and handed them to Tori. The applause, if possible, grew louder, and the audience was on its feet. In the front row, her friends were cheering her on.

Nora finally had to resort to the microphone, saying,

"I think Tori will be happy to do one more number."

The lights dimmed. Tori handed the roses to Nora and returned to the bench for the first encore. When she finished, the applause and cries for more echoed. Even after a second and then a third encore, the audience still clamored for more.

Nora walked on stage. As the voices and applause faded away, she said, "I hope we can convince Tori to perform here again. Thank you for coming, and have a safe trip home."

Dwayne escorted her off the stage, where the crew was waiting to congratulate her. Nora pulled her to one side. "I didn't want to say anything before your performance, but we'd like to offer you a position on the board."

With a slight frown, she said, "Myra Swanson resigned. She said they're selling their home and moving. It's understandable considering their legal difficulties with the FBI and police."

She squeezed Tori's hand. "I don't need an answer tonight, but ... please think about it. You would be such an asset. And I am going to ask for another concert. So be warned."

Before Tori could respond, Linc approached, his eyes filled with regret.

Nora said, "Hi, Linc. Isn't she special?" Her face glowed with delight. "Tori, I'll talk to you later." She turned and walked away.

Tori eyed him with guarded suspicion. The FBI

investigation into the murder of the Interpol agent had garnered widespread publicity, and he was undoubtedly aware of the complicity of the Swansons, especially Carly's role in the murder.

He drew in a deep breath. "Nora's right. You are indeed special. I wanted to tell you how wrong I was. I had no idea of the extent of your talent, and it was a privilege to hear you play and sing. I won't spoil your evening with comments about Carly, though what she did was unbelievably wrong. I hope that, down the road, you and I will be able to mend fences."

Though his apology seemed earnest, Tori knew she couldn't trust him again. Unwilling to voice her distrust, she simply replied, "Thank you."

When Mia, David, Parker, and the rest of her team rushed toward her, her last glimpse of Linc was the piercing look he directed toward David, then to Parker. The anger simmering in his eyes sparked a fleeting unease.

But as her friends surrounded her with laughter and hearty congratulations, handing her a glass of champagne, the disquiet slipped away, swallowed by the jubilant atmosphere.

The backstage area soon became swamped, with many of the audience staying to congratulate Tori. The curtains were drawn back, spilling the overflow onto the stage.

Reporters from Dallas and Fort Worth, drawn by her newfound notoriety, clamored for an interview, showering her with praise.

Tori was overwhelmed. She hadn't been prepared for such a frenzy. David and Mia stayed by her side as a buffer, though Parker was never far away, nor were Heidi, Cammie, and Tina. One reporter asked about her future plans as a concert pianist. Would she consider a musical tour?

She glanced at the friends and loved ones surrounding her. She slipped her arm through Mia's. "No. I wouldn't be interested. My heart is here."

As she twisted her head to smile up at David, her gaze drifted beyond him, catching sight of Linc standing in the shadows of the curtains. An uneasiness stirred.

I hope you enjoyed the latest adventures of Tori Winters and her friends. If you did, please consider leaving a review on Amazon or your favorite book retailer.

For more insight into the story's background,
The Story Behind the Fiction follows.

Best Wishes

Anita Dickason

The Story Behind the Fiction

I couldn't have chosen a better setting for my Tori Winters Mystery Series than Granbury, Texas. The town's rich history, striking architecture, and storied landmarks provide the perfect backdrop for mystery and suspense.

When I began *Deadly Keepsakes*, Book One of the series, I never imagined how deeply Granbury would influence my plots and characters. Each book has uncovered new layers of this unique and intriguing town with unexpected mysteries and suspense.

Within this latest book, Granbury's iconic landmarks, Granbury Opera House and Hood County Jail Museum, as well as the eerie folklore of Granbury's ghosts, became the inspiration for my storytelling, shaping the twists and turns of Tori's latest mystery.

Granbury Opera House

The beautifully restored 19th-century theater stands as a testament to the town's vibrant history. With its elegant architecture and longstanding tradition of live performances, it has served as a cultural cornerstone, showcasing plays, musicals, and concerts.

After visiting Granbury, I was enthralled by the Opera House's timeless appeal. It was impossible not to be inspired. Not only did Tori Winters take center stage at the

Opera House, but this magnificent building and its events became central to *Murder with Wine.*

While the setting is rooted in reality, I did take a few liberties with the events and characters, all of which are fictional.

Hood County Jail Museum

Built in 1885, the building served as the county jail until 1978. The site retains much of its historic past with preserved jail cells, an iron cage, and even a gallows room. The museum features exhibits of local legends, lawmen, and the outlaws who once walked its halls.

Where better to place a dangerous encounter with a cryptic warning on a dark night during a ghost tour?

Granbury
Ghosts and Legends Walking Tour

While the *Granbury Ghosts and Legend Tour* is very much a real event, the version I created in *Murder with Wine* is entirely fictional. Much like the Opera House, I took a few liberties in crafting my ghost tour and its characters.

The real tour is a fascinating journey through the town's historic square, where eerie tales and local folklore are shared. It's a must-visit for anyone exploring Granbury, offering chilling stories about legendary figures like the Lady in Red, the Faceless Girl, and even mysteries surrounding John Wilkes Booth and the infamous outlaw Jesse James.

For those interested in learning more, the tour's owner has written two books I highly recommend.

Haunted Granbury by Brandy Herr

The Ghostly Tales of Granbury by Brandy Herr (adapted for children)

About the Author

I'm a twenty-two-year veteran of the Dallas Police Department, which means I write about what I know—cops and crimes. I served as a patrol officer, undercover narcotics detective, advanced accident investigator, SWAT tactical officer, and the team's first female sniper. That diverse experience has provided an endless source of inspiration for my plots and characters.

Writing the *Tori Winters Mystery Series* was a gamble. One that required a style different from my acclaimed crime thrillers. Needless to say, self-doubt crept in. But taking that risk paid off. From the many heartwarming reviews and comments I've received, it's clear readers love the *Tori Winters Mystery* series. For an author, that's what matters most—crafting a story people enjoy.